the Whisper of Dawn

the Whisper of Dawn

Of Wind and Sky

~ Book 2 ~

By Rebekah Colburn

For my daughter, Grace.

May she never forget what a treasure she is.

And for all who have yet to discover their true value.

"Because of the tender mercy of our God,

whereby **the sunrise shall visit us** *from on high*

to give light to those who sit in darkness

and in the shadow of death

to guide our feet into the way of peace."

Luke 1: 78-79 (ESV)

Prologue

Wyoming Territory, Fall 1866

"I've come to say good-bye," Annette announced solemnly. Her blue eyes were intense with purpose, though her knuckles were white where she gripped the pommel of the saddle.

The wind tugged at tendrils of blond hair that had slipped free from her braid. She pushed them from her youthful face with a thoughtless gesture, eyeing the man before her as cautiously as if he were a maverick bull who could charge at any provocation.

His green eyes mocked her, but beneath his dark mustache, his lips thinned with impatience.

"What are you talking about?" Ricky demanded, striding toward her and grasping the reins of her brown and white stallion.

"We can't keep doing this, Ricky," she'd explained in a voice trembling with grief.

"Oh, darlin'," he'd crooned in his seductive southern drawl, releasing the reins to take her hand. "I wish there was another way for us to be together." He lifted her hand to his lips. "Perhaps we can find a way."

He looked up to meet her gaze, eyes burning with intensity as he declared, "Annette, you know I can't live without you."

"But Ricky, I can't live like *this*!" she'd sobbed.

"Come here," he urged her gently. "Come here." He helped her down from the saddle, enfolding her in his embrace and letting her weep into his shoulder.

She pushed against him, but he drew her close with his strong arms. The smell of coffee and bacon clung to his chambray shirt under the leather duster.

"This is wrong!" she cried, trying unsuccessfully to free herself of his hold.

He pressed a kiss into her cheek, wiping away her tears with his thumb. "Don't cry now, darlin'. There, there."

And before she realized what was happening, his mouth was mingling with hers, tasting the saltiness of her tears. He scooped her into his arms and carried her toward the cabin.

"But what about your—" she'd protested. So many emotions warred inside her.

"She's gone for the day," Ricky had assured her.

"Please. I should go," Annette tried again to resist him, but he pressed a tender kiss to her ear.

"Stay with me, love," he'd begged, his voice husky with longing. "Please don't leave me."

Her determination faded as he kissed her again, repeating his plea into her ear. The hands that had been pushing him away now wrapped around his neck and held him close. She tried to remember her anger and resolve. But her thoughts were like thin wisps of steam hovering over the creek in the fall. They drifted away before she could grasp them.

He carried her into the bedroom. She let herself get lost in him.

And for a moment, she even allowed herself to forget he didn't belong to her.

It had been easy to reduce Mrs. Lawson to a mere idea: the wife. But the moment Annette heard her horrified gasp and looked up to see Vivian standing in the doorway, face ashen with the jagged pain of betrayal, she had become a woman of flesh and blood.

Ice-cold terror coursed through Annette's veins that had only seconds before run hot with passion. Then the heat of shame warmed her again.

Sick to her stomach with disgust, Annette clutched the blankets in a vain attempt to cover herself. She heard Ricky spew out Vivian's name as if it were a curse—as if it had been she who was caught in a grievous wrong.

Anguish twisted his wife's features as she turned and fled from the cabin.

Ricky rapidly pulled on his clothing, bolting from the room after Vivian, leaving Annette trembling upon their bed. She dressed herself with shaking hands, heart in her throat. What would happen to them now?

From the front steps of the Lawsons' cabin she watched Ricky chase after his wife, calling desperately for her to stop. Suddenly his pursuit came to an abrupt halt. He fell forward into the waving knee-high prairie grass and disappeared from Annette's sight. She watched, paralyzed, as his wife ran back to him, then suddenly sat still and rigid next to him as the buffalo grass billowed around her.

Annette felt a growing dread in the pit of her stomach as she realized the horrible truth. Ricky was dead.

Frightened, Annette ran to the barn and leapt onto her stallion, digging her heels into his flanks and urging him to flee this horrible place. Her heart pounded in her chest as his hooves thudded over the dry earth. Tears of confusion streaked her cheeks.

What had she done?

I. Conviction

"My guilt overwhelms me—
It is a burden too heavy to bear."

Ps. 38:4 NLT

Chapter One

*W*ith a sigh, Annette settled against the trunk of an aspen tree. Arranging the brown cotton skirt around her ankles, she retrieved a book from her apron pocket and turned to the marked page. The afternoon sun was unrelenting, but the shade afforded a cool place to rest.

Her sunbonnet hung from its strings around her neck and she smoothed her damp blond hair away from her face, squinting against the harsh light on the white pages. Finally, she gave up and leaned her head against the tree behind her. The soothing babble of the creek rushing over the rocks and the whisper of the wind through the tall buffalo grass calmed her spirits.

She relished the peacefulness of the moment. The complete absence of chaos and commands that filled her family's cabin.

Her reverie was disrupted by the bawling of a calf. Having grown up on a cattle ranch, she was accustomed to the Longhorns roaming the open range. The calf bawled again, and Annette registered the call of distress.

Peering around the tree she had been reclining against, she saw that the calf had approached the creek in hopes of alleviating his thirst. But there had been a severe thunderstorm the night before, accompanied by heavy rainfall. The bank of the creek, usually rock solid, had been reduced to a thick mud that sucked the calf's narrow hooves down and held them captive. The calf threw his head back and cried pathetically.

His mother looked on helplessly and bellowed in fear. Annette sighed as she removed her boots and hoisted up her skirt, tucking it between her legs and into the waistband in the front. She could hardly leave him there to break a leg. She waded into the shallow water, hoping the cow would understand her desire was to help.

She approached cautiously, arms outstretched. Speaking softly in low tones, she kept one eye on the cow as she took another step toward the mired calf. His eyes rolled in his head, revealing the whites as he strained against the mud. Annette took a deep breath and wrapped one arm around his neck and the other around his belly.

"What do you think you're doing?" a male voice demanded behind her.

Startled, Annette lost her footing in the slick mud and landed squarely on her bottom. From this disgraced position, she glared up at the stranger on horseback. "Well, I'm not rustling cattle," she grumbled indignantly, surveying the mud coating her entire backside.

He had an odd way of turning his head away from her while his eyes were shifting to look at her. She wondered if he was insane or some sort of criminal, and fear coiled in her belly. He looked away, his Adam's apple bobbing in agitation as he swallowed.

The man dismounted, but made no effort to help her to her feet. Instead he observed the trapped calf she had been attempting to free.

While his back was to her, Annette slowly came to her feet and began to edge away from him. She held her hands out to either side for balance, glancing warily over her shoulder one more time as she waded into the cold waters and began to make her way over the rocks to the opposite bank.

She was alone on the vast prairie with this man. He could do to her whatever he wished. No one would hear her cries for help.

"Hold on a minute," she heard him call gruffly after her. "I'll get him out. You just hold on."

She paused to watch as he scooped both arms under the calf's belly and easily lifted him from the mud. The calf's protests were stilled as the stranger placed him in the grass a few feet away from his mother. The cow bellowed, and with a happy little bleat, the calf bounded up to her and began nursing.

"Are you all right?" the man turned toward her, his head still angled slightly to the right while his eyes peered to the left in order to look at her.

Annette let out her breath slowly. While he had been tending to the calf, she had glimpsed the jagged scar running the full length of his right cheek. It narrowly missed his eye, and the pucker of scar tissue pulled at it oddly. It ran through the corner of his mouth, tugging his lips downward.

That was why he was facing away from her. He didn't want her to see. Compassion calmed her earlier fear.

"I'm fine," she assured him. "I'm glad you came along when you did. I'm not quite strong enough to lift him."

He nodded, tipping his dusty brown Stetson. He wore the standard uniform of a cowboy: leather duster, cowboy boots, and a Stetson. Annette had seen enough of them to know.

"My name's Jesse Stone," he tipped his hat again, politely.

"My cabin's just over that rise," he indicated the direction he had come from.

So he's living in Ricky's old cabin, Annette thought.

"It's good to meet you," she replied. "I'm Annette Hamilton. My pa's your neighbor, Walter Hamilton."

"Figured as much," Jesse stated.

Annette's toes were going numb from the icy water. She carefully made her way across the slippery rocks to the other side of the bank, then turned to face him, the water gurgling quietly between them.

"Well, good afternoon," she said in dismissal. "Thank you for your help."

"Yes ma'am," he tipped his hat, swallowing again. "Good afternoon."

Annette picked up her boots and climbed the small embankment to where she had been resting among the trees. She twisted to view the back of her skirt. Her mother would be furious with her. She sighed as she dried her feet on her skirt and stuck them into her boots. Nothing she could do about it now. She laced up her boots, made a futile attempt to brush the mud from her clothes, and set off at a brisk walk.

She shook her head, wondering what the man had hoped to accomplish by barking at her that way when it was perfectly obvious her intention had been to free the calf. She wondered if he knew the first thing about cattle. Jesse Stone was just another pioneer to stake his claim on one hundred and sixty acres of free land offered by the government. All a man had to do was live on it for five years and make improvements, then file for a deed of title. Jesse was the third man to stake his claim on this particular piece of property.

Ricky Lawson had been the first. After his death, his wife, Vivian, had lived with the Gibson family until she remarried—to the very man who purchased her deceased husband's herd and filed a claim for his homestead.

Then, she and Rob Hudson had only stayed for a year and a half before giving up and heading back east.

Though why, she didn't understand. Why would they abandon ranching when it was such a sure thing? There were times when she wondered if Vivian had convinced her husband to move away because she was uncomfortable with Annette so close by. And Annette couldn't say she blamed her.

Although the conversation they'd had the last time she had seen Vivian Lawson Hudson still perplexed her.

It was the spring of 1868. She remembered their meeting vividly. Annette had taken her basket and went to the creek to pick chokecherries. She had been so absorbed in her own thoughts, she hadn't been aware of another's presence until she heard a female gasp. Startled, she had peered around the bush and found herself staring into the wide brown eyes of Vivian Hudson, whose fear was quickly replaced with embarrassment.

Vivian had immediately apologized for startling her, and the two women had stared at one another awkwardly for what seemed like an eternity. Annette's mind raced to find some polite way to extricate herself from this uncomfortable encounter.

But Vivian spoke first. She had smiled as if they were friends and resumed picking berries, saying, "It's a lovely day today, isn't it? I'm so glad the snows have finally melted and everything is beginning to grow again. There are enough berries here for us both, I think."

Then she'd added, as if these words had special meaning: "I love it when spring finally warms the land. It's like a fresh start, every year."

A fresh start. Annette had caught herself staring at Vivian dubiously. Why should Vivian talk to her about a fresh start? As if it was just that easy. And why should Vivian even care about offering her a word of hope?

Annette had pondered the exchange over and over again. It seemed that in Vivian's warm brown eyes, she had seen forgiveness.

But how could Vivian possibly forgive her for what she had done? And if she had, why had Vivian been so quick to move away with her new husband?

Annette's attention jerked to the present as the sound of her siblings' wailing could be heard before the cabin came into view. She braced herself as she quickened her pace. There was no good excuse for her muddy skirts, and if the mayhem was any indication, her mother would be in a foul mood.

"Annette!" her mother scolded as she approached. Agnes Hamilton sat on a stump outside the cabin, wiping the tearstained face of five year old Mary.

Agnes had once been an attractive woman, though never quite as stunning as her firstborn daughter. Time, however, had left its unyielding mark on her. Her blond hair was streaked with gray, and her face creased with wrinkles. Annette assumed it was the strain and fatigue of raising five children over a period of eighteen years that had taken its toll. Her dress fit snugly across her midsection, and her temper was often just as strained.

"Get inside and tend to your brothers and sisters," Agnes snapped. "Where have you been?" Then, as her eyes took in Annette's skirts, she gasped. "What is that?"

"Sorry, Mama," Annette muttered as she hurried toward the door.

"I asked you where you've been," her mother reminded her irritably.

"You told me I could—"

"You need to stay within earshot. I've been calling you for half an hour."

"Yes ma'am," Annette said as she opened the door of the cabin. She groaned inwardly as she saw the baby, Howard, in his cradle howling at the top of his lungs.

Mary's twin sister, Janice, sat on a stool with her nose in a corner, making as much noise as the infant. And ten year old Ernest sat on the bed with his hands over his ears, scowling at her as if all the racket were Annette's fault.

Gritting her teeth and wishing for patience, Annette went to the infant and scooped him up. She bounced him gently as she hummed soothingly. Within seconds Howard had quieted. He stuck his fist into his mouth and sucked on his knuckles.

"Janice," she knelt down in front of her sobbing sister. "Why don't you calm down and tell me what happened."

Janice sniffled. "I hit Mary."

"Want to tell me why?"

"She stepped on my doll and got her all dirty."

"I'm sure it was an accident. When Mama lets you out of

the corner, be sure to apologize to your sister."

Janice nodded, pouting. But her crying had ceased.

"Ernest, can you please hold Howard? I need to start supper."

"I don't want to hold that stinky Drool-Baby," the boy protested.

"Hold him anyway. I need to start supper before Mama gets upset."

Reluctantly Ernest accepted his infant brother.

Annette went outside and joined her mother and Mary in the vegetable garden. She said nothing, but held out her apron for the produce to be deposited into it.

"You know I need your help, Annette. You can't just run off like that," Agnes chided.

"Sorry, Mama," Annette replied. But anger burned silently on her tongue. Her mother had told her to go out and get some fresh air while the little ones napped. She had been gone for less than an hour.

"Why are you so dirty?"

"I fell in the mud," she answered simply.

"Get these vegetables washed and peeled, then change your skirt before your father gets home."

"Yes ma'am."

After pulling a bucket of water up from the well, Annette rinsed the vegetables and took them inside. Howard was settled into his crib again, but was quietly staring at the ceiling. Janice looked like she had found something to play with in the corner.

Ernest was kneeling at the fireplace, stoking the coals.

Depositing the vegetables onto the table, Annette proceeded to prepare them for supper. As her hands worked, her mind drifted to their new neighbor, Jesse Stone. She wondered if he had gotten that terrible scar in a fight with wild Indians or if he had been attacked by a Longhorn steer on a cattle drive to the railhead in Cheyenne. Either way, she felt sorry for him. It was terrible to always be judged by a face you didn't choose.

Chapter Two

*J*esse watched the young woman as she walked away from him, carefully making her way through the tall grass in her bare feet. She didn't look back as she climbed up the slope to the grove of trees, where she freed the front of her muddy skirt from her waistband and stooped to retrieve her boots.

He turned away quickly, fearful she might catch him staring. He couldn't remember ever seeing such a lovely woman. There was no flaw in her appearance: fair skin, golden blond hair, sparkling blue eyes, high cheek bones, and full, pink lips. He resisted the urge to look back at her one more time.

Heaving a bitter sigh, Jesse slipped his left foot into the stirrup and swung his right leg over the saddle. He had to look down to make sure the toe of the boot was placed properly in the stirrup before nudging his horse forward. He rested his right hand on his thigh, wondering if he would ever find a woman who was interested in a mangled wreck of a man like him.

Well, there's more to a man than just his face or having two good legs, Jesse reminded himself. He was well on his way to making it rich in this land of opportunity. He wasn't sure why Rob Hudson had chosen to sell now, when beef was a prime market and he had everything he needed to build a fortune. With the completion of the railhead in Cheyenne, shipping beef to the east at a higher rate was guaranteed. Last year alone, the ranchers boasted a profit almost double what they had earned the year before, when they had been harassed by Kansas farmers as they drove their herds to Abilene.

In 1862 President Lincoln had passed the Homestead Act, which provided a way for men with ambition and an adventurous spirit to succeed by the sweat of their own brow as an alternative to the slave labor economy of the South. Any man over the age of twenty-one brave enough to make his way into the western territories (who had never taken up arms against the federal government), could file an application for one hundred and sixty acres. After living on the land for five years and providing proof of having made improvements to the property, he could then file for a deed of title and the land would become his. Without any money ever changing hands.

If the five years of occupation was not completed, the ownership of the land reverted back to the Government and became available for another individual to claim it. As Jesse understood it, he was the third man to apply for this particular claim. Ricky Lawson had died before his time was completed, and Rob Hudson had changed his mind.

Mr. Hudson said he missed the waters of Maryland's Chesapeake Bay. Jesse thought it sounded more than a little crazy to abandon a flourishing enterprise and head east to gamble on a far less profitable venture. But Mrs. Hudson had smiled as her husband explained their reasons for leaving. She had seemed at peace with the decision, so who was Jesse to argue? Their foolishness was his hope.

He had big plans for this ranch. He was going to buy five hundred more head of the Longhorns from Texas. Longhorns were quick to reproduce, and adding to what he had bought from Rob Hudson, he estimated by the fall he would have two thousand head. He figured at least half of the animals would be mature and ready for market, not including those he wanted to keep for breeding purposes. At between forty and sixty dollars a head, he would make a tidy profit.

He would convert the little cabin into a bunkhouse for the hired cowboys and build a grand three-story house with a fireplace in every room. He might not have a handsome face or an able body to offer a woman, but he could promise security and comfort. There were more and more folks coming into the territory all the time. There was bound to be a young woman who would find that a fair offer.

Jesse shook his head. Who was he fooling?

He'd never been brave enough to court a woman. Anytime he was attracted to a young lady, he began to swallow nervously, his palms would sweat, and he felt like his heart would pound a hole through his ribcage. Trying to manage the physical discomfort always made him speak abruptly. He usually frightened a woman off before he had the chance to slow his pulse.

Jesse snorted, disgusted with himself. He was twenty-one years old and he'd never kissed a woman. He couldn't even bring himself to look a woman squarely in the face for fear she would be repulsed by the jagged scar marring his features. He reached up now to trace the puckered skin with his gloved hand. How could any woman stand to look at that?

What difference did it make if he was a war hero? There were plenty of men who could claim the same status, and still had a handsome face to win a woman over. He'd known the cost of fighting, but he'd been so determined to prove himself as brave and valiant as his older brothers that he'd worn his mother out with his pleading until she granted him permission to enlist.

Now all he had to show for it was a disfigured face and black loathing for his greatest act of courage.

And a cattle ranch in Wyoming Territory.

That Johnny-Reb had done him a favor when he caught him in the leg with a well-aimed rifle shot. Jesse may have lost his right leg below the knee, but he'd been sent home to Springfield, Massachusetts with permission to live a civilian life. Oh, there were some men who did choose to return to the front after losing a limb, like his brother Stephen, but Jesse wasn't like them. He'd seen enough of war and was happy to find another way to contribute to the cause.

As soon as he was well enough he had taken a job at the National Armory. Jesse had signed on to make the Springfield rifles the boys at the front would hold in their hands as they marched out to meet the enemy. And he was paid fair wages for the job. He gave half of his earnings to his mother to help pay the mortgage and keep food on the table for them and his two sisters. And the other half he put in a jar under the bed.

His father had died of influenza when Jesse was ten, but he'd never felt the brunt of caring for the women until his brothers were off in the war. His father had left enough money to manage their affairs for several years, but it had eventually run out. Tending to the finances had always been Peter's concern, until it fell on Jesse's shoulders after his return from the war. His mother said if he was old enough to fight, he was old enough to be the man of the house.

Joseph Stone had been a loving father and husband, and a man of a strong moral character. Jesse had felt his loss keenly as a boy, and in his father's absence, he had looked to his older brothers for the example of what was required to be a man.

And, in a time of war, it had seemed the answer was simple: Fight. But Jesse should have known he didn't have the stomach for it, considering his revulsion the time his cousin Garrett had brought home a deer for supper when his family was visiting their home in the country.

Garrett had taken the boys outside to show them how to dress the deer and prepare the venison. Having grown up in the city, Jesse had never seen meat that wasn't cut and hanging in the butcher shop. He had embarrassed himself thoroughly by vomiting in the bushes and subjected himself to brutal teasing.

He should have known he wasn't made to be a soldier.

After the war had been won, the Federal Government decided that all the men who had suffered amputation of an appendage while fighting to defend the Union were due a monthly pension of eight dollars and a prosthetic limb as compensation. Jesse had accepted the prosthetic foot with gratitude despite the pain it caused. He could discard the crutches and walk like a man instead of a cripple, wearing a boot over the artificial foot. He added the eight dollars a month to his jar.

If only that dirty Rebel hadn't sliced his face with a bayonet, Jesse might have been able to live a normal life. But even more crippling than the shame of his appearance was the guilt eating away at his conscience. Some choices seemed wise in the moment, but later proved themselves to be as bitter as poison.

Jesse pushed these thoughts away. The past was a closed door that could never be walked through again. Once done, a deed could never be undone.

He'd saved his earnings and pension money for four long

years, waiting until both of his sisters were married off and in the care of their husbands. His mother had wept the day he announced he was moving west to stake his claim on a plot of land and raise cattle. Jesse had held her in his arms, but remained unmoved by her tears. He knew the only hope he had of finding peace was to leave the familiar world of New England and prove himself in an unknown place.

Maybe Jesse could never outrun the guilt following at his heels like a stubborn hound, but at least he could build a life that was his own. Here, the war seemed far away and forgotten. No one knew his brothers. No one knew his own story. It was a fresh slate.

He remembered the angry look on Annette Hamilton's face as he had barked at her. Why couldn't he speak to a woman without offending her? Of all the stupid, foolish things he could have said! It was perfectly obvious what she was trying to do. He could have rode down there and been her hero instead of setting her against him before they were even introduced. He sighed again as he rubbed his gloved hand over his chin. When would he ever learn how to act calm and debonair around a woman?

The wind had tugged strands of blond hair from her braid, and they slipped free under the sunbonnet she wore to wave like flags around her shoulders. She had sat there in the mud, bare ankles exposed to the sunlight, having fallen in her effort to hoist the bawling calf from the mud. He laughed at the memory of it!

He guessed women behaved differently out in the west. No respectable woman in Massachusetts would have ever been allowed to wander unescorted, and certainly it would never have entered her head to remove her shoes. She would have stood by and watched the calf struggle until its fragile legs were broken, forcing Jesse to shoot it if a mountain lion hadn't already dragged it off. But Annette had grown up on the frontier as a rancher's daughter and would probably end up a rancher's wife.

Even in mud-splattered calico, she was a beauty. Jesse swore under his breath. Some men seemed content to live and die alone. He wasn't one of them.

He nudged the mare into a canter. *I'm going to build my own life right here in the Wyoming Territory, even if I have to spend it alone.* He just didn't have the heart to follow in his brothers' footsteps any more. Stephen would graduate next year from Harvard with a law degree. Albert was completing coursework to become a clergyman in the Unitarian church. They both were married.

Jesse was the black sheep. He was stepping out and walking alone.

He had left behind cobblestone sidewalks and orderly streets with houses lined one after the other for a windswept prairie as far as the eye could see. He'd never felt crowded in Springfield, where the houses were close enough to peer into a neighbor's window and see what they were eating for dinner. But he felt like he had space to breathe and grow in this wild, open land. There was freedom in this untamed wilderness. Freedom to *be*.

Jesse watched the wind whip over the buffalo grass, buffeting the long blades wildly about as it swept over the hills and swells of the prairie. He breathed deeply the fresh smell of it. There was no hint of factory smoke, nor any indication of any human presence. He knew there were folks coming into the territory all the time, that he had neighbors to his left and to his right, but not for miles and miles. He had one hundred and sixty acres to call his own, and that was just the kind of yard he wanted.

Rob Hudson might have been homesick for the east coast and the rise and fall of the waves, but Jesse couldn't imagine a more magnificent view than the one confronting him at that very moment. He loved the feel of his horse underneath him, the wind against his skin, and the sunshine warm on his shoulders. The vast, wild splendor of these grassy plains made him feel lost in something bigger than himself.

The day he left Massachusetts, his brother Stephen had driven him to the train station to see him off. His penetrating eyes had searched Jesse's for a moment before he said, "You know you're breaking Mother's heart."

"I know it," Jesse admitted. "But she's got you and Albert, and soon she'll have grandchildren to sit on her lap. I'll write often. She'll get used to it."

"You don't have to go so far away. There are plenty of opportunities in the east. You don't have to go to college if it doesn't suit you. There are other choices." Stephen was a lawyer. He enjoyed using his powers of persuasion.

"Look, Stephen, I know the family will miss me. I love you all, and this isn't an easy decision for me. But sometimes a man needs to find his own way. Respect that this is my choice." Jesse hadn't meant to sound so angry.

Stephen toyed with the left sleeve of his linen suit jacket, secured under the armpit. Just below the elbow, his arm ended in an abrupt stump. Jesse knew he had a habit of fidgeting with the loose sleeve when he was thinking.

He came at Jesse from a new angle. "Annie ran into Sophia

a few nights ago. She said Sophia looked very crestfallen at the news of your departure. You know that girl's had her eye on you for years now. You could marry her and settle here, let our children grow up together. Cousins should know one another. She's a fine looking girl, and from a nice family. She'd make a good wife."

Jesse knew Stephen spoke truly. Sophia had seemed to strategically make herself available whenever Jesse was in the room. He couldn't pretend he hadn't noticed. How she could stand to look at him or tolerate his brusque ways, Jesse couldn't imagine. Sophia was pretty enough, and she seemed kind and soft spoken. But she was in love with an ideal Jesse knew he could never live up to.

"I'm looking for a pioneer wife," Jesse countered with a crooked smile. "I want a woman who can shoot a mountain lion with one hand and cook beef stew with the other."

His brother's eyes narrowed at the joke. "You might want to reconsider that idea. Besides," Stephen let out a frustrated sigh, "you know Mother's still grieving over Peter. She can't stand the idea of losing you, too."

"She's not losing me. I'm not even leaving the country. I'll write. I'll come back to visit someday. Don't try to play to my emotions like I'm a feeble minded jury member."

"No need to get belligerent. I'm just fulfilling my duty to ask you to stay. Have you considered—"

Jesse brought his right hand up to his brother's chest, holding his argument at bay. "Stephen. Just let me go." He lowered his hand and offered it in peace as he added, "And wish me luck."

Stephen clasped his hand firmly, his lips thinning into a line. "I wish you would stay, Jesse. But I wish you luck wherever you choose to go."

Jesse held fast to the handshake while he wrapped his left arm around his brother's shoulders. "Tell Mother I love her."

He broke free and grabbed his suitcase, striding away before Stephen could see the doubt in his eyes and pounce on his weakness. Leaving had been more difficult than he'd expected.

But once he was on the train, listening to the wheels whirring over the steel tracks and watching the world race past his window, Jesse had felt the first stirring of hope he had known in a long time. Maybe his life wasn't a closed book, but a story he could write for himself in the wild west.

Jesse was startled from his reverie as his mount climbed a rise and he saw the herd stretched out below him, grazing quietly and murmuring to one another in low tones. He smiled as he descended the grassy knoll. Their horns were dipped low to the ground, but still held a promise of danger. Tip to tip, they could extend up to seven feet in length. There was no uniformity in the color of their coats. They speckled the prairie with hues of red and brown and black and white. And when he looked at them, Jesse saw his future.

Chapter Three

The cast iron pot in the fireplace was bubbling. Annette lay baby Howard down in his cradle and hurried across the room, using her skirt to lift the lid. She carefully swung the iron hook the pot was resting on outward, removing it from the fire. She stirred hopefully. It didn't appear to be scalded, and she sighed with relief as she replaced the lid and checked the corn muffins.

Her mother had left her to prepare supper and care for the baby and the twins while she went to the well to draw water. Ernest was in the barn, helping their father with the evening chores. No sooner had her mother left when the baby had begun to spit up. Annette had rushed to tend to him, fearful of the reprimand she would receive if either of her parents returned and found him wearing vomit and crying.

She sighed wearily as she removed the corn muffins, reminding her little sisters that they had been asked to set the table. The five year old girls chattered and giggled as they grudgingly obeyed.

The cabin door opened and Agnes entered, carrying the bucket of water. Annette would have preferred to fetch it herself, but supposed her mother needed the moment of fresh air and silence as much as she did.

Annette pushed an errant strand of hair back from her face as she announced, "Supper's ready, Mama."

"All right. Girls," she addressed Janice and Mary, "come sit down at the table and wait for Papa."

The twins skipped and bounced to the table, climbing onto the bench seat next to one another and folding their hands in their laps. They looked like little angels as Walter and Ernest entered the cabin and took their places. Annette and Agnes served the men, then seated themselves.

"We'll be having company next Sunday for supper," Walter informed them with apparent satisfaction.

"Yes?" Agnes asked, her blond eyebrows lifted in curiosity. "Who's coming?"

"Bryan Hunt," he replied, addressing Annette. "He's our neighbor to the south. He's been out here for about two years and hasn't found a wife yet. Maybe he was waiting for the train to bring more ladies from the east to choose from. You'd better grab him before someone else does."

"What man wouldn't be interested in our daughter?" Agnes demanded, her blue eyes lighting up with pride.

Annette felt her stomach convulse with dread.

"I told him my daughter was the prettiest girl this side of the Missouri," he declared in response. "That Hunt's a good catch," he assured Annette.

She forced down the bite of stew lodged in her throat. Her father's brown eyes surveyed her response quizzically. He placed his fork on the table and demanded, "Don't you want to have a house and family of your own?"

"Of course I do, Papa," Annette assured him quickly, forcing a smile. "I'm just nervous about meeting him, that's all."

Walter laughed, lifting his fork for another bite. "Don't worry. He's a bit older than you, probably thirty if I had to guess. But he's easy on the eyes and seems nice enough. I think you'll like him."

Annette nodded, as if reassured. Her father had good intentions, she was sure of it.

Walter Hamilton wasn't the tallest man Annette had ever met, but he had a presence that filled the room when he entered. He was broad shouldered and barrel-chested and spoke in a booming voice that commanded attention. Annette didn't dare go against him.

Her supper churned in her stomach. What was she going to do?

~

The cabin was finally silent. Annette waited just a few more minutes, to be sure everyone was sleeping. The twins were breathing evenly in their bed against the far wall. She quietly slipped into her boots and draped a shawl around her shoulders. After carefully descending the ladder from the loft room she shared with her sisters, Annette tip-toed across the main room of the cabin where her brother, Ernest slept. Her parents and baby Howard had a room to themselves.

She cautiously lifted the hinge and let herself outside. The stars twinkled overhead in the black expanse of the sky. The vast prairie stretched out before her like an endless sea, the buffalo grass appearing almost blue in the moonlight. The chirping sounds of insects in the grass met her ears like music. Closing her eyes, she breathed the sweet smell of the night into her lungs.

With one backward glance over her shoulder, Annette

hurried away from the cabin. If her parents knew she was wandering about alone in the darkness, they would have been both terrified and furious. Annette knew there were dangers, both from nature and mankind. Wolves, mountain lions, horse thieves, Indians, and any other number of threats lurked in the darkness. But Annette felt safe.

This prairie land was her home. Her father had come west to mine for gold in '49, where he had met and married her mama in San Francisco, California. But after a time, he decided ranching would be an easier and faster way to make his fortune. And so he had moved his young family to Wyoming where there was free fodder for cattle to graze.

Annette carried a bowie knife in her waist, assuming it would provide some means of protection if she found herself attacked by either man or beast. She had slipped out undetected for these nighttime excursions more than once and never experienced an encounter of any kind. Her parents may not understand why she chose to place herself in jeopardy, and Annette wasn't sure she could explain it herself. She simply felt the need to escape, to be in isolation and hear the voice of nature.

She enjoyed her moments of solitude during the afternoon, whenever she could manage to get away. But there was something about the moonlight and the silence of the night that spoke to her heart. Sometimes she would look up at the sky stretching as far to the left as it did to the right, sprinkled with dancing white stars, and feel the urge to pray. But why should God listen to her prayers?

The prettiest girl west of the Missouri, her father had called her. There had been a time when such a compliment would have been welcomed. She had appreciated the attention she received from men. Anywhere she went, men couldn't keep their eyes off her. She used to blush under their gaze, enjoying the warmth flushing her cheeks as they winked or waved at her.

Now she wished she could hide from the eyes of men. Their attention made her feel uneasy, for now she knew what they were thinking when they stared at her. If they knew the truth of what she had done, of *who* she was, some might lose respect for her while others would simply want to stand in line to exploit her. And if she fell into the hands of another man like Ricky, would she have the strength she lacked the first time or once more yield to the loneliness inside her?

She stood still as she crested a rise in the undulating prairie. From there she could see a light shining in the distance. Now it was the light from Jesse Stone's cabin. But once it had belonged to Ricky Lawson.

Annette had thought herself in love with him. What a fool she had been.

He had been so handsome and debonair, and had made her laugh so easily. She'd enjoyed his attention, never realizing the danger he posed. When Ricky was flirting with her, she had felt her insides melt and her heart flutter. She had felt wanted, not for her ability to cook dinner or change a diaper, but as a man wants a woman. Ricky had made her feel special.

She had been sixteen years old. She'd never been alone with a man before, other than her father or brothers. She had been innocent.

Annette had been wholly unequipped to deal with the calculated intentions of the older man. It all seemed so clear to her now, so very obvious. But then, all she had known was that when he looked at her with his green eyes full of desire, she felt a fire spring to life within her. A harmless touch of his hand to her elbow would spark a yearning she had never known before. His jokes and charming manner had disarmed her. His eyes burning with longing had conquered her.

A tear trickled down her cheek. Shame consumed her.

She had let it happen. Though she'd never meant to. It was true she'd enjoyed the warmth that his lingering smile had given. The way his eyes said so much without a word passing his lips. He wanted her near him, and Annette couldn't help but respond to his longing for her. She wanted to be near him, too. There was a deep ache in her heart that his presence filled.

And so she had sought ways to be in his company. She had been happy to deliver the message that a traveling photographer was coming through, documenting the changing west and the families that were part of its story. She had spotted him near the cabin and waved to him, watching as he hurried down the slope to meet her at the place where the creek meandered past his home.

She had seen the pleasure her arrival brought him before he ever opened his mouth. But she had enjoyed hearing him admit it. "Annette Hamilton! You're a pleasant surprise!"

"Hello, Mr. Lawson. My mama sent me to tell you that there's a photographer coming through. She thought you might be interested in getting your picture taken."

"I appreciate the thoughtfulness. Is your family going to let him take a photograph?"

"Yes. Papa says one day we could be in a book, back east. The man's giving us a copy, and keeping one for himself. He's making a collection of all the families he meets as he travels west to Oregon."

"You'll make a fine subject for his camera," Ricky had drawled in his Southern accent that made anything he said sound just a little more flirtatious. "You're pretty as a picture as it is."

Annette had responded with a blushing giggle. "Thank you, Mr. Lawson." She had glanced down at his feet nervously, her eyes darting back to his at the sound of his deep chuckle.

He'd smiled then, a different kind of smile. There was something in his expression that melted her insides like butter in a skillet. "I like your giggle," he'd told her, grinning.

"I like your laugh, too," she'd admitted, realizing her own smile had changed. There was something passing between them she'd never known before. Something elemental. Like the charged air around a bull when he sensed a female nearby.

"Would you like me to give you a ride home?" he'd asked then, his eyes hopeful.

"Oh, no thank you," she'd hastily declined, afraid of what her parents would think if she arrived home with Mr. Lawson.

"Are you safe, out on the prairie alone?" he'd asked then, doubtfully scanning the horizon.

"Yes, I'm fine. I grew up on this prairie, and I know how to take care of myself."

"Do you walk alone often?"

Annette hesitated. She sensed it was a leading question.

Her pulse accelerated as she admitted, "I do like to walk alone."

"Well," he grinned then, "maybe I'll run into you sometime

soon. Would that be all right?"

´ The spiral of heat grew in her stomach. She smiled and nodded, unsure of how to answer. "I'd better head home. Good evening."

"All right then," he'd replied reluctantly. "You be careful now."

"I will," she'd promised, turning to leave. She'd walked the distance of several yards when something compelled her to look back. Ricky Lawson stood rooted to the spot, watching her go.

He grinned broadly and waved when he saw he'd been caught, and Annette felt a flutter of her heartbeat as she waved back. This time, he turned away first and headed back to his cabin.

Where his wife was most likely preparing his supper. A sinking feeling had quickly replaced the exhilarated racing of her heart. She had let herself forget there was a Mrs. Lawson. The look in his eyes and the tone of his voice made it easy to forget.

Annette had resolved to keep her distance and to be on guard against those green eyes and that Southern drawl of his. But when he'd come to find her the next day in the grove of aspens where she often retreated for a moment of afternoon solitude, she'd found she was no match for his charm.

Mama always said, "If you play with fire, you shouldn't be surprised if you get burned." She had thought of that saying as she watched him approach, a look of pure satisfaction registering on his handsome face.

She had stood up, determined to be polite and greet him, then quickly take her leave. She watched as his horse crossed the creek, water splashing into the air. Ricky had brought it to a halt just a few feet shy of her and dismounted. The black leather duster brushed against the back of his legs as he closed the distance between them. He'd removed his black Stetson, running a hand through his hair.

"I was hoping I'd see you today," he'd admitted, a slow smile curving his lips.

Annette felt her cheeks warm with the admission. She smiled at him shyly. She wasn't sure how to respond. The man was married.

They talked quietly for a few moments, then Ricky had left with a tip of his hat and a grin. But not before he had promised they would meet again soon.

Annette's head had swirled with confusion. Was she making too much of the man's interest? Perhaps he was just being polite or brotherly. Though she knew there was nothing brotherly in the way he looked at her. She considered mentioning the meeting with her mother that night, but didn't want to paint Mr. Lawson in a dark light if it was undeserved.

Annette stayed close to home for a few days, but eventually her need for solitude overcame her fear of the flirtatious Mr. Lawson. The only way to preserve her sanity and find the patience to care for her younger siblings was to take some time alone to herself.

Soon she fell back into her old routine, and worries of Mr. Lawson's intentions slipped from her mind. Until the afternoon she saw him riding his mount across the creek toward her. She felt warm from the tip of her toes to the top of her head. She was surprised by the sense of elation his appearance brought her.

Once again the conversation was brief, but Ricky mentioned

he had missed seeing her and hoped he wouldn't have to wait so long to see her again. Annette made no promises, but she let herself fall back into her usual routine of visiting the aspen grove. And he made it a habit to visit her there.

After a few weeks, it seemed thoughts of him were all that filled her mind. As she washed the breakfast dishes, she was preoccupied with hopes of an encounter that afternoon. And at night before she fell asleep, she replayed their last meeting in her mind.

Then Ricky made his confession: "I think I've fallen in love with you, Annette," he admitted quietly. "You're all I ever think about."

Me too, she had thought silently. She was short of breath and unable to step away from him. She felt as though she were under his spell, unable to make her body obey the commands her mind was giving.

"Walk away from him. You need to put distance between you. Tell him to leave, to stop saying these things!" her instincts screamed. But she couldn't force herself to look away as he reached out and gently caressed her cheek, his touch igniting a fire within her.

At her sudden intake of breath, he had stepped closer. She had to lift her chin to look into his face. He hesitated, giving her time to run away if she wanted. But curiosity and yearning held her captive.

His fingers trailed from her cheek until they were tangled in her hair just behind her ear. Her heart pounded like an Indian drum in her chest. She knew he was going to kiss her. And she longed to feel his lips pressed against her own.

When finally his mouth met hers, she felt something awaken inside her. She ached to feel his arms around her, and was pleased when she felt them pulling her to his chest. She sighed into him, letting the kiss deepen, carried away by sensations she never imagined possible.

She didn't realize her eyes were closed and she was clinging to his neck until the kiss ended. Annette abruptly opened her eyes to find him gazing down at her, smiling like a king surveying his treasure. She'd felt a weakness in the pit of her stomach, as if something had given way. In that brief moment, everything had changed.

In his face she saw both tenderness and possession. He had claimed her. She knew her heart belonged to him, and there was no joy to be found in it. He was married.

But the wild beating of her heart spoke another story. Ricky's touch made her feel alive; his eyes made her feel wanted.

"You're so beautiful," he'd whispered huskily, letting his mouth graze her cheek.

What good could come from this secret love affair? She should push him away from her and curse him as a rogue. But how could she turn away from the deep emotions he awakened in her soul?

He'd broken the embrace then, taken her hand and led her to sit beside him on a fallen log. "I've wanted to do that for a long time," he confessed, his eyes studying every detail of her face. He reached out to stroke her hair. Her sunbonnet had fallen over her shoulders.

Trembling, Annette couldn't speak.

"Are you all right?" he'd asked with such gentle concern that any fear or regret she'd felt disappeared.

She nodded. He put his arm around her shoulders and drew her close. She rested her head against him, feeling the pounding of his heart.

"I wish I never had to let you go," he whispered into her ear, wrapping both arms around her.

Annette closed her eyes, relishing this moment, dreading when it must end.

"Can I see you tomorrow?" he'd asked.

Annette consented with a silent nod of her head.

"That seems so far away." His voice was thick with longing.

Annette tried to find her bearings. The world seemed to be spinning around her, out of control. In the span of half an hour, her entire life had changed. Nothing would be the same again.

Ricky rose from the log, and Annette knew he was going to leave her. She clung to his hand, hating the thought of his departure. But she said nothing. She let him lead her to where his mount waited. He leaned down to brush a gentle kiss across her lips.

"I'll miss you," he whispered. His eyes locked with hers, and she felt her heart wildly thumping in her chest. He smiled. "I'll look forward to tomorrow," he promised.

Then he swung up into the saddle, and with a wave of his hand, rode away.

Annette had returned home in a daze. Her heart soared and yet her mind was tortured. She busied herself with preparing supper and tending her siblings, fearful that her parents would notice the change in her. For she knew she was different now. She had tasted the forbidden fruit... and longed for more.

Chapter Four

*A*nnette released her sadness in a long sigh as she watched the distant light twinkle across the prairie. She wondered why Jesse Stone was awake so late into the night. Perhaps he was writing a letter to a sweetheart back east about his new life in the cattle country.

Many lonely nights she had gazed across the miles at that small flickering light while she thought of Ricky and his wife alone in their cabin. Jealousy had twisted her insides with pain. The very possibility of him kissing his wife's lips made her sick with envy.

And shame. For Vivian was the one who had rights to him.

After that first kiss, Annette had spent the night weeping as she tossed and turned with tortured emotions. She'd heard stories of the wondrous spark that a man and a woman could share, of the way they longed to be together until the moment when they were. This was her first love. She had discovered there was more to a kiss than just the lips touching. It was something that happened deep inside her, not just in her physical body, but in her being. As if something had been shared and now they were joined by a tenuous bond.

She knew she should tell Ricky to stay away from her. He was wrong to kiss a woman who was not his wife. But Annette longed to feel the warmth of his kiss again. Her imagination conjured their next meeting.

What harm could there be in stealing another kiss?

But far more had been stolen than a mere kiss. Annette hadn't known what to expect. She had been innocent to the ways of the world. Of course, she knew there was a special way that babies were created between a man and a woman. She had seen her mother grow round with child several times.

What she hadn't known was that it was possible to get caught up in a whirlwind of sensations until her reasoning was clouded and her good judgment lost. That what had felt like bliss could end in pain. And that she would be left alone to stare her loss in the eyes.

Looking back, she wondered if he had been preparing her for what he certainly had known was coming. It seemed each time they met, he hungered for a little more of her until he had taken all she had to give. And then he had returned to his wife while she lay alone in the barn and sobbed brokenly, wondering how she would hide her disgrace and humiliation.

Tormented by guilt, and equally sick with longing for Ricky to be hers alone, Annette had stood in this very spot and watched as the candle light from the Lawsons' cabin flickered in the night. She had fallen on her knees and begged for God to forgive her of her sins, vowing she would never again allow herself to be swept away in a tempest of desire.

Yet even as she uttered the words to the heaven, she knew them to be a falsehood. If a simple kiss had bound them together, how much more intricately woven were they after having shared the intimacy of husband and wife? She had allowed herself to be driven into a corner where there was no escape. If she remained in this relationship, she would be tormented with envy and shame. But if she ended it, she would be haunted by loneliness and sweet memories of the passion they had shared. What hope was there for her now?

Realizing the ugly truth of her situation, Annette had decided to go to the aspen grove the following afternoon and wait for Ricky to meet her. She was certain he would after what had transpired in his barn the afternoon before. And when he did, she would tell him they must never meet like this again. She could not continue to be his mistress. It was a horrible mistake and she was sorry it had happened.

But as he had appeared over the rise, black duster stretched taut across broad shoulders, his Stetson shading a handsome face that wore a seductively crooked grin, Annette knew she didn't have the strength to follow through with her resolution. His hold over her was too strong.

There in the shadows, in the midst of the vast prairie, he held her against his chest and kissed her deeply. Despite the sweet words and hollow promises he whispered in her ear, a dark resentment began to mingle with the tender feelings in Annette's heart. The joy began to fade into anger, and the longing into loathing.

Ricky could never give her his last name or a home to call her own. He could only give her moments of ecstasy in a life of loneliness.

Determined to end their affair once and for all, Annette had asked permission of her parents to take a ride and look for the late blooming buffalo berries. Agnes had agreed, and Annette had saddled her horse and rode straight to the Lawson's cabin. She had circled wide around the cabin itself, approaching from the vantage point of the barn and keeping a watchful eye for Mrs. Lawson. She hoped she could produce a believable lie if she found herself confronted with the woman.

But it was Ricky who spotted her. He was saddling his own stallion in the barn when he heard the sound of hooves approaching. He had emerged from the barn, his green eyes lighting with excitement at the sight of her.

She should have anticipated his response to her announcement. From the beginning, he had been both persistent and persuasive. He wasn't going to just let her walk away.

Her shoulders drooped with the weight of brutal honesty as she admitted that she should have known her own weakness and inability to follow through. She had known at the onset that they were flirting with danger. Perhaps she should have gone to extreme measures to ensure she was never alone in his presence again.

If she had written him a note detailing her decision to end their relationship, it would have precluded the opportunity for him to seduce her one more time. It would have prevented the outcome of her good intentions: Vivian's discovery of their affair and Ricky's unlikely death.

Yet, it would have left physical evidence of their relationship. It was just as possible that he wouldn't have destroyed the note immediately, as he should have, but instead left it lying around to be discovered by his wife. Then what might have happened? If Ricky hadn't died on the spot, certainly Vivian would have been more inclined to publicly indict her.

Annette had tried to resist Ricky that fateful day, but she hadn't tried hard enough. Never could she have imagined how this twisted drama would unfold. Even now, two and a half years later, Annette shook her head in disbelief at the memory.

If she had been stronger in her resolve, never dismounted from her stallion or let him put his arms around her, whisper sweet words in her ear or kiss her cheek, how would the story have ended? She could never take back what she had given away. She could never pretend the whole sordid affair hadn't happened.

It was her history now. It would forever be a part of her life's story.

Oh Lord, is there no way to erase my guilt? Annette breathed into the still night as painful regret assaulted her.

Now her father had a suitor in mind for her. She was lucky it hadn't happened sooner. Perhaps if her parents didn't rely so heavily on her to help with the younger children and household chores, they would have seen her married off sooner. With four children younger than herself to care for, Annette's capable hands and strong back had been sorely needed. She wondered how they would fare if she ever did leave home.

But marriage wasn't a realistic prospect for her. What respectable man would want her? A man brought his money and home to the marriage, the promise of security and shelter and a respectable name. A woman's gift was her purity and the ability to care for her husband and their home.

If she did marry Bryan Hunt, how would he react to the discovery that she was a soiled dove? In this wild territory, there were few respectable women worthy of marriage. The other kind of loose women could be found in every railroad town across the prairie. But when a man chose his wife, he wanted her to be untouched. And if she misled Bryan into believing she was, he would only resent her once the truth came out.

But regret wasn't powerful enough to change the past. Only

powerful enough to cripple. Annette hung her head. What was she going to do?

No one knew of her terrible secret except Vivian Lawson Hudson, who had carried it with her on the train back east. Her father would never understand why she should resist marriage, and how could Annette confess the reason why she was unsuitable for it?

The day she had giggled under Ricky's appreciative eye, she'd had no way of knowing just how much he would take from her.

Why hadn't Vivian announced her sins to the world? Annette had ruined Vivian's marriage. Why hadn't Vivian ruined her reputation? Why had she let the secret go quietly with Ricky to his grave?

A fresh start, Vivian had said. How could she ever have a fresh start?

~

Jesse leaned over to blow out the oil lamp resting on the table. The snoring of the three men who shared the cabin with him seemed loud in the silence. Jesse slipped into his bunk and pulled the blankets up to his chin. His mind was racing.

Claude Montgomery, the ranch foreman, shifted in his bunk, producing a series of loud snorts and groans that only further prevented Jesse's mind from resting. Claude had been with Rob Hudson before Jesse arrived, and with Ricky Lawson before him. He had come into the territory from Texas, with experience in ranching valuable to the newcomers who wanted to gain a fortune in beef but knew nothing about the Longhorn cattle.

Jesse had wondered why Claude had chosen to work for others instead of staking his own claim on the land. When asked, Claude had explained that the Homestead Act offered land only to men who had never taken up arms against the federal government. And Claude had fought for the Confederacy. Which Jesse found particularly interesting since Jim Ingram, one of the two cowboys who worked the ranch with him, was Negro. Jesse had been surprised by it at the first encounter. He supposed he shouldn't have been. Negroes could make a new life in the West just as easily as broken down veterans. Everyone, it seemed, was trying to escape their pasts.

"Rattlesnake" Rupert Sheldon, the other cowboy, was from England. He claimed he had come to America seeking adventure, but Jesse suspected a deeper reason for leaving his homeland. Rupert had earned his nickname when he shot a rattlesnake dead with a single well-aimed shot, saving Claude as it slithered up behind him.

Jesse was relieved that Claude and Jim seemed to have reached an understanding and worked together without conflict, for the most part. Claude admitted he'd resented the Negro's presence when he was first hired, but the strong, black man had eventually won his respect with patience and hard work. Jesse admired Claude's broad-minded wisdom to grasp the equality of mankind despite the prejudice of his upbringing. It took moral courage and free thinking, which were qualities Jesse greatly respected.

In Massachusetts, the only Negroes Jesse had known had been free. He had been raised surrounded by abolitionists and antislavery activists. He was well acquainted with the words of former slave Frederick Douglass, and the brave acts of Harriet Tubman. As a boy, he'd read *Uncle Tom's Cabin*, by Harriet

Beecher Stowe, and his father had known William Lloyd Garrison, editor of the abolitionist newspaper, *The Liberator*. Stories of the courageous John Brown and his siege on Harper's Ferry, Virginia had been legend in his household.

It seemed ironic to Jesse that they should all now sleep under the same roof: the rebel from Texas, the former slave, and himself. Rattlesnake was the only one set apart from the influence of their civil conflict.

Rolling over on his bunk, Jesse tried to quiet his mind. He had discussed the future of the ranch with Claude that evening. He was in the financial position to begin building the house he'd envisioned when he left Springfield. He would build it on the tallest rise, so he could sit on his front porch and look out over the vast acres of swaying prairie grass and grazing cattle, like a king on hill.

Staring up at the rafters, draped in shadows, he considered something Claude had revealed in the course of their conversation. Jesse had heard, and wanted to believe, that all the odds were in his favor as a cattle rancher. The government provided the land and the land provided the fodder. It was as simple as buying a few head of cattle and watching the herd grow. Longhorns were known to be hardy and fast producing.

But there was one threat to his success. The same threat that was posed to any cattleman on this land of the open range. Cattle rustlers. His ranch foreman told stories of men weeding out unbranded calves, or mavericks, and marking them as their own. Or changing an existing brand into one uniquely his own. It was an easy way to build a herd without ever spending a penny.

Since the law wasn't a strong presence out in this wild territory, it was up to the ranchers and their cowboys to watch out for these thieves and to dispense justice when necessary. This frontier justice was usually served with a rope under the nearest tree. It was an unsettling prospect, and Jesse rolled onto his side, hoping to shift his thoughts as well.

He winced as the stump of his right leg tingled painfully, routing his thoughts back to the past. To the war.

His mother had made him wait until he was sixteen to enlist, although he would have gone sooner if she'd allowed it. He had been so eager to prove himself, to be a war hero like his brothers. He should have understood the cost fighting would demand.

Certainly he had known the risk involved. Peter, the eldest, had been one of the first to enlist after Fort Sumter fell to the rebels in South Carolina in 1861. He had managed to keep himself alive and all his limbs attached for two years, killing so many rebels he was promoted from Private all the way up to First Sergeant and was in line for a promotion to Sergeant Major at the time of his death. He also boasted a Medal of Honor for gallantry and bravery in battle.

Stephen was the second eldest. He wore the rank of Corporal at the time he was wounded and the amputation of his left hand required from the splintering of his bones and resulting infection. His injury had occurred while in the act of capturing the Confederate flag, an act which also earned him a Medal of Honor.

Despite his disability, Stephen had re-enlisted and served in the Invalid Corps as a cook. Jesse validated his decision not to re-enlist on the basis that his amputation was more incapacitating than his brother's. At least Stephen could walk without a crutch. One could get by much more easily without a hand than without a foot.

Albert had fared the best of all of the Stone brothers. He had earned a Medal of Honor for bearing the colors despite great risk to himself and returned from the war unscathed. Well, perhaps not completely unscathed, but at least with all of his vital appendages intact. He had lost his hearing in one ear from the blast of cannon fire at close range.

Jesse had wanted to avenge Peter's death. He'd wanted to prove he was just as strong and brave as his three older brothers. He'd resented being left behind with his sisters while they were celebrated and revered.

He had marched off to war after three weeks of training, which had consisted mostly of learning to drill and the thirteen steps necessary to loading his rifle. After two weeks of marching and one horrific battle, Jesse had been wounded severely enough to require the amputation of his right leg and transport to a military hospital for recovery. He had then been honorably discharged and sent home as a veteran at the age of sixteen.

Tracing the jagged scar lining his face, Jesse tried to push down the terrible sense of failure.

He remembered the plans for the home he had sketched. He was only twenty-one. There was plenty of time left to prove himself.

Chapter Five

*A*nnette spent the morning over the boiling wash tub, stirring the dirty clothes and scrubbing them against the washboard, then transferring them to the rinse bucket. She removed the last item from the wooden tub, wrung it out and hung it on the line to dry. Now that her work was done, perhaps she could slip away for a little while.

She peered over her shoulder at the silent cabin. She doubted her absence would even be noticed. Her mother had been preoccupied with teaching the twins their letters while little Howard slept. Ernest was pulling weeds in the garden and his back was to her, absorbed in his own thoughts.

Annette let her feet carry her through the windswept prairie to her quiet place. She had always found solace in the shade of the aspen trees, though she had not returned to it for several months after Ricky's death. She settled herself now on the fallen log where they had sat together, wishing she could free herself both of his memory and of the consequences he had brought to her life.

Tomorrow Bryan Hunt would eat supper with them. She hoped he was either unattractive or unlikeable. It would make rejecting him far easier. And more understandable to her parents.

Despair welled up inside her until she felt nauseous with it. She closed her eyes, leaning her elbows on her knees and holding her head in her hands. What had she done?

If Bryan Hunt should find her to his liking, he would request permission to call on her. If she allowed it, in time he would likely ask for her hand. And then where would she be? She could never carry her shame into a marriage.

Without the hope of marriage, what hope did she have? To flee to Cheyenne or any one of the towns that had sprung up along the railroad tracks that offered "entertainment and comfort" for the lonely men on the plains? It would be better to be dead than to live the life of a prostitute. But any woman who wasn't pure was automatically reduced to the same status.

Oh Lord, can You hear me or have You turned Your face away from me and made Your ears deaf to my voice? What can I do?

The whistling of the wind through the waving grass was the only reply. The blue sky overhead was silent as white clouds slowly drifted by. Annette sighed. Had she really expected an answer?

Tears of self-pity traced a wet trail down her cheek. She had no one to blame but herself for her predicament. Except perhaps Ricky, and what good was it to blame a dead man?

Annette was distracted from these morbid thoughts as a man crested the hill on the opposite bank. For a moment her heart caught in her throat, until she blinked away the past and saw that this man's Stetson was brown, and his horse was white with dappled gray on the haunches. It was her new neighbor, Jesse Stone.

She intended to march off with a haughty glare in his direction, until she saw his posture change the moment he noticed her in the shadows. She scoffed at her own conceit as she realized he hadn't come seeking her out. He had merely been checking on the cattle and stumbled across her today as innocently as he had the week before.

He shifted in the saddle, tipping his hat in greeting and looking as though he might continue on his way. But then he seemed to suffer a change of mind as he brought the reins to his mount's neck and urged him across the creek to where Annette watched his approach with wary eyes.

"Good afternoon, ma'am," he greeted her awkwardly, keeping his scarred right cheek turned away from her view as he twisted his slate gray eyes to meet hers.

"Good afternoon, Mr. Stone," Annette replied, wondering again how he had come by the scar.

"I just wanted to say I'm sorry for my behavior the last time we met. I didn't mean to be rude." He swallowed nervously, wishing he had been able to speak without sounding gruff again.

But after a moment of silent study, Annette answered, "Apology accepted," as she came to her feet. She felt so sorry for his obvious discomfort that she wanted to put him at ease. "I suppose it's an uncommon sight to see a woman wrestling a calf in the mud, and bound to distract any man into a state of irritation."

Caught off guard by the pretty smile that accompanied her teasing tone, a laugh passed Jesse's lips. Her smiled broadened, and Jesse's heart began to pound in his chest.

"If I may ask, where are you from, Mr. Stone? I don't recognize your accent?" she asked him then in a conversational manner that both thrilled and frightened Jesse with the prospect of prolonging the encounter.

"I wouldn't think so. I'm from Massachusetts," he

explained.

At her quizzical expression, he added, "It's one of the northern states. New England," he added.

But at her blank look, he realized geography must have been an area of oversight on the part of her educator. Most likely her mother, he supposed, as there were no schools to be found in this section of the country.

"Let's just say it took me about three weeks to get here, by train."

Her eyebrows lifted in curiosity. "Is Massa...?"

"Massachusetts," he supplied.

"Is it very different from the Wyoming Territory?" she asked sincerely.

Jesse smothered a laugh, but allowed himself an amused smile. "Yes, ma'am. It is indeed very different."

"How so?" she queried.

Jesse scratched his forehead under his brown beaver Stetson. "The landscape is different. The people are different."

"What makes them different?"

Jesse wasn't confident he could explain, but he was loathe to end the conversation with her. He decided to veer the exchange in a direction that required her to do the talking.

"I guess you've only ever known the western states, have you, ma'am?" he asked as he swung down from the saddle, belatedly realizing he should have done so before offering her the apology.

She nodded. Her eyes turned away from him to scan the

vast landscape surrounding them. Jesse could see the admiration she had for the wild open prairie. Her profile presented against the blue sky was more exquisite than Jesse could have created in his imagination. He was grateful for the opportunity to stare while her eyes were averted elsewhere.

"My Papa came west to California in '49 to pan for gold," she swung her blue gaze back to his. "He'd hoped to get rich but ended up dirt poor. My Mama's family came west about the same time. Her pa owned a mercantile and sold to all the miners. Her ma ran the boardinghouse. I was born in San Francisco," she told him. "Pa thought he'd try his hand at ranching and moved us out here when I was just a girl."

Jesse found he couldn't meet her gaze. He watched the clear waters of the shallow creek rushing over the rocks and forming little eddies and currents instead. "I guess he made a good choice," he said. "The beef industry is on the rise."

"Did you—" she caught herself before she asked about his scar. He had put such effort into keeping it hidden from her, she didn't want to admit to having already noticed it. "Did you fight in the War Between the States? My Papa says the North and the South were at each other's throats, and we were lucky to be clear of the killing here."

Jesse was silent, watching the creek pensively for a moment.

The battlefield stretched out for miles, filled with men engaged in combat against one another. Blue and gray uniforms as far as he could see. Men fighting one another with rifles, bayonets, bowie knives, and fists. The sounds of their straining and the groans of their pain filled his ears. They were all streaked and splattered with blood. The smell of it mingled with it the odors of gunpowder and smoke. It was unnatural, all this killing. Cold terror and sick revulsion filled every fiber of his being.

He blinked away the memory and answered simply, "I did."

She saw the way his mouth tightened at her question. "I didn't mean to bring up a difficult subject."

"Not at all," Jesse assured her. "I'm just not very good at conversation. I mean, I like to listen, but I'm not very good at talking. I'm sorry if I offended you."

Annette smiled as she reassured him. "No offense taken."

Jesse couldn't have been much older than she was. Annette hadn't realized how lonely she was until this moment. Jesse's discomfort put her at ease. She liked the way he kept his eyes averted instead of staring at her like a prized heifer. She even appreciated that he was rather withdrawn, instead of being flirtatious. His awkward ways made her feel safe. He wasn't a thing like Ricky Lawson.

"Yes, I did fight in the war," Jesse returned to her question. "But only briefly. I was wounded and sent home to heal. It wasn't as glorious as I had imagined."

His voice sounded so grim and dark that Annette wondered what he had seen on the battlefield. His expression was guarded, but Annette could see the pain he tried to hide as unsuccessfully as his scar.

"I suppose not," she said solemnly, trying to imagine how young he must have been when he had taken up arms to fight.

"Don't you have trouble with Indians out here? I can't

imagine there's a truly peaceful place on this planet."

"For years there was trouble with the Sioux, but last summer Chief Red Cloud signed a treaty at Fort Laramie. Now the Indians are supposed to stay on their own land, on a Reservation. I've never even seen an Indian."

"I did, at the fort. He was a handsome fellow, bronze and covered in animal skins."

"Well, I guess I have seen an Indian—but not one like that. Mrs. Gibson, on the other side of your claim, is a Lakota Sioux. But she wears calico and a sunbonnet."

"Yes, I've met her. She seems very civilized."

"You'd hardly know she was an Indian," Annette affirmed, wondering again if Vivian had confided in her.

Jesse quietly surveyed the fluffy white clouds scuttling by overhead, and the shadows forming underneath them in the thick grass. A comfortable silence fell between then.

Suddenly Annette took notice of the changing angle of the sun and leapt to her feet, exclaiming, "Oh! It's getting late. I have to get home or my folks will be worried about me."

Jesse realized he had almost turned to face her, so startled had he been by her outburst. He carefully kept his right cheek averted as he stood and said, "It was nice seeing you again, Miss Hamilton."

"It was nice seeing you as well, Mr. Stone. I'm sure we'll meet again," she threw over her shoulder as she hurried away.

Jesse watched her retreat until she had disappeared into the vastness of the prairie, then turned and mounted his horse.

~

Annette slipped quietly into the cabin. Her sisters were busy at the table, drawing letters and pictures with their chalk and slate. Ernest was in the barn, milking the dairy cow. Her mother was bent over the baby, changing his diaper. Without looking up at Annette, she said, "Run out to the garden and bring in the vegetables for supper."

"Yes ma'am," Annette answered, and went to obey. Apparently she hadn't been missed.

Over supper, her mother informed her that tomorrow they would scrub every inch of the cabin and iron the curtains and tablecloth Annette had washed the day before. She wanted the twins to gather wildflowers to place in a cup on the table, and everything in perfect order when their guest arrived.

Her mother's nervous fluttering made Annette's stomach cramp with anxiety. Her father grinned and winked at her, assuming her nerves stemmed from excitement.

She spent the following morning churning butter and forming it into perfectly round pats using the mold Papa had given Mama for Christmas last year. Then she joined her mother and siblings as they worked together to clean the cabin until it was virtually antiseptic. The ironing was finished by the mid-day meal, and then they began to work on preparations for supper: roast beef with boiled potatoes, carrots, and turnips, flaky sour dough biscuits, and a berry pie for dessert.

Then Annette was sent to change into her best dress, and her mother fussed over her hair for half an hour. It was brushed until it shone, then part of it was braided and wound with the rest into a chignon at the base of her head.

She regarded her reflection in the mirror with disdain. She looked for all the world like an innocent, young woman ready to meet her first suitor. The deception curdled her stomach.

Then came the cries of her sisters: "He's here! Oh, look, he's here!"

Annette peeked discreetly out the window. She sighed in resolute disappointment. He was the most handsome man she had ever seen.

Was this the way men felt when they stared at her? She had never felt as though her breath was taken away merely by beholding a man. Ricky's charm had come from his charismatic personality and southern drawl, though he had been handsome. But Bryan Hunt had the same effect without ever saying a word.

Her father stepped outside to greet him, and Annette studied the man carefully as they exchanged pleasantries. Mr. Hunt didn't carry himself with conceit or arrogance, although he certainly had to know the affect he had on women. He was soft-spoken despite the deep timbre of his voice, and had an almost gentle demeanor despite his thickly muscled physique. Annette was intrigued.

She blushed crimson as her father brought him into the cabin and they were introduced. He had the palest blue eyes she had ever seen paired with such dark hair. The contrast was very appealing.

She remained silent throughout the meal, unless forced to answer a direct question. Annette listened with curious ears as her father drew out the story of how Mr. Hunt had grown up on a tobacco plantation in Maryland that kept slaves, but was drafted into fighting for the Union despite his family's loyalty to the Confederacy.

He explained how his father had fallen ill after the war ended, and he had chosen to sell the plantation and use the profit to buy cattle in Wyoming. There was such sadness in his voice as he spoke, Annette suspected there were details he had chosen to withhold.

"Growing tobacco is constant and back-breaking work," he told them. "It makes cattle ranching seem like a vacation. Those Longhorns just wander the prairie, eating the fodder God has provided, and growing fat for market. I can't imagine why anyone in his right mind would fool with tobacco when he can do just as well with cattle."

"I'm glad someone makes the effort," her father had laughed, patting the pipe that waited in his pocket for after supper.

Bryan Hunt chuckled, admitting, "I brought a supply with me to use for trade on the wagon trail. I must say it served me better than cash." When he smiled, a dimple formed in his left cheek.

Annette sighed. She liked Mr. Hunt. He was well spoken, courteous, and honest. She found herself desperately wishing she could rewind the clock of time and undo her past mistakes.

If she had met Bryan Hunt before she'd met Ricky, she could have easily fallen in love with him and welcomed his advances.

But that opportunity would have to pass her by. Bryan Hunt deserved a young woman who was everything he assumed Annette to be: virtuous and untouched. Annette shifted in her seat, feeling the filthiness of her sins as if Ricky's hands had branded her just as permanently as her father branded his cattle. She would forever carry the black scar upon her soul.

"It is good for a man not to touch a woman. Nevertheless, to avoid fornication, let every man have his own wife, and let every woman have her own husband." The words of the Apostle Paul haunted her. *"Flee fornication. Every sin that a man doeth is without the body; but he that committeth fornication sinneth against his own body."*

The roast beef had been cooked until it almost melted in her mouth. But it lodged like sawdust in Annette's throat. God would surely be satisfied with the grief that gripped Annette as she glimpsed what her future might have been like if she had been strong enough to resist temptation. She supposed she deserved whatever misery came upon her.

Chapter Six

*J*esse grinned widely. He had spent two weeks traveling to Fort Laramie and the new town, Weston, to get a lead on an architect and builder for the house he had planned, and then actually tracking the men down and convincing them to take him on. But it had been time well spent. Before winter arrived, his three story dream house would be a reality.

He hoped he would be able to commission a photographer to capture its image once it was completed. His mother and his sisters and brothers would all see he was more than just a visionary or a fugitive, running away from his past. They would see he was successful in this western frontier, and had been wise to leave home and forge his own destiny.

Perhaps they would send him their blessings, instead of constant words of regret. He thought of the letter in his pocket he had picked up at the post office in Weston. His mother was still baffled by his choice to leave the place of his birth in New England to move to a stark and empty landscape in the middle of nowhere. She longed to have all of her children in her parlor once again. Jesse wondered if she would ever realize it was an impossible dream. Peter was dead, and Jesse was gone forever.

He had written and mailed a reply to her before leaving town. He assured her he loved and missed her and the rest of the family, but he was making a new life for himself and was quite satisfied with his choice. He briefly described the tranquil landscape, trying to help her see that it was neither stark nor empty. It was filled with rolling hills covered in tall grass that waved and billowed in the wind, dotted with sagebrush and Indian paintbrush, with a sky above it reaching as far as the eye could see. The seeming endless prairie was interrupted with shallow creeks flowing through hidden valleys, providing water for the cattle and a place for trees to grow and offer shade from the summer sun.

He looked about him now as he urged his mare homeward. Why would he ever trade this picturesque beauty for the industrial chaos of Springfield, Massachusetts?

As if afraid her emotional pleas weren't enough to make Jesse feel guilty, his mother had also written about a banquet to be held the following month to honor all the city's men who had fought to preserve the Union. There would be special honors given to those families, like the Stones, who had given all their sons to the cause. Stephen and Albert would receive engraved plaques citing the city's indebtedness to their selfless contributions to freedom and equality. She grieved that neither he nor Peter would be there to receive theirs.

Jesse let out a low sound, somewhere between a chuckle and a groan. His mother had no idea how glad he was to miss that event! If anything, the news had confirmed his decision to leave Springfield when he did.

He had already received far more adulation and praise than he deserved. He had thought the respect of others would fill him up, but it had only left him feeling more aware of the emptiness. Jesse wanted no more undeserved awards and would be happy to never again hear spoken such words as "valiant, brave, or gallant." It was all just romanticized murder and glorified butchery, and hero worship for those guilty of such crimes. He wanted no part of it.

He supposed some men were indeed heroes, for their sacrifice had allowed for the freedom of the Negroes as well as the legal unification of the country. But Jesse wasn't one of them.

His thoughts drifted back to the plans he had drawn up with the architect for his new house. When he had a photographer take a picture of it, he would have one taken of him in his cowboy attire. It was a far cry from the suit and bowler he had worn back east. His mother would hardly recognize him.

Jesse could hardly recognize himself. His skin was still learning to accept the change in climate. It seemed he always had a strip of red sunburn across his cheeks and nose, and his skin felt dry and itchy from the sun and wind. He'd actually bought a facial cream while he was in town to give him some relief.

His hands had been utterly transformed. Once soft and smooth as a woman's, they were now work-hardened and callused. He even had dirt under his nails from working in the garden, growing vegetables to add to their simple diet. He liked their new strength.

Everything about this new life suited him. He had no regrets over his choice to move west.

Although sometimes he did long for the soft voices and gentle ways of womenfolk. His world now was filled with the brusque, grumbling ways of men and cattle.

Perhaps this longing explained why Jesse had suffered a moment of weakness while shopping in town. He'd felt a tug on his heartstrings as he'd walked through the mercantile and saw a basket filled with sleeping pups, and a sign explaining that they were orphans in need of care. His mother would have smiled to see the tenderness touching her son's scarred face as he gently lifted the brown and white puppy in his hand, stroking its nose with a work-hardened forefinger.

According the store owner, the puppies were Bull Terriers and were bred for herding cattle. Jesse told himself it was a practical decision. He was taking the puppy back with him for the purpose of training it to work on the ranch. But there was a tell-tale warmth in his chest as he cradled the animal against his belly, safely tucked into his shirt for the journey home. For some reason, just feeling its small form pressed against him for comfort made him feel less alone.

He smiled now as he thought of his sisters and how they would have adored the round, little pup. Their first question, after they had finished cooing over it, would have been, "What's his name?" Jesse figured he would have to teach it to come to something, but what, he had no idea.

The men were just as pleased to see the puppy as his sisters would have been. Jesse stood back and smiled as they took turns holding it and stroking its silky fur.

"He's a fat little thing," Claude commented. "Round as a ball."

Rattlesnake reached over to rub the exposed belly as Claude cradled the animal in the crook of his arm. All four little paws dangled in the air limply, and small brown eyes looked up at them with curiosity and trust.

Jim chuckled. "Now dat right there, dat looks like trouble to me!" he stated in his deep, rumbling voice.

"Not my dog," Jesse countered. "He's going to be a working dog. He'll earn his keep."

Jim just shook his head as Claude scratched it behind the ears. "What you goin' to call it?"

Jesse retrieved his puppy from Claude's arms and stared down into the little face. "No idea," he confessed.

"Had me a dog named Blue once," Jim suggested.

"This ain't Alabama," Claude reminded him, with a playful punch to the shoulder. "We don't call our dogs Blue 'round here! Besides, he's brown."

"I had a dog named Templeton once," Rattlesnake Rupert offered.

Claude scoffed and Jim stated, "This ain't no England here, neither!"

Jesse lifted the puppy into the air and met its gaze. He felt something soften deep inside him, something he didn't even realize had become hard. "We're calling him Lucky. And that's final."

"Half the dogs in America named Lucky," Claude mumbled under his breath as he turned away. "At least Blue's a little more original," he nodded at Jim.

"Mind your own business," Jesse retorted, settling onto his bunk with the bundle of fur in his lap. He leaned his head back against the crude wooden wall and stroked the soft puppy.

His grandfather had died just as Jesse was starting to sprout up and his voice to deepen. Just a year or so before the war had changed everything. His grandfather had kept a big black dog named Lucky, and Jesse had loved to sit on the floor in front of the fireplace and pet it while he listened to his grandfather's stories. Jesse sighed at the memory of earlier times. It wasn't often he could recall life before the war.

The memory reminded him that he hadn't always carried these burdens of guilt and shame. But looking around him, he supposed every man there could say the same. At one time, they had all been innocent young boys dreaming of a future that President Lincoln's war had shattered in one way or another.

Even Jim Ingram. He might never have to plant cotton for a white man again, but he was still viewed by many as a lesser citizen because of his dark skin. He had run away from his master in Alabama and fled to Pennsylvania where he had joined the Union army. But instead of giving him a uniform and a rifle, they'd given him grunt work to ease their load. Jim did what was asked of him, and when the war was over and he was granted his freedom, he returned to the plantation to find his wife and children. But they had disappeared into the chaos of a ravaged South.

Jim carried them as quietly in his heart as the scars lining his back. He said his wife was a beautiful woman with skin the shade of coffee laced with cream. Her mother had been a slave, and her father had been a white man. Her mother's master. Jim worried a similar fate might have befallen Martha. But he would never know.

Jesse scratched the white spot behind little Lucky's ears. He guessed some things were just like his foot. Once taken, there was no replacing them. You had just had to learn how to keep limping along.

~

Annette draped the wet clothes over the line. She paused to wipe the sweat from her eyes, then bent to retrieve another garment from the basket. She had spent the morning boiling the laundry in hot water and lye soap, and then scrubbing it against the washboard until her fingers were red. After rinsing the clothes clean and wringing the water out, she must hang them up to dry before helping her mother prepare supper.

She sighed. With seven people in the house, there was never a shortage of work to be done.

Mary and Janice made an effort to help, but created more of a distraction than anything else. They had abandoned the pretense of helping and were now using the clothing pins for dolls and acting out dramatic and lively scenes. Annette just let them play. They were only five years old. One day they would have to spend every waking moment cooking and cleaning as she did. They might as well enjoy their childhood freedom while they could.

The hot, dry wind flapped the sheet against her face, and Annette sighed wearily as she secured the clothing pins. "Girls, I'm going to need those pins now," she said as she pulled out the last item and fought the wind to drape the quilt over the line.

"But we're not done!" Janice whined.

"I'm very sorry," Annette offered as she held out her hand. "But we can't let mother's quilt blow away. I don't think father would be very pleased if you let that happen."

Grudgingly the girls surrendered the pins and scampered off to occupy themselves with a new game.

"Don't go far," Annette called after them. "It will be suppertime soon."

She cringed as she entered the cabin, the empty basket on her hip, and heard the ear-splitting wails of her infant brother. Her mother looked close to tears herself as she bent over the baby to change his diaper.

"Annette, can you start supper?" she shouted over the din.

Annette nodded as there was no use in answering with Howard's cries filling their ears. She set to work retrieving meat from the smokehouse and dicing vegetables for stew. She thought it convenient that Ernest wasn't around to help.

She had the table set and was just pulling the cornbread from the fire when her father came through the door, water dripping from his chin from washing the dust and sweat from his face. Her mother stood and placed Howard in his cradle, rubbing her temples and sighing.

"He had another one of his crying fits," Agnes said. "I wish I knew why. None of my other babies cried like this."

Walter grunted in acknowledgement before demanding, "Where's Ernest?"

"I'll get him," Annette offered, "and the girls." The sooner she rounded up her siblings and her father could eat, the better the evening would go for all of them.

She found him in the stable, carving a wolf out of piece of wood. Though tempted to chide him for hiding out instead of helping, she simply told him to wash up for supper and went to tell her sisters the same.

In minutes they were all assembled around the table. Her

father bowed his head to give thanks for their food. They ate in silence until Walter leaned back in his chair and said, "Saw young Mr. Hunt today. He seemed quite taken with our Annette. Asked if he could come by and go for a walk with her." He grinned broadly at this news. "I told him he could come by any time."

"But Papa, don't you think he's a little too old for me?" Annette ventured.

"Don't be absurd. He's only ten or twelve years older than you. He can give you security a younger man can't. He's got tobacco money from back east and a good mind for the cattle business. He's a wise choice for any woman, and if you don't move fast, you might lose your opportunity. More respectable ladies are coming into the territory all the time."

Annette shifted in her chair. "Yes, I know, but—"

"Don't talk with food in your mouth," he interrupted. "No use being the prettiest girl in the territory if you have manners like a pig. What man wants that?"

"Yes, papa," she said, falling silent again.

"I've found you the best catch I can, girl, and I don't want you to throw it away or mess it up out of some silly notion that you need a man closer to your age. You've got to leave home sometime and get married, and Bryan Hunt's going to own half this country in just a few years if I've got him pegged right. He'll give you a good name and a good home, and that's all you need."

"Yes sir."

She tried to quell the sick feeling that rose up in her throat every time the subject of marriage or Bryan Hunt came up. She genuinely liked the man. There wasn't anything she would enjoy more than a leisurely stroll at sunset by his side, listening to his deep, gentle voice. But it wasn't fair to lead the man on. If he wanted a respectable, virtuous woman as his wife—as all men did—then he didn't want her.

"Don't be afraid," her mother said gently, placing her hand over Annette's. "Marriage isn't the end of the world."

Annette swallowed tears at her mother's misunderstanding of her anxiety. "Yes, I know," she began, "but you and Papa need me here. How will you manage with the baby and the twins?"

Her mother's eyes fell to her lap, as if she dreaded the day herself, then came back to Annette's with false brightness. "We'll miss your help, of course, but we'll manage just fine. You can't waste your youth on your brothers and sisters. You need a husband and babies of your own."

"I don't want to hear another word about it!" Walter slammed his fist on the table. "I don't understand why you wouldn't be glad to have a wealthy, handsome man want to court you! Do you really think you can do better than Bryan Hunt? I swear, I'll never understand what goes on in a woman's head," he grumbled as he pushed back his chair and stomped from the cabin to complete the evening chores.

"Ernest, go help your father," Agnes instructed. She waited until the door closed behind him to lean forward and admonish, "You must stop aggravating your father this way. He's trying to take care of you. There's no good reason why you shouldn't welcome Mr. Hunt's attention. I don't want any more complaining on the subject. Do you understand?"

"Yes ma'am."

Annette quickly rose from the table and began stacking the dishes to wash. She didn't want her mother to see the tears welling in her eyes. Sometimes she wished she could confess what had happened and ask for advice. But she knew better than to do that. She was locked in a prison of shame and isolation, with every hope for her future trampled like the prairie grass after a stampede.

Lord, You're the only one who knows the truth of who I am and what I've done. Can't You help me find a way out of this mess? I don't want to die a spinster, but what man will ever want to marry me? I can't let anyone know what happened, but how can I explain why I can't marry Bryan Hunt? And worse yet, I wish I could.

A ragged sob tore from her throat as she rushed outside into the fresh air, the dry wind tugging at her long, blond hair. She pumped water into a bucket and began to scrub the dishes, thankful for an excuse to be alone while she gained control of her emotions.

One sin, one stolen kiss, had led to this. Like a runaway train, her life seemed to be careening wildly out of control, and all she could do was wait and see where it would stop and what destruction would lie ahead.

Lord, please hear the cries of my heart! What can I do?

Chapter Seven

*P*atriotic music floated cheerfully over the dull murmur of conversation. Atop a platform in the center of town perched a violinist, a cellist, and a flutist, surrounded by the red, white, and blue bunting of the American Flag.

Every year there had been fireworks at Fort Laramie, but the celebration had moved to the newly developed town of Weston. While most young women would have looked forward to the opportunity to visit with friends or flirt with young men, Annette would have preferred to stay home. Surrounded by the laughter of those who hadn't seen one another in months and listening as they called out greetings and exchanged hugs only brought home the reality of her own loneliness.

Other girls had never liked her. They stood at a distance, staring at her with blatant jealousy as all the single men (and a few married) ogled at her. They all assumed that because she was pretty, she was happier than they were. That her appearance would afford her a love they couldn't know.

Annette wished she could tell them how wrong they were. She wished she was a plain Jane whom a man would fall in love with for all the attributes that *weren't* visible to the eye. But that opportunity had already passed her by.

She retrieved a glass of lemonade for herself and another for her mother and carried them back to where her family sat on a quilt spread over the grass. She settled down next to them, watching her younger sisters and hoping their stories turned out much happier than her own. And when it came time for Ernest to marry, she hoped he picked a young woman for her intelligence and kindness and not her comeliness alone.

Gazing past the musicians on the platform, she watched the wispy white clouds drift by in the blue sky and wished she could have brought her sewing to pass the time. The fireworks wouldn't begin until after dark, leaving her at least two blank hours to fill.

"Miss Hamilton, how nice to see you this evening!" she looked up to find Mr. Bryan Hunt standing over her with his hand outstretched. She accepted it, setting her lemonade aside and allowing him aid her to her feet.

"How nice to see you as well," she replied demurely, feeling a flush come to her cheeks and a quickening of her pulse.

The skin at the corners of his pale blue eyes crinkled as he smiled, revealing even white teeth. The wind stirred his dark hair as he removed his hat in greeting. Why did the man have to be so handsome?

"I was hoping I would have the chance to visit with you tonight. Would you like to walk with me for a bit, before the fireworks begin?" he asked in his deep, quiet voice.

Annette nodded shyly. She felt liked a trapped rabbit, with no polite way to decline. And no real wish to.

He offered his arm, and she accepted, hoping she wasn't sealing her fate by being seen in public on his elbow. She could feel the bulge of his muscles through the layers of his coat and shirt, and her own hand seemed delicate by comparison. She stared down at the toes of her shoes as she walked, hoping he would lead the conversation.

"I'm looking forward to the fireworks," he began, and she heard the tell-tale tightness in his voice and realized he was as uncomfortable as she was. "They're always spectacular against the wide open sky."

Annette nodded in agreement.

"Where I come from there isn't much open sky, except where the land has been cleared for fields. We have dense woodlands, which might hinder the view but offers shade and a beauty of its own." He paused awkwardly. "Would you like some lemonade?"

She supposed he was too nervous to realize she had set her glass down on the quilt when he had taken her hand. "Yes, thank you," she said, appreciating the diversion.

He steered her toward the beverage table and she accepted a second glass, sipping at it daintily. She searched her mind for something to say. "I can't imagine what it's like to be closed in by all those trees. I enjoy the shade of the aspen grove by the creek in the summer. But all I've ever known is the open prairie."

She noticed the creases on his forehead smoothed as she began speaking. He seemed relieved she was finally engaging in conversation with him. "I notice the cattle like it too," he smiled. "Gets hot out here in the dead of summer, doesn't it? And dry. My plantation was next to the Potomac River, and between that and the trees, the air could be so damp in the summer you could breathe the moisture in the air."

Annette cocked her head, trying to imagine what he meant.

"I guess that's hard to picture," he smiled at her puzzled

look.

She realized she had been furrowing her eyebrows and laughed at herself. "I'm afraid it is. Do you miss it?"

Bryan's eyes grew distant, and an expression of painful longing haunted his features. A dark shadow seemed to pass over him, and Annette sensed a silent grief that was deeper than she could fathom. He forced the edges of his mouth to lift, but the effort was still too sad to be called a smile. "Yes I do, Miss Hamilton."

Curiosity superseded good judgment, and Annette blurted, "What is it you miss the most?" hoping to know the reason for the grief she had just witnessed.

He looked away, not just into the clouds, but far away into the past. Annette regretted her question immediately, realizing she had trespassed into a private loss. She wanted to take it back, but still longed to know his secret.

"My wife," he finally whispered. "I miss my wife the most."

Annette fumbled for a response. "I'm so sorry. I didn't mean to pry."

"You should know," Bryan turned to meet her gaze, his light blue eyes staring into hers. "She died in childbirth. While I was away in the war."

He was telling her because he intended to court her. She saw it in the way he searched her face for a reaction. She tried to mask her expression as she answered, "I'm truly sorry for your loss. I understand now your reasons for selling the plantation and moving so far away."

He nodded slowly. "I'm sorry to ruin the festive atmosphere," he forced another sad smile. "I never meant to talk about her tonight."

Suddenly the deceased Mrs. Hunt felt as real as Mrs. Lawson had been. Because she still held Bryan's heart. This much was obvious.

Annette looked down at her hands, searching for something to say. If she had been intending to let him court her, if she had pinned her hopes on him, she would have been sorely disappointed to know that she was moving into another woman's shadow. As it was, she had known all along there was no future with this man. And his confession only confirmed it. She never wanted to love in the presence of another woman again. Whether it was a man's wife, or merely her memory.

"Would you like some pie?" she asked, intentionally breaking the mood. She wished she knew how to extricate herself from this awkward situation without bringing him further pain. But if he only knew the truth, he would thank her for gently pushing him away.

A small but genuine smile curved his lips at the lighter turn in conversation. "That would be fine."

She accepted his arm again and walked with him to the refreshments. When her pie was finished, she turned to him and said, "Thank you so much for our walk. I'm sure my parents need help with the children now, so please excuse me."

He nodded in understanding. "Thank you, Miss Hamilton. I hope you enjoy your evening."

"And you as well, Mr. Hunt," she answered politely before turning away.

She was weaving her way through the throng when she spotted Jesse Stone standing on the edge of crowd. He wore his hat pulled low over his forehead, as if to hide beneath it. But his eyes caught her gaze by accident, and reluctantly, he nodded in acknowledgement.

His reticence to engage in even the smallest exchange with her was intriguing. Annette noticed his discomfort as she approached, but hoped to quickly put him at ease.

"Good evening, Mr. Stone. I'm happy you made it to the fireworks display tonight. I think you'll enjoy it."

Something sharp against her toes caused her to jump back, gasping.

"I'm so sorry," Jesse leapt forward and pulled the puppy away. She looked down in surprise at her drool-covered shoe.

She laughed. "No harm done. He simply startled me."

The brown and white puppy lunged at her again, tail wagging in excitement. "Sit, Lucky," Jesse commanded, and the dog obeyed. But only for a fleeting second before he was straining against the rope again, his whole body moving back and forth with the force of his tail-wagging.

Annette watched as Jesse knelt down to control the dog, unable to guard his face and manage the puppy simultaneously. The ragged edges of the scar ran along his eye down to his mouth, turning the corner downward in a perpetual frown. Aware of her gaze, he tugged at his hat and stood, angling his face to the left to hide his disfigurement.

Feeling oddly guilty for having looked, Annette hastened to redeem her mistake. "He looks like a handful." She knelt down to rub him behind the ears. Lucky flopped to the ground immediately and rolled onto his back, tongue lolling onto the ground. She smiled as she rubbed his belly for a moment, then stood again and said, "Would you like me to bring you some refreshments? I'm sure you don't want to take him into that crowd."

Jesse's chin dipped in what could be perceived as a nod. He grumbled something she couldn't quite make out.

"All right then," she answered brightly, "I'll be right back."

She half expected him to have disappeared before she could return, but he was standing where she had left him, wearing a scowl. He accepted the lemonade and pie with a grunt, having already tied the brown and white bundle of energy to a nearby fence post.

"He's just a baby," she commented, kneeling down to pet the puppy again. Lucky rested his chin on his paws and yawned. Annette scooped him up and cradled him in her arms. "He's precious."

"He can't be more than nine weeks old," Jesse finally spoke. "I'm going to train him to herd cattle."

"I know a lot of ranchers do that," Annette replied. "My father says it's just one more mouth to feed."

"I guess it is," Jesse admitted. "But he's good company, too."

Lucky licked her hand steadily, pausing to look up at her with round, contented eyes. "We have barn cats," she commented. "Since they eat the mice, they earn their keep. But they're good company too."

She didn't realize she was swaying back and forth,

bouncing the dog gently as if he were an infant. A smile curved Jesse's lips. "He's a puppy, not a baby," he said with the first hint of humor in his voice Annette had ever heard.

She grinned and admitted, "I'm used to tending my baby brother. He's eight months old, so I do a lot of rocking. But I think Lucky enjoys it, too."

Jesse just shook his head. "You remind me of my sisters," he commented.

Annette looked up, hoping he would say more. He responded to the encouragement in her eyes and continued, "They loved dogs. My grandfather had a dog, a big black animal, but as gentle as I've ever seen. His name was Lucky. I named this little guy after him. Helps me to remember better times, when my family was whole." He patted his right thigh, "When I was whole."

She observed the gesture and lifted her eyebrows quizzically.

"I was shot in the leg, and they had to amputate below the knee. There's a false foot inside that boot," he explained with a chuckle. "It's better than a peg-leg."

Jesse had wondered what Annette would say to this disclosure, and was surprised at the pleased look she wore. He was baffled by it for a moment, then realized she was pleased he was talking to her openly. He suddenly felt his throat tighten, and swallowed to ease the pressure.

"I never even noticed a limp," she reassured him. "Does it hurt?"

He nodded. "Sometimes."

"I've seen men walking with peg-legs and always wondered how they kept their balance. I'm sure it's easier with the false foot."

Jesse had to smile at her use of his joking term. "They call it a 'prosthesis,' or a 'prosthetic foot.'"

"Oh," she said. "I never knew they made such things."

"It's a rather new invention. So many men lost limbs in the war."

"Oh," she said again, trying to process this information. "I'm very sorry."

"My brother, Stephen, lost his arm. But he refuses to wear a prosthetic hand."

"The war must have been very ugly," she commented softly, as her understanding of the word began to expand.

He nodded. "It was."

Lucky yawned expansively and let out a high-pitched whine before curling up against Annette's chest and closing his eyes. She held him close and rocked him unconsciously, her thoughts drifting to other questions she wanted to ask.

But Jesse shifted his weight to his good foot, shifting the conversation as well. "How many brothers and sisters do you have? You look like you have experience with rocking."

She grinned, becoming aware of her swaying motion again. "I have four siblings, in all. Two brothers and two sisters. Ernest is thirteen, the twins, Mary and Janice, are five, and then there's baby Howard. It's difficult to find a quiet moment at home. That's why I go to the aspen grove whenever I can. It's peaceful there."

"I share a cabin with three ranch hands. Hard to find a quiet moment there too," he replied, grinning back at her.

Although he had to know she had already seen his scar, Annette observed he continued to keep the right side of his face averted. But she noticed that when he smiled, the left side of his face was enjoyable to look at. Not handsome like Bryan Hunt, perhaps, but the transformation was remarkable. She had wondered if he ever wore an expression other than a scowl or a frown. And now that she knew, she wished she could see more of this relaxed side of him.

"Not for long, though," he continued, and she was confused at the sudden comment until he explained further: "I have plans to build a house for myself. The ranch hands will keep the cabin."

"Then you plan to stay?"

His eyebrow lifted. "I just got here. Of course I plan to stay."

She laughed. "Not everyone who comes west chooses to stay. But if you're building a house, I guess you will."

"I don't wish to ever return east," he confessed. "I feel more at home in this wilderness than I did in Massachusetts."

The approval in her eyes made him swallow nervously. He lifted his lemonade glass to his lips to take a drink, only to realize with embarrassment that it was empty. But she was looking down at the puppy, and didn't seem to notice.

"What is—"

"'Evening, Mr. Stone," Walter Hamilton interrupted his daughter. "Good to see you."

Jesse nodded in greeting, noting the irritation in her father's voice.

"Annette, the fireworks are about to begin."

"Yes sir," she answered quietly, as if reprimanded. "Good evening, Mr. Stone," she said in parting as she offered him the puppy, then turned to follow her father back to the quilt where the family waited for her.

Once settled on the blanket, her mother demanded, "Annette Hamilton, what on earth were you doing with that boy all this time? You walked away with Mr. Hunt!"

Her father's eyebrows creased into an ominous 'V' between his eyes. "And Mr. Hunt noticed how much attention you were giving that Jesse Stone. He didn't look pleased. What are you thinking?"

"I'm sorry," Annette offered. "I was just visiting. He's a nice young man."

"Well, you should spend your time visiting with the man who's courting you," her mother snapped.

"I did—I just was walking back to join you and noticed Jesse—"

"You shouldn't have stood there with him so long, Annette," her father chastised. "You spent more time with that crippled eyesore than you did with your suitor."

Annette sighed in frustration. Perhaps she was more comfortable in Jesse's company for that very reason: he wasn't a suitor, or even a prospect as a suitor.

But she had to disagree with her father's unflattering description. Jesse was not a "crippled eyesore," and she didn't appreciate the derogatory judgment.

"He was injured in The War Between the States," she defended him.

"Watch your tone, girl," her father retorted, his eyes narrowing on her in warning.

"Yes sir," she whispered quietly. She had finally found a friend, someone she could talk to who was neither jealous of her nor interested in pursuing her. And she would probably never have the opportunity to visit with him again.

Chapter Eight

*J*esse accepted Lucky from Annette, feeling oddly like they were children who had been scolded for some misbehavior. Though what the trespass had been, he wasn't sure. As he saw it, the only misconduct Annette was guilty of was conversing with him. It would seem that for whatever reason, Mr. Hamilton didn't approve of him.

He gently placed the sleeping puppy on the grass at his feet and squatted down beside him to watch the light display. A heavy mantle of loneliness settled on his shoulders as he watched Annette walking away. He wasn't sure what had prompted him to open up with her the way he had. He couldn't recall ever talking with another woman like that, except his sisters. And Annette was by far the most appealing woman he had ever met. It was strange that he should feel so at ease with her.

She seemed determined to be his friend, which was another thing Jesse found odd. He'd always assumed women were repulsed by his scarred face, and he knew he wasn't good at making conversation. In Springfield, he assumed it was either his family name or his hero status prompting Sophia's interest in him. He couldn't quite figure out what Annette's interest was, or if she simply was as desperate for a friend as he was. Either way, he was sorry her father had pulled her away.

~

Annette sat quietly throughout the evening, allowing her sisters to lean against her and to point and talk excitedly as the lights burst into the dark expanse of sky and lit up their faces. The acrid smell of smoke filled her nostrils. She felt a growing sense of loss. Her mother was always reminding her that she needed a husband and children of her own. She put her arm around Mary and pulled her close. Would she ever have a daughter of her own? Or had she forfeited that blessing too?

She couldn't see Jesse from where she sat, but she knew he was there, watching the fireworks from the outskirts of the crowd. When the festivities ended and her family was making their way to their wagon, she saw Bryan Hunt at a distance and dipped her chin in shy acknowledgement. He had waved in greeting, but made no effort to speak to her.

She woke to the usual Sunday morning routine of helping the girls to dress, eating breakfast, and then a time of Bible reading around the table. Her father seemed as bored with it as Ernest, but her mother insisted they have their own service every Sunday morning since there was no church nearby to attend. Sometimes Annette paid more attention than others.

Sundays were supposed to be a day of rest, but her father found the inactivity frustrating and preferred to stay busy. And her mother found it more peaceful to just let him be. Annette spent the afternoon unstitching an old dress that was beyond repair and using the fabric to make an apron and sunbonnet. She set aside some fabric to make matching dresses for the twins' ragdolls.

Her focus was intent upon the needle and thread in her fingers when she heard her mother gasp, "Oh, Annette! Mr. Hunt just rode up and he's talking with your father!"

"Oh dear," Annette murmured before she could think.

Her mother glared at her sharply, and Annette quickly added, "I look like a mess."

Agnes rushed across the room and hastily tucked loose strands of hair behind Annette's ears and smoothed the wrinkles from her skirt. "You look just fine, dear. You're too pretty to ever worry about that."

They sat primly and waited until the door opened and Walter entered with Bryan Hunt on his heels. "You have a visitor," her father announced, grinning broadly.

"Good afternoon," Annette said politely, feeling butterflies dance in her stomach as she glanced up at her suitor.

"Good afternoon, Mrs. Hamilton," Bryan first greeted her mother, then redirected his gaze to the object of his visit. "I was hoping Annette could take a brief walk with me this afternoon."

"Yes, yes of course she can!" Agnes insisted, with what Annette thought was too much enthusiasm.

She rose quietly and reached for her sunbonnet, placing it on her head as she walked toward the door and followed Bryan out into the bright sunshine. She blinked as her eyes adjusted to the light.

"I'm sorry to surprise you like this," Bryan apologized after they had walked several paces in silence. "I felt I needed to talk with you after our conversation last night."

Annette's mind raced. Her pulse raced as well. What was it he felt the need to say? "Oh?" she asked cautiously.

He didn't answer immediately, as if he were searching for the right words. Which only served to brew more anxiety in Annette's mind. Finally he said, "I shouldn't have spoken of my wife so soon, but she was on my mind and I felt it wasn't fair to keep it from you. I understand you didn't know I was a widower, and it might change how you think about me…"

He paused, and Annette waited in silence for him to continue. She had no idea how to respond.

He stilled and turned to face her, his pale blue eyes gentle and sincere. "I loved my wife very much. But I know my heart can learn to love again, and I'm certain I could make you very happy, if you would let me. I know it's too early to speak of marriage, but I want to make my intentions clear at the outset. I can see that you're a kind and gracious woman, and you deserve to be loved fully and wholly. I'm still learning how to set old memories aside and live with my losses." He paused again, releasing a sigh as he pulled off his hat and ran his fingers through his dark hair. He turned away, and Annette stared at his strong profile silhouetted against the blue sky.

"What I'm trying to say is this," he continued with an uncertain laugh, "I would like to get to know you better, and I hope you wouldn't mind spending more time with me."

The vulnerability in those handsome eyes took her breath away. She swallowed nervously, and was reminded of Jesse. She forced a smile and said quietly, "I would like that." What else could she say after such a heartfelt request? And sadly, she found that it *had* changed how she felt. He was handsome and strong, sensitive and attentive. And wasn't afraid to share his thoughts and feelings. He *was* a rare catch, just not for the reasons her father supposed.

How was she ever going to push him away without breaking his heart, as well her own?

~

The days passed, but Annette couldn't get Bryan Hunt's blue eyes out of her mind. The sadness and longing she saw in their depths. She lifted the iron from the fire and began making circles over the fabric, smoothing away the wrinkles. Her hand worked methodically while her mind drifted to the dilemma she faced.

This Sunday, she could expect him to arrive in the afternoon and invite her for another walk. And as much as she might desire to walk with him, to spend time and get to know him better, she knew that the sooner she ended this charade, the better off he would be. All she was doing was prolonging the inevitable.

She wondered what his wife had been like. What she had looked like and how old she had been when she passed. What a tragedy, to lose both wife and child while he was away fighting in the war. She felt a pang of grief in sympathy. She truly hoped that one day he found a woman to love again. A woman who deserved him.

"Ouch!" she cried as she burned the thumb on her left hand, holding the sheet still to accept the iron. She set the iron aside and ran outside to the well. A bucket half-full of water sat beside it, and she plunged her hand in. But the water was lukewarm and did nothing to alleviate the pain. She closed her eyes and took a deep breath. Then she drew some fresh water from the well and let her hand soak for a moment.

Her mother would chide her for not paying better attention to the task at hand. And Annette wished she had been paying better attention. The sting on her thumb was not pleasant. She only wished it was the biggest worry on her mind.

Squaring her shoulders, she returned to her duty, cringing at the stack of diapers left to be ironed after she finished the sheets and aprons. There was no use complaining. She put her back into the work and set about finishing more carefully.

Just as she wiped the sweat from her brow and folded the last diaper, Howard began screaming. Her mother hurried from churning butter and scooped him up to nurse. The girls took this opportunity to burst into the cabin, shouting loudly.

Annette hushed them and directed them outside. "What's the matter, girls?" she asked, trying to keep her voice patient and calm.

As she listened, Annette realized they were over-tired and taking offense where none was warranted. "Sit down here and I'll read you a story," she offered.

She went inside to retrieve a book and saw her mother holding back tears as Howard alternated between nursing and screaming. She wished there was something she could do to help with the baby, but at least she could keep the girls distracted.

Annette read to them until they began to droop forward. Silence came from the cabin. She slowly opened the door and peered inside. Her mother nodded wearily for her to enter.

"I'm going to lay down for a bit myself," Agnes whispered, gently lowering Howard into his cradle.

"I'll tell the girls to come in and take their naps," Annette replied.

Once everyone was settled and the cabin was quiet, Annette tip-toed toward the door. She broke into a run as soon as she had carefully latched the door behind her. There wouldn't be enough time—there never was—but she didn't want to waste a moment alone.

Resting her back against an aspen tree and allowing its leafy branches to offer shade against the summer sun, she opened the book tucked in her apron pocket. She was quickly lost in the story, and almost forgot to watch the progress of the sun until a movement in the corner of her eye caught her attention.

Glancing up, she saw Jesse riding his horse across the rise. She lifted her hand to wave, and was disappointed when he merely tipped his hat in greeting and continued on his way.

She lowered her gaze to the novel in her lap and resumed reading. It wasn't until a strand of hair tangled in her eyelashes that her attention was brought back to reality and she saw the wind had picked up. The sky had darkened to an ominous shade of charcoal gray, the temperature had dropped, and there was a different smell to the air. Earthy and moist and threatening.

She knew this prairie, and storms could sweep up out of nowhere. She looked up at the sky with apprehension, wondering if she had enough time to run home before the clouds burst open. Annette decided to risk it, tucking the book into her apron pocket as she took off at a run.

She hadn't gone very far before she cried out in pain as she was pelted with hailstones. Raising her arms to cover her head, she continued forward blindly, stumbling over sagebrush and prairie dog holes. Bruises formed on her shoulders and arms, and she decided she should turn back and huddle under the canopy of the aspens.

Suddenly a rider appeared out of the gray haze. He called out her name and offered his hand. *Jesse!* Annette accepted, and he swung her up onto his lap, urging his horse into a gallop toward the aspen grove. He halted the stallion and helped

Annette down, then quickly removed the saddle and blanket from its back.

Draping the gray saddle blanket over his head, he told Annette, "Come under the blanket. It will help protect us."

The inappropriate intimacy of their make-shift tent hardly mattered in the face of the hailstones striking against her body. She hurried into the shelter he offered, aware of his breath as it mingled with hers in the darkness, her shoulder pressing into his.

"Are you all right?" he asked, raising his voice to be heard over the sounds of the storm outside their flimsy refuge.

"A little bruised," she admitted. "Thank you for coming back for me."

"It's a good thing you're wearing that blue sunbonnet or I never would have spotted you," he admitted. "I've never seen anything like this! The sky turned black in an instant and then the hail started! How do the cattle survive?"

She let out a little sigh. "Some won't. They're hardy animals, but the young or the weak won't make it."

Silence fell as Jesse and Annette both wondered how their herds would fare in this storm. There was nothing they could do to save them. Hopefully they had found shelter under trees as they had, or in one of the enclosures made for their protection. They would simply have to wait until the storm had passed to investigate.

Moments passed as they huddled quietly under the blanket. The dampness brought out the scent of the horseflesh mingled in the wool. Annette lifted the edge to allow some fresh air in. Her eyes had adjusted to the darkness, and she could faintly make out Jesse's eyes and the outline of his nose. Without thinking, he had allowed her to settle on his right side. The side that bore the scar. Annette couldn't quite make it out in the shadows, and she was thankful for his sake. She knew he wouldn't want her to look at it, and she wanted to be able to look at him.

"Where's Lucky?" she worried. "I hope he's safe."

"I hope so, too. I left him tied up at the cabin. Rattlesnake Rupert was there, so I'm sure he brought him inside."

"I'm sure he did," Annette affirmed.

"Your parents will be worried about you," Jesse stated, thinking of how furious her father would be if he knew they were sitting together under the same blanket, bodies making contact. The awareness of it brought a flush of heat, and he swallowed reflexively.

"How old are you?"

He was startled by the sudden question, but thankful for the conversational tone in her voice. There was no telling how long the storm would last.

He relaxed his body and leaned back against the trunk of the tree. "I'm twenty-one."

"Do you think your parents are worried about you?"

He chuckled. "My mother begs me to come home in every letter she sends. She never understood why I chose to come west."

"You won't go back, though. Will you?"

Jesse allowed himself to smile in the darkness at the hopeful tone of her voice. "No, I won't go back. One day I might return for a short visit, just to put her mind at rest that I'm healthy and thriving out here. But that's all."

"What about the rest of your family?"

"My father passed when I was young. I had three brothers, but one was killed in the war. And I have two sisters. None of them wanted me to leave."

"Are they older or younger?"

Jesse smiled again, enjoying the way she led the conversation so comfortably. He began to hope the storm would never end.

"They're all older than me."

"Oh. That's probably easier," she sighed.

"You have to help out with your younger siblings a lot, don't you?" Jesse observed.

"I do. The baby has a delicate stomach, and he cries a lot. It puts a strain on my mother. The twins are still young, and they can be trying. Ernest is old enough to start pitching in more, but since he's a boy, he's exempt from household chores and caring for children."

"I'm sure you're a great help to your mother," Jesse said. "I'll bet they're missing you right now."

Annette imagined the cabin cramped with everyone inside as the hail beat down on the roof. She was sure Jesse was right. She let out a long, aching sigh.

He hesitated, then asked, "What is it?"

"Sometimes they act as though they can't survive without me; other times I feel like they're trying to push me out of the door."

"Push you out?"

She sighed again, bitterly. "They want me to get married."

Chapter Nine

$\mathcal{J}$esse felt like a fool for the sudden weight of disappointment that sank in the pit of his stomach. Of course her parents were encouraging her to marry. Of course one day she *would* marry. And it could never be to a man like him.

"I suppose that's a normal thing for them to want," he finally forced out in the most casual voice he could manage.

Annette nodded slowly. "Yes. I suppose it is."

"Why does it bother you?" He would think she would long to get married and get out of her parents' cabin.

She was silent for so long that Jesse was beginning to worry he had said the wrong thing and ruined this rare moment of camaraderie. Outside the cozy confines of their blanket, the storm still raged. It sounded as though the size of the hailstones had diminished, but they were still pattering down on the tree limbs and prairie grass. Thunder reverberated through the heavens, and beside him, he could feel Annette's body tense.

He decided to change the question. "Do you already have a suitor?" He had noticed the way Bryan Hunt had singled her out the night of the fireworks. Even the memory of it brought a sharp pang of envy.

She let out a long sigh. "Yes, I do. Mr. Bryan Hunt, to be precise."

"I know him. He's a handsome man. Owns a sizeable head

of cattle. Seems like a nice enough gentleman."

"Yes."

Jesse's confusion was beginning to breed frustration. But he tried to keep it from creeping into his voice. "Then I don't understand your reluctance."

Silence was her only reply.

"You think he's too old for you?" Jesse tried to prod her into talking again. Now more than ever, he wanted her to voice her thoughts to him.

"No. It's nothing to do with him."

Thoroughly baffled, Jesse demanded, "What then?"

Again she answered with a lengthy silence. Jesse was beginning to think they would have to wait out the remainder of the storm in this way, as he had given up on the conversation.

Finally she spoke in a voice so soft that Jesse almost couldn't hear her over the sound of the hail falling around them. "I made a terrible mistake."

Now Jesse's entire being was focused on the words coming out of her mouth. "What mistake?"

"Promise you will never speak a word of this to another living soul," she demanded.

Jesse would have promised anything just to hear her confession. "I swear," he vowed. "It will stay between us."

"I… There was…" she halted, as if trying to gather her thoughts into the right words.

Jesse felt like he would explode with impatience, but forced himself to remain still and silent. He didn't want to do anything that would keep her from telling her secret.

"I was seduced by an older man," she whispered so low that Jesse had to lean forward and strain to hear her words. "I didn't know what was happening until it was too late."

For a moment, Jesse was still baffled. Then comprehension dawned. Followed by disbelief. She couldn't possibly be saying what he thought she was telling him.

"What are you saying?"

The muffled sound of her sobs as she lowered her head into her arms, resting upon her knees, was the only answer. Jesse sat in stunned shock.

His first response was disgust. She was soiled. Just as dirty as a prostitute. But as he listened to her crying, he felt compassion moving into his heart. She said she hadn't meant for it to happen. That she was seduced by an older man. A man who probably knew exactly what he was after and how to get it from her. Then left her to live with the consequences.

He wanted to put an arm around her and draw her close, but that was something he could never do. Instead he said gently, "I'll never tell."

She lifted her face and Jesse fervently wished it was brighter under the blanket so he could see the expression she wore. "You don't hate me now?" she asked in a tearful whisper.

Jesse thought of his own deception, which had been completely voluntarily. "I don't."

A small breath of relief passed her lips. "Thank you."

"What will you do?" he asked, suddenly understanding her predicament.

"I don't know," her voice was so small and defeated, Jesse again resisted the urge to draw her into the protective shelter of his arms.

They fell silent again, each of them contemplating the impossible situation. Jesse realized that outside their make-shift tent, the world had also fallen silent. "I think the storm has passed," he said as he lifted the blanket from their heads.

The sky was lighter, though still heavy with gray clouds. The grass around them was as battered and beaten down as Annette's spirits. He could see her now in the dim light, her eyes averted, shame and vulnerability marking every feature.

"I need to get you home," he said.

She glanced up at him then, and he hoped she saw the acceptance in his eyes.

He turned away from her and began to look over his stallion, carefully running his hands over his neck, back, and legs.

"Is he all right?" Annette asked.

"He seems fine," Jesse answered. "Can you ride behind me?"

She nodded, and he swung up into the saddle from the left side, then reached down to position his right foot in the stirrup. He offered his hand and pulled her up behind him. She gripped the back of the saddle, and Jesse instructed softly, "Put your arms around me. I don't want you to fall off."

Annette complied without comment. He nudged the stallion forward and tried not to imagine what Mr. Hamilton's response would be to seeing his daughter riding home in this fashion after having been stranded on the prairie with him for well over an hour's time. He also tried not to think about her soft body pressed against his back, her arms holding him tightly.

They rode this way for several minutes until he saw a rider up ahead and recognized his identity. He slowed to a halt and allowed Walter Hamilton to ride alongside him. He tipped his hat and said, "Good evening, Mr. Hamilton. I was just bringing your daughter home."

"Is she all right?"

"Yes sir. I happened by her during the storm and gave her the saddle blanket to cover her. Under the trees, it wasn't so bad." He was careful not to reveal that he had been under the blanket with her.

Walter nodded slowly, eyeing him distrustfully. His gaze swung to his daughter, sitting behind Jesse on the back of his horse. "Are you all right?" he repeated, this time directing the question at her.

"Yes, Papa. I don't know what I would have done if Jesse hadn't come along."

"Well, then, I owe you my thanks for keeping my daughter safe," Walter said resentfully. "Come on, Annette. Let's get you home." Annette slid down from behind Jesse and allowed her father to pull her up behind him.

She looked at Jesse from across the short distance, and he registered her gratitude and tipped his hat to her. "Good evening," he said to her father.

Mr. Hamilton nodded, then urged his horse forward. Jesse pressed the reins to his stallion's neck and rode in the opposite direction. But his thoughts followed Annette as she made her way back to her cabin.

~

Sunday morning dawned, and Annette fidgeted her way through breakfast and the Bible reading. Her stomach felt twisted into knots, like the braided rag rug covering their floor. She knew in the afternoon Bryan Hunt would appear and invite her for a walk. What she didn't know was how to push him away without revealing her secret or breaking his heart.

Dear God, what can I do? I'm trapped like a bull in a pen on branding day. I can't escape my sins or their consequences. If only Providence would have mercy on her and send a miracle.

"Annette!" her mother snapped sharply.

She looked up, startled, at her mother's narrowed gaze.

"I've asked you three times to bring me my sewing basket. Are you all right?"

"Yes, mother," Annette answered quietly, running to retrieve the basket.

"Why don't you go change into your blue calico and smooth your hair. Mr. Hunt will likely arrive soon to visit you," her mother encouraged.

Annette complied, not knowing what else to do. Guilt ate at her conscience for her continued deception. All she was doing was giving her parents and Mr. Hunt more false hopes about the future of their relationship. She just couldn't think of a believable reason to send him away. If she could only discover some flaw in him, some excuse that her parents would understand.

But as she walked with him through the green prairie grass, she could only find reasons to love him. He was always a gentleman, treating her with nothing but respect and kindness. She enjoyed listening to him tell stories about his childhood on the Potomac River and his dreams for his cattle ranch. He didn't stare at her overlong or let his eyes drift downward to her body. He asked questions, and listened carefully to her answers as if her thoughts were valuable to him. There wasn't a single thing she could hold against Bryan Hunt.

Her heart began to yearn for him. As she walked alongside him, she wondered if perhaps God hadn't offered a way of escape because this was the man she was supposed to marry. If she told him of her affair with Ricky Lawson, would he forgive her as Jesse Stone had or turn away in disgust? Her heart hammered in her chest at the very idea of confessing to him.

Dear God, let me know if I should I tell him. Will he understand?

Then it seemed as if God did indeed give her the answer. Bryan began to reminisce about his wife.

"Her name was Virginia. We had known one another all our lives. Her father owned a neighboring plantation and it was always assumed we would marry." He shrugged and sighed. "We fell in love so young, it seemed like it took forever for her to come of age. As soon as she turned sixteen, we were married." He gazed off into the distance again, and Annette tried to imagine him as a young man with his new bride.

"I admired her for her gentleness, as well as her spirited nature," he continued. "One time it rained for days on end, and Virginia had so much pent up energy that she actually ran barefoot through the mud in the lane and horrified her mother."

He shook his head and chuckled at the memory. "But what I loved most about her was her sweet nature and purity of spirit."

His voice trailed off and Annette bowed her head and blinked back tears. There was her answer.

~

Bryan took supper with the family again, and then took his leave. Annette had remained withdrawn and sullen throughout the evening. Hopelessness had taken root with Bryan's description of his first wife. *Purity of spirit.* Annette was exactly the opposite.

She leaned against the wooden structure of the well, pausing before pulling up fresh water to wash the supper dishes. Her gaze spread out to the western sky where the sun was sinking below the horizon. Streaks of violet and pink filled the great expanse, and the great orange ball of the sun hovered over the rim of the earth, offering its last golden rays of light for the day. She sighed wearily, wishing that when morning came again, she would have a reason to face it.

The sound of an approaching rider startled her from her reverie. She turned to see Jesse Stone riding toward her, and her eyes widened in surprise. He tipped his hat in greeting, then dismounted to the left side of his horse.

"I'm here to visit with you, if that's all right. I'll go in and ask permission from your father, if you don't mind," he said quietly, keeping the scarred side of his face averted out of habit.

Baffled by his presence, Annette nodded. "Yes, that's fine."

She waited outside until he returned, carrying his hat in his hands. "Come with me," he said, purposefully stepping to her right side so she would be speaking to his unblemished cheek.

Annette glanced up at him in curiosity. "Is everything all right?"

"Yes, I just had an idea I wanted to discuss with you. A possible solution to your problem."

A flush of embarrassment warmed her cheeks at the mention of her "problem." She was a fallen woman, ineligible for marriage with a respectable man. That was her "problem." The familiar hand of shame squeezed her heart, and she wondered what possible solution Jesse could have contrived for her.

"What is it?" she asked, searching his face where he allowed her to see it.

Jesse glanced back toward the cabin, then said, "Let's walk a little further before we discuss it."

Intrigued, Annette continued walking alongside him. The prairie stretched out with the appearance of being level, but hidden in the undulating waves of prairie grass were swells and rises. They walked down into a small depression that hid them from the prying eyes of her parents, and he paused.

Just as when she first met him, Jesse met her gaze by twisting his head at an unusual angle while keeping his scar hidden from view. "I've been thinking about what you told me, and I…" he paused, removing his hat again and twisting it in his hands. The glinting rays of evening sunlight shimmered on his golden brown hair. "I mean, a solution occurred to me, if it's agreeable to you."

Annette's blond brows came together in puzzlement. "What is it?"

"I remember when my sister, Caroline, came of age. She had two suitors competing for her hand, and she had to choose between them."

"Two suitors?" she repeated, still confused.

"Yes. So if you had another suitor…" his voice trailed off.

Annette couldn't understand what he was suggesting until she saw his Adam's apple working.

"Do you mean…?" she began tentatively, wanting to be sure she understood him correctly before she gave an answer.

"I've started construction on a three-story house," he responded, almost defensively. "I may not be as wealthy as Mr. Hunt, but I can offer you a respectable name and I have every reason to believe that over the next few years, my herd may double or even triple in size."

His slate gray eyes had been fixed somewhere behind her as he spoke, and now they shifted to meet her gaze for only a second before bouncing away again.

Annette let out her breath slowly. This was a proposal of marriage. Her mind reeled. This was a solution she had never anticipated. Jesse knew the truth, but was offering her a way to preserve her reputation and that of her family as well. Everyone would assume she was a virgin wearing white on her wedding day. She would be able to marry a respectable man, and have a husband and a home of her own.

"Jesse, I…" she wished he would meet her gaze squarely and she stepped in front of him, forcing him to look at her head-on. "I don't understand why you would do this."

She noticed how he wiped his palms on his thighs and

swallowed again before answering. "You're the only woman I've ever been able to talk to."

This honest answer brought a faint smile to Annette's lips. He had turned his head away and was staring at the ground now, and she stepped again into his line of vision and waited until his gray eyes met hers. "I'm honored," she answered softly. "Thank you."

"Your father won't approve," Jesse said hastily, unsure how to respond to the emotion that had crept into her voice and the tender gratitude in her vivid blue eyes.

"Mmm. My father. Well, I suppose I will have to deal with him," she admitted. "As you said, if I have two suitors to choose from, I can choose the one I wish. He can't force me to marry anyone."

"He won't understand why you chose me," Jesse blurted resentfully.

Shame and regret silenced Annette. Jesse knew she would never have chosen him if her compromised virtue hadn't forced her into it. She laid her hand gently on his arm and was startled as he flinched and stepped away from her.

"You're the only man I can talk to," she tried to reassure him. "You're the only person I've ever told."

He nodded in recognition of the admission, understanding the significance of her trust in him. "The house should be finished by late September. We could be married in October."

"All right," she agreed quietly, her head spinning.

"What will you tell Bryan Hunt?" Jesse wondered aloud.

"That I've chosen you," she answered steadily, wishing he

could understand how much his offer truly meant to her.

Chapter Ten

*A*nnette sat in the grass, her back resting against the log walls of the cabin. Overhead, the stars twinkled brightly in the distance. She breathed in the sweet smell of the prairie at night, listening to the gentle rustling of the wind in the grass.

She had tried to sleep in the room she shared with her twin sisters, then finally stepped quietly around their trundle bed and slipped out into the main room. Ernest slept on a cot in the kitchen, and she could tell by the rhythm of his breathing that he was sleeping soundly. She tip-toed outside and closed the door behind her.

But she felt a loyalty to Jesse that prevented her from walking alone in the darkness. If any harm fell to her, by man or by beast, she would have no one to blame but herself. And now that mattered in a way it hadn't before. She didn't want to put herself at risk. She knew Jesse would never agree to let her ramble alone at night, and she wanted to honor him.

She still could hardly believe he had suggested marriage. He could barely meet her gaze, and he still attempted to keep his scar hidden from her. When he did talk to her, it was often abrupt and awkward. She wondered what being married to him would be like.

But it was an act of mercy, and she was grateful for it. He was giving her a great gift, and she finally felt as if perhaps she did have a reason to hope. Jesse may not be the husband she imagined for herself, and he certainly wasn't as handsome or confident as Bryan Hunt, but he must have a kind heart or he wouldn't have agreed to keep her secret and take her as his wife. And that mattered far more than a flawless face or two good legs.

Not only did she feel indebted to Jesse, but also to Providence Himself. That morning her father had read from the book of Genesis, the story of Sarah's handmaid, Hagar. Although the story wasn't quite the same as her own, Annette had found her ears perking up as she listened to the way Abraham had slept with Hagar to get her pregnant, in order to preserve his family lineage since his wife was unable to conceive. It had been his wife's idea, oddly enough, but once Hagar was actually pregnant, Sarah had become jealous and sent her handmaid out into the desert to die.

God could have left Hagar to her fate, but instead had mercy on her and not only intervened in her life, but promised He would make a great nation of her son.

Annette was baffled by the mercy God showed Hagar, as much as she was by the mercy He was showing her now. She was perhaps more culpable than Hagar, who had been following orders, but both of them had been guilty of committing adultery with a married man. When God appeared to Hagar, she seemed surprised He had seen her. Just as Annette was. The Lord would have been justified in turning His back and leaving both of them to their consequences. But He hadn't.

Thank You, Lord, for answering my prayers. You truly are "The God who sees me."

She knew she would still live with the regret of her past, and that some consequences could never be taken away. But at least she had been preserved from public humiliation and the resulting spinsterhood.

Jesse and Annette had agreed he should not request permission from her parents to court her until she had first explained that she was partial to him. They both knew her father would have dismissed him with a curt laugh. Her parents already had their minds made up that she would marry Bryan Hunt.

When she returned from her walk with Jesse, her father's eyes were riveted on the door behind her.

"Where's young Mr. Stone?" he demanded.

"He wanted to head back before dark fell," Annette answered.

"What did he want with you?"

"He wanted to declare his intentions toward me," she said quietly, heart pounding as she braced herself for the storm that would inevitably follow.

She watched the dark clouds roll into her father's eyes as his brows drew together. "His intentions?"

"Yes, Papa."

"He wants to court you?" her mother blurted, as if to be sure she had heard correctly.

"Doesn't he know that you're already courting Mr. Hunt?" Walter demanded.

"I prefer to marry Mr. Stone," Annette declared. She had decided to be as straightforward and simple in her arguments as possible. She just wanted it settled.

"*What?* Over Mr. Hunt?" Agnes' voice was high-pitched

with disbelief.

"Why?" her father's voice came out low and accusing, and Annette didn't understand the implication until her mother added, "Did something happen between you two, that day in the storm?"

Annette raised her eyebrows. "In the hail, Mama?" she asked sarcastically, thinking how uncomfortable and awkward that would have been.

Her mother's eyes narrowed angrily. "Don't be impudent, child!"

Walter closed his eyes and shook his head, as if to clear the cobwebs from his thoughts. "I don't understand why you would turn down Bryan Hunt in favor of Jesse Stone."

"Mr. Hunt is a very nice man," she began, trying not to sound as if the line had been carefully rehearsed. "But Jesse is closer to my age and we have more in common. I'm more comfortable with him, and I have stronger feelings for him."

"This is the most ridiculous thing I've ever heard!" Walter Hamilton erupted, slamming his fists down on the table violently and sending the twins running to their mother's arms.

"There's nothing ridiculous about me choosing one man over another," she countered.

"But…" he sputtered, "you would choose that crippled eyesore over Mr. Hunt!" his voice was incredulous.

"I have chosen Jesse."

"My daughter is the most beautiful girl in the Western Territories," he boomed, "and she wants me to let her marry a one-legged man with a scar from one side of his face to the other!"

"How dare you judge him for his battle scars!" she screamed furiously. "You can't force me to marry against my will. I've chosen Jesse, and that's final!"

"Oh *yes I can* force you to marry against your will," Walter replied threateningly.

Annette met his gaze squarely, her blue eyes as hard as sapphires. "But you won't," she answered certainly, turning on her heel and retreating to her bedroom.

She leaned against the wall, shaking. Through the door she could hear her father demand of his wife, "What does she mean?"

"Walter Hamilton, if you force her to marry against her will, she may never speak to us again. She could run off and marry Jesse anyway, and then we would never see our grandchildren! I don't like this any more than you do, but you have to let her make up her own mind."

Annette couldn't make out her father's grumbled response.

"Maybe if we go along with it, she'll come to her senses on her own and change her mind," her mother suggested in a despondent tone. "What else can we do?"

The heavy footfalls of her father's feet were followed by the banging of the door as he made his exit in reply. Annette went to her bed and sank down on it. At least that was over.

As she watched the stars twinkle in the distant sky, she prayed her parents would one day be able to see past Jesse's amputated foot and scarred face. And she prayed for the wisdom to explain to Bryan Hunt why she had chosen another man. She dreaded the look of pain and disappointment that she knew would transform his handsome face when she told him. How was she ever going to be strong enough?

She let out a long sigh and shook her head sadly. How many people had Ricky hurt when he decided to seduce her? Vivian and Annette were the first victims, but Bryan and Jesse were affected by it too. And she suspected that Vivian's second husband could say the same. Five people hurt by one man's selfish decision.

And if Jesse hadn't offered to protect her secret, it would have torn her family apart as well. They were upset by her decision, but at least there was no shame and judgment involved.

~

After several days of contemplation, Annette decided that the sooner she informed Bryan of her rejection, the sooner she could stop worrying about it. And it would be better if she made the trip to inform him before he rode over on Sunday with thoughts of courting her. Her parents tried to dissuade her in hopes she would give up on the idea, but in the end, they allowed her to ride to Bryan's homestead with Ernest for chaperone.

As the brown and white stallion plodded his way across the miles of dry grass, Annette prepared the words in her mind. Her palms sweated and her stomach twisted with nerves. She desperately wished there was a way to avoid this confrontation. But there wasn't.

She was almost relieved when they reached his cabin and found it deserted. He and his men must have been out checking on the cattle. She settled on the front porch with Ernest to wait. He had been quiet throughout their ride but now heaved a sigh and said, "Really, Annette. You're ruining everything."

"Oh hush," she snapped irritably. Bryan's absence meant that her agony of waiting was prolonged. She tapped her foot and paced back and forth, searching the horizon. She wasn't leaving until this was done.

When she saw a group of riders approaching, she told her brother to stay put and began walking toward them. She wiped her sweaty palms on her apron and tried to steady her erratic breathing. How did one stick a knife in a man's heart while looking him in the eyes?

"Miss Hamilton!" Bryan had spurred his horse forward and called out her name in surprise. "Is everything all right?"

"Yes." She noticed his men approaching to see if they could offer assistance and said, "I was hoping to be able to speak with you."

A flicker of concern showed in his eyes before he urged the cowhands to go on without him. He dismounted and stood in front of her, waiting. To Annette, he looked like a man before a firing squad and she cursed herself as a fool for the thousandth time. But the reminder that he deserved better than her gave her the courage to follow through with what she must say.

"Mr. Hunt, I have thoroughly enjoyed getting to know you in recent weeks, and I am honored by your interest in me. However, I have received a proposal of marriage from another man and I have decided to accept it. It is not because of any error on your part or any fault that I have found in you. I only want you to know that I hold you in the highest of regards and hope you will be able to forgive me." She let her gaze settle somewhere beyond his right shoulder as she delivered her speech, knowing she would not be able to finish if she were to actually meet his gaze.

"Look at me," he said quietly, and she slowly let her eyes lock with his. There she saw exactly the wounded confusion she had expected.

"Have I offended you in some way, Miss Hamilton? Because if I have, I would like to apolo—"

"No, not all. As I said, my decision is not because of anything you have or haven't done. It really isn't about you at all. I don't know how to make you understand, but I truly think you are a wonderful man and I hope one day you meet a woman who will love you the way you deserve. A woman like your Virginia." She drew a deep breath and added, "But I am marrying Jesse Stone this October."

Bryan's pale blue eyes bored into hers, searching for answers. Finally he said, "Then I wish you happiness."

"I wish the same for you," Annette replied sincerely, wishing she could say more. But knowing that the wisest thing to do was to leave before she did.

Afraid he would see the truth of her affection in her eyes and confuse the matter further, she stared down at her feet. "I should go," she whispered.

"Annette, I—"

"Please don't," she interrupted. "I really must go."

They walked back to where her brother waited with her mount in silence. She hurried to step into the saddle before Bryan had the chance to offer his assistance. She let her gaze meet his one last time in parting, then turned and rode away.

Chapter Eleven

*J*esse searched Annette's face as she saw her future home for the first time. He was satisfied with the surprise and awe he saw registered in her expression.

It stood on the hill, overlooking the prairie just as he had envisioned. Three impressive stories, the siding painted white with black shutters at every window, and accented with a two story front porch trimmed in white dentil molding. Two brick chimneys were built onto either side of the house.

The interior wasn't completely finished, and freight wagons loaded with supplies were stationed outside the front door. Occasionally, workmen could be seen coming and going as they retrieved tools or materials.

For the last few weeks, he hadn't been able to visit Annette very often. Duties at the ranch and overseeing the construction had taken all his time. But now that the house matched the drawings he had sketched with the architect, he wanted her to see it. And he was pleased with her response.

"Oh, Jesse!" she exclaimed. "I've never seen anything like it!"

Jesse just smiled and watched her. He shifted his weight to his left foot to relieve the pressure on his amputated leg where it rested in the prosthesis. It had been hurting him more than usual over the last few days. Maybe it was the weather, as the sweat caused it to swell and chafe. But he would far rather tolerate the pain than the humiliation of hobbling about on crutches.

He had told Annette it was to be a grand three-story house, but he suspected she believed him to be exaggerating. As he stood next to her, watching the way her eyes took in the details of it, he felt proud of his lovely wife-to-be and the grand house he was able to provide for her.

Annette had grown up on the western prairie where crude log cabins were the only form of structure. Jesse had designed the house based on what he knew back east. And although it may have seemed a little out of place in its setting, there was no denying its stately presence.

"How many rooms does it have?" she questioned, taking in the size of the structure and noting the number of windows. There were thirteen just on the front side of the house.

"Four bedrooms," he replied, trying to keep the pride from his voice. "There's a spacious living room, a separate room for dining, and the kitchen's in the back. Perhaps in a year or two, we could hire someone to cook and clean for you."

She let out her breath slowly.

"Each bedroom has a fireplace. The uh… master bedroom is the largest," Jesse added, almost saying "*our* bedroom," but finding the implications too intimate. He swallowed, shifting his feet again.

He noticed a faint blush color her cheeks, and he knew similar thoughts must be coming to her mind. Only a span of a few weeks' time separated them from marriage. His pulse accelerated at the very idea.

How had *he* managed to secure the prettiest wife in the territory?

Annette knelt down to pet Lucky, who had been nudging her and begging for attention since she'd arrived. Jesse watched as she stroked the dog's brown ears and rubbed the white patch on his nose, crooning to him softly.

Clearing his throat, Jesse continued, "I'm going to order furniture from a company back east that will ship it by train. Is there anything in particular you would like?"

She stood and faced him, and as much as Jesse wanted to meet her gaze, he kept his scarred cheek averted and tilted his eyes to see her. She looked upset, and Jesse couldn't figure out why she should be. Had he said something wrong?

"I'm sure whatever you choose will be fine," she said quietly.

Jesse shoved his hands in his pockets and stared at the toes of his boots.

"I don't deserve so much," she whispered beside him.

Understanding brought relief as Jesse lifted his eyes to his new home. "Neither do I."

Suddenly Lucky jumped up to lick Annette's cheek, almost knocking her over.

"No, Lucky!" Jesse pushed the dog away with one hand while grabbing Annette's elbow with the other to steady her.

"I'm sorry. He's just excited to see you," he apologized.

Annette chuckled. "So I see." She reached down to rub the puppy's head and received sloppy kisses on her hand in exchange.

"I've made arrangements with the preacher in town," Jesse told her, still not quite believing she would follow through with it.

She nodded.

"Should I invite any of the neighbors, or did you want it to be a family affair?" Jesse continued uncomfortably.

"I suppose your family won't be able make it," she realized.

"No. The train tickets are too expensive."

"Well then, if there's anyone you would like to invite, that would be fine."

"Isn't there anyone you want invited?" Jesse persisted, certain she had friends whom she would want present at her wedding.

She shook her head silently.

Jesse almost pushed the matter further, until he remembered the Fourth of July. He had noticed the way she stayed with her family, with the exception of a brief walk with her former suitor, Bryan Hunt. He had observed the way the men gawked at her and the women glared. It had never occurred to him that perhaps it was just as isolating to be gorgeous as it was to be disfigured.

Jesse cleared his throat. "If I invite all the ranchers I know, I'll have to invite Bryan."

Her eyes flicked to his, then turned back to watch as a painter carried his brushes up the front steps. "I suppose so. I guess he'll have to decide if he wants to attend or not."

Jesse watched her carefully from the corner of his eye. Did she want Bryan in attendance, or was she hoping the handsome widower wouldn't come? He still sensed some attraction on her part, and he tried to quell the rise of jealousy at the thought. Jesse knew the only reason she had turned Bryan down in favor of his proposal was because she had to. It wasn't as if she had pretended to be in love with him.

But, he reminded himself, he would never have found a wife for himself otherwise. In time she might learn to care for him. Though the thought of her ever seeing his stump or being close enough to examine his scar was mortifying.

How was he ever going to go through with this?

~

Agnes slowly pulled the wedding gown from the trunk, listening to the soft rustle of satin. A wistful smile touched her lips. "Your father and I were married in San Francisco in 1850..." She shook her head as she stood. "Where did the years go?"

Against the white fabric, her hands showed their age as she smoothed them over the familiar gown. Leathery and wrinkled, they were the hands of a woman who had worked hard all her life. Annette looked down at her own hands, still smooth even if browned from the sun, and wondered what the years would bring to her.

Agnes held up the gown, and Annette stood and allowed her mother to pull it over her head.

"Hmm. You're so much thinner and taller than I was. But I think I can make it work," her mother pursed her lips together as she turned Annette in a slow circle, gathering folds of fabric and sticking pins in them.

Since Annette had offered no compromise in her decision, her parents had become unusually silent on the matter. Annette had been surprised and touched when her mother had offered the use of her old wedding gown.

"It's beautiful," she said softly, appreciative of the gift even if it wasn't quite her taste. The lines of the dress looked as if they'd been the fashion twenty years ago. But nothing about this wedding was like the dreams Annette had nurtured since she was a small girl.

Agnes paused as she leaned over to stick another pin into the white satin. "My mother made it for me." She glanced at Annette briefly. "You know, she didn't approve of my choice for a husband either. But your father and I have worked out just fine." She allowed her eyes to meet her daughter's as she added, "I do hope you'll be happy."

"I know you do, Mama," Annette assured her. "I didn't know your parents didn't approve of Papa."

"Well, they thought he was just a grubby gold-miner who didn't have the means to take care of me. But cattle ranching has done us well, and I guess you'll be all right too. No matter who you marry."

"Jesse's a good man," Annette asserted quietly.

"I'm sure he is," Agnes replied in the tone of voice she used when she was simply agreeing to avoid an argument. Annette had heard her use it many times in conversation with her father.

They fell silent as Agnes continued to spin Annette in a slow circle, sticking pins here and there. Looking down at her mother's head, bent to her work, Annette noticed the gray woven through her mother's blond hair. Her breath caught in her chest. As much as she resented the constant nagging and demands of home, Annette knew she would miss her family.

Finally Agnes straightened and said, "All right. I'll see what I can do with it."

Careful not to get poked with one of the many pins, Annette removed the gown and stepped back into her every day dress. She was moving toward the door when her mother stopped her.

"Sit down," she ordered in a suddenly tense voice. "I want to speak with you."

Curious, Annette sat down on the edge of the bed. She looked up at her mother and waited.

Agnes cleared her throat, then lowered herself onto the bed next to Annette. "My mother didn't prepare me for my wedding night, and I always wished she had," she began. Annette tried to mask the inward cringe as she realized what the topic of this conversation was to be. Having no idea how to reply, she simply nodded.

The box of pins was still in Agnes' hands and she fidgeted with them in her lap. "The first time is the worst. It gets better after that. In time, you might even find you look forward to it. Just tell him to be patient and gentle with you, and it'll go easier."

Numbly, Annette nodded, wondering what she would be thinking if she didn't already know how it happened. She tried to close her mind to the memories that threatened to surface. The smell of the hay, the way she'd cried when Ricky had left her alone in the barn only moments after it was finished.

After she'd cried herself sick, she'd climbed onto her stallion and rode quietly away. She'd stumbled tearfully to the creek to wash her dress. As she had knelt by the creek, scrubbing away the tell-tale signs of her sin, she'd known that the romance was over. The spell was broken. In the place of infatuation, there was only a heartache that would never be healed.

She had given away the gift meant for her husband. She had already given it away to someone who didn't deserve it, and she could never take it back.

Tears threatened, and Annette blinked them away.

Agnes gently took her chin in her hands in a rare moment of tenderness. Mistaking her tears for fear, she said, "Don't worry. You'll be fine."

"Thank you for everything, Mama," Annette managed to whisper.

II. Repentance

"Purify me from my sins, and I will be clean;
wash me, and I will be whiter than snow."

Ps. 51:7 NLT

Chapter Twelve

P ink light glowed through the thin curtains with the dawn. Annette lay awake, watching the weak light brighten as the sun climbed in the sky. Her eyes were fixed on the ceiling above her. Today was her wedding day.

For hours she had lain awake trying to think of a way out. Not because of Jesse, necessarily, but simply out of fear. After the Reverend proclaimed their marriage legal and she took Jesse's name, it was almost irreversible. She would spend the rest of her life as Mrs. Jesse Stone—and what did she really even know about him? Truth was that she barely knew him at all. And although she found him companionable, he wasn't at all the kind of suitor she had imagined becoming her husband.

As she had told her mother, he *was* a good man. A little odd, perhaps, and clearly unsure of himself, but he had a kind heart. She didn't fear mistreatment at his hand, and she couldn't imagine he would ever break his commitment to her. That would require *speaking* to another woman, and his shyness prevented that.

She had to smile as she remembered his visit the evening before. He had arrived unexpectedly as she was up to her elbows in suds, washing the supper dishes. She had heard the sound of a rider, and assumed it was one of her father's ranch hands. Annette had looked up in surprise as her father opened the door to invite Jesse in, hat suffering abuse in his tense hands.

"Good evening," he'd said, staring at the back wall. "I was hoping I could speak briefly with Annette."

"Yes, of course," Agnes answered, though her voice sounded uncertain.

Annette smiled in greeting as she wiped her wet hands on the dish rag. She left her sunbonnet on its peg since the sun was too low in the sky to be a threat to her pale skin.

"Is everything all right?" she asked him when they had walked a fair distance from the cabin.

"Everything's fine," he answered, as if surprised she had asked.

"Oh, I just didn't expect to see you tonight," Annette admitted, studying the side of his face he revealed to her. A heavy shadow of whiskers darkened his jaw, and she presumed he would shave it in the morning. She found herself wondering if it was difficult to work the razor around the scar that pulled at his mouth.

She watched as he stared down at the toes of his boots and shoved his hands into his pockets. He cleared his throat. "I just came by to see you." He shifted from one boot to the other. "I brought you a gift."

Brushing a wisp of blonde hair away that the wind had blown into her eyes, Annette looked up at him with a smile. "That's very thoughtful of you," she said, wondering what it could be.

Jesse lifted his chin and gazed out at the distant horizon, the sky darkening into dusky purple and slate. "When I left home, my mother gave me something to keep with me until I met the woman I would marry. She said my grandfather had given it to my grandmother as a token of love and commitment." He cleared his throat, glancing at her briefly, then looking away again. "I want you to have it, Annette."

"Thank you," she answered softly, wondering if he had forgotten to actually give it to her.

Finally he drew his right hand out of his pocket and glancing down at the object, transferred it to his left hand, then held it out for her to receive. She wished that in such moments he would face her, instead of keeping his scarred side averted. But she reached out and accepted the gift, opening her hand to reveal an exquisitely engraved silver brooch, encrusted with pearls and sapphires. It was the most extraordinary—and expensive—piece of jewelry Annette had ever seen.

"Oh, Jesse!" she exclaimed, looking up to find that in his delight over her response, he had forgotten to keep his face turned away from her. And the opportunity to meet his gaze squarely felt like an even greater gift.

Annette quickly returned her gaze to the brooch, knowing he would regret his moment of openness. "It's lovely!" she whispered. She looked up at him again, aware he was meeting her eyes with that familiarly odd tilt. "Thank you," she repeated sincerely, touched by the sweetness of the gesture.

Jesse's smile was very satisfied as he removed his hat and ran his fingers through his hair before replacing it. "You're welcome."

"I'll always treasure it," she said softly, letting her fingers trace over the intricate design and the sparkling stones. Annette swallowed down tears. "I'm honored by your kindness."

She wanted to say more, but shame silenced her tongue. She

didn't deserve such a gift. But then Jesse knew that, and gave it to her anyway. Which made it even more precious to her.

"I'm glad you like it," he said, and Annette's eyes lifted from the brooch to search his face at the husky timbre of his voice.

But whatever emotions moved him were already hidden. He tipped his hat as he said gruffly, "I need to be going."

"I'll see you tomorrow, then," she answered softly, waiting for him to meet her gaze. When he did let his eyes settle on her, she smiled up at him.

As soon as Jesse had taken his leave, Annette had burst into the cabin and ran to her mother's side, exclaiming, "Mama! Look at what Jesse gave me!"

"For heaven's sake, girl, quiet down before you wake the children!" her mother scolded, setting her mending aside to accept the item in Annette's hand.

When Agnes saw what her daughter placed in her palm, she gasped in disbelief. "Why, Annette! It's breathtaking!"

"I know," Annette answered quietly, feeling a sudden flush of pride in her future husband. He was a man of worldly means, but also a man of unspeakable kindness. "I want to wear it tomorrow, on my wedding dress. I think he would like that."

Agnes sprang from her chair and hurried into Annette's room, despite that the girls were sleeping on the trundle bed. She tread softly to where the gown was draped carefully over a chair, already ironed smooth and shimmering in the candlelight. Wordlessly, she spread the dress over the bed, pointing to the scooped bodice. Annette pinned the silver brooch to the lace.

~

Propping herself on one elbow, Annette let her eyes fall on her wedding dress. In the pink light of dawn, the gown took on a rosy hue. Probably more suitable than the white intended to represent purity, but Annette pushed such thoughts away. After today, her past mistakes could be swept away as if they had never happened. She would become a wife, a respectable woman with a household of her own.

The wedding was scheduled for three o'clock in the afternoon at Jesse's homestead. The morning was a whirlwind of preparations. Everyone was loaded into the wagon, along with the finery that would be donned just before the ceremony. When she arrived, Annette was taken aback by the flurry of activity as tables were set up and laden with food, an archway erected with flowers for the bride and groom to stand beneath, and white ribbons and decorations hung on the porch and tables.

Jesse had even hired a photographer to capture the day's festivities. Annette was astounded by his attention to even the smallest details. It was more elegant and elaborate than she had ever imagined her wedding would be. Gratitude and respect continued to blossom in her heart as she peered down from a second story window at the grandeur of it all.

Then it was time to dress and prepare for the event. Her heart began to race as she carefully stepped into the satin gown and let her mother adjust it over her shoulders and button up the back. Then Agnes sat her down to style her hair. She brushed until it shone, then began weaving flowers into braids that wound around her head and through a chignon at the base of her neck. Finally, the veil was carefully pinned into place.

Annette looked into the mirror and let out a breath of disbelief. She was stunning. She had to admit it even to herself. She looked like a bride fit for such a grand wedding. If only the truth matched the image in the reflection.

The sins of the past would soon be covered over forever, she reminded herself. Once she had taken Jesse's name, no one ever need know. The saying, "Dead men tell no secrets" came to mind, and she thought of Ricky buried on a nearby hill. A shiver ran down her spine.

She would be living on the very land that Ricky had owned. What a peculiar twist of fate.

She closed her eyes and sent up a quick prayer to heaven. *Let us forget the past and find happiness and peace.*

Annette turned to find her mother's eyes misted over. "You're the most enchanting bride I've ever seen. I'm so glad there will be a photograph to remember how you look today."

A knock at the door signaled that the time had come. "We're waiting for you," her father's voice summoned them.

Trying to calm the racing of her pulse, Annette smoothed her hand over the satin skirt. She nodded at her mother. "I'm ready."

Opening the door, she took her father's elbow and let him lead her down the stairs and outside where a crowd of guests rose from their chairs to watch her procession to stand beside the groom. Jesse was half-turned to face her, keeping his scarred right cheek averted as always. He was dressed handsomely in a fine black suit with a white flower in his buttonhole and his hair neatly combed. His blue-gray eyes said everything. He looked both proud and terrified.

Walter lifted Annette's veil to kiss her cheek, then placed her hand in Jesse's. Only Annette knew how much this gesture had cost him.

As Jesse's fingers curled around hers, she noticed that they trembled. She squeezed his hand gently, hoping to reassure. In the back of her mind a question lingered. *Does he regret his offer?*

Annette tried to focus on the words of the preacher, but her thoughts drifted in and out of the present like the flowers woven into her hair. She had spotted Bryan Hunt as she had walked slowly down the aisle between the guests. The jagged pain in his eyes had been hard to ignore.

The Reverend spoke her name and she realized it was time to recite the vows. She lifted her chin and willed her voice to sound confident and sure. Jesse was instructed to face her and take her hands, but it seemed his head tilted right out of habit and his eyes only held hers for a second before dancing away to some point beyond her shoulder.

Then it was finished. They were husband and wife. He leaned forward and brushed his lips across hers so softly and so quickly that it was over before she had a chance to register it had happened. His cheeks burned pink as he took her hand and they turned to face the friends who applauded as they were announced as "Mr. and Mrs. Jesse Stone."

It was done.

~

The abundance of food spread out upon the tables at the reception made Annette's eyes grow wide. How had Jesse financed such an extravagant event? Even her father appeared to be impressed.

Most of the folks in attendance were neighboring ranchers whom Annette had known through the years, although some were new to the territory and merely acquaintances. Annette smiled and nodded politely as she was hugged and congratulated by what seemed to be hundreds of people. Jesse was even more uncomfortable with the attention, and whenever possible, Annette tried to take the brunt of the socializing for him.

As Annette spied the couple approaching, her thoughts turned backward once again. It seemed that every time she had seen Vivian at an event, Sarah Gibson had been by her side. They had been the best of friends, and if Vivian had disclosed her secret shame to anyone, it would have been the Indian woman.

Frank Gibson was the first to congratulate her, nodding his head at her before turning to shake Jesse's hand. Annette put him somewhere in his mid to late forties. His hair was thinning and mostly gray, and his beard was streaked with silver.

His wife followed at his side. Sarah's jet black hair gleamed in the autumn sunshine, revealing a few silver strands of her own. Her tanned skin crinkled around her eyes as she smiled kindly. "Congratulations, Mrs. Stone. I wish you every happiness."

"Thank you," Annette answered for what was surely the hundredth time in the last hour, but this time the words seemed caught in her throat.

"My husband and I are your closest neighbors," Sarah continued. "If you ever need anything at all, we're just over that rise," she pointed in the direction of her cabin. "I hope you won't mind if I stop by to visit from time to time. I get lonesome for female conversation."

Annette nodded mutely, hoping the woman never followed through on her threat.

Sarah's brown eyes, dark and round as almonds, held Annette's gaze for a second longer. Then she took her husband's elbow and let him lead her to where the fiddlers played and couples and children danced. Annette glanced back at the couple discreetly. If it wasn't for her dark hair and skin, Sarah Gibson could have been mistaken for a white woman. Annette hadn't sensed any hostility in her eyes or manner, but perhaps it was as well hidden as Sarah's heritage.

"Are you going to dance with your bride, Mr. Stone?" demanded Mrs. Pearson as she appeared at his elbow. She was an elderly woman with a reputation for both her outspoken opinions and her love of gossip. "I declare she's tired of all the well wishes by now!"

Annette looked up at Jesse and smiled, "I'm fine. But I would like something to drink."

"Nonsense! It's your wedding day! You must share a dance," the old busybody insisted.

Jesse shifted his feet. He nodded politely at Mrs. Pearson and offered Annette his elbow. She realized that he was leading her past the beverage table to where a wooden platform had been erected for dancing. She glanced up at him in surprise.

"I can't promise I won't fall," he admitted, and remembered his false foot.

"If you do," she teased, "I'll be sure to catch you."

A hint of a smile touched his lips. He took her right hand in his and let his left hand rest gently on the small of her back.

"You wore the brooch," he commented with satisfaction, his voice close to her ear.

"It made my mother's dress feel more like my own," she admitted gratefully.

They moved to the music rather carefully, both of them praying for Jesse to be able to execute the steps successfully. When the song concluded and he had managed to avoid any mishaps, he bowed at her dramatically, then led her to the beverages.

"Thank you for the dance," she said.

"It *is* our wedding day," he replied, and Annette was unsure if he was in earnest or poking fun at Mrs. Pearson.

"Let's find something to eat," he said then, and Annette was grateful for the opportunity to rest her feet even though she wasn't sure she could eat a bite. She wondered if his amputated leg hurt after hours of standing, and she discreetly observed that he walked with a slight limp.

Before long, families began to take their leave and the crowd began to dwindle. The pale light of dusk settled on the horizon, and a knot of anxiety formed in Annette's stomach as she thought of the wedding night ahead.

Her sisters suddenly appeared at her side, wrapping their arms around her waist. She drew Mary up onto her lap first, then Janice. "Are you leaving?"

"Yes, but we want you to come home with us!" Janice cried.

"You can't leave us," Mary added petulantly.

Agnes approached, carrying baby Howard in her arms. "Now, let your sister be," she admonished the twins. "It's her wedding day. She's a married woman now and this is her home. She'll still come to visit."

But her eyes held loss. Annette placed her sisters on the ground and stood to embrace her mother. "I'll visit," she promised.

Walter shook Jesse's hand again and embraced his daughter silently. Ernest, standing off to the side of his parents, nodded his head in acknowledgment, hands stuffed in his pockets.

"We'll miss you," Agnes admitted. "But I pray you will find happiness here." She turned to survey the three story mansion towering over them. "It's quite a home you have," she offered admiringly.

"Thank you for everything, Mama," Annette clung to her mother's hand, fighting off the guilt that niggled at her conscience.

"It's time to go," Walter said, taking Agnes by the arm. "Good night," he included both his daughter and her new husband in his abrupt farewell.

"Good-night!" chimed the twins as they turned to follow their parents.

Annette felt a sudden chill of loneliness as she watched her family walking away. She was no longer a Hamilton. She was to make a new family with the man who stood by her side.

Within minutes, the last guest had departed, leaving Annette and Jesse standing with the hired help as they began the task of cleaning up the aftermath left from the day's celebration.

Realizing this was their cue, Jesse cleared his throat and offered his arm. Wordlessly, they walked back toward the grand white house together.

Annette wished he would at least look at her, but tension seemed to have eclipsed the festive mood. He swallowed nervously as the door closed behind them. They were utterly alone in the house, though someone had been thoughtful enough to light the lamps and dispel the darkness.

In the soft glow of the oil lamp that graced the wall, Jesse's features were heavily shadowed. She looked up at him expectantly.

He actually looked quite handsome in his linen suit with a flower in the buttonhole. She had never seen him without his hat, with his hair combed so neatly and his face clean shaven.

Affection warmed her heart. He was her husband.

Chapter Thirteen

I figured I'd sleep on the couch," he announced. "You can have the bedroom," Jesse offered, anticipating her relief at the arrangement.

Instead, she registered surprise just before a wounded expression moved into her eyes. She straightened her shoulders and blinked back tears.

He stared at her helplessly, utterly confused.

Her gaze lifted to the darkened stairway. She looked back at him, then turned abruptly and almost ran up the stairs. Jesse stood alone, looking up at the retreating form of his wife. He let out a sigh of frustration and ran his fingers through his hair.

Lucky was tied up outside, and Jesse went to retrieve him. The dog was used to sleeping on the floor next to his bed. He scratched the dog behind the ears, puzzling over the way Annette had responded to his suggestion.

He had thought it all over and assumed she would want some time to get comfortable with him before they shared a bed. It wasn't as if she had married him out of love. Besides, he couldn't bear the thought of her seeing the grotesque stump of his right leg, the skin chafed and swollen from hours of pressing against the prosthesis.

Settling onto the couch, Jesse leaned over to pull up his pant leg and loosen the leather straps that held it in place. Carefully he removed the device that allowed him to walk on two feet, staring at the deformity protruding where an ankle and foot should have. Blisters had formed from rubbing against the rounded depression where his stump rested. Usually he made it a point to sit regularly throughout the day, even if it was mounted on his horse. But the wedding ceremony and reception had allowed him little opportunity.

He had ointment he could apply to the blisters, but he hadn't thought to remove it from the bedroom in which Annette was now sleeping. If the ointment could have soaked into his skin while he slept with the stump exposed to the open air, it would have hastened the healing.

He ran a hand gingerly over the tender, discolored skin and winced with humiliation. How could he ever let his flawless bride look at him without his false foot and the pants that covered it? The mere idea of her seeing him as he was, all his scars revealed, made his face burn hot with shame.

Leaning back into the pillows and cushions of the sofa, Jesse tried to get comfortable. He let his hand hang down to the floor, where Lucky licked it affectionately.

It wasn't fair to put Annette in a situation where she must feign indifference to his appearance while trying to mask her revulsion. How could he ever attempt intimacy while wondering if his wife was disgusted by him? He shook his head. How could he ever get close enough to even kiss her when he couldn't bear the thought of her looking him full in the face?

Jesse traced the line of the scar that ran the length of his cheek, starting at his temple and moving downward along his cheekbone to the corner of his mouth, pulling his lips into a perpetual frown. Annette was everything lovely that a woman could be. And he was a mangled cripple.

Lord, I rescued her from shame and a life of loneliness, but now what do I do? I don't know how to love her. I'm too ashamed to let her close.

It had been a long time since he had felt the need to ask God for help. His mother had knelt on the carpet in her bedroom every morning and prayed. Jesse had seen her. When asked, she said she was praying for the safety of her sons in the war, for him, for the future of her daughters, and for any of life's trials that she might be facing that day. She said she prayed about everything.

Religion and prayer had always seemed rather feminine to Jesse. True enough, his brother Albert was a clergyman. But his faith had always seemed rather vague and incomplete. Jesse didn't understand it. What was prayer supposed to accomplish, anyway?

His mother had prayed for the safety of her sons, but only three of the four had returned home, and Jesse and Stephen with vital limbs missing. It seemed to him that Providence sat back and watched as life on earth transpired based on the will of mankind. How He could let the years of killing one another drag on the way He had, Jesse couldn't comprehend.

The war had been directed by President Lincoln and Secretary of War Stanton. Not God. If God had involved Himself anywhere along the way, Jesse couldn't imagine where.

The only time Jesse had felt a desperate need to pray was that horrible day he had been sent out into battle. He had never seen anything like it. Not the brutality and viciousness that moved men to strike out at one another with every weapon available to them, nor the hatred that powered it. They all looked the same to him, no matter what color uniform they wore. He could not bring himself to see these soldiers in gray as enemies, regardless of what they believed or what they had done. They were just men. Just men fighting for their lives. They were all fighting for a cause they believed in, whether it was the preservation of the Union or the preservation of the South.

That day, he had prayed. Maybe Providence had answered. Maybe He hadn't. But Jesse had made a decision and directed his own fate from there. And he had managed for himself just fine.

But now he felt as helpless and unsure as he had the moment the first shot had been fired and the battle had erupted. Just as ill equipped to face the situation confronting him. He was married to the most beautiful woman in the Wyoming Territory. She was upstairs in his bedroom, at that very moment. And he had no idea what to do with her.

~

Jesse startled awake. He listened, and from the sounds coming from upstairs, Annette was already up. Through the window, he could see the gray edges of the sky brightening with the dawn. He wished he could light the lamp, but he didn't dare take the time.

He fumbled in the darkness beside the couch, searching for the prosthesis. His movement woke Lucky, who jumped up to lick his face.

"Down, boy," he pushed the dog away.

His neck ached. The couch was not designed with a good night's sleep in mind. His fingers closed around the metal rod and he quickly pulled up his pant leg and positioned his stump into place, tightening the buckles carefully in the dark shadows.

Straightening, he buttoned his shirt at the neck and ran a hand through his rumpled hair. He could hear her at the top of the stairs, slowly descending the steps. A circle of light preceded her as she held the candle high to illumine her way. In the pale glow, her hair shone like burnished gold.

Jesse quickly rose to light the oil lamp on the table, then turned to greet her.

He was silenced by the stony expression on her lovely face.

Lucky bounded over and greeted her with an enthusiastic, slobbering kiss on her hand. She leaned over to rub his head and scratch his ears.

After a moment, the dog flopped onto the floor at her feet. Annette turned to look at Jesse. "Good morning," she said coolly. "I'll make your breakfast before you head out."

Jesse had planned to stay around the house until late in the afternoon. He was reluctant to face the teasing of the men if he didn't. But now it seemed as if he was being dismissed. She seemed angry, and Jesse couldn't imagine why.

Did she want to share a bed with me last night? It wasn't possible.

He swallowed nervously. "I won't be riding out this morning. I have some work to do around here," he finished lamely. Claude had taught him how to braid rawhide strips into a whip, and he wanted to make a new one for himself before the fall roundup. Today was as a good a day as any.

She merely nodded and walked to the cast iron stove Jesse had bought for her and stared at it. "I've never used a stove like this," she admitted.

She studied it dubiously. The black cast iron box only reached to above her knees. It stood about two feet from the wall, connected by a pipe allowing the smoke to exit the chimney. It had four burners on top, and two doors on the side. Stooping to inspect it more closely, she opened the first door to reveal an ash-filled chamber where firewood would burn. Behind the second door was a small oven where bread or other dishes could be baked. A warming tray was positioned at the front of the stove. It was nothing like she was accustomed to.

"We always used the fireplace," she informed him, coming to her feet.

"I'll start a fire for you," Jesse volunteered.

Walking to the pantry, she pulled out cornmeal and salt for the johnnycakes. "Should I go out to gather eggs?" she asked.

"I'll get them," he quickly offered. "And fresh milk, too."

When he returned, he found her standing at the window, gazing out as the sun touched the distant horizon with hues of crimson and violet. Her silhouette against the sunrise was enough to stop him in his tracks. Her blond hair was pulled back into a simple bun at the neck, and she wore a pink apron. Even though she was not as elegantly attired as the day before, she was just as beautiful.

She turned to face him, and he was startled by the sadness in her eyes. Silently, she accepted the eggs and milk and set about making breakfast.

Never having used a modern stove, she had trouble getting the temperature just right by adjusting the dampers and flues. The eggs came out a little runny while the johnnycakes burned at the edges. Flustered and frustrated, she placed the plate before him.

"I'll have to get used to it," was all she said.

Jesse wondered if they would ever get used to living together. Before the wedding, it had been easy to be together. Easy to talk. Now it was stilted and he didn't know why, let alone what to do about it.

"Would you like to take a ride with me, while the sun is still coming up?" he asked, wishing he could explain that he wanted to share the morning with her, while the air was still crisp with the fresh scent of a new day and the sky ablaze with the brilliance of sunrise. But it was the best he could do.

She shook her head. "No thank you. I think I'll unpack my things after I clean the dishes."

Retracing his steps to the barn, Jesse retrieved the rawhide strips and returned to the house. He would have preferred to sit out on the front porch and enjoy the morning while he worked, but he didn't want to be spotted alone on the day after his wedding and subject himself to teasing.

He settled onto the couch where he had spent the night, and set to work weaving the strips into a sturdy whip. While his fingers worked, his mind drifted. The wedding had been more impressive than he had hoped. He was glad he had been able to find a photographer willing to come out and take pictures of the momentous day. And grateful Annette had chosen to wear the brooch on her wedding gown for his mother to see.

Before the ceremony, Jesse had commissioned a picture of the house, adorned with wedding decorations, and another of himself, mounted on his appaloosa and wearing his Stetson, duster, and spurs. He would send copies of them with the wedding photo to his mother. He knew she would show them to everyone in Springfield, Massachusetts.

And everyone would wonder how in the world he had managed to catch such a gorgeous wife.

~

In the bedroom, *her* bedroom apparently, Annette had finished putting her few items of clothing in the fancy armoire and flopped down on the bed. She stifled back more tears as she curled onto her side.

Jesse had been so sweet the night before their wedding when he had given her the exquisite silver brooch. She had thought he genuinely cared for her. Why else would he have offered to give her his name knowing the truth about her? But whatever affection he felt was not enough to permit him to touch her. Perhaps he was afraid he would be stained by her sins if he lay with her.

He had taken her as his wife, but apparently had no desire to consummate their vows.

The marriage was a farce. She had let herself believe that being married would wipe clean her past as an adulteress. But it was foolish and wishful thinking, she realized now. Her past could never be undone.

She wished she could have lied to Bryan Hunt, could have found a way to trick him. If she had, she would be held warmly in his arms right this minute instead of crying tears of rejection and grief. But it wasn't within her to live a lie.

The worst part was that Annette had determined to close her thoughts and heart to Bryan. She had felt new feelings budding for Jesse as he demonstrated kindness and generosity toward her. And now it seemed even he didn't truly want her.

She looked around the spacious bedchamber. Was she just another accessory to add to Jesse's life to make him feel complete? A cattle ranch, a big house, and a trophy wife. Whatever he had left behind, he seemed in a hurry to prove himself a success out west. And she was just another prize on his mantle.

Everyone would look at him and think how lucky he was to have her. Only she and Jesse would know the truth: he married her because no one else would, and he couldn't bring himself to touch her.

Sitting up, Annette dried her tears. He had still done her a favor. Even if they never knew the kind of love she had hoped for, she still owed him. He had saved her. And she would show her gratitude by being the best wife she could be. She would keep his grand house spotlessly clean, all his clothing washed and darned, and learn how to cook delicious meals on the cast iron stove. She would get up early to gather eggs and milk the cow, and have breakfast waiting for him when he woke up.

On the couch.

She sighed. At least he hadn't made *her* sleep on the couch.

She had been hurt, but also a touch relieved, when she realized he didn't expect her to share the intimacies of husband and wife. The only experience she had with such things was with Ricky, and he had made her pulse race just by the way he looked at her. She couldn't imagine what it would be like to have Jesse touch her when all they shared was an oddly awkward friendship. There was no passion between them, no sparks of desire.

There had been a longing on her part to feel wanted, to be his wife in the fullest sense of the word. She had been disappointed when he had sent her up the stairs alone. But—and she felt uncharitable admitting it, even to herself—the idea of being in intimate proximity to him made her uncomfortable. His face was badly scarred.

Annette stood, smoothing her clothes and patting her hair into place. There was no point in hiding in the bedroom all morning. Although she had no idea what needed to be done in this big, empty house without muddy boots tracking the floor and diapers needing to be changed, she was sure she could find some useful way to occupy her time.

As she descended the stairs, she saw the back of Jesse's head, bent to the work in his hands. He turned and said, "I'm not sure this is turning out as well as I planned. Perhaps you can help me."

Curious, Annette circled the couch to join him. She sat down beside him, keeping a generous distance between them, and observed the strands of rawhide he was attempting to braid. Parts of it were woven together well, but it appeared he had lost his rhythm when trying to weave in a new strand.

Wordlessly, Annette took the rope from him and demonstrated how to seamlessly introduce a new section of leather.

She noticed his eyes moved from her hands to her face and back again. She returned the rope and said, "There, you see."

"Thank you," he answered quietly.

"You're welcome," she replied politely, coming to her feet.

Jesse stood too, stuffing his hands into his pockets and

clearing his throat. "Umm… I was hoping you would take a ride with me. I noticed the leaves on the aspens have turned, and they're the only trees here that change color in the fall. It reminds me of home." He cleared his throat again. "Would you come with me?"

Annette hesitated. She had already declined to ride with him once that morning. Clearly it was important, and she wanted to please him. "All right," she agreed.

He almost smiled as he said, "I'll saddle the horses."

Annette retrieved her sunbonnet and a sweater and joined him in the barn. Ricky had built this barn when he first settled on this plot of land. They had shared more than just a clandestine kiss in its shelter. She pushed away the memories as she watched her husband saddle his appaloosa mare. Her mount was already prepared and waiting.

It was a sleek, black mare, who tossed her silky mane and snorted at Annette as she approached. "She's magnificent," Annette commented softly, reaching up to rub the velvety nose.

"She's yours," Jesse said.

"I beg your pardon?" Annette said, thinking she had misheard him.

"She's your horse, whenever you want to ride. I bought her for you."

"Oh…" Annette fumbled for words. She didn't understand this man. Not one bit.

"Thank you, Jesse," she finally managed. "What's her name?"

"Bella," he said. "I didn't name her."

Annette had to smile. "I like it." She fingered the black mane and Bella turned her head to nuzzle Annette's shoulder.

"They said she was very gentle, and would make a good lady's horse," Jesse explained.

He came over to Annette and offered his hand. Although his assistance was unnecessary, Annette allowed him to play the gentleman. After all, he had just referred to her as a lady. She settled her skirts over the saddle and waited for him to mount up.

She followed Jesse as he led them out of the barn and into the sunshine. It was a crisp fall day, perfect for riding. The sky was a cerulean basin over their heads, with not even a wisp of white clouds to interrupt its endless blue. The air was brisk enough to merit the sweater, but the sun felt warm on her back.

They rode in silence, each one absorbed in their own thoughts. Annette reached down to pat the sleek black neck of her mare. Bella was a fine horse, and Annette knew enough to guess at the price Jesse had paid for her. It hadn't been a small amount. Nor had the wedding celebration been an inexpensive event. Why on earth was Jesse being so generous with her?

She glanced over at his smooth left cheek exposed to her view, wishing she could know his thoughts.

He turned his head slightly to meet her gaze as he asked, "What do you think of her?"

"She's sure of her footing, but has a smooth and almost delicate gate. She's responsive with the bit, and almost seems to read my mind," Annette replied.

"You're familiar with horses," Jesse observed.

"I don't get to ride often, but I enjoy it when I can," she

replied.

Jesse's lips curved upward as he urged his mare into a fast canter.

Annette gently nudged Bella in the flanks and fell into step beside him. He responded by coaxing his mount into a loping gallop. Bella kept pace.

Jesse shot her a brief look, his eyes challenging as he sped off at full gallop.

Annette threw back her head and laughed. She knew she and her light-footed mount could easily race him as far as he wanted to run. She leaned into Bella's neck and urged the mare forward. They sped over the ground at lightning speed, the grass beneath them only a blur of green and brown. Annette grabbed hold of Bella's long black mane and gave the horse her head. They became one animal moving fluidly over the uneven ground, the wind rushing against them as they heaved forward.

As the grove of aspens came into the view and the earth sloped downward to meet the creek, Annette tugged softly at the reins to slow Bella's descent. Jesse had fallen a few paces behind, as she halted Bella at the creek waters, Annette turned in her saddle to gloat.

He tugged his hat forward and grinned. "You're quick," he said with approval.

"Bella's fast," Annette replied with a laugh as she dismounted and knelt down to cup a handful of water to her mouth.

She stood and turned to find Jesse standing by her side, shaking his head and chuckling under his breath.

"Is something funny?" she demanded.

Again he grinned, a rare sight Annette was finding she enjoyed. "I was just remembering the first time I saw you," he explained. "You were barefoot in the mud, wrestling with that little calf. I'd never seen anything like it in my life!"

"I'm sure we were quite a sight," she admitted with a laugh. "I went home covered in mud from head to toe!"

"He was almost as big as you were," Jesse chuckled again at the memory. "But you were giving it your best."

"Now don't make fun of me," Annette retorted. "You accused me of cattle rustling!"

"I did no such thing!"

"You did. And I hardly look the part," she giggled again, imagining how ridiculous she must have looked to Jesse as he came over the rise and spotted her ankle deep in mud.

He appeared to be thinking the very same thing and burst into deep, hearty laughter. Annette had never seen him like this before. She threw back her head and let the moment take over. They laughed until their sides felt as though they were splitting.

"Oh, that was funny," Jesse said as he squatted down to rest against the trunk of an aspen.

Annette wiped at her eyes as she joined him. "I can't remember ever laughing like that," she tried to catch her breath.

Jesse's smile was natural and full as he turned his head three quarters of the way to look at her, just short of letting her see his face full on. "I enjoyed it."

Annette smiled back at him, joining him on the ground. Overhead, the branches of the tree stretched out, clothed in the crimson leaves of fall. "It's lovely here, Jesse. I'm glad we came."

"So am I," he answered sincerely.

Chapter Fourteen

Jesse had to chuckle at the letter in his hands. His mother couldn't have been more shocked by the pictures he'd sent if he had been standing next to the Queen of England. He'd written to inform her of his engagement when Annette had first agreed to marry him. No doubt, his mother had pictured a woman equal to him in physical appearance.

That any woman would so quickly agree to marry him must have come as quite a surprise, since he had only been out west for several months. He suspected his family had given up on him ever finding a wife. But then to receive the pictures and see that his bride was an exceptionally attractive woman must have been an absolute shock.

"*I can hardly believe my eyes,*" she'd written. "*Your new wife is quite simply stunning. And I was so pleased to see she was wearing my mother's brooch! We would truly love to meet her, and deeply regret we could not attend your wedding. Please give her our warmest congratulations and convey that we welcome her into our family with open arms.*"

Jesse could only imagine the conversations that had taken place as his brothers and their wives, and his sisters and their husbands, had gathered around the table to examine the photos. They hadn't believed he would survive in the wilderness, let alone succeed. Yet there in front of them was the unbelievable evidence.

"Your home is far grander than I imagined. The western territories must be growing more civilized with the advancement of the railroad. We are all so happy for you, and very much enjoyed the picture of you playing the cowboy."

Jesse shook his head. *Playing the cowboy.* They still didn't get it. This was who he had *become*, not just a part he was playing until he grew bored with it or stumbled into failure. He was a cattle rancher now and forever.

He turned over the package that had arrived with the letter, sliding his thumb along the edge of the brown paper to reveal its contents. His father's Bible. He placed it on his lap and opened the front flap, reading the list of births and deaths chronicling his family's history. The last two deaths were the nearest to his heart. *Joseph Stone, deceased 1857. Peter Stone, deceased 1862.*

He traced his finger over their names. He wondered what his father would have thought of the war, of all his sons going off to fight for the sake of the preserving the Union and abolishing slavery. He would have approved at the start, but as the war dragged on and turned into butchery, would he have changed his mind? There was no way to know.

But if his father could look down from heaven, as some supposed, Jesse only hoped his own days of soldiering had been shielded from his father's sight.

His mother had written, *"Son, I know the eldest son should receive the Family Bible, but we are all in agreement that it should be yours. You are removed from us by time and distance, and we hope this sacred gift will help you cling to your heritage. I pray you will spend time in this great book with your new wife, and that God will bless your marriage."*

More guilt and sentimentality. Yes, he had chosen to move

away. Would she never understand it had nothing to do with a lack of love for his family? He left home to get away from the past. To start over. And with every fiber of his being, he believed he had made the right choice.

He had survived the rigors of the round-up, which was far more grueling than he had imagined. The hours spent in the saddle had been hard on his rear-end and his amputated leg. But he had managed.

All the ranchers had worked together to round up the vast numbers of cattle grazing the open range. Then they were sorted by brand. Once his own herd had been set apart, the calves were cut out. The hardest part had been the branding, dehorning and castration of the calves. Jesse had made it a point to stay as far away from those pens as possible.

Claude had helped him to determine which animals were ready to be sold at the market in Cheyenne, and he had made a tidy profit, making the exhausting drive to the railhead worthwhile. He had spent days in the saddle, coated with dust kicked up by the hooves of the great beasts, watching always for strays that needed to be cut back into the herd, or for mountain lions that might prey on the weak or young. At night, he had taken turns watching the sleeping animals to ensure nothing startled them into a destructive and terrifying stampede.

Nothing in his prior life had prepared him for this sort of work. And against all logic, he loved it. The sweat, the dirt, the danger. It made him feel like a man: strong, brave and competent.

And then there was Annette. If he had stayed in Massachusetts, he would still be tongue-tied around every woman he met, watching as his brothers and sisters had children and his friends found wives. She made all the achievements seem worthwhile. Every time he rode through the waving prairie grass toward his grand house, he knew she was inside waiting for him to come home.

~

Annette lifted the dash in the butter churn in a rhythmic pattern: up and down, up and down. Inside, she could hear the milk sloshing around, slowly thickening into fresh butter. She paused to wipe at the opening where a bit of buttermilk had splashed out.

The churn was white pottery with a blue flowered pattern painted on the front. Her mother's churn was wooden, serviceable and plain. It might not make the work any easier, but there was something about a thing of beauty that made the work more pleasant.

She couldn't complain. Jesse treated her well. He wasn't the most talkative man, but at times she could lure him into conversation. They had been married almost a month now, and were easing into a comfortable routine.

Though she still slept alone in the master bedroom. Jesse had relocated from the couch to the second bedroom since the furniture had been delivered. It had been transported by train and then carried by ox-drawn freighter to their homestead. It was just as fine as the furniture he had installed in the rest of the house.

She sighed, plunging the dash into the butter again. It certainly wasn't the way she had imagined marriage would be.

Her thoughts still sometimes drifted to Bryan Hunt in the quiet moments of the day as she kneaded dough for biscuits or swept the floor. She wondered if he had forgiven her for leading him on and then suddenly marrying another man. Sometimes she worried he might have quickly forgotten her, turning his interest to any one of the other young ladies that had moved into the territory.

Annette wouldn't blame him if he had. There was no reason why he shouldn't. But the thought of him walking in the sunset with another woman did cause a twinge of envy, accompanied by a pang of loss. Bryan Hunt had been everything she had dreamed her one-day suitor would be.

But the gate was closed on that dream, and she had been corralled into another life. This life, here with Jesse Stone. And she was trying to make the best of it.

The days passed more slowly here. She didn't really miss the chaos of her family's cabin, but she did find the hours of silence oppressive. The house was much larger, but two of the four bedrooms were unused, and since Jesse was the only one tracking mud on the floor, it remained relatively clean. Mostly, it was Lucky's fur littering the floor. Though she didn't mind the housework: the cleaning, laundry, ironing and cooking. It was the loneliness that bothered her most.

One afternoon, she had saddled Bella and ridden home to visit her mother. She had looked forward to some female conversation, but instead had found she was pulled back into the role of older sister. There had been no time for the visit she longed for, as she was occupied helping with baby Howard and the twins while her mother took advantage of the opportunity to complete household chores uninterrupted. They had sat for a few moments and shared a cup of tea, but even then, there were constant interruptions.

Since then, Annette hadn't visited her family again. She had gone hoping to find herself refreshed, and had instead returned home exhausted.

The butter had thickened, and she removed the lid and poured out the remaining buttermilk. She placed the butter in a container and put it in the cellar to keep cool.

When she returned to the kitchen, a movement through the window caught her eye. She peered out and saw a wagon approaching. It appeared to be a woman with a passel of children in tow. And it wasn't difficult to guess who it was. Sarah Gibson, the Indian woman who had been friends with Vivian Lawson Hudson.

Annette groaned. Honestly, she was surprised the woman had waited this long to follow through on her threat to visit. She had to admit, she wished she could let herself become friends with Sarah. But if Sarah knew about her affair with Ricky, she could only be there to snoop for a tidbit of gossip to write to Vivian about. And if she didn't know, then Vivian and Sarah hadn't been as close as they appeared.

It was safer to assume this woman knew her darkest secret and had the power to ruin her with it. Though if Sarah had intended to use it against her, she surely would have done so by now. Still, Annette wasn't about to trust her.

She went to the front door and saw the wagon come to a halt. Taking a deep breath, she went outside to greet her visitor. Descending the porch steps, she smiled graciously and said, "Good morning, Mrs. Gibson."

"Please, call me Sarah," the Indian woman replied warmly. "I hope now is a good time for a visit?"

"Yes, it's perfectly fine. Please come in and I'll prepare

some tea."

Three children clambered down from the wagon, all with hair just as dark as their mother's. Sarah put her arm around the oldest girl's shoulders and asked, "Have you met my children?"

Annette had certainly seen them around, and had likely been introduced at some point through the years. But she couldn't remember their names. "No, I'm afraid I haven't," she answered, wondering if the children had ever overheard any conversations between their mother and her closest friend.

"This is Elizabeth," Sarah indicated her daughter, who appeared to be at the tender age between girl and woman. "Then there's Frank Jr.," she indicated the boy who Annette guessed to be about the same age as Ernest. "And that's Miriam," she said as the little girl came over and shyly grasped her mother's hand. She couldn't have been more than a year or two older than the twins.

"It's nice to meet you," Annette told the children. "Please, come in," she indicated for them to follow her into the house.

"You have quite a home," Sarah told her. "I've never seen anything like it."

"Thank you," Annette said, taking in the luxury of her new home with some pride.

She ushered them into the spacious kitchen and invited them to sit at the table while she put water on to boil. "Would the children like a slice of berry cobbler?" she offered, hoping there was enough left over from the evening before to go around.

"I'm sure they would, thank you," Sarah replied, and Annette excused herself to retrieve it from the cellar.

She paused in the cool darkness to take a breath. She hoped it would be a short visit.

After the children and Sarah were all settled with a very small portion of cobbler, Annette set about making tea. This was her first time playing hostess in her own home, and that combined with the identity of her uninvited guest made her feel a bit flustered.

The children devoured their cobbler in seconds. Annette wondered what she was supposed to do with all three of them staring at her with their big, curious eyes. She smiled uncertainly.

Sarah seemed to sense her unease and suggested, "Would you like to take the tea on the porch? Then we can keep on an eye on the children while they play outside."

Annette nodded gratefully. They herded the children out the door, and Annette brought two chairs from the kitchen. She was thankful the day was pleasant, although she did drape a shawl around her shoulders. All too soon winter's chill would keep them inside.

She sipped at her hot tea, wondering how long Sarah intended to stay.

"Are you settling in all right?" her guest asked in a motherly fashion. "I remember those first weeks of marriage were a time of learning."

Annette didn't know how to reply. She suddenly realized that she wished she *could* confide in someone about the odd nature of their sleeping arrangements, but the cause for it was never far from her mind.

She had hoped the shame would fall away, like a cast off

garment, and she would step into the life of a respectable wife. But she didn't feel like a wife when she fell asleep alone every night. She felt like a housekeeper who had changed her last name.

"Yes, we're doing fine," she managed. Annette struggled to think of something more to add. "Although it is an adjustment." She hoped she sounded like a new bride should.

Sarah's dark eyes seemed knowing, but she only said, "It takes time. Two separate individuals learning to share one life." She chuckled. "It is more difficult than two streams running into one river. The currents collide and churn up the waters. But then they learn how to flow together and there is calm."

Unsure how to reply to these words of wisdom, Annette merely nodded. It felt more like she and Jesse were two streams running parallel to one another than merging into one greater river.

"The great mystery of the two becoming one flesh," Sarah chuckled. "Just remember that all rivers have rapids and waterfalls. They do not *always* flow peacefully along!"

Annette appreciated this more realistic picture of conflict and struggle. She smiled. "Would you like more tea?"

"No thank you," Sarah declined. "How is your family? I'm sure you are missed at home."

"They're well. I went to visit them while Jesse was away on the cattle drive. My mother has her hands full with the little ones, and my help is missed," Annette admitted, grateful the conversation had turned away from marriage.

"Yes, I'm sure of that. How was the cattle drive for Jesse? This was his first."

"He seemed to enjoy it," Annette answered. "He's a cowboy at heart."

"Some men are. It is a good time to be in the business of cattle," Sarah nodded. "Though the railroad may also bring trouble, it has brought prosperity for the ranchers."

Unsure of what she meant, Annette merely nodded. She supposed the Indian woman referred to the way the railroad had cut through lands occupied by native peoples who had roamed the great prairie and hunted the buffalo. The railroad had brought change to the prairie in more ways than one. Where travel to the west had once been a grueling trip that required months of toil and hardship, now anyone who could afford the train ticket could come to the open frontier.

Annette had heard stories of the slaughter of the buffalo by men who did it for the sport, or were paid by the railroad to eliminate the danger of the herds damaging tracks or interfering with the train's progress. She knew there was injustice against the Indians, though she had to admit she had given little thought to it up until now.

"The railroad has been the salvation of the rancher," Annette quoted Jesse. "And Jesse said he's even heard of inventors building refrigerated cars so the cattle can be slaughtered before it's shipped out. They haven't been successful at it yet, but Jesse says it's bound to happen."

Sarah nodded slowly. "The world is always changing... for better or for worse."

"Many of these changes are for the better—" Annette began, but was interrupted when little Miriam ran up onto the porch, hands clasped together, dark eyes sparkling.

"Mama, look!" she exclaimed. She slowly opened her hands to reveal a fat, fuzzy caterpillar with black and red stripes. "It's a woolly bear!" she grinned.

"That means winter's coming," Sarah said as she reached over to run a finger across the furry creature.

Miriam turned to Annette and held out her find for display. "Do you want to pet it?" she asked sweetly.

Annette shook her head. "No thank you. I'll just look at it."

The little hand shot out to hold the caterpillar just a few inches from Annette's face. "But it's soft," Miriam explained, bringing it closer for Annette to inspect.

Annette had to smile. "It does look soft," she admitted as she gently took the little girl's wrist and pushed her hand away to a more comfortable distance. "But I don't think I want to touch it."

"Why not?" Miriam asked, curiously.

"I don't like bugs very much," Annette confessed.

"Oh," Miriam said, disappointed. "But do you like butterflies?"

"I do. They're very pretty."

"This caterpillar will turn into a moth, and that's almost like a butterfly," the little girl explained.

Annette laughed. "Maybe I'll let it land on my finger when it's a moth," she offered, pleased when the child smiled in response.

Sarah laughed. "Miriam is fascinated with insects."

"And," Miriam said, her eyes widening with excitement,

"did you know that when you touch him too hard, the woolly bear curls into a ball? Like this," she demonstrated for Annette, pinching the unfortunate creature between her fingers until it pulled itself into a tight ball.

Sarah came to her feet. "Miriam, can you put the woolly bear back where you found him and tell your brother and sister it's time for us to head home?"

"Yes ma'am," the little girl replied, but her lower lip jutted ever so slightly and her steps were slow as she went to obey.

Annette was surprised to feel disappointed at the announcement.

"We'll let you be now," Sarah smiled. "I just wanted to be neighborly. I hope you'll come pay me a visit one day. It must be lonely for you here."

"Thank you for coming," Annette replied, surprised at the sincerity in her own voice.

Chapter Fifteen

*A*nnette watched from the porch until Sarah Gibson and her children disappeared into the distance, swallowed up by the vast prairie. The tall grasses were beginning to brown with the coming of winter, and as she watched them swaying in the afternoon breeze, Annette felt melancholy settle on her shoulders.

It had been refreshing to hear the children's laughter without bearing the responsibility of caring for them. But mostly, she'd enjoyed having another woman to talk to. She had to admit that it didn't seem as if Sarah was prying her for secrets to share with Vivian. She genuinely seemed to be reaching out as a friend. And a female friend was something Annette had never known before.

Sarah had to be close to twenty years older than Annette and was happily married. For these reasons, there was no cause for jealousy or envy to divide them. Although Sarah was much older, and probably closer to her mother's age than her own, Annette knew she could come to think of the woman as a friend.

But did Sarah know about her affair with Ricky? That was the question that troubled Annette. She had seen no condemnation in Sarah's eyes when she looked at her. Had Vivian been too ashamed to tell her closest friend of her husband's unfaithfulness?

If Annette hadn't seen Ricky's death with her own eyes, she

might have wondered if Vivian had been at fault. Annette had seen the rage and hatred in Vivian's eyes when she saw them together. Vivian had even grabbed the poker from the fireplace to use as a weapon, then thought better of it. Perhaps she had been afraid of being blamed for her husband's death.

Annette sighed. She wished her past sins could be wiped away as easily as Jesse's muddy footprints on her kitchen floor.

The swaying brown grass of the prairie stretched out on all sides around her, with not a soul in sight. Though it wasn't, it seemed empty. Entering the quiet house, Annette felt the crush of silence pressing against her eardrums. She sat heavily on the couch, loneliness her only companion.

She leaned her head back and closed her eyes. It was a big house to live in all alone. Jesse was home so little. Every day, she only had her thoughts to listen to.

The afternoon sunlight glinted through the window and slanted across her face. She squinted against the brightness assaulting her eyes. It suddenly struck her as odd that there were no curtains to close. Jesse had thought of furniture items, but such things as rugs and curtains had escaped his interest.

An idea sprang to life in Annette's head. She smiled as she came to her feet. In the trunk she had brought from home was an old dress belonging to her mother. Annette had only worn it once out of duty. She thought the pattern was outdated and the skirt far too wide. But the fabric was still in nice condition, and there was plenty of material to work with.

Annette smiled as she leapt to her feet and darted up the stairs. She would surprise Jesse with curtains on the windows when he came home. Immediately, she set to work unstitching the dress. She measured out sections to make panels and began

178

cutting with her sewing shears.

Looking at the work in front of her as she began stitching the seams, she realized she would have to finish the project tomorrow. At least it would give her something to look forward to.

The following day, after her usual chores were completed, she returned to her bedroom and pulled the unfinished curtains from the trunk. She spread everything out over the bed and set to work.

Humming a tune, she put the thimble on her finger and bent her head to stitching seams. After a while, she had to stretch and walk about the room. She hoped Jesse would be pleased with her gift.

But when he came home that evening, he surveyed the new curtains hanging at the window with a dark expression.

"What's the matter?" Annette worried. "I thought that shade of green would complement the red couch..." she trailed off. Was it the stripes? Was the fabric not as fine as he would have wished?

"Did you make them?" he demanded.

Annette's hands twisted together in a knot of worry. "Yes," she answered, unsure of where she had gone wrong.

"You know I would have been happy to order you curtains. All you had to do was ask."

"I know, I just had this old dress..." she stopped as his eyes widened, and she wished she could take the words back.

"You made these curtains *out of an old dress*?" he exclaimed angrily.

"I'm sorry, Jesse! I was only trying to be helpful!" she cried as she turned and ran up to her room.

Slamming the door behind her, she fell onto the bed. Tears came and she wiped them away with trembling hands. All she had wanted was to show her appreciation for the lavish home he had given her by adding to it with her own work. Why had he reacted that way?

All the disappointments of her marriage seemed to rise up like demons, larger than life, and dance in dark and threatening circles around her. How many evenings did he do little more than grunt in response to her attempts at conversation? He never touched her, not even her elbow or her hand.

If she had married Bryan…

More tears came. If she had married Bryan, he would have learned her dirty secret and hated her for it.

Jesse might be withdrawn and unsociable at times, but she had never seem him behave in such an unpredictable and volatile manner. He seemed insulted by her gift. Annette shook her head. Perhaps he came from a wealthy family and his mother never had to make anything for herself. Perhaps he was embarrassed by the home-made curtains sewn from an old dress. After all, he had worked so hard to have a grand house filled with fancy furniture from back east. Her simple curtains must have seemed inadequate.

She would have to find a way to apologize and make amends. But when she went downstairs, Jesse was gone. With a sigh, Annette set about removing the curtains she had worked so hard to put up.

By dinnertime, there was still no sign of him. She prepared

supper, then after eating her own portion, left Jesse's on the stove to warm and went up to her room.

She sat down in a plush armchair in the corner, closing her eyes with a sigh. Whatever chaos had reined in her parent's cabin, at least she hadn't been alone. She had felt lonely, at times. Invisible, misunderstood, exhausted, or frustrated. But she had never been alone.

Reaching for a book to fend off the quiet shrouding the house, Annette found comfort in the familiar words of an often read story. The hours passed until the only light came from a single flickering candle. Finally, she blew it out and prepared for bed.

Slipping into her long, white nightgown, Annette let down her hair and brushed it thoroughly before plaiting it into a thick braid. She pulled back the comforter and slipped into the sheets. But the silence seemed as loud as before. The loneliness just as dreadful.

Sleep would not come. Only thoughts of shame and disappointment.

Finally, she threw back the covers and reached for a shawl. Annette pushed open the glass door leading to the second level porch and slipped out into the moonlight. Pale white light spilled across the wooden planks of the floor and the white painted railing. She went to lean against it, staring out at the eerily serene landscape stretching out for miles before her. Rolling, windswept hills illumined by the full moon above.

Startled by a sudden noise behind her, Annette spun around to see the form of a man emerging from the shadows cast by the house. She had forgotten the guest room also had a door opening onto this porch.

~

"I didn't mean to frighten you," Jesse apologized as he stepped forward. "I couldn't sleep."

"Neither could I," Annette replied, eyeing him warily.

Jesse swallowed. The moonlight shone brightly on her blond hair and white nightgown. Her features were cast in the pale glow, and miraculously made her more stunning than he'd ever seen her before. With her hair down and in her nightclothes, he felt he had trespassed on her privacy and intruded on her vulnerability.

He saw the way she stepped back as he approached, how she studied him nervously as if he were a snake that might strike at any second.

"I..." he began uncertainly. He knew he owed her an apology, but where to begin?

"The way I spoke to you earlier," he tried again, "I didn't mean to sound... What I'm trying to say is that I'm sorry," he finished gruffly.

The injured expression on her face, the distrust, never changed. It hadn't been enough.

Jesse took another step toward her. Suddenly it was vitally important to see the openness in her face that had been there before. She was the only friend he'd ever really had. And he wanted her to feel safe with him.

"Annette," he took a deep breath, "I should never have spoken to you the way I did," he said sincerely. "I put the curtains back up for you. It looks like you put a lot of work into them, and they turned out well."

One blond eyebrow arched. "Then why were you so angry?"

He let out a long sigh. "I never thought of curtains for you. I wanted to provide you with everything you needed. I didn't want you to have to make them yourself."

Finally the hurt and wariness began to fade from her eyes. She studied him silently before she said, "I think I understand. But I didn't mind. I enjoyed feeling like I was contributing to our home." She paused, "Jesse, I never imagined I would live in a place like this or have so many fine things. I wanted to surprise you, to give you something."

Our home. Jesse's breath caught in his throat.

"Why were you gone so long?" she asked him then.

"I'm sorry I wasn't back for dinner," Jesse answered. "I never meant to be gone so long. I just wanted to take a ride to clear my head. But I came across a cow that had been attacked by a mountain lion, and I didn't want to leave it roaming around. So I went to get the men to help me track it."

"Did you find it?"

"No. We'll have to go out again tomorrow."

It was the truth, but not the whole truth. Claude indicated that the cow may have been recently deceased when the mountain lion came across it.

He said that cattle rustlers were most likely to steal calves which were unbranded, but already weaned. Though sometimes they did stoop to taking younger calves, which were still nursing. Since Longhorn calves and cows had a strong instinct to be reunited and had been known to find one another, even if

183

separated by miles, rustlers would go to cruel measures to ensure they didn't.

He'd cringed when Claude revealed that rustlers sometimes cut the muscles supporting the calf's eyelids to make it temporarily blind, or even applied a hot iron between the toes to render its feet too sore for walking. Less common was the practice of splitting the calf's tongue to prevent suckling. Or killing the mother and thus making the calf a genuine orphan.

Jesse never thought he would sanction hanging. And he still wasn't sure that he did. Stealing was one thing, but going to such lengths to hide it, was another.

"I always felt sad when my father had to shoot one of the cats," Annette admitted, and Jesse turned to her in surprise.

"Have you ever seen their faces?" she asked, and he shook his head. "They have pink heart-shaped noses and big eyes. They don't mean to hurt anything. They're just hungry."

Jesse smiled at her defense of the animal. "You think I should let it go?"

She hesitated. "I know it's a threat to our herd. I just wish there was another way."

He nodded.

"Co-existing isn't always easy, whether it's with animals or one another," he said thoughtfully, letting his gaze move past her face to the moonlit prairie below them.

"We're learning," she ventured softly.

Jesse met her gaze. The softness there made his knees feel weak. "No," he was quick to explain, "I was thinking of Jim Ingram, one of my cowhands."

She turned away from him. "Is he the Negro?"

"Yes, he is. And our foreman, Claude, was raised with the southern way of thinking that darker skin color makes you less human. They worked through their differences a while back, and normally they get along all right. But sometimes it's hard to let go of your earliest learning, and sometimes Claude's prejudice slips out. I don't think it's anything against Jim personally, but I still hate to hear that kind of talk."

"What happened?"

Jesse was grateful they seemed to have resumed their easy camaraderie. He tried to forget that she was wearing only a nightgown with a shawl draped over her shoulders. But he found it rather distracting.

"In the darkness, someone let a shot go thinking they'd spotted the cat. But it turned out to be nothing but a shadow. Claude told me to tell the nigger he'd better calm his trigger finger. That he'd better be careful no one fired at him, being black as night to begin with."

Just remembering the incident riled Jesse's fury. "Turns out it was Rattlesnake who fired the shot. Honest mistake, but we were lucky no one was hurt. I made Claude apologize."

"You feel strongly about the Negros, don't you?" Annette asked. "You fought to set them free," she added.

Jesse rubbed a hand over his eyes, finding the truth painful. "I didn't set anyone free. President Lincoln did that."

"But you fought?"

"I fought with the Union," he conceded.

"Jim's the only Negro man I've ever seen," she admitted.

"I only knew a few, and they were all free. But it was different in the South. Jim was a slave in Alabama. He was considered property, and treated like no more than an animal. He ran away, hoping to get to freedom and then find a way to get his wife and children there with him. But after the war, he could never find them again. There's no way to ever know what happened."

Annette studied his face in the moonlight. "How sad," she said quietly.

"I wish the world could change faster," Jesse continued. "The Thirteenth Amendment declares them free, but now the true battle lies in the hearts and minds of men. And that's a war that can't be won with weapons or force."

"Do you truly believe they're the same as us?" Annette asked, but her question held only curiosity.

"I don't think any of us are the same," he replied.

A brooding silence fell over them. Then Annette stated: "I think we *are* all the same. We all have hearts that can be broken. We all want the same things, whether we're Indian, Negro, or White."

Jesse regarded her thoughtfully. "What do we want?"

"Love and acceptance," she whispered into the darkness, her eyes fixed far away on the pale horizon.

Jesse swallowed nervously. She was speaking of herself.

Did she want *his* love? *His* acceptance? How could it matter to her?

The answer came as she slowly moved her hand across the rail until it came to rest on his.

The Whisper of Dawn

Chapter Sixteen

*A*nnette lit a candle, placing it on the table next to her chair as she picked up her sewing. Pale gray light filtered through the windows but offered little illumination for her eyes as she wove her needle through the fabric. She had wanted to make curtains for the kitchen windows, red and white checked to match the tablecloth, but she had been hesitant to suggest such a project after the way Jesse had responded to the living room curtains she'd made.

But the leaden sky greeting her each day through the bare windows was more than she could tolerate. *It might be the man who provides the house, but it's the woman who makes it a home by adding her feminine touches.*

Annette scooted her chair closer to the fireplace, both for light and warmth. She'd come to appreciate a blaze in the fireplace. Her parents' cabin had never been so cozy on a cold winter's day. She focused on making neat, little stitches as she hemmed the fabric on her lap. The curtains would add much needed cheerfulness to the kitchen.

When she'd tentatively broached the subject to Jesse, he had actually seemed pleased by the idea. She had to shake her head. She never quite knew what to expect from him.

She hadn't touched him again since that night on the moonlit porch. Jesse had stiffened instantly as her hand rested gently on his. Such a light touch. But he had immediately pulled away and quickly excused himself. What a cruel joke that all of her life men had desired her, and now the man she married couldn't tolerate her touch.

As long as she left well enough alone, he seemed content to have her company. As long as she slept in her room and made no effort to touch him, everything moved along smoothly. They might as well be brother and sister.

And Annette was realizing as each day passed that she wanted a different relationship with him. Something was blossoming inside her, a bond growing stronger with each shared meal, with each shared laugh.

Couldn't Jesse feel it too?

She sprang to her feet at a sound outside the door. She hadn't expected Jesse home so soon, but found herself eager to see his face as she moved to greet him. It was impossible to always keep his scarred cheek hidden from her now that they lived together, and eventually he had begun to relax in her company. Annette tried to be respectful to him by never staring and always sitting to his left when possible. But often she found she didn't even see his scar anymore, even when it was right in front of her.

But as the door swung open, Annette was startled to find it wasn't her husband's pale gray eyes meeting hers.

"Sarah!" she exclaimed, genuinely pleased to see her neighbor smiling back at her.

"I hope you don't mind a visit," Sarah began. "I brought you a pie and some noisy children for company," she grinned.

"Oh, please come in," Annette stepped back from the door to allow her guests entrance. "And thank you for the pie."

"You're welcome. We were in a need of a change of scenery today," Sarah said. "The walls of our cabin were growing tiresome."

"I'm glad you came," Annette said as she gathered up her sewing and put her thimble and needle into the sewing kit to avoid the grasp of little hands.

"Here, let me take your coat, then I'll put some water on for tea," she invited.

As she helped Sarah remove her coat, Annette couldn't help but notice the transformation in the older woman's figure. Her eyes moved to Sarah's questioningly.

Smiling, Sarah nodded. "I'm in the motherly way again," she admitted.

"Congratulations," Annette replied, but a heavy, sinking feeling grew in her own stomach.

All her life, she'd dreamed of being a mother. There were still two empty rooms in this big house that might never be filled. As long as Jesse couldn't even hold her hand, there was little hope of ever making babies with him. The thought brought a sharp pang of grief and longing.

Why did Jesse keep himself so aloof? Didn't he long for more, just as she did?

"When do you expect it?" Annette asked, more to make conversation than out of interest.

"In the spring," Sarah replied. "Just as the snows are melting away. It's a good time for a new life to enter the world."

Annette forced a smile, but was thankful she had a reason to turn her back to her guest as she stoked the fire in the oven and placed the teapot on top.

"Would you like me to cut the pie?" she asked.

"Oh no, save it to share with Jesse," Sarah insisted. "I'm happy to have tea and conversation."

"What shall I serve the children?" Annette wondered.

"Tea for Elizabeth, milk or water would be fine for Frank and Miriam."

Annette set about serving the children, then seated herself at the table. "It won't be long before Christmas," she commented, watching the smiles that lit the young faces.

"I know what Daddy's giving Mama," Frank announced conspiratorially.

"Well, don't tell!" Elizabeth admonished, reminding Annette a little of herself as she tended her younger siblings.

"I want to give the baby a gift," Miriam said, "but Mama said the baby wouldn't know. But I think I'm going to make it a little dolly, just in case it's a girl."

"That's a very nice idea," Annette had to smile.

"I think it's going to be a boy, though," Frank Jr. countered certainly. "You'll see."

Miriam just looked at Annette and shook her head knowingly.

Sarah smiled as she rested her hand on the roundness of her belly. "Well, we'll have to wait and see, won't we? And we'll be just as happy if it's a boy *or* a girl. As long it isn't both!" she laughed.

Annette watched the children as they giggled together. She

felt a twinge of envy, then laughed inwardly at herself for all those days she had longed to get away from the noise and demands of her parents' cabin—from the children—and just be alone. Now she was alone so often that the voices of children were a welcome diversion.

"Do you like to play games?" Annette heard herself asking the younger two children.

"We do," they chimed.

"Have you ever played Hide the Thimble?"

"Yes! Miriam's awfully tricky at hiding it," Frank Jr. warned.

Annette smiled. "Well, let's go into the living room and I'll get my thimble."

Frank Jr. spoke truthfully. Miriam always found the best hiding spots for the thimble. Although Annette had them searching for quite some time before it was discovered in her secret place. Elizabeth was hesitant to play, struggling with wanting to be viewed as a young woman but still being a child. When she saw Annette was going to play, she decided to play, too. Sarah just looked on and laughed.

After the game had worn itself out, they all collapsed onto the couch and laughed.

"That was fun, Annette," Miriam declared.

"Mrs. Stone," Sarah gently reprimanded.

"Can we come play with you again, Mrs. Stone?" Frank Jr. inquired.

Annette looked over at Sarah and answered, "I would like that."

"Well then, we'll have to come by again sometime too. But you're welcome to drop by our place if you need some company. You're welcome any time," Sarah offered.

"Thank you, Sarah," Annette answered warmly, thinking that if the weather held out, she would pay both Sarah and her mother a visit the following week. So far there had been little snow, which suited Annette just fine.

She walked them out to the wagon and helped the children get situated. Then she stood by the barn waving until they were out of sight.

~

Maybe she just needed some time away in order to appreciate coming home. But as Annette mounted Bella and pulled the scarf over her face to ward off the bitter wind, she found herself longing for the familiar shape of the cabin, the welcoming voice of her mother, and even the sweet hugs of her little sisters.

She glanced up at the sky. The heavy clouds had been hanging in the sky for weeks without producing snow. Annette only hoped they didn't unleash their wintry fury as she made her way across the open plain.

Suddenly a figure appeared over a ridge to her right, startling her as he interrupted the loneliness of the landscape. She waved in greeting, assuming it was either one of her own or one of her father's ranch hands. He waved in reply and spurred his horse toward her.

As he drew near, Annette recognized the rider. She groaned inwardly. Bryan Hunt.

"Annette!" he greeted her warmly. "What are you doing

riding alone today?"

"I'm on my way to visit my family," she explained.

"Allow me to ride with you part of the way," he said, bringing his mount alongside Bella.

Annette nodded and smiled politely. "We haven't seen very much snow this winter," she said, trying to make conversation.

"No. But winter's not over yet. I admit I'm looking forward to another Wyoming blizzard."

"Well, I hope you enjoy it," she replied drily. "I hate the way the wind blows the snow all about and causes drifts that are dangerous to cattle, horses, and men. In this rolling landscape, it's difficult to know how deep the snow is until you're into it."

"True enough," he replied. "But it's part of the adventure."

They rode in silence for a moment before Bryan asked, "How are you doing?"

Annette recognized the underlying question. Was she happy in her marriage? Did she regret her decision?

She turned to him with a bright smile. "I'm doing very well. How are you?"

His returning smile lacked sincerity, as did his reply. "I'm fine."

"Well," he said as they crested a rise and the Hamiltons' cabin came into view, "I hope you enjoy your visit. Stay safe." He tipped his hat and guided his mount in the direction he had been traveling before their paths had crossed.

"You too," Annette answered softly.

~

Jesse reined in his appaloosa mare and dismounted. He thought he'd spotted mountain lion tracks in the soft mud along the creek. But as he knelt to inspect it, he realized it had only been his imagination. He'd been wary of the animals ever since finding the mauled cow. Its tender hide had been shredded by the sharp claws, and its flesh ripped out by razor sharp teeth. It had left a sick feeling in his stomach as he looked at the bloody carcass.

The cat had been found, and he was sorry to have to report to Annette, shot and killed. But Jesse rode a little easier knowing the predator was gone.

Though Claude's comment about the possibility of cattle rustlers being involved in the cow's death continued to plague his thoughts. If men could be so ruthless toward a helpless animal, how vicious would they be to anyone who threatened their schemes?

But if there were rustlers helping themselves to his herd, he and his men would have to find and stop them. Jesse had worked too hard to let any unscrupulous characters just take it away from him.

Climbing back onto his mount, Jesse's eyes swept the sea of waving brown grass. Perhaps in winter the prairie was more like his mother imagined, barren and desolate. But even then, it had a wild freedom in the vastness of its rolling plains that made Jesse's spirits feel alive.

Suddenly he saw Annette riding Bella in the distance. She had told him she was planning to visit her family today. He thought of calling to her, but her back was to him and the wind would carry his voice away.

Just then, a man on horseback came over a ridge and Annette waved to him in greeting. It only took Jesse a second to recognize the man's big white stallion. Bryan Hunt waved in reply as he rode toward her. Raw jealousy twisted Jesse's gut.

Had she planned this meeting, using the visit with her parents as an excuse for her absence? His eyes narrowed as he watched Bryan ride alongside her. Perhaps she had grown tired of her husband sleeping down the hall and wanted a man who could make her blood race. If she had been with a married man before, why should infidelity bother her now?

Jesse followed them at a distance, sweat beading his forehead and moistening the back of his neck despite the cold. He could hardly believe he was spying on his own wife. But what was she doing out here alone with her old suitor?

Then suddenly Bryan tipped his hat and rode away. Annette halted her mount, and watched as he disappeared over the rise. She stared at the empty space where he had been for just a moment, then nudged Bella on her way.

Jesse felt a wash of relief, followed by a hot wave of guilt and humiliation. He whirled his horse around and rode hard in the opposite direction. He felt like a fool.

Still, the seed of doubt had been planted. Had they spotted him following them, was that why they had so quickly parted ways? Had this been a chance encounter, but they had made plans to meet again? How was Jesse ever to know?

He couldn't shake the memory of them riding side by side in conversation. Annette on her small black mare, and Bryan on his big white stallion. Even at a distance, the man cut a striking figure. Together, he and Annette made a striking couple.

Jesse knew everyone wondered why the prettiest girl around would choose to marry a man with a disfigured face. Anyone with half a brain knew there had to be a secret explanation for it. Especially those who knew Bryan Hunt had been pursuing her as well. He wondered how many people had guessed the real reason for their marriage.

Still, sometimes he heard a softness in her voice or noticed a tenderness in her eyes, and it made him wonder if she hadn't developed deeper feelings for him than the friendship that had originally brought them together. But every time he began to let himself believe it might be true, he would catch a glimpse of his reflection in a glass window and scoff at his own foolishness.

Why should Annette ever love a man like him?

And perhaps the worst part of all was that Jesse felt consumed with his desire for her. Not just physically, although being in close proximity to her every day was becoming increasingly frustrating for him. But also emotionally. He longed to be able to stroke her blond hair and whisper the words, "I love you," in her ear. He longed to kiss her, to pull her body close to his…

He caught his breath. Didn't she understand the effect she had on him? When she touched his hand that evening on the porch, as the moonlight emphasized the thin nightgown she wore and spilled over her long, blond hair, Jesse had felt as if his whole body had caught on fire. Startled by the intensity of his sudden yearning for her, he had spun around and rushed back to his room, rousing Lucky as he burst through the door.

Many times he had remembered that evening. Why had she touched his hand? And what if she had wanted the same thing he had—for him to put his arm around her waist and draw her close to his chest? What would she have done if he had tried?

But what if she had pushed him away, affronted by his presumption? He couldn't bear the thought of her rejecting him like that. Most likely all she wanted was simply to demonstrate her friendship with him and her appreciation of his compassion for Jim Ingram and other Negroes. It was probably better that he embarrassed himself with a hasty retreat than with an unwelcome advance.

Chapter Seventeen

A light snow fell from the leaden clouds above. Jesse pulled his collar higher around his neck and adjusted his hat lower over his eyes. The air was biting cold and a steady wind blew the snowflakes directly into his face. His mare stepped carefully through the snow covering the ground like a white blanket. Jesse's eyes scanned the landscape, searching for the windbreak where he had spotted a small herd retreating for shelter.

This could be his last chance to check on them before the weather became unsafe for riders. The snow showed no sign of letting up, and the temperatures continued to plummet. He carried sacks of hay and grain in his saddlebags, to supplement the animals during the winter storm when fodder was covered by snow.

He finally saw them in the distance and breathed a sigh of relief. He was eager to return home and sit by the fireplace with a hot cup of coffee in his hand and his wife by his side.

Guilt prodded his conscience. His ranch foreman and cowhands were all riding in this weather. Claude had suggested going into town to ask around if anyone had heard or seen anything suspicious. The Texan was certain a herd of about thirty head had vanished into thin air, and a band of crafty rustlers were to blame for it. Jesse had granted permission for them to pursue any leads they were given in Weston.

He wondered if he should have insisted on going with them. But Claude had argued that it wasn't wise to leave Annette alone in such savage weather. It would be better for him to remain to look after his wife. Jesse knew there was wisdom in the counsel, but his pride chafed at being left behind.

The large animals lifted their eyes to watch him warily as he approached, but were too cold to do more than that. They huddled together for warmth under the wooden structure protecting them from the fierce wind and the snowdrifts it created. A small calf bleated in protest at the cold, pressing tighter against its mother.

Quickly, Jesse unloaded the hay and grain in the interior corner of the windbreak and remounted. He pitied the beasts for having to remain outdoors throughout the long winter, but was grateful for the warm home awaiting him.

Jesse nudged the mare forward, feeling lost in the vast expanse of white and gray. The sky and the snow-covered ground were the same dull shade, and his own appaloosa mount blended into the landscape. He was part of it, this great land of wind and sky, and he knew it was where he belonged even when his fingers grew stiff with cold and a shiver worked its way down his spine.

Suddenly the mare lost her footing in a hidden drift, plummeting sideways and throwing Jesse from her back. His right foot caught in the stirrup, the dead "false foot" he couldn't control. The mare fell to her knees and Jesse grabbed at the stirrup and shook his boot free. But he could feel the damage that had already been done.

He winced as he lowered himself back onto the ground. Pain seared the stump where the prosthesis was attached. He knew he should examine it, but was afraid of what he might find.

Finally he leaned forward and pulled up the leg of his pants. Red blood trickled down the metal brace, dripping onto the white snow. He loosened the leather straps holding it to his leg, gritting his teeth at the bruises and cuts they had bit into him. The skin had never healed properly from the amputation and was always aggravated by chafing and pressure. Now it was a bloodied mess.

He cringed at the realization that he couldn't put the prosthesis back over the wound. He would have to ride home without it, and enter the house without it. In the absence of his cowhands, he would have to ask Annette to care for the pathetic stump where once his foot had been. His pride ached even more than the wound.

Squeezing his eyes shut, he prayed for strength, then pushed himself up onto his elbows. The mare stood at least three paces away. He dragged himself until he was beside her, then rolled onto his knees and used the stirrup to steady himself as he stood on the one good foot. Mounting the horse was going to prove an even greater challenge.

He situated the prosthesis into the saddlebag and reached up to grab the pommel of the saddle, then pulled himself up until he could get the toe of his left boot into the stirrup. Shifting his weight to his left leg, he settled himself into the saddle and let out a slow, anguished breath. Now he had to make it safely home.

~

Annette hummed a familiar song to chase away the quiet. The only sounds in the house were the crackling and hissing of the fire as it devoured the logs in the fireplace. The orange glow glinted off her knitting needles as they chased one another through the yarn. Lucky curled up at her feet, sleeping peacefully.

She was making a scarf for Jesse. She'd noticed the one he used hadn't been made with a Wyoming winter in mind. She hoped he would appreciate her thoughtfulness.

Suddenly she heard the kitchen door burst open, followed by the banging of furniture. She sprang to her feet, the knitting dropping to the floor. The dog also leapt to his feet, barking at the startling noises. Annette's heart pounded in her chest.

Then she heard Jesse calling her name in a voice strained with pain. She raced to the kitchen and gasped in disbelief at what she saw. Jesse had flopped into a chair and was resting his head on the table, clearly exhausted. A trail of blood dirtied the floor from the doorway to the empty fabric of his right pant leg.

Lucky ran to his master, sniffing him over with concern. Before he could cause further injury, Annette took the dog by the collar and tied him in the corner.

She quickly turned her attention back to her husband. She had never seen Jesse without the prosthesis. There was something strange about the way his pants puffed out on the floor, absent of a foot. The pool of blood was growing there, and Annette swallowed her revulsion and stepped toward him.

She knelt down beside him and gently lifted the pants until she could see the wound. She wished she could take back the gasp that escaped her lips. Whatever it was she had expected to see, this was worse.

"We need to get it cleaned and wrapped," she tried to sound confident, but the catch in her voice gave her away.

Her mind raced. She grabbed a kitchen towel nearby used for drying dishes. She wrapped it around the damaged stump to slow the bleeding. "Jesse, I need to get you to the couch. You need to lie down."

He lifted his head and opened his eyes. Annette swallowed again. He must have lost a lot of blood. He looked ready to pass out. She desperately wished Claude, Rattlesnake and Jim were around to offer their aid.

"Lean on me," she said, hoping she could hold his weight.

He put an arm around her shoulders and she pushed him up until his weight rested on the good foot. She stumbled as he lifted the foot to move forward in an awkward hopping motion. She wondered how she would ever get him as far as the living room, but she gritted her teeth and determined not to let him fall.

By the time he had been lowered onto the couch, Annette was covered in perspiration and her breath came in heavy puffs. But she hadn't let him fall. She pushed a loose strand of hair out of her eyes and set about preparing a basin of hot water and finding cloths to bind the wound.

Jesse seemed to have slipped into unconsciousness, which made the task easier to perform. When she had finished, she wanted to sink into a chair and cry, but the trail of blood now stretched from the doorway to the couch.

When it had been cleaned, it occurred to her that he would have been unable to unsaddle his mare in his condition. As she opened the door, her hand went to her mouth. She could see he had dragged himself from the barn, leaving a crimson path in the white snow.

Tears sprang to her eyes. She found the mare standing in the barn, and went to tend to her. The right stirrup was covered in blood.

Annette had never seen so much blood in her life, and her stomach churned. But she quickly set about unsaddling the mare and cleaning the mess.

Finally, she returned to the house and checked on Jesse. He was still sleeping on the couch, his skin an unhealthy pallor. Covering him with blankets, she sat down in the chair beside him, her thoughts in a jumble.

From the kitchen came the keening sound of a dog whining.

With a sigh, Annette went to untie him. Not so much because of his whimpering, but because she wanted the comfort of his warm body pressed against her knee.

Jesse had always worn the prosthesis around her. She had known he'd lost a foot in the war, and that he wore the false foot in place of using crutches. But she had never given it much thought. Suddenly, she understood his shame. And his pain. All this time he had kept it from her. The puckering, scarring, and discoloration of his skin revealed the constant process of injury and healing.

She shook her head sadly. The poor man. He couldn't hide the scar on his face, but he had done everything he could to hide his amputated leg from her. Annette scooted her chair closer to him. He slept the deep sleep of a man who had lost too much blood and struggled against pain and weather to get home. His breathing was shallow and slow, and his sandy blond hair fell across his forehead. With a gentle hand, Annette pushed it back, then with the tips of her fingers, traced the cheek marred by a jagged scar.

If only he would let her touch him when he was awake.

~

Jesse heard a soft sound near his left ear but he was too disoriented to place it. Slowly the fog cleared and he recognized it as a human voice, humming a tune quietly. His eyelids felt as though they were made of lead and he could hardly force them open. As consciousness returned, so did his awareness of the searing pain that ripped through his entire right leg. An involuntary groan escaped his lips.

Instantly, Annette was beside him. "Jesse, are you all right?"

He closed his eyes, searching for a way to reply. "Yes," he lied.

Lucky rose from the floor and rested his chin on Jesse's chest, licking his chin. He reached up to scratch the dog behind his ears.

"You need to eat to stay strong, so you can heal," she whispered close to Jesse's ear. "I've kept some soup warm on the stove. Let me get you a bowl."

Jesse didn't reply, but silently watched her retreating form. Part of him enjoyed the attention. Part of him resented it. He despised the weakness holding him captive to her care.

In just a moment, she returned, setting the bowl of soup down as she instructed, "Sit up slowly. You lost a lot of blood. Do you want me to help you?"

The thought of her arms around him was certainly appealing, but not under these circumstances. He grunted in response as he pushed himself up. A wave of dizziness washed over him, but he tried to hide it from her.

"Keep your leg up," she cautioned. "Do you want me to put a pillow behind your back?"

Jesse nodded and leaned forward. He felt like a helpless child.

Annette pulled her chair close as if she intended to spoon the soup into his mouth. "I'll take it," he informed her brusquely.

The soup was as delicious as it smelled. Jesse took several spoonfuls before looking up to see the expression on her face. He wasn't sure what it meant, but he suspected he'd hurt her feelings with his resistance to her fussing over him like a mother hen.

Guilt pricked his conscience as he remembered how she had

supported his weight as she brought him into the living room to clean his wound. "Annette, thank you for everything," he offered quietly.

"You're welcome," she replied, a smile ghosting her lips.

"The soup's delicious," he added for good measure.

"I'm glad. If you want something more substantial, let me know. I wasn't sure what you would be ready for."

"This is fine for now," he admitted, wondering how long it would take him to recuperate this time and hoping it wouldn't be long.

~

Pulling back the bandage covering his stump, Annette cringed. The smell was putrid, but the sight was far worse. It had been almost a week since his accident, and the wounds refused to heal. The skin was angry and red around the edges, and oozing green in the center. She had tried changing the bandages frequently, carefully cleaning the abrasions with iodine, but it hadn't improved.

She touched his forehead. He was burning up with fever.

Jesse lay weakly against his pillow. Annette had managed to get him to his bed the day after the accident. Jesse had crawled awkwardly up the stairs with her supporting him at the elbow to steady his balance. It had been slow and painful progress, and Annette's heart had ached to ease the shame she saw in his eyes.

Five days later, he remained prostrate in his bed. His irritability had faded away into a silence that disturbed Annette even more. His eyes were dull and his voice expressionless. He ate when she offered him food, but in such a half-hearted and listless way that Annette often took over feeding him to ensure the plate was emptied.

She had hoped his leg would show signs of improvement by now, but instead it was growing worse each day. And Annette had no idea what she could do to help him. She wished the men had come back from town, but Jesse said he'd given them time off as there wasn't much they could do in the dead of winter.

Her mother would probably know how to treat the infection, but Annette dreaded leaving Jesse for the length of time it would take to ride to her parents' homestead and get back. She tapped her chin thoughtfully. Sarah Gibson was her closest neighbor. Sarah might be able to help.

"Jesse," she said quietly, "I need to ride for help. Your leg isn't healing."

He opened his eyes halfway and looked at her from across the bed. "Where are you going?"

"To see Sarah and Frank Gibson. Maybe they know of a remedy I don't."

"The snow..."

Annette stood at the foot of his bed, her hand resting on the wooden frame. She looked out the window at the snow the wind had pushed around until parts of the earth were exposed and others were covered in drifts. "I'll be careful." She walked around the bed to sit at the chair by his head. "You need help, Jesse. I have to go find it."

He closed his eyes and nodded imperceptibly.

"I'll be back as soon as I can. Do you need anything before I go?"

Silence.

Annette stood. "I..." She wished she knew what to say to comfort him. But she wasn't sure he would appreciate her words if she had any to say. "I'll tie Lucky up in the kitchen, where he'll be warm."

She turned and left the room. Donning her heaviest coat, she went out to saddle Bella. She would have to take her time and be careful, trying to stay on ground that was clear enough to promise safe footing. At least the sky was clear and there was no threat of more snow.

Lord, please give Sarah the wisdom she needs to help Jesse's leg. And show me how I can help his spirits to heal, she prayed as she made her way across the desolate landscape.

When she reached the Gibsons' cabin, Sarah flung open the door and greeted her with a welcoming smile. "I'm so glad you came!" she exclaimed. Guilt pierced Annette at these words, for she had never followed through with her intention to visit.

"I'm sorry, Sarah, but I've actually come for help," she confessed.

"What's wrong?" Sarah drew her into the cabin and closed the door. Over her shoulder, she called, "Elizabeth, put water on for tea, please."

"It's Jesse," Annette explained. "His horse lost her footing in the storm last week and threw him. His prosthesis caught in the stirrup and damaged his leg when he fell. I've been caring for it, but it's become infected and only getting worse. He has a raging fever, and I don't know what more to do." Tears threatened as she thought of what might happen if they couldn't heal his leg.

"I know how to treat bad infections," Sarah assured her. "But I will need some time to get what I need."

"How long?"

"Drink a cup of tea to warm yourself, then go back to Jesse. I will come as soon as I can."

Annette tried to hide her disappointment at this answer. But Sarah seemed confident she knew a way to heal it, so waiting was her only option.

She returned home and checked on Jesse. He appeared to be sleeping, so Annette left him alone. She stoked the fire to keep him warm and settled into a chair to read until Sarah arrived.

Three hours passed before she heard a knock at the door. Annette bolted down the stairs to open it, relieved to see Sarah standing before her with a look of purpose on her brown face.

"Where is he?" she asked.

Annette led her up the stairs. "What do you have?" she asked anxiously.

"Bacon."

At first Annette thought she had heard incorrectly. "Bacon?"

"Yes, it will draw out the infection and the wound will heal."

Annette stared at her as they walked into Jesse's room. "Are you sure?"

"I have seen it done many times," Sarah assured her, producing a cloth-covered package from the bag she carried and proceeding to unwrap it.

Jesse's eyes opened and he regarded Sarah warily. "You're going to put raw meat on my leg?"

"I am," she replied.

She immediately set to work, pulling back the covers and removing the bandages to reveal his wounds. "It is bad," she admitted, "but I've seen worse." And she began to apply the raw bacon to the infected skin, binding it on with the fresh bandages.

"There," she pronounced when she was finished. "By morning, all will be well."

Chapter Eighteen

*A*nnette was dubious that the raw meat could produce healing, but Sarah's certainty couldn't be argued. The Indian woman offered at least a hope for Jesse's recovery, and it was the only one they had.

"Where did you find fresh bacon?" Annette wondered aloud.

"In the little pen behind my cabin," Sarah smiled. "That's why I needed time."

"You mean… you slaughtered your pig just so Jesse could have raw bacon?"

"God was watching over your husband," Sarah replied. "We just bought two pigs a few months ago."

"To breed," Annette realized, humbled by the sacrifice. "We can buy you another, in the spring."

"A gift does not require payment. It is given freely."

Annette reached over to grip Sarah's hand. "We are grateful to you."

"It will soon be dark. I will stay the night, if that is all right with you?"

A sigh of relief passed Annette's lips. If the remedy didn't work its magic and Jesse took a turn for the worse, at least Sarah would be there with her. "I would like that," she smiled.

The women worked together to prepare supper, and Annette had to admit it was a far more pleasant experience when shared with another woman. They ate their meal in Jesse's room, and he also seemed to be encouraged by the company and ate with more gusto than usual.

After the kitchen had been cleaned up and the dishes put away, they returned to Jesse's room. He was sleeping soundly, but still burning hot to the touch, and so they situated themselves by the fireplace to keep a close watch on him.

Sarah settled into the chair, resting her hands on the rounded swell of her abdomen. In all her concern over Jesse, Annette had quite forgotten Sarah carried a child hidden safely inside her.

"How are you feeling these days?" she asked now.

"A little tired, but otherwise I'm fine. This baby is going to be a big one. My belly is growing so fast!" she laughed.

Annette had to silently agree that Sarah's belly appeared considerably rounder than the last time she had seen her.

"I hope it wasn't too much for you, riding out here in the cold," Annette worried.

"I am a strong Lakota woman," Sarah replied with a teasing grin. "My family lived in tipis made of buffalo hide, although they stayed warmer than you might think. My mother raised seven children, and she never let the weather or child-bearing slow her down."

"Do you ever visit your family?" Annette asked, thinking of how she missed her own.

"It has been a while. Since they were told by the white

government to live on a reservation, it has become more difficult. They're supposed to be allowed to leave the reservation to hunt, but the soldiers do not look kindly on it."

"I'm sorry," Annette admitted, "I remember my father talking about it but I didn't pay attention."

"Last year there was a treaty signed at Fort Laramie restricting my people to a certain plot of land. It may seem like a large plot to the white government, but for us, it is not enough. The Lakota people are wanderers, following the buffalo for our livelihood. We are not used to living in one place, as the white man does."

"But you do," Annette noticed.

"I do. But my story is different. I chose to marry Frank, and I chose to enter into the white world and take his ways. This was not forced onto me."

"Will your people be able to hunt buffalo on this reservation?"

"Some, perhaps. But the railroad has brought hard times to the buffalo. Many men have shot them to make more room for the trains to run through without fear of the herds. And many have shot them for the price of their hides. The Lakota wasted not a single part of the buffalo. But these poachers take the hide and leave the carcass to rot." Sadness and grief entered Sarah's voice as she spoke. "The ways of my people have changed forever, I'm afraid."

Silence fell between them. Annette pondered what Sarah had revealed, but felt unequipped to respond.

Finally, Sarah interrupted the quiet to ask, "Shall I get the Bible and read? I noticed it on your table downstairs. Frank reads the Bible out loud every night to us."

"Of course," Annette answered, surprised.

When Sarah returned with the large, family Bible and settled it upon her lap, Annette commented, "Did you take Frank's religion too?"

"Frank says it is not a religion. It is knowing Jesus as savior. And I did not take it, but I believe Jesus took me," she smiled.

Annette's brows wrinkled in confusion. "What do you mean?"

"Ah," Sarah said, "let me show you." She flipped through the pages of the Bible until she had found the passage she desired. "'For all have sinned and come short of the glory of God, being justified freely by His grace through the redemption that is in Christ Jesus.' You see, religion is the idea that good works achieve salvation. But only faith in God's son, Jesus Christ, brings salvation."

When Annette did not reply, Sarah continued. "Here, let me see…" she turned more pages. "'For the wages of sin is death, but the gift of God is eternal life through Jesus Christ our Lord.' It means we are all sinners, without hope apart from the work of Jesus."

Annette nodded slowly. Her father read the Bible, but she'd never heard it explained like this before.

Sarah returned to the book and began flipping more pages. Annette watched in awe. She had no idea what was within the book, and certainly no idea where to find specific words!

"Here it is. *'If we confess our sins, He is faithful and just to forgive our sins and to cleanse us from all unrighteousness.'"*

"So, God can forgive *any* sin?" Annette asked hopefully.

"He can and He will. If you confess your sins and believe in Jesus, who already paid the price for your sins when He died on the cross."

"Frank taught you this?"

"Yes. And when I heard it, my heart sang. I found new peace, never offered through any teachings I had heard before."

Annette opened her mouth to reply, but Lucky chose that moment to bound around the corner and onto her lap, knocking her from her chair. She landed on the floor with her feet in the air and her skirt puddled around her waist.

"Oh!" she cried, pushing him away as he covered her face in wet kisses.

Sarah jumped to restrain the animal while Annette situated her skirt and gained her feet.

"He must have chewed through the rope," Annette said, shaking her head. From the bed, she heard Jesse chuckle.

"It's not funny!" Annette fumed, embarrassed by the unladylike position the dog had placed her in.

But Jesse's chuckle deepened until his whole body shook with laughter. And the sound was so contagious that both women couldn't keep themselves from joining in. Lucky smiled, tongue lolling from his mouth, as he looked up at Annette lovingly.

"You are a rotten beast!" she declared to the bull terrier, who only wagged his brown tail in response.

~

When morning came, Annette hovered over Sarah's shoulder as she removed the bandages from Jesse's damaged leg. Oddly enough, the bacon appeared cooked. And even more amazing, when she peeled it away to reveal Jesse's skin underneath, it was as if a miracle had occurred. The infection was gone. Completely gone, and the skin appeared to have begun healing.

"Bacon..." Annette mumbled. "I can't believe it!"

From his pillow, Jesse raised his eyebrows in curiosity. "How does it look?"

"Much better," Sarah informed him. "You'll need to stay off it for a few more days, but you are on the mend."

"Sarah, I can't thank you enough," Annette exclaimed.

"I'm glad I could help," Sarah smiled. "And I'll have fresh pork to prepare when I get home."

"How can I ever repay you?"

"One day I will have a need, and you can help me," Sarah replied.

"I will be happy to," Annette vowed, wondering how she could ever be of help to this dear woman who seemed so self-sufficient.

~

Jesse shifted his weight to his elbows, then pushed himself into an upright position in the bed, reaching behind his back to adjust the pillows against the headboard. He leaned against them and tried to calm the restless feeling beginning to overtake him as his health improved and he remained restricted to the bed.

He was just as dumb-founded as Annette by the success of

Sarah's unusual treatment. But the infection was gone, as was his fever. His head felt clear again, and the pain in his stump was reduced to a manageable degree.

Claude had come to visit him after Sarah had taken her departure. He'd been given a lead by the bartender in Weston. There was a new homesteader northwest of the town by the name of Harvey Simons. He'd been in to visit the saloon recently and taken to bragging once the liquor loosened up his tongue. He'd talked about how his herd was multiplying faster than anyone else in the west, almost as if by magic. Then he'd laughed loud and long, as if it was good joke.

Claude and the boys had waited for the snow to let up, then rode over to Simons' ranch to investigate. They hadn't found anything conclusive, but Claude had snooped around the barn after dark and found a handful of bawling calves. It wasn't enough evidence to hang the man, but certainly enough to warrant keeping close watch on him.

Now that his leg was healing, Jesse would soon be able to get back in the saddle and help his men keep closer watch on his herd. If Claude was right, this Simons fellow was lining his own pockets by thinning Jesse's. And Jesse wasn't going to sit idly by and let it continue, even if it meant this Harvey ended up dangling from a rope.

Jesse figured Harvey Simons was familiar with the form of punishment given cattle thieves when he chose to pursue it as a career. So if justice found him, it would be on his own head.

To this point, Jesse had appreciated the friendship Annette found in Sarah, but now he was even more grateful for the woman's knowledge and kindness. It just went to prove what he had believed all along, that skin color had no bearing on the character of a person.

After the women had left the room, Jesse called Lucky to him and praised the dog for his bad behavior. Jesse chuckled just remembering the shocked expression on Annette's face as she sat on the floor on her backside, her skirt hiked up to her waist. He'd had a nice view of her petticoats and her slim ankles above the boots. The dog had done him a good deed.

But his smiled faded away as he reflected on the conversation his faithful dog had interrupted. Though his eyes had been closed, he had been listening to every word Sarah spoke about the price of sin and the forgiveness of God. His heart had quickened as Annette had asked if God placed restrictions or limitations on the sins He would forgive. Because if such forgiveness was possible, he wanted it too.

It just seemed too simple. You were to pray to God, confess your sins and believe in Jesus, and—just like that—your sins were forgiven? It seemed there should be a penance attached. Some way to prove your sincerity. Why would God want to forgive either him or Annette? It just didn't make sense. They had both broken the rules and deserved punishment for it.

Annette's was having to give up Bryan Hunt and marry him. Who knows if that wasn't part of his own punishment too? Was his amputation, or the scar on his face, all part of his punishment? Who could say? Maybe those were just random coincidences and his only punishment was the burden of guilt he carried.

Sarah had said that her "heart sang" when she knew she was forgiven by God. That she had found new peace. Jesse fervently wished both he and Annette could know this kind of peace. But it seemed just beyond their reach.

Chapter Nineteen

*W*ith Jesse disabled, Annette's floors stayed much cleaner. Apart from when the men came to visit him or give their reports. But the honest truth was Annette didn't mind sweeping up the dirt they left behind. It gave her a sense of purpose.

She settled down to knit, but her heart wasn't in it. Jesse was upstairs reading a book, with Lucky curled on the bed at his feet.

Soon he would be ready to move about, but Annette had examined the prosthesis and was worried the tender skin would break open if he tried to wear it too soon. And he seemed determined to never be without it. She supposed it was much easier than walking on crutches, but if the wound reopened he risked another infection.

Perhaps she could convince him to let his pride suffer for the sake of his health. But where were his crutches? Annette was certain he should have a pair lying about somewhere, though she had never seen them.

She remembered him mentioning that the house had an attic. And she suspected if Jesse owned crutches, he would have hidden them away up there.

Other than occasional cleaning, Annette seldom visited the third floor. Now she searched about for an entrance to the attic. She found a door that opened to a narrow, dark staircase. After retrieving a candle, she climbed the stairs to investigate. It was a large, open space with the same wood flooring as was throughout the rest of the house. It was amazing to Annette how quickly the bugs and spiders had taken up residence.

Brushing away a spider's web, Annette held her candle high to look about for Jesse's crutches. A trunk in the back corner caught her eye. Careful not to become entangled in any other webs, Annette went to the trunk and knelt down before it. She hesitated, hoping Jesse wouldn't mind her looking through his things. After all, she was only trying to help him regain his mobility.

Inside the trunk, she found several items of clothing, a blanket, and a few books. It appeared he had put the trunk in the attic and forgotten all about it. She was about to close it when something caught her eye. It was a black leather box, rectangular in shape. When she opened it, she found a blue velvet background with the Medal of Honor pinned to it.

Why was something like this tucked away in a trunk? She ran her fingers over the five pointed gold star, in the center of which was a symbolic picture Annette didn't quite understand, and above it was an American eagle resting atop crossed cannons. It was suspended from a ribbon striped white and red at the bottom, with a rectangle of solid blue at the top. The clasp above the ribbon was a bar with two cornucopias and a shield of arms in the center.

Annette studied it in the flickering candlelight. It was a remarkable pendant. She turned it over in her hand. His name was engraved on the back side.

Pride at her husband's bravery filled her as she looked at the medal. It should be on display for everyone to see, not hidden away with the spiders in the attic. She would mount it to the wall in the living room and surprise him when he was well enough to come down the stairs.

Which reminded her that the original purpose of her search was to locate the crutches. Standing, she waved the candle above her head again, laughing at herself as she spotted the crutches tucked behind the trunk on the floor. They were far too long to fit inside it.

Considering the excursion a success, Annette carried the crutches and the Medal of Honor to her room. She would need to wipe the crutches down before she gave them to Jesse, and she would have to wait for the right moment to broach the conversation. She hoped after the time spent caring for his wounded stump, he would realize the absurdity of trying to hide his disability from her. And above all, she hoped he would understand it didn't matter to her.

The medal needed polishing. Months of neglect in the wooden trunk had left it tarnished brown. She rubbed away at it until it shone. Then she examined the velvet background to which it had been pinned. She suspected she had a picture frame that would hold it if she removed the glass. Retrieving the frame, she took out the picture it contained of her grandparents on her father's side. She had never met them, and although it might matter to her father if the picture was set out in her new house, Annette thought it was more important to celebrate her husband's achievements.

It wasn't a perfect fit, but she was able to work at it until the blue velvet lay neatly in the frame and the Medal of Honor was show-cased in its center. On the wall at the bottom of the stairs was a needle-point picture of roses that had been given to her as a wedding present. She could find another place to display it, she decided, as she hung the medal in its place.

She smiled up at it, imagining Jesse's face when he saw her gift to him, meant to honor him a second time for his valor in war. And perhaps it would help him to remember how he had received the wounds that led to the amputation of his foot as well as the scar on his face.

He had fought for a cause he believed in and sacrificed for it in ways that could never be ignored or forgotten. That was something worth being proud of.

~

Jesse opened his eyes as he heard his wife's footsteps entering the room. She smiled cheerfully and asked, "How are you feeling?"

"Too good to lay in bed another day," he answered.

"Let me take a look at your leg," Annette cautioned. Jesse grit his teeth at the maternal tone. He was no stranger to pain. He knew his own limitations.

But he lay silently as she pulled back the blankets and adjusted the loose pant leg. He watched her face as she examined his stump. She was so flawless, it still took his breath away just to look at her. That perfectly shaped jawline, so delicate and refined. The slope of her nose, too, was perfect, and her wide blue eyes framed in dark lashes were more exquisite than any he had ever seen before. Her blonde hair was swept up at her neck in a chignon, with a few stray tendrils curling around her face.

How could she look at him without revulsion clouding her expression? He didn't know, but all that registered on her lovely face was concern. She pulled down the covers and sat down at his feet.

"It looks like it's healing up really well, Jesse. But I'm afraid if you try to wear the prosthesis too early, it will rub the tender skin and we'll be starting over again."

"I can wrap it. I'm used to the pain."

She winced at his words as if feeling the pain for him. "But it could become infected again," she protested gently.

Jesse heaved a frustrated sigh. "I can't tolerate spending another day lying here like an invalid!"

"You could use your crutches," Annette suggested tentatively. "I found them in the attic."

Jesse pushed himself up into a sitting position against the headboard. He rubbed at his eyes wearily. There was no use pretending he was a whole man any longer. The charade was over. He nodded in defeat. At least it would be better than lying in bed.

"I'll get them for you," she said as she sprang from the bed with what Jesse thought was unnecessary enthusiasm.

He watched as she rushed from the room, only to return in seconds holding the wooden crutches in front of her. Annette had already wrapped the curved rests that went under his arms with strips of fabric to soften them. She had used fabric that was dark blue, Federal Blue. She smiled as she handed them to him, seeming pleased he was willing to use them.

He wished he could understand her kindness toward him. He wished he could feel as though he deserved her.

"Thank you," he choked out, humiliated all over again by his weakness and dependency.

She stood back and watched as he used one crutch to push himself into a standing position, then adjusted them both under his armpits. It had been a long time since he had used crutches. He wished Annette wasn't observing as he carefully swung the crutches forward and hopped a step. Jesse felt awkward and imbalanced, and trying to ignore his wife hovering nearby, he practiced getting the feel of it as he maneuvered around the bedroom.

"How do you manage the stairs with them?" she asked suddenly.

Jesse heard the curiosity in her voice, untainted by judgment, but felt the shame of his condition just the same. He closed his eyes, trying to remember how he had managed the stairs.

"Very carefully," he finally smiled at her, watching the returning smile that grew on her face.

"I'll help you," she promised.

Jesse's heart thudded in his chest at the thought of her arms around him, her body pressed close as they descended the stairs. He had to admit that she had been an angel of mercy throughout his convalescence, always caring for him with tenderness and patience. And never making him feel as though she was disgusted or burdened by his injury.

He felt another pang of regret that he couldn't be the man she deserved.

"Just be careful I don't knock you down the stairs and land on you," he forced out in a teasing tone, and was rewarded with another sweet smile.

At the top of the stairs, Jesse took a deep breath. "Stand

beside me, but down one step," he instructed. "Just be ready to steady me if I lose my balance." He looked down again. "Here," he handed her one of the crutches. "I'll hold the railing with this hand."

Annette accepted the crutch and stepped down, facing toward him, her hand hovering in close range should she need to grab hold of him. The stairs were illuminated by oil lamps that burned at the top and bottom of the stairwell. The pale yellow light flickered around them on the plaster walls, and the steps themselves were hidden in shadow. Slowly, one painful step at a time, they made their way to the bottom.

"You did it!" she beamed, handing back the other crutch.

"I did," Jesse admitted, though it had been a greater feat of strength and agility than he had anticipated. How pathetic that something as simple as descending the stairs was a great accomplishment. He let out a sigh of exhaustion and frustration. His body was unused to the exertion.

"Jesse," Annette said quietly, and he turned in curiosity at the tone of her voice. "Look," she indicated to the wall beside him.

Jesse turned his head and peered up at the Medal of Honor hung ceremoniously upon the wall, glinting golden in the pale dancing light of the oil lamp.

~

"I'm so proud of you," Annette said. "I thought it should be on display where—"

But her words were interrupted as he threw down one of his crutches and reached up to snatch the medal off the wall. "You had no right!" he gasped out in fury as he hurled it across the room, narrowly missing the window. It crashed into the wall and bounced back, sliding under an armchair.

Annette gasped and backed away from him, eyes wide with fear.

"Jesse, what did I do?" she cried.

"You had no right to go through my things! If I had wanted it on the wall, I would have put it there!" he spat angrily as he hobbled toward the kitchen on one crutch.

Trembling, Annette sank down on the couch.

It was meant to be a gesture of acceptance and affirmation. Why had he reacted with anger? She had put such thought and care into the gift, certain it would be appreciated, and instead he had thrown it across the room. Why?

For a moment she had been afraid he would strike *her*. The raw fury in his eyes had been both unexpected and intense. A small gash in the wall revealed where his crutch had struck it before landing on the floor at his feet. Annette slowly stood and went to retrieve it, propping it against the wall within his reach should he decide to come back for it.

Then she went over to the armchair and knelt on the floor. She leaned down and peered under it, searching for the framed Medal of Honor. The frame had split apart, and she pulled the two pieces out from the under the chair and placed them in her lap.

The fragmented gift, meant to symbolize honor and acceptance, signified a deeper truth. There was more to this than she could imagine. There was a secret explanation that would make sense of his behavior if only she knew it. Annette remembered how he had responded to the home-made curtains. It had been pride then that caused him to disdain her gift. What was it now?

Her thoughts were interrupted by a crash coming from the kitchen. Annette winced as she realized he had fallen to the ground. She sprang to her feet, then stopped herself. She didn't dare offer him help in his current state of mind.

Instead, she placed the Medal of Honor and the broken frame on the table next to the family Bible and took the stairs to her bedroom. There she knelt down in front of her bed and prayed.

Lord, heal Jesse's wounded heart. I don't understand him. But there's more pain he endures every day than I can even imagine. Bring him peace. And mend the tear in our relationship. I so desperately want us to have a real marriage.

~

Jesse lay on the hard floor in the kitchen, ashamed of the tears dampening his cheeks. A man's pride could only take so much beating. Exposing his injured stump to Annette had been difficult enough, but having to allow her to care for him for days on end, even aid him down the stairs, was all too much. Then seeing the Medal of Honor where she had so proudly displayed it on the wall...

He had fled to the kitchen to leave her presence, wishing he hadn't thrown the second crutch on the ground where it was impossible for him to retrieve it. Then, when he went to lower himself into a kitchen chair, he had lost his balance and tumbled gracelessly onto the floor in a broken heap. He had waited a moment, dreading Annette's arrival and offer of assistance. But she hadn't come. And Jesse couldn't blame her.

He pushed himself upright and leaned back against the wall. He remembered the way she had looked at him after he had hurled the medal across the room, her blue eyes filled with fear. He covered his face in defeat. Once again, she had reached out to him in the most sincere and thoughtful way, and he had ruined it.

But she was his wife. She was all he had. Jesse had to find a way to make things right.

Swallowing down the anxiety churning in his stomach, Jesse reached for the crutch and used it and the wall to support himself as he stood. Then, using the one crutch, he carefully made his way to the living room. It was empty, of course.

But he saw that she had left the Medal of Honor for him on the table next to the Bible. He closed his eyes briefly, then reached for it. It had been a long time since he had seen it. He had closed the box, thrown it in the trunk, and tried to forget.

Now he placed it in his shirt pocket, left the crutch Annette had propped against the wall where it was, and took hold of the railing. Step by step, he laboriously made his way to the second floor and stood outside his wife's bedroom door.

Hesitating, his heart pounding, Jesse rapped on the door.

When she opened it, her eyes were rimmed with red from crying.

"I'm so sorry, Annette," he blurted. "I hope you can forgive me."

"Come in," she said, gesturing to the armchair by the fireplace.

Jesse didn't protest, but hobbled over and lowered himself

down. His entire body ached.

"Why?' she asked simply.

Jesse hung his head.

Chapter Twenty

I don't deserve it. Not the medal, and not your pride in me."

Annette searched his face. "What do you mean?"

"I didn't earn that medal. It should have gone to someone else."

He looked up from his hands, shaking in his lap, to her clear blue eyes. She studied him quietly, waiting for him to continue. How could Jesse tell her the truth and expect her to care for him the same way in the future? Any respect she had for him would be lost.

But he owed her the truth, once and for all. And finally, he would know a moment of true courage.

"I should have known I wouldn't make a good soldier," he began quietly. "I never could stand the sight of blood. It makes me queasy. But my older brothers had all gone off to fight and I wanted to prove I was just as much a hero as they were. My brother, Peter, was killed. And I suppose I thought to somehow avenge his death. I wanted to set the slaves free, too. I just wanted to be a hero, like Stephen and Albert and Peter. They all earned medals.

"But I wasn't prepared for what real battle would be like. They taught me how to load and fire my musket. But nothing can prepare you for the ugliness of war. When the battle erupted, I saw men cut down all around me…" He paused, closing his eyes as he went back in his mind to that day on the battlefield.

"There was blood everywhere," he shuddered. "Spilling from chest wounds and face wounds and from arms and legs... It was awful! And the sounds of men screaming in agony were as loud as the gunfire and the grenades. Smoke filled the air. I just stood there, gripping my rifle. I couldn't shoot anyone! I was terrified. I was only sixteen years old and I didn't want to die."

Jesse closed his eyes, ashamed of his selfish cowardice. "I saw five men running toward the woods. I followed them. They were Federal soldiers, like me. I thought they were deserting, and all I wanted was to get away from the screaming and the blood. I-I didn't know they had been given the order to capture a medical supply wagon from the rebels. When I saw the enemy camp and the Corporal gave instructions on how we were to seize it, I realized my mistake. What could I do but act as if I had planned to join the mission?

"I crept low along the ground with another private, approaching the wagon. I prayed no one would spot us and we could just take the wagon and ride away. But the rebels saw us. They shot the soldier next to me. I dropped to the ground and rolled behind a log, peering up as another rebel charged at me. I had no idea how to fight. I stood up and held up my gun, but I knew I didn't have time to shoot. He had a bayonet fixed at the end of his rifle, and he lifted it over his head. I blocked it with my rifle, but he was taller and stronger than I was and it slid up my rifle and ripped into my face." He reached up to trace the jagged scar running the length of his face from his right lip to his eye.

"I've never felt such pain. I slammed the butt of my rifle into his face and when he fell to the ground, I slammed it into his stomach. I heard his ribs crack." He swallowed back the bile that rose with the memory.

"Then I saw Corporal Adams. In such swift, polished motions that my eyes could hardly follow, he shot one rebel down as he came at him from the side, knocked another out cold with his rifle when he came at him from behind, and took down a third with his saber. Then he leapt onto the seat of the wagon and whipped the horses into action. I took off at a run and leapt up onto the seat beside him. I thought we were going to make it, but then he took a bullet in the back. He just slumped over, right beside me, with the reins in his hands.

"I grabbed the reins and I..." Jesse found tears streaming down his face as he admitted, "I pushed him out onto the ground and rode out like the hounds of hell were chasing after me. Then I felt a bullet rip through my leg, and I thought about how injured men were sent home. I didn't even mind the pain. I rode back to camp and I took credit for everything. They had to take my foot, but I let them send me home and give me a medal. That was my one and only battle."

Jesse thumbed the tears from his eyes. "Corporal Lewis Adams is the real hero. He deserved a Medal of Honor for his 'act of valor in acquisitioning medical supplies from enemy forces at great personal risk,' not me. I was just a coward."

Annette stared at him mutely in disbelief, her mouth open. When she realized he was finished with his confession, she whispered, "Jesse, I don't know what to say."

The disappointment in her eyes said enough. Jesse felt as though his heart were squeezed in a vice. "Well," he managed in a voice raw with pain, "now you know the truth."

He pushed himself up onto his crutch and slowly hobbled from the room.

~

Annette stared at his empty chair, her mind reeling. All this time, she had believed he was a true war hero. The medal had indeed reminded him of how he received his injuries, and it wasn't at all what Annette had imagined. At least now his reaction made sense.

His story played through her mind. She tried to imagine the battle scene he had described: the smoke, the gunfire, the bloodied men. His fear made sense to her. A young boy, unequipped for such violence and chaos, panicking and wanting to run for safety. That made sense. But claiming credit for another man's bravery, since dead men tell no tales, was an entirely different thing.

Then she remembered the story of the three brothers. How one had died, but all had fought in the war. They had all earned medals for their bravery, and young Jesse had just wanted to follow in their footsteps.

Annette closed her eyes, remembering the mistake she had made at sixteen, when she let a married man woo her into his bed. Who was she to judge Jesse for his sins when she was guilty of her own? She would never forget the look on Vivian's face when she saw Annette in bed with her husband. Even now the shame burned her cheeks.

Jesse had stolen another man's reward. But Annette had stolen another woman's husband.

If Annette could turn back the clock of time and relive her life, she would spurn Ricky Lawson from the first moment she clapped eyes on him. She would never have given him the chance to break his wife's heart and steal her innocence. But she

236

couldn't go back.

And neither could Jesse, no matter how much he might wish he could. They had both made their choices, and now they carried the burden of their guilt.

All this time, he had known her secret. Now she knew his.

Jesse had chosen to help her carry her burden. And now she had the chance to help him carry his.

~

"Jesse?" Annette called softly at his door. "I want to talk to you."

"It's open," he replied dully.

Jesse's room also boasted a fireplace, and he was seated in the armchair before it. He held the Medal of Honor in his hands, staring blankly at it, not even looking up as Annette entered the room.

Annette settled on the footstool and waited for him to lift his eyes, but he never did. Finally she said gently, "Jesse, look at me."

When he did, the brokenness Annette saw there brought tears to her eyes.

"I'm so ashamed," he whispered. "I've never told anyone. My mother wanted to hang all our medals on the wall. She told everyone about her sons, how they were all war heroes who would have made their father proud. He died when I was a boy. He was a man of principal and character. He would be so ashamed." Jesse's voice broke.

"Jesse, listen to me," Annette chose her words carefully. "Some men are born with the constitution of soldiers. Some

237

aren't. You were sixteen. You made a bad decision, to be sure. What you did was wrong. But it doesn't change how I think about you. You know my past. You chose to marry me anyway. I think your confession only reveals to me a truth I already knew. You are gentle man who hides behind his stern ways and his scars." She paused, seeing the word "gentle" had only turned him away. "And I respect a man who is strong—as you clearly are, to suffer all the pain you do and continue ranching—but has a gentle nature," she hastened to assure him. "You don't have to hide anymore." She leaned forward, her eyes boring into his. "Don't hide from me."

He looked as vulnerable as a little boy as he stared back at her, trying to understand her words. Annette wished with all her heart he would stop hiding, stop pushing her away, and just let them discover what love could be like. She knew that together they could, if only his shame and pride didn't stand in the way.

She waited, watching his eyes move about the room as he searched for a reply. His hand reached up to trace the scar marring his face. He dropped his hand back to his lap as if the scar had burned him.

Annette sighed. He wasn't ready yet to step out from behind his defenses yet. But one day he would.

"You don't hold it against me?" he finally asked.

Annette shook her head. "Would that be fair?"

Jesse nodded understanding. He looked down at the medal in his fingers. "I wish there was something I could do to make things right."

Annette met his gaze squarely. She didn't need to say it.

"But if I turn the medal in and give it to his family... mine will know the truth."

Annette reached over and laid her hand upon Jesse's. "You don't to have to explain it to me. I understand." She would do anything to keep her family from knowing her secret shame.

"I know," Jesse answered softly, surprising her as he placed his other hand over hers.

~

Weeks passed, and Jesse's leg healed over better than it had been before the injury. He was able to wear the prosthesis again and return to his usual routine. Although he was unable to ride out to check on the cattle because the heavy winter snows had resumed, keeping them trapped inside.

They read books, played checkers, and shared quiet conversation by the warmth of the fire. There was a new intimacy in their camaraderie, their bond strengthened by the trials and discoveries this winter had brought.

Annette was grateful when the sun began to warm the earth again, and all the snow had either blown away in the fierce wind or melted into the grass. At last, Jesse could feel ownership of his ranch as he rode his mount over the prairie to inspect his cattle. And Annette could take Bella out for a ride and visit her family.

But first, she felt a call was due to her neighbor, Sarah. After all, without Sarah's help, Jesse probably wouldn't have survived the winter.

As she approached the cabin, she saw Elizabeth seated on the front porch watching her younger siblings play. Annette waved a greeting to Miriam and Little Frank as she dismounted.

The children waved back and came running to greet her, then just as quickly scampered off to enjoy the spring day.

But when Elizabeth strode forward to take her by the elbow and lead her away from the front door, Annette knew something was wrong. The young girl's face was lined with worry, her blue eyes much older than her twelve years.

"What is it?" Annette worried.

"It's Mama. She lost the baby. She's not doing well."

"Oh no!" Annette cried. "Can I help?"

"It isn't her health," Elizabeth assured her. "She's so sad. She won't get out of bed. Mama just lays there, staring at the wall. She won't talk to anyone."

Annette pulled the girl close for a hug. "I'm so sorry," she whispered through her tears.

"May I come in and say hello?" she asked.

Elizabeth shrugged. "You can try."

Annette took a deep breath. She had no idea what Sarah was feeling or how she could offer comfort.

When she entered the cabin, her eyes were temporarily lost in the darkness. She blinked as her sight adjusted from the bright sunshine to the dim, candlelit interior. The door to Sarah and Frank's bedroom was open, and she called out in greeting as she approached.

"Hello, Sarah. It's Annette."

She found Sarah, just as Elizabeth had described. Sarah lay on the bed, her hair unbrushed, staring blankly at the log wall in front of her. Her brown face was empty of every spark of vitality, and the absence of it made her seem like a shell of her former self.

"I'm sorry to hear of your loss," Annette offered tentatively.

Sarah glanced at her, but her only response was the tears rolling down her cheeks.

"What can I do for you?" Annette begged, her heart breaking.

Finally Sarah spoke in a low, raspy voice. "He was perfect. But the cord was around his neck. The very thing meant to give him life."

"Oh, Sarah…" Annette wished she knew what to say in the face of Sarah's tragedy. But she knew no words of comfort or hope.

And so she sat down on the bed next to the Indian woman and stroked her head as if she were a child. Sarah just closed her eyes and cried fresh tears. And Annette cried with her.

After a time, Annette slipped away and brought Sarah a cup of water. To her relief, Sarah sat up and accepted it.

Handing the cup back to Annette, Sarah wiped the tears from her eyes and leaned back against the wall. "I know I must get up and go on for the sake of the other three. But I don't know how," she admitted, her voice flat and weary.

"Where is Frank?" Annette wondered.

"Looking after the cattle," Sarah replied.

Annette hesitated. There was more to this answer than what was said.

"He doesn't understand my grief," Sarah explained. "He did

not nurture this child inside himself through the long winter or struggle through the pangs of childbirth only to hold—" a sob of grief stole her breath, "to hold a lifeless baby."

"He grieves too," Annette assured her. "In a different way."

"Yes," Sarah answered, but her voice lacked conviction.

Annette was at a loss for words. Sarah had given her so much, and she only wished that now in her moment of need, she had something to offer back.

Chapter Twenty-One

*A*nnette had just placed the pancakes on the griddle and was thinking again how grateful she was for the cast iron stove when something brought her attention to the window. Beyond the red-checked curtains she had made, in the pink light of morning, Annette could see a wagon rolling across the plains toward her.

It must be Sarah, she thought as she hurried to put a pot of water on for tea before heading for the door. Five days had passed since her visit, and Annette had struggled with what to do. Go back and have nothing more to offer than she did the first time, or give the woman time to recover from the physical symptoms of childbirth as well as the suffering of her heart? She remembered her mother's emotions always seemed more intense after the birth of a child, and she hoped with time Sarah would learn how to live with this great loss.

But when she opened the door, Sarah looked no closer to coping with her baby's death. Her tanned face was lined with grief, and her dark eyes were dull with pain.

Annette couldn't help but stare, for the woman had always worn tight-waisted dresses made of calico with her hair twisted up in chignon. Today Sarah wore a buckskin dress, with fringes that swayed with her movement. The dress only reached to her knees, leaving the buckskin leggings underneath visible, as well as the beaded moccasins on her feet. Her long black hair, woven with silver, was plaited into a thick braid that hung down her back. She looked very much like the Indian woman she was.

"I'm leaving," Sarah announced abruptly.

"What do you mean?" Annette asked, taken aback by the uncharacteristic rudeness.

"I'm taking the children and going back to my family. Just for a while. I will be back. But for now I need to have the comfort of my mother's arms. She will understand another mother's heartbreak."

"Frank...?" Annette fumbled for a way to ask the question. She couldn't imagine how Frank must feel, having just lost the infant and now being left behind by his wife and three children.

"He understands," Sarah stated matter-of-factly. "I will be back when the time is right." She paused before adding, "Perhaps you could send Jesse by to check on him from time to time."

From the kitchen came the sound of Jesse returning from the barn. He joined Annette at the door, greeting Sarah with a nod of his head.

"Would you like to come in for a moment? I put water on for tea." Annette offered, but wasn't surprised when Sarah declined.

"Thank you, but I have a long journey ahead," Sarah answered. To Jesse, she asked, "Your leg is well?"

"Very well, thanks to your magic bacon," Jesse replied. "I'm in your debt."

Sarah shook her head. "God is the healer. I only supplied the material."

"Your family is on the reservation?" Annette wondered

aloud, thinking of the miles that lay ahead of Sarah, alone with the children.

"They are, but I do not know exactly where. It will take time to find them."

"Are you safe, traveling alone?" Annette worried.

"I carry a gun. I shoot as well as any man."

"I will pray for you," Annette offered, hoping her prayers meant something—to God and to Sarah.

"Thank you," the older woman replied sincerely. "And I will pray for you."

Annette almost asked why Sarah assumed she needed prayer, but knowing there were so many reasons why she did, she decided to hold her tongue and just be grateful.

"When I return, I will come visit you," Sarah promised, and Annette moved forward to embrace her.

Jesse surprised both women by reaching forward to squeeze Sarah's hand. "I wish you safe travel."

Then they stood, shoulder to shoulder, in the doorway and watched as Sarah returned to the wagon. The children sat quietly in the wagon bed, looking downcast and anxious at the trip their mother had planned for them. They had been raised as white children and knew nothing of the Lakota people or their ways.

Annette raised her hand in farewell, and all three children waved back.

"Why is she going to the reservation?" Jesse asked, having missed the beginning of the conversation.

"To be with her mother. She doesn't feel like Frank

understands her grief."

"I'll ride over later and see how he's doing," Jesse said. "I suspect she doesn't understand his."

~

As Jesse made his way to Frank Gibson's homestead, he breathed deeply the sweet smells of spring. The buffalo grass was still brown from winter, but new shoots were springing up from the earth and adding their aroma of new growth to the air. The perfume of sagebrush warmed by sunshine filled his nostrils as he trotted his appaloosa across the open prairie.

The sky was clear and blue overhead, and Jesse wished his thoughts were as bright and cheerful. He liked Sarah Gibson. She reminded him of his mother, with her strength and nurturing spirit. He hated seeing her so grieved, and he was certain Frank just carried his grief in a different way. Silently, inside, with the need for movement and action to distract him from his pain.

Ever since Sarah's visit, her words about forgiveness and peace had stayed with him. The words she quoted from the Bible: *"For all have sinned and come short of the glory of God, being justified freely by His grace through the redemption that is in Christ Jesus."*

All have sinned... but all can be justified freely through redemption in Jesus Christ. The words played through his head. It was a comforting idea, to be forgiven by God, but Jesse couldn't imagine why the Creator would ever send His son to take the punishment mankind deserved. If all had sinned, shouldn't all take their own punishment?

As Jesse neared the Gibson cabin, he saw smoke coming from the chimney and was relieved Frank was at home. If he had been out, Jesse would have made the trip for nothing.

He staked his mount near the cabin to let him roam and eat new spring grass. Then Jesse went to the door and knocked. After a moment, Frank answered it. He was much older than Jesse, perhaps old enough to be his father. His face was lined with years of working in the sun, and his hair gray and thinning.

"Jesse Stone," he said in surprise. "Come on in."

Jesse stepped inside and removed his hat, hanging it on the peg near the door. The Gibsons' cabin was rustic, but there was a charm in the primitive functionality of the place. He took the seat Frank offered at the table and accepted a cup of coffee.

"Sarah stopped by to tell Annette good-bye," Jesse said, to explain his presence.

"Hmm," Frank nodded. "I thought as much."

"I'm sorry for your loss," Jesse added, wishing he was better with words.

"I appreciate that," Frank said. He reached for the open Bible on the table, which he must have been reading when Jesse arrived. "I wish I knew how to help Sarah. She's so torn up about it." He rested his elbows on the table and dropped his head into his hands. "It was a little boy. He was fully formed, round and strong. But when he came out, the cord was tangled around his neck. I slipped it off as soon as I could, but it was too late. His face was already blue…"

Jesse's eyes widened. He hadn't thought about that detail, that Frank would have been the one to deliver it. There weren't any doctors riding around the prairie offering to help bring babies into the world. It was all on the parents. And God.

"You did what you could," Jesse assured him, knowing the words fell flat in the face of such a loss.

"I did," Frank agreed. "Sarah knows that. It's just hard to let him go."

Jesse nodded as if he understood, but he was well aware that he didn't.

"She hasn't seen her family in a long time," Frank went on. "I wish it was under better circumstances, but perhaps only a mother can comfort another mother."

"Well, if you need a good meal while she's away, just come by our place," Jesse offered, not knowing what else to say.

"I will," Frank said. "I'm glad to see you walking around on that leg. She said it was messed up pretty good."

"It was. I'm grateful you were willing to slaughter your pig for me to have the bacon. I never heard of such a thing, but it did the trick."

"Nothing's worth having if it doesn't serve a purpose," Frank replied.

Jesse paused. He'd never heard anyone speak like that before. Jesse always thought everything was worth having just for the sake of having it: for the comfort it brought, or for the wealth it represented. But this idea of what one had serving a purpose... this was a foreign idea.

"Does Sarah blame God?" Jesse asked the question weighing on his mind. "Do you think He was punishing you for something?"

Frank studied Jesse silently before he answered slowly. "Our God is the God of Abraham, Isaac, and Jacob. He has existed throughout all time." He paused, his tone softening with sadness. "Life is a delicate thing. All men suffer. All men are tested. Job said: 'The Lord gave, and the Lord hath taken away; blessed be the name of the Lord.'"

Jesse nodded slowly, unconsciously tracing the scar along his cheekbone. "Sarah told us you taught her about your God. About how sins can be forgiven," Jesse heard himself saying, and suddenly he hungered to hear more, to understand this faith that Frank could cling to even in the face of unspeakable loss.

"*'For God so loved the world, that He gave His only begotten Son, that whosoever believeth in Him should not perish, but have everlasting life. For God sent not his Son into the world to condemn the world; but that world through Him might be saved.'*"

"Is that from the Bible?" Jesse wondered.

Frank nodded. "The book of John, chapter three. It's my favorite passage."

"That was the part I didn't understand," Jesse realized. "Why God would send His son to die. But I'm not sure I understand why He would love us enough to send Him, either."

Frank let out a humorless laugh. "I'm not really sure either. It's not because we deserve it, that's certain. I guess it's because He created us in His image, and He was committed to loving us from the beginning. When Adam sinned, He broke fellowship with God. But through Jesus, that fellowship can be restored."

Jesse pondered these words, certain he didn't understand them in their fullness, but a glimmer of insight was opening in his mind as well as in his heart. "Sarah said God can forgive any sin. Is that true? If you say you're sorry for your sins and believe

Jesus is the Savior, He just forgives you? Don't you have to do something to make up for your wrong-doing?"

Frank cocked his head to the side, as if thinking deeply. "Well, that's what religion teaches. That you have to do some kind of penance before God forgives you. But if you look at the Bible, Jesus forgave the thief hanging on the cross next to Him, just because he admitted he was a sinner and said he believed Jesus was Who He said He was."

Jesse nodded. He had come to offer Frank some encouragement, and instead Frank had given him hope. He stood, offering Frank his hand.

"Thank you for taking the time to explain it to me. I need to head back, but please let me know if there's anything we can do for you."

"Sure thing," Frank nodded, walking with him to the door.

Once outside, Frank said suddenly, "We buried him over that rise, just under that tree."

Jesse took a step forward, sensing the unasked question to join him at the gravesite. Frank fell into step beside him, and together they walked to where the ground was turned over in a very small mound. Jesse stared at the size of it, reminded of the little infant lying underneath.

Frank knelt down and took a fistful of the soft earth in his hand. "We named him Joshua," he whispered, his voice breaking. "It means 'God is my salvation.'"

~

Riding home, Jesse couldn't shake the image of that small grave from his mind. Nor the picture of a broken father kneeling over it, grieving his son but still claiming God as his salvation.

For so long, Jesse had felt alone. He'd felt alienated from his family because of his lie. He'd wanted to be called a war hero, but once he was, it only reminded him that he didn't deserve it. He didn't want his family to know what a coward he really was, and so he had lived with the dark shadow of guilt over his head. His mother celebrated his valor as if he deserved it the way his brothers did, but only because Jesse had taken credit for another man's bravery.

He tried to remember the safe feeling he had known as a boy, before the war, even back before his father died. When he had been young enough to sit on his father's lap and listen to him talk of things that mattered in this life. Jesse was too little to remember the words now, but he remembered that feeling: loved, accepted.

When Frank talked of Providence, he seemed to have a relationship with Him. Jesse had heard men pray to God as "Heavenly Father" and always thought it sounded pompous and remote. But suddenly it sounded intimate and real. Frank had lost something more precious than anything Jesse could imagine, and yet he still knew he was loved. He still trusted God.

Jesse wanted that. He wanted to walk through life with his head held high, instead of hanging low with the weight of shame. He wanted to be able to breathe in the fresh prairie air as he surveyed his land claim and herd of cattle, and not feel burdened believing he didn't deserve it because of his sin. He wanted to be free of the burden. He wanted to know the peace that Sarah claimed made her "heart sing."

Halting his appaloosa, Jesse dismounted. And there in the midst of the greatness of the rolling plains, the sky a wide basin of blue stretching overhead from one horizon to the other, Jesse knelt down upon his knees. He felt the crunch of the dry winter grass under him, but he saw the starts of new spring grass pushing their way through the earth. He felt God's presence, listening.

Jesus, I know I've done something awful. And that's probably not the only thing I've done I deserve punishment for. But I understand now that you've already taken my punishment. I believe You are God's son. I believe you can set me free, and give me peace with God and with myself.

Jesse lifted his head and looked around at the swaying buffalo grass and the blue sky. He didn't know what words he was supposed to say, he only hoped God would take what he had to offer.

God, I don't know if there are certain words I'm supposed to say or if you just know my heart. But I'm sorry, truly sorry, for stealing another man's glory and claiming it as my own. I'm sorry for all the lies I've had to tell to keep it through the years. I don't want to lie any more. I want to do what's right. Please forgive me for this and for all my other sins. I give you my life.

He let out his breath as he felt the weight lift that had been pressing so hard upon his shoulders. He couldn't explain how he knew, but somehow he knew it had been enough. God had forgiven him, out of His great love. And it was such a reassuring certainty that it flooded Jesse's heart and brought tears to his eyes. After all the years of guilt and shame, he was truly forgiven.

Chapter Twenty-Two

*T*he smell of freshly baked bread filled the kitchen, mingling with the aroma of beef stewed with carrots, potatoes and onions. Annette covered the bread with a cloth to keep it warm, peering out the window at the darkening sky and wondering when Jesse would return.

She retrieved the crock of butter from the cellar and set it on the table, trying to decide if she should take her meal alone or continue waiting for her husband. Finally, her hunger won out and Annette prepared a bowl and settled at the table to eat.

Sarah's grief-stricken face weighed heavy on her mind as she ate. Annette said a prayer for Sarah's safety as she traveled, as well as for her healing. She had come to rely on the woman far more than she ever imagined, and now she waited eagerly for her return. She hoped Sarah found the comfort she needed with her family on the Great Sioux Reservation.

A sound outside revealed Jesse's return. Annette moved to the stove to prepare his supper. He came through the door with a nodded greeting and removed his hat and coat, hanging them on the pegs by the door. Then he took his place beside her at the table.

"Thank you, Annette. It smells wonderful."

Settling back into her chair, Annette said, "I was just thinking about Sarah when you came in. How was Frank?"

Jesse shook his head. "I don't know how to explain it. He's

obviously just as upset as you would expect him to be, but somehow he's at peace too." He shrugged. "He showed me where they buried the baby. They named him Joshua."

"So sad," Annette murmured quietly as she sliced the bread and offered a piece to Jesse.

"I heard what Sarah said to you the night she was here, about how God forgives sin. I asked Frank about it," he admitted.

Annette's head lifted. "What did he say?"

"He quoted a verse from the Bible, about how God so loved the world…" Jesse paused. "Let me get the Bible and see if I can find it."

He came back and spread the family Bible on the table, moving their bowls of stew aside so no food was spilled onto it. "He said it was in the book of John, wherever that is." He flipped pages for a while until he found it.

"Chapter three," he muttered, turning more pages. His eyes scanned until he recognized the words. *"For God so loved the world, that He gave His only begotten Son, that whosoever believeth in Him should not perish, but have eternal life. For God did not send His son into the world to condemn the world, but that the world through Him might be saved."*

"It's funny," Annette commented. "I've heard that verse before, but never really understood it. That it meant we could be forgiven by believing in Jesus."

She pulled the Bible closer and began reading for herself.

"And this is the condemnation, that the light has come into the world, and men loved darkness rather than light."

Jesse listened to her reading the scripture, and when she fell silent, their eyes met.

"The light shone in our hearts, revealing our sin," she said quietly.

"So we ran from it," Jesse finished grimly.

"But if we believe in the name of Jesus, we can come into the light without shame," Annette realized, feeling a spark of hope take fire in her soul.

"On the way home from seeing Frank, I prayed to God and asked for forgiveness. And I felt it—I felt like He heard me and I was forgiven," Jesse exclaimed. "I felt like," he paused, suddenly embarrassed, "I felt like that light was inside me."

"I think I understand…" Annette's voice trailed off. "I just wish I could know the peace Sarah and Frank, and now you, have found. But what I did was so awful… I feel like I don't deserve to be forgiven."

Jesse smiled gently. "Frank said that doesn't have anything to do with it. None of us deserve it. It's about God's love, like the verse says."

Annette nodded slowly as understanding began to push back the doubts. "I do believe in Jesus, and I am sorry for what I did. Is that enough?"

Jesse nodded, reaching over to place his hands over hers in an uncharacteristic gesture of intimacy.

Annette bowed her head. *Dear God, if you can see into my heart, you can see both the darkness there and the sorrow. I don't want to live with this heavy burden of shame any longer. I want to know forgiveness. I do believe Jesus died to redeem me, and more than anything, I'm sorry for my sins. I want to feel Your love and acceptance. I want to be who You want me to be.*

Suddenly Vivian Lawson's words flashed through Annette's mind. *"I love it when spring finally warms the land. It's like a fresh start, every year."*

Vivian's words held an underlying message to Annette, revealing forgiveness and encouraging her to make a fresh start with her life. Annette had thought that was impossible, but now she saw a glimmer of light on what had been a dark horizon.

She felt a whisper of dawn in her soul with the realization that her sins had truly been pardoned by God. Despite all she had been and done, God had chosen to love her anyway. She could have a fresh start. She could step into the light.

~

This new sense of peace and joy was too great a gift to keep to herself. Annette had planned on visiting her family as soon as the weather changed, and now she had a new reason to see them. Without revealing her secret guilt, she wanted to share with them the marvelous freedom that came with knowing she was forgiven.

The Bible said all had sinned, and so regardless of what their sins might be, it stood to reason that all should rejoice in being forgiven.

She knew her parents considered themselves Christians. They read the Bible and didn't claim any other religion. But now Annette knew they had been missing something vital: it hadn't changed them.

Jesse admitted the same was true of his family. "My brother

Albert is even a clergyman," he admitted. "And it always seemed like an intellectual matter. The Bible was just a collection of stories and a guideline to moral behavior. There was never any passion or excitement over the message it contained. How could we have all read the Bible but missed the most important thing?" he wondered.

Annette repositioned her mending on her lap, enjoying the camaraderie they shared. In the fireplace, a log crackled as it erupted into fresh flames. Although the days were warming, the evenings were still cool and Annette enjoyed the warmth of the fire, and even more, sharing it with her husband.

"Jesse," she ventured, "would you go with me to visit my family?" Before he could protest, she continued, "I know my father has never made you feel welcomed... and I don't blame you for not wanting to come... but they're my family. And you're my husband," she finished simply.

She watched the uncertainty flicker in his eyes. He tapped his fingers on the red padded armrest of the chair. "If that's what you want," he said finally.

"Thank you," Annette smiled at him.

But once they reached the cabin the following afternoon, doubt set in as to the wisdom of her good intentions. It had been some time since Annette had seen her father, and she knew he had never fully forgiven her for what had seemed to him to be a critical failure in judgment. He had hand-picked the perfect husband for her, and she had chosen a scar-faced cripple instead.

Only now Annette wondered if Jesse hadn't been the perfect choice for her, after all.

She spotted her father emerging from the barn and

straightened her shoulders, preparing herself for a less than welcoming reception. He nodded in greeting and came to take the reins of her mare.

"Weather's turned," he stated. "Glad winter's over. Go on in and I'll put your horses in the barn."

She dismounted, glancing over to see Jesse do the same. He handed the reins to his father-in-law, saying, "Thank you, Mr. Hamilton. Good to see you."

"Mm-hmm," was the only reply Walter bothered to give.

Jesse turned to Annette as if to say, "I told you so," but she only gave him an encouraging smile. She knew this wasn't easy for him. Which was why she appreciated it so much.

"Come on," she said, "Let's go in and see Mama."

She rapped at the door instead of just entering, so her mother would know she had guests. When Agnes saw Annette standing there, she threw her arms around her shoulders with a squeal of delight.

"Oh, Annette! I was hoping it was you!" Then, noticing Jesse standing off to the side, she said, "And Jesse, too! Come inside and I'll start some supper."

The twins, hearing their sister was home for a visit, raced across the room and flung themselves into Annette's arms. Ernest stood back, too old for such emotional displays, and offered her a solid handshake. But his smile was warm and welcoming, and Annette drew him into a reluctant hug just the same.

"Oh my goodness," she exclaimed when she saw baby Howard. He was hardly recognizable. Round and chubby, sitting up and laughing, he was dark-haired and bright-eyed. "The last time I saw you," she said, scooping him up, "you were just an infant. Now look at you!" She kissed his cheek and was rewarded with a happy gurgle.

"I was afraid he wouldn't recognize you," Agnes admitted, "but it seems he does."

"I missed you, Mama," Annette confessed, sitting down on the bed with her twin sisters and tweaking their noses, "and you too!"

The girls giggled. Agnes only turned her back to Annette as she stoked the fire.

In the silence, Annette glanced about the cabin. She had grown accustomed to her three-story brick mansion with a cast-iron stove in a separate kitchen and a fireplace in every bedroom. Her family home seemed basic and rustic by comparison. The heavy iron pot was suspended by a hook in the fireplace, with a wooden board before it for the bread to cook from the heat of the flames. When a chill wind blew around the cabin, a draft whistled through the chinks in the logs.

"How are you and Jesse getting along?" her mother asked over her shoulder.

"Just fine, ma'am," Jesse answered awkwardly and silence descended until Walter entered the cabin with a cut of beef from the smokehouse.

He handed it off to his wife without a word and settled into the chair by the fireplace.

Annette let baby Howard tug on her braid as she searched her mind for something to say. Finally Agnes said, "Annette, come out to the well with me and help me pump some water."

Annette cast an apologetic glance at Jesse, sympathizing with the sudden dread registering in his eyes at the prospect of being left alone with her father.

Once outside, alone at the well, Agnes leaned forward and whispered conspiratorially, "Are you all right?"

"Yes, Mama. In fact, there's something I wanted to tell you," she began nervously.

Agnes' eyes lit up. "I knew it! I thought you had a glow about you!"

"What do you mean?"

"You're expecting, aren't you?" her mother asked hopefully.

Annette reached for the bucket. Her mother's words had cast a dark shadow over her newfound joy, like a black cloud obscuring the sun. But she took a deep breath, determined not to let this reminder of her longing ruin the reality of her joy. She could never admit to her mother that they had never consummated their marriage. And sometimes she was afraid they never would.

But she felt new hope in this too. Without their shame and guilt to separate them, there was at least the possibility of discovering the intimacy of a real and loving marriage.

Blushing at the very idea of sharing such intimacy with Jesse, Annette answered her mother, "No. I'm sorry." She brushed her hair out of her eyes, regretful she couldn't say yes. "That isn't why I'm glowing."

Agnes leaned against the wooden frame of the well. She couldn't mask her disappointment. "Why then?"

Hesitating, unsure of her words, Annette fumbled. "I... I discovered something in the Bible."

Raising an eyebrow in mockery, Agnes took the bucket from Annette's still hands and dropped it down into the dark opening. They remained in silence until the distant splash reminded Annette she must answer her mother's question.

She wished she had Sarah's gift for words.

"Well, it's just that I never realized how personal the message of forgiveness is," Annette began slowly, wanting to articulate the reason for her great joy over a few printed words in a well-known book. "Jesus died for *my* sins, Mama, and *yours*. Because of God's great love for us."

Her mother turned to regard her with such an expression of disdain that Annette felt as if she were the age of her twin sisters, corrected with a simple look. "Did you attend one of those Methodist tent meetings? I've heard about those."

"No, Mama," Annette hesitated. "Mrs. Gibson shared some scriptures with me when she came to tend Jesse's leg over the winter."

"She's Indian," Agnes declared, leaving Annette unsure what conclusion to draw from her obvious statement as she turned the handle and pulled the bucket up out of the darkness.

"Yes, she is," she finally agreed.

"So why is *she* teaching you about our Bible?"

"Well, she was only sharing what her husband Frank had taught her," Annette explained.

Agnes wrapped her hand around the handle of the bucket and stated: "I'm glad you're happy, Annette. And I'm glad you're reading your Bible."

Watching her mother's retreating form, Annette heaved a disappointed sigh. Whatever she had expected or hoped to come of this conversation, it certainly hadn't.

Lord, I'm not sure if I just didn't say it right or she just doesn't understand the enormity of the gift. But I do. And I'm so grateful.

As she followed her mother into the cabin, she heard her father's voice and hoped he hadn't said anything awful to Jesse while she was out of hearing.

"Well, I say we'll all be sorry sooner or later," Walter insisted.

Annette shot Jesse a curious look. He took the cue and explained, "We're talking about sheep sharing the open range with cattle."

"Ah," Annette said, vastly relieved.

"I heard two brothers by the name of Durbin brought eight hundred sheep into Wyoming, over near Cheyenne. He's going to let them share the land with the cattle," her father elaborated. "It's a mistake, I'm telling you right now. Sheep are like parasites. They eat the ground bare and there's nothing left for the cattle. All I can say is he'd better keep them far away from here."

"Oh, Cheyenne's a far piece from here," her mother assured. "So, Jesse," she changed the subject as if it was one that had already worn itself out, "what happened to your leg?"

Annette realized her mistake when she saw the daggers Jesse shot at her with his gray eyes. She knew he didn't want to remind her father of his weakness, and with good reason.

"Horse lost her footing in a drift," Jesse said curtly, "and I took a fall. I hurt my leg, but it's healed up fine now."

"That's good," Agnes nodded, cutting vegetables for stew as she talked. "Annette said Sarah Gibson came over to help you. Must've been a nasty fall."

Annette knew her mother meant no harm and was merely trying to promote conversation. But she wished Agnes had found another topic to encourage.

"It just had a bit of an infection," she spoke up. "But Sarah knew what to do for it."

"Which leg was it?" Walter asked pointedly. Shame burned Annette's cheeks. He was reminding her she had chosen a crippled man against his wishes. And reminding Jesse, too.

Jesse swallowed. If Annette had been close enough, she might have been tempted to take his hand. Which would have only made his humiliation complete.

"It was my amputated leg, sir," Jesse finally answered, looking Walter squarely in the eyes.

"Hmm," was the only reply Walter bothered to offer.

"Well, we're glad Sarah was able to help," Agnes assured him, trying to smooth over her husband's blunder.

But the remainder of the visit was stilted by an underlying tension not even the children's cheerful banter could dispel. Annette was as relieved as Jesse when the time was appropriate for them to take their leave.

She hugged her mother warmly good-bye, but only offered her father a nod. Jesse did the same.

III.   Redemption

"Oh, what joy for those whose disobedience is forgiven,
whose sin is put out of sight!"

Ps. 32:1 NLT

Chapter Twenty-Three

They rode parallel to one another, in complete silence, for the greater part of the way home. Jesse's appaloosa seemed to be keeping time with the little black mare.

Finally Annette broke the silence.

"Jesse," she sighed, "I'm so sorry for my father's behavior. I'm really glad you came. I wanted to see my family and to tell my mother about God's forgiveness. She didn't understand," she admitted, "but at least I tried."

Jesse reached up to trace the scar marring his cheek, a gesture Annette was becoming familiar with. "It's not your fault," he answered in a defeated voice.

"No, but I'm still sorry. He can be overly opinionated, I'm afraid. Don't take it to heart."

Jesse's head lifted at the protective tone of her voice. He could see in the angry tilt of her chin that she resented her father's comment—and not just because of its rudeness, but because it had hurt him. And knowing she cared so much about his feelings almost made up for the slight.

He studied her profile cut against the rose hues of the setting sun. The fullness of her lips, the elegant line of her nose, her delicate chin. She was breathtaking. The wind tugged at loose tendrils of her blond hair, contrasting against the black mane of her mount as it too was tossed by the spring breeze.

Could she learn to love me? The question rolled around in his mind, echoing back to him. It was ridiculous to think she could... and yet, sometimes he wondered if the impossible could be true. Why else would his feelings matter so much to her?

But they had always been good friends. She felt safe with him. And while he cherished her friendship, he wanted so much more from her. He resisted the urge to touch his scarred cheek again, but he could see it in his mind as he had seen it that morning in the mirror. A face that had never been handsome torn from eyebrow to mouth, rendered grotesque and repulsive. A woman like her might appreciate him as a friend, but how could she ever take him as a lover?

"You're every bit the man that he is," Annette added, when he failed to reply. "He just has two feet."

A hint of smile touched Jesse's lips at the way she said it. She glanced over at him, and he was surprised at the laughter that burst forth from within him.

Annette was as startled by his outburst as Jesse was, and raised an eyebrow in question. "What did I say?"

Jesse found the laughter had taken over him. It had been a long time since he had laughed until the tears came to his eyes. "I don't know," he admitted. "It just sounded funny!"

Unable to resist the contagious effect of his spontaneous humor, Annette joined in the laughter. Then, to Jesse's immense surprise and delight, she urged Bella closer to him and reached over to knock his hat down over his eyes in a playful gesture.

Jesse pushed it back up and found her watching him with a mischievous twinkle in her eyes. Then she dug her heels into her mare's sides, yelling *"Heeya!"* and darting off into the swaying buffalo grass.

It only took Jesse a second to curb his surprise and spur his mount to follow. Delighted at this turn in the evening, he leaned into his mare's gray mane and urged her forward.

As he raced toward Annette, he felt gratitude for her faith in him to keep his seat as they galloped across the uneven ground. He was thankful she didn't treat him like an invalid, advising against anything that might result in further injury. Although to be honest, since his fall over the winter, there was a small seed of fear whispering caution in his ear. But almost nothing would have held him back after the adorably taunting expression Annette had been wearing just before galloping away.

He slapped the reins against the appaloosa's neck, urging her to even greater speed. She stretched out, and within a few paces, Jesse had caught up to Bella's flanks. He leaned forward and tugged at the long blond braid hanging down Annette's back. She turned to look over her shoulder at him, blue eyes dancing.

Jesse's pulse kicked up a notch at the way she smiled at him. Almost like a woman would when she was enjoying a man's company. A man she felt attracted to. He swallowed.

She slowed her mount and Jesse tugged at the appaloosa's reins to match her pace. "You can't outrun me," he grinned.

"I didn't think so," she retorted. "But I thought you'd enjoy the chase."

He laughed at her response. "I did, Nettie." The nickname rolled off his tongue before he had a chance to think about it. But once it was out, he liked the sound of it. He watched her face to gauge her reaction.

She smiled as she told him, "No one's called me that since I was a little girl."

"You reminded me of one just now," Jesse laughed, knowing she wouldn't take offense.

"I enjoy riding with you," she answered. "We should do it more often."

Unsure how to reply, Jesse simply nodded. *Could she...?*

The sun was slipping beneath the horizon, and the sky was painted with crimson and gold, then fading into violet before disappearing into the cobalt hues of night. The breeze carried the smells of sweet grass and sagebrush. She wore such a tender smile in the fading light that for a second Jesse entertained the thought of closing the distance between them and kissing her gently on the lips. The setting couldn't have been more romantic, or the timing more perfect.

But fear of her reaction rooted him firmly to the spot. He didn't dare risk losing this easy camaraderie they shared. It meant too much to him.

Although the thought was now imbedded in his mind, and his eyes seemed riveted to the sweet fullness of her lips. He blinked to clear his mind and swallowed. What would it be like to take her in his arms?

"The sunset is beautiful tonight," he forced himself to say in a casual voice, though it still sounded rather strained to his own ears.

She turned her head to the western sky and sighed. "We should get back before darkness falls." Though Jesse noted she made no move to do as she suggested.

They sat together astride their horses, side by side, watching the sun slip beneath the rim of the earth and plunge it into darkness. Then in the dusky shadows, they made their way back home.

~

Sighing as she sank down into the plush chair before the mirrored vanity, Annette ran her fingers through her long hair, untangling the windblown plaits. She set about brushing it with rhythmic strokes, but her mind was elsewhere.

It had been good to see her mother and the twins, and Ernest and baby Howard. And even though he hadn't been very welcoming, it had been good to see her father too. Despite his rudeness, Annette knew he loved her and only wanted the best for her. He just couldn't see she already had it.

Somewhere along the way, she had fallen in love with Jesse. She wasn't exactly sure when it happened, only that it had. His scar didn't matter. His amputated leg didn't matter. He could be difficult and volatile and frustrating at times, but he had given her everything she had thought was impossible. He had offered her acceptance, a respectable name, a home of her own, and even though he hadn't told her, she knew he had given her his heart.

For a moment, she had thought this time he really was going to kiss her. Her heart had hammered in her chest and she had longed to feel the softness of his lips against hers, to feel the strength in his hands as he drew her close to him. But then the moment had passed and he seemed oblivious to her disappointment.

He does love me, doesn't he?

She felt certain it was in his eyes when he looked at her, in his voice when he spoke to her. Did he not yet know it himself or was he unwilling to act on it, to be with a woman who had lost her virginity to a married man?

Annette set the brush aside and walked to the bed, pulling back the quilt and slipping beneath it. The logs in the fireplace crackled and she watched as they glowed orange, consumed by the fire until they were gray with ashes. Her eyes began to droop, but her mind still pondered.

If he loved her as she loved him, couldn't they have a normal marriage? The empty space next to her in the bed seemed larger and colder than usual. She rolled onto her side, staring at the pillow meant for Jesse. Would she ever know what it was like to fall asleep in his arms instead of holding herself tightly to push back the loneliness?

Sometimes she wanted to take him by the shoulders and shake him. But what if she was wrong? What if he couldn't allow himself to love her as a man loves a woman? What a fool she would be, with her heart twice broken.

She closed her eyes. The only hands that had ever touched her and awakened a fire within her belonged to Ricky Lawson, husband to another woman. She remembered the way his green eyes had lingered over her lips, before he ever leaned down to kiss her. The anticipation as she waited for him to finalize what his eyes merely suggested. The dark hairs of his mustache had tickled against her skin. His hands had been firm and possessive as they gripped her waist.

She should have slapped him soundly across the face. But she hadn't.

Rolling onto her other side, pulling the blankets into a bunch, Annette heaved a sigh. When would those memories be replaced? Any lingering emotions she'd harbored for Ricky—dark and twisted as they might have been—had long since faded with time. Now all she wanted was to know the way it was between a man and a woman when there was mutual love and not a trace of guilt.

Annette remembered the expression on Jesse's face as his eyes had lingered over her lips. She pushed back the quilts, feeling warmth spread over her.

They were making a life together. She had delighted in the deep rumble of his unexpected laughter. If there was one thing about him she would like to change, he would laugh more often. She wished the seriousness pulling down at his lips would smooth out into laugh lines that crinkled around his mouth, and yes, puckered his scar.

She smiled in the darkness as she remembered the easy way he had spoken her nickname, "Nettie." She liked it. It made her feel like she belonged to someone who knew her well enough to call her by her childhood name.

She liked feeling like she belonged to Jesse.

Chapter Twenty-Four

Next door, in the smaller room intended for guests—or perhaps children—Jesse lay awake in his bed. Lucky was curled at his feet, snoring. He hadn't planned to let the dog sleep with him, but the puppy's whining and his own loneliness had eventually worn him down.

He rubbed his hand over his face in frustration. When the sky had been afire with color and the timing had been so perfect, he wished he could have known how Annette would have reacted if he'd made an advance. She was, after all, his wife!

But the circumstances of their union were hardly typical. It had been a marriage of convenience for both of them. Yet… something seemed to be changing between them. And Jesse only hoped it wasn't his own imagination.

The fire hissed and crackled in the fireplace, and Jesse felt a fire burn within himself as he imagined feeling her soft lips against his, her body pressed against his chest… He shook his head. He was never going to fall asleep this way!

Pushing himself upright, he leaned against the headboard and reached over to the bedside table to light a candle. Then opening the Bible in his lap, he flipped through the pages until he found the book of John. He had learned that whenever his sense of peace began to falter, the words of scripture restored it.

Disturbed by his master's movements, the brown and white

bull terrier relocated himself at Jesse's side, flopping down next to him with his chin in Jesse's lap. Jesse stroked Lucky's silky ears absently as he read.

After a while, his eyes began to droop and the words on the page began to blur. Returning the Bible to the table and blowing out the flame, Jesse curled onto his side and Lucky nestled in close to his shoulder.

His last thoughts before drifting into sleep were a prayer. *Lord, help me to love Annette the way I should. Even if she never can love me back.*

His first thoughts upon waking were of Annette.

He imagined her lying in her bed, in the white nightgown she was wearing the time she had startled him on the second level porch. Was her hair braided and stretched out on the sheet behind her, or did it spill like a banner of golden silk across her pillow? Did she wear a peaceful expression, with her hands tucked under her cheek like a little girl? Or were her brows knit together in worry from a fitful dream?

With a sigh, he sat up and swung his legs over the edge of the bed. Reaching for the prosthesis, always kept within close reach, he began attaching it to the amputated stump on his right leg. Ever since Sarah had applied her "magic bacon," it seemed to have healed completely. He was far more careful with it than before, not daring to risk another infection. He routinely applied ointment to the skin before sleeping, as a precautionary measure, even though there didn't appear to be a need for it. The tingling of the severed nerves still plagued him at times, but there was nothing to be done about that.

Carefully pulling his trousers over the false foot and then stepping into it with his good foot, he finished dressing and tugged on his boots. An idea was budding in his mind. A surprise for Annette which he hoped would bring another smile of delight to her sweet face.

He would invite her to go into town with him and go shopping. She could buy new material for sewing or anything else she wanted. They could walk the planked walkway along the storefronts with her hand tucked into his elbow. And everyone who passed could marvel at his good fortune and her bad judgment.

A slight smile tipped the corner of his mouth at the thought. He had stopped trying to hide his scar from her, and more often than not, he actually found himself forgetting to worry about it. She never seemed bothered by it, never seemed uncomfortable or put off. He only wished *he* could look in the mirror without being repulsed.

When he returned to the kitchen after milking the cow and retrieving eggs from the chicken coop, he found Annette stoking the fire in the cast iron stove. Though she had been new to it when they married, she had adapted quickly. And the view she presented as she bent over to add more logs couldn't be faulted, either.

She turned to find him standing in the doorway, the grin on his face revealing his thoughts, and quickly straightened. He thought she looked a little flushed at having caught him staring, and he quickly handed her the milk and eggs, saying, "I was thinking we could go into town after breakfast, if you would like."

Her blue eyes brightened and she exclaimed, "Oh, I would love that!"

He smiled as she set about making breakfast with new

purpose, his recent indiscretion already forgotten. *Although*, he reminded himself, *she is my wife*.

As soon as breakfast had been eaten, Jesse hitched up the wagon while she washed dishes. It was a long ride into town and if they wanted to get back before dark, they would need to get an early start.

Jesse smiled as he helped her onto the buckboard, noticing she'd pinned the wedding brooch to the lapel of her coat. And as they traveled, he was aware that she didn't seem to mind when their shoulders and thighs were jostled together as the wagon rolled over rocks or prairie dog burrows. He knew he certainly didn't mind.

When they reached Weston, Jesse felt the usual discomfort he felt around people unaccustomed to his scar. He knew most folks didn't mean any harm, and it was a natural response to stare at someone who was different. But it didn't make being the object of such unflattering attention any easier.

Suddenly an old memory rose up from when he was a boy and the soldiers first began returning from the front. His mother had jabbed him sharply with her elbow for staring at a man who was badly maimed from a grenade explosion. Jesse had been unable to keep his eyes from it, fascinated by the red puckering flesh twisting the man's face into something that looked almost inhuman.

It had been mere curiosity that held his gaze fixed on the young soldier, nothing more. But his mother had reprimanded him later, out of the soldier's hearing, telling him, *"It's unkind to bring attention to a man's scars. Always look him in the eyes to acknowledge his humanity."*

Jesse hadn't thought of the incident in years, and wasn't

sure why he had thought of it now. But it helped him to feel a little more forgiving toward those whose eyes lingered over his right cheek before darting away guiltily. He determined to try to meet their gaze and smile, and so remind them of their shared humanity.

His wife tucked her hand into the crook of his elbow and walked alongside him, seeming to be either unaware or unaffected by the looks he received. Her quiet acceptance gave him confidence, and he lifted his chin, intentionally smoothing the lines of the scowl he felt shaping his expression. He looked down at her and couldn't help but respond to the smile on Annette's face. She appeared to be enjoying the outing just as he had hoped.

"Are you hungry?" he asked her.

"A little. I forgot how long it takes to get here. I should have packed lunch for us," she admitted.

"There's a little diner up ahead. Let's eat there," Jesse suggested.

"I've never eaten at one before," Annette said, looking up at him eagerly. "What will we eat?"

Jesse laughed. "We'll have to see what's on the menu."

"It seems like the town has grown just since the last time we were here," she commented. "Don't you think so?"

Jesse looked around. The railroad was changing the face of the west. It was so much easier to travel, and so many less casualties along the way. There was so much more space, so many more opportunities out west. Jesse didn't wonder that the town was growing. What he wondered was if the east would ever be able to heal from the ravages of a war that had torn it apart.

Out here, it was easier to forget and begin again.

The words "Home-cooked Food" were painted in red on the glass windows, and a sign above the door boasted: "Maggie's Restaurant." Annette seemed a little unsure of herself as she walked into the establishment, looking around at the tables all set with red and white checked tablecloths to give it a homey feeling. Jesse led her to an empty table in the back corner.

Handing her a menu, he said, "What will it be, Nettie?"

She smiled, "I think I'll have the chicken pot pie."

"Roast beef for me," he replied.

Conversation came easily as they ate, and Jesse realized he had forgotten to be self-conscious of his scar. It was the first time since the injury he could remember feeling relaxed in a public setting. And here he was sitting across the table from the prettiest girl in the territory. And she was his wife.

"So, Nettie," he asked when the empty plates had been cleared, "what do you want to buy while we're here?"

She smiled. "I'd love a new pair of shoes. I saw a woman with high heeled white boots once, and I've always wanted a pair since!"

Jesse had never paid any attention to her shoes. He glanced down at them now and noticed they were simple brown boots, probably polished many times over. He wished he had thought of it first, but today he would make her feel treasured. He would buy her absolutely anything her heart desired!

"Well then, let's go find you a pair," he grinned as he came to his feet and offered his elbow.

She stood, taking his arm and grinning. Jesse couldn't help

but feel pride at the joy in her eyes. Just knowing he was responsible for that wide smile and the sparkle lighting her blue eyes made him feel like a king.

~

Annette held on to Jesse's arm as they crossed the street, lifting her skirt to reduce the amount of mud and horse droppings soaking the hem. She glanced over at Jesse and wasn't surprised to notice he was watching her. He grinned, and she laughed at the fun they were having. She felt like a little girl, carefree and excited to have a day out in town. With her best friend.

She wondered if Jesse knew how different he was now from the man he had been when they first met. He had worn a perpetual frown, his brows drawn together fiercely. Annette wondered if people hadn't stared at him more in response to his intimidating expression than because of his scar. She did notice that the townspeople they passed either averted their eyes or honed in on the right side of his cheek as he passed. But it was just human nature at play, and Annette truly believed if any one of those people were given the chance to talk to Jesse, they would treat him with respect.

To his credit, he seemed largely unaffected by it. Annette was proud of him. Just in choosing to bring her to town today, he had shown bravery. She hoped his new confidence had something to do with her.

As he opened the door for her to precede him into the mercantile, Annette turned to ask, "What do *you* want today, Jesse?"

"Only to take you shopping," he answered flippantly, but there was tenderness in his eyes.

Annette paused, feeling her throat tighten with emotion. "Thank you," she said softly. What he wanted wasn't simply to take her shopping, she knew, but to make her feel cherished. And she did.

"If they don't have what you're looking for here," Jesse told her, "we can try the dressmaker's shop. I thought I saw some shoes in the store window there."

The mercantile carried everything from rakes and seed, and pots and cook stoves, to clothing and shoes. It was much easier to get goods from the east now that the train was cutting through the territory. Freighters still had to load up their mule-drawn wagons and haul the merchandise to the various towns scattered across the prairie, but it was far easier than hauling it all the way from Missouri.

Annette spotted the shelves lined with women's boots and hurried to peruse the selection. On the top shelf were white kid boots, delicately shaped with feminine high heels. "This is what I was looking for!" she exclaimed. "I hope there's a pair that will fit me!"

Jesse scanned about and pulled a chair over for her. "Sit down and we'll try some on."

"What?" she exclaimed. "Right here?"

"You'll want to know if they fit," Jesse replied matter-of-factly.

Annette took a seat and leaned down to untie her boots, careful to keep her skirt covering her ankles. She watched with amusement as Jesse picked up a pair of boots, sized them up, and reached for another. But when he handed them to her and she slipped them on, she was surprised to discover he had chosen well.

"They fit perfectly!"

She put both boots on and laced them, then slowly stood on the delicate heels. She took a few steps. "It'll take some getting used to," she laughed as her ankles wobbled.

"They look very pretty," Jesse said, and Annette looked up to find him studying her—not just her feet—with approval.

Annette was used to the attention of men. She'd been receiving it ever since she was twelve or thirteen and her body had begun to fill out with the curves of a woman. As they'd passed the saloon coming into town, she'd seen the way the men had gawked at her. It didn't feel like a compliment. It made her feel as if her femininity had been cheapened, as if she were no more than a sexual object, created solely to produce lust in men.

Under Jesse's longing gaze, she felt appreciated and adored. She was glad her appearance pleased him.

Jesse looked almost guilty at having been caught staring at her, just as he had that morning in the kitchen. Annette's smile was hidden from his view as she knelt down to remove the new boots. Any other man would have taken her for his pleasure a long time ago. But Jesse hadn't.

Annette returned the old brown boots to her feet and adjusted her skirt over them. Jesse stood holding the white boots, waiting for her.

"Is there anything else you want while we're here?" he asked.

Not wanting to take advantage of his generous nature, Annette shook her head. "Oh, this is all I want! Thank you," she said softly.

He nodded, his gray eyes locking with hers. There was more she wanted to say, and she could see there was more he wanted to hear. But she would wait until they were alone in the wagon for the long ride home to say it.

As they walked down the narrow aisles toward the counter to pay for their purchase, Jesse paused to look at some rope. Lucky had chewed through three in the last few weeks.

Suddenly, a patron walking past the end of the aisle caught Annette's eye. Then her breath caught in her chest as she recognized him. He paused and stared back at her.

His dark hair had grown since the last time she'd seen him, but he was just as handsome in his duster and Stetson. Bryan's blue eyes penetrated her gaze with such intensity that she took a step back. Then he smiled tightly, tipping his hat before continuing on his way.

Annette felt a familiar flutter in her stomach, and although she had done nothing wrong, she hoped Jesse hadn't noticed their little exchange. But glancing back at him, she saw the expression on his face and knew she hoped in vain.

He said nothing as he picked up a length of rope, wound up and knotted in the middle. Annette followed behind him and stood silently by his side as he counted out payment for the items.

Annette wished she could say seeing Bryan again hadn't affected her. But it had. In that brief instant when she realized who was standing there, a flood of longing and regret had washed over her afresh. And his eyes had spoken volumes without his mouth ever moving. His very silence spoke to her.

He was still hurt by her rejection.

Which only served to remind Annette why she had been forced to turn him down.

The ride home with Jesse was a silent one. The playful, jovial mood had evaporated. Jesse sat pensively beside her, clearly lost in his own thoughts. And it was just as well. Annette couldn't have forced a cheerful conversation if Jesse had expected it.

All she could think about was that look on Bryan's handsome face. And how he had walked away without offering the simplest of pleasantries.

Ricky's face appeared in her mind's eye, wearing the smug smile he often wore when he knew she was under his spell. He had told her he loved her, but he'd taken everything from her. And she had let him. When she chose to let Ricky kiss her for the very first time, she had chosen to forfeit Bryan Hunt. Even if she didn't understand it at the time.

Annette had believed the blood of Jesus washed her clean, but suddenly she felt like a whore again. She had felt satisfied in her life with Jesse Stone, but suddenly she was reminded of what she'd lost with Bryan.

It wasn't that she didn't value Jesse and all he had given to her. Because she did. She just felt confused by the unwelcome reminder of what might have been.

Chapter Twenty-Five

*A*nnette pressed her forehead against the glass, watching Jesse ride away into the waving green prairie grass. Her heart sank. She knew she had hurt him, though it had never been her intention. There was still something unsettled between her and Bryan Hunt, and Jesse had the unfortunate opportunity to witness it.

She watched until he disappeared into the prairie, her thoughts in a turmoil. Then with a heavy sigh, she went out back where Jesse had heated tubs of water for laundry.

Tied to a fencepost, Lucky strained against the rope, crying after his master. Jesse had been working with him for the last few weeks, teaching him how to walk alongside the horse as well as introducing him to the cattle. She tried to comfort him, but the dog was wounded at being left behind.

Hoping the bull terrier would soon calm down, Annette rolled up her sleeves and set about the unpleasant task. As her hands worked, her mind also worked to find resolution to the conflict gnawing at her insides.

Lord, I felt at peace. But all it took was one reminder of my past and that peace is gone. Was it ever real or did I just fool myself because I wanted it so badly?

She used a long stick to work the clothes around in the boiling hot water and lye soap. She wished she could find cleansing that would last instead of so quickly disappearing and leaving her feeling as sullied as Jesse's socks.

She tried to remember the verses she had read, the words Sarah had told her, but all her mind could produce was the memory of Bryan's blue eyes burning into hers. If he knew the truth about her, his expression would have held judgment, not just the sting of rejection. Because she wasn't the woman of virtue he believed her to be.

Whether from the strong smell of lye or from her own deep sense of worthlessness, tears gathered in Annette's eyes. She remembered the tenderness in Jesse's voice as he'd said, "I only want to take you shopping." She couldn't imagine why he, of all people, should love her when he knew the truth of her impurity.

Throughout the morning, her thoughts circled like a vulture around a carcass. She scrubbed the clothes on the washboard, rinsed them in a tub of clean water, and then hung them on the line to dry. Leaving the heavy tubs for Jesse to empty later, she returned to the house to make dough for biscuits.

But the weight of despondency rested so heavily on her shoulders, she instead went into the living room and slumped down onto the couch. Tears streaked her cheeks.

She wanted to know again the freedom that came from the knowledge of God's forgiveness.

Finally, she went up the stairs to retrieve the Bible. The last place she had seen it was Jesse's nightstand, and sure enough, that was where she found it. Sitting in the armchair by the fireplace, which lay cold due to the warm weather outside, Annette opened the Bible on her lap.

She tried to remember where the verses were that Sarah had spoken to her about. The book of Romans seemed familiar.

As she skimmed through the verses, her eyes fixed on verse eight of chapter five. *"But God demonstrated His own love toward us, in that while we were still sinners, Christ died for us."*

While we were still sinners...

Slowly, the way the sun rises and pushes back the night's shadows, peace seeped into her heart once more. Even while she was foolish enough to allow a married man to seduce her, God had still loved her. He'd loved her even before she was sorry for letting it happen.

God loved her then, and loved her still.

She took a ragged breath as the arms of security wrapped around her once more.

Her thoughts returned to Jesse, to the withdrawn manner he'd adopted since their encounter with Bryan the day before. She missed him. She missed the openness beginning to transform him. She missed the closeness they'd shared as they laughed and giggled on their shopping expedition.

Lord, how do I reach him again?

Closing the Bible, she leaned her head back against the soft cushion of the armchair and closed her eyes. Jesse's face was before her, his gray eyes looking at her with a mixture of adoration and longing. His sandy blond hair tumbled over his forehead, and a smile tipped the corner of his mouth and made the scar pucker. Annette longed to touch his face, to let her fingers smooth over the ragged places on his skin and let healing soak through her fingertips into his heart.

And suddenly she understood.

The reason he didn't make love to her wasn't because he

didn't believe *she was unworthy*. It was because he didn't believe *himself worthy*.

All this time, their mutual shame had been keeping them apart. Their fear of rejection had been the wall between them, dividing them as surely as the walls between their bedrooms kept them apart. The only way to breach the gap was for someone to walk through the door.

Her heart pounded at the very idea, but it was time—past time—for them to come together.

If she was wrong in her interpretation, and he turned away from her in disgust... She covered her face and took a deep breath.

When had Jesse taken such possession of her heart?

~

The gray and white appaloosa stretched out, her hooves making a soft thudding sound as she galloped over the hard earth. Jesse leaned into her neck, urging her forward. He wanted to feel the wind in his face. He only wished he could outrun the familiar pain gripping his heart.

The sky above was blue, and the grass beneath his mare's hooves was lush and green. If his mind hadn't been so tortured, he might have enjoyed the peace and splendor of nature surrounding him. But his eyes were oblivious to it. All he could see was the way Annette had stilled when Bryan Hunt had appeared at the end of the aisle at the mercantile, and the cryptic look they had exchanged.

In a fraction of a second, the camaraderie he and Annette shared had been divided. A fragile bud of hope had been blossoming in his soul, fed by her kindness and attention. He had dared to believe she could love a man like him, mangled and crippled, but the truth had always been right in front of him. She was grateful to him for saving her from the embarrassment of being discovered as an adulteress and shaming her family. She saw him as a benefactor. Nothing more.

He spurred his mount to a faster pace, letting the breeze cool the anger that flushed his cheeks. He wasn't angry with her. She had never said she loved him, had never let on that she had feelings for any man but Bryan. No, Jesse was angry with himself. He had let his imagination get the better of him, dreaming that one day she could see him as a man and love him—emotionally and physically—as her husband.

He had a thriving ranch and the promise of financial success. He had a grand home and a beautiful wife. But as he raced madly across the open prairie, it didn't feel like he had anything.

Finally he slowed the horse to a walk. He pulled off his beaver Stetson and ran a hand through his hair. *Oh God, why did you bring her into my life? Why did you let me glimpse what love could be like only to withhold it from me? I've said I'm sorry for my cowardice and lies a thousand times over. Is it not enough?*

Jesse replaced the hat to his head and squared his shoulders. Ahead of him, climbing a rise, was Rattlesnake and Jim Ingram. He urged the appaloosa forward to join them. Sometimes he still felt like a city slicker greenhorn around them, humbled by their knowledge and experience as cattlemen.

The more time he spent with them, the more comfortable he felt in his role of rancher. But today he felt like the same little boy who had sat cross-legged and enthralled as he listened to his older brothers, dressed in their smart blue uniforms, recounting tales of bravery and heroism in war. And knowing he could never be like them.

No matter how he tried, he couldn't seem to silence the voice that whispered *"Failure"* in his ears. He was still nothing more than an imposter.

His gloved hand reached up to trace the scar marking his face. The memory of the fear that turned his blood to ice and held him captive sickened him. He had been given a chance to prove himself, to be a gallant war hero, and he had only been worried about saving his own sorry skin.

~

A flash of movement from within a grassy depression caught his eye and jarred Jesse from his somber thoughts. He spurred his horse toward the spot, certain it was another rider. As he slowed his mount, he saw there were two cowboys circling a small herd of cattle. His cattle.

As he approached, the young man wearing a plaid shirt and white Stetson brought his horse to a sudden halt, as if surprised by Jesse's unexpected appearance. But he quickly pasted a friendly smile onto his face.

Jesse disliked him immediately.

He was a tall, lanky fellow and his grin was wide and toothy. Jesse suspected women found his tanned features and dimples attractive. But instinctively, Jesse distrusted him and his cohort, who rode abreast of him and tipped his hat.

Jesse tipped his hat in return. "Afternoon," he greeted. "I'm Jesse Stone."

"Harvey Simons," the smiling young man answered.

"George Harper," his companion introduced himself. He was a few years older than Simons, his face shadowed with a scraggly beard.

Jesse perused the pair silently. Harvey Simons was the man Claude suspected of stealing his calves. It was odd that they were riding through his herd, but not uncommon considering the nature of the open range. It was difficult to recognize the brand at a distance, and sometimes the herds intermingled. Jesse couldn't accuse them of any wrong-doing, but his gut told him they were up to no good.

"Don't believe we've met before," Jesse commented, trying to match the fellow's friendliness, but hearing the undertone of challenge in his voice.

"My homestead's a few miles northwest of town," Harvey answered, completely unconcerned. "We're just out looking for any of my cattle that wandered out here. Trying to bring 'em a little closer to home before the round-up."

Jesse nodded. It was a plausible answer. But he still didn't believe it.

"Well," Jesse hesitated, "good day to you." He tipped his hat again and urged his appaloosa forward.

They tipped their hats in reply and rode off in the other direction. Jesse halted his mount to watch their departure.

If they were stealing cattle—and he was inclined to think they were—what were they doing so far from their own land, riding around *his* herd? It was the just the two of them, on horseback, and they hadn't even carried saddlebags on their mounts. What were they up to?

Not knowing what he hoped to find, Jesse dismounted and walked among the herd, studying them carefully. Nothing seemed out of place, but Jesse couldn't get Harvey's smug grin out of his mind. He searched the ground for hoof prints, then rode in the direction it appeared they had been coming from.

Father, you've given me this land and this opportunity. Don't let thieves take it away from me. If there's something going on, help me to find a clue.

He nudged his mount into a fast canter, his eyes scanning back and forth across the horizon as he rode over the vast green landscape. Another small herd came into view, and he rode toward them, circling the herd cautiously and searching for any signs that something was amiss.

His first find was a blackened ring where a campfire had burned. He dismounted and knelt down to examine the ashes. There was still the faint smell of wood smoke to them. Jesse looked around. It was possible this fire had nothing to do with Simons and Harper, but he strongly suspected it did.

At first glance, nothing appeared out of the ordinary. Then Jesse's eyes narrowed as he let out a gasp.

He stepped closer to inspect the brand seared into the cow's hide. His brand, the "open hat," had been altered into a "flying T." By adding a straight line to the center of the open hat, it had been transformed into a new brand, and it didn't take much imagination to guess to whom that brand belonged.

The original symbol, shaped as it was described, like a cowboy's hat, was as brown as the animal's hide. The straight line which rendered it a "flying T" was pink in the center and blackened around the edges where the hot iron had seared the flesh.

They weren't just stealing his unbranded calves. They were rustling mature cattle to be sold for profit at this year's market.

Jesse let out his breath in a low, angry hiss. These cattle were the ones Simons claimed had wandered far from his ranch and he was working to bring closer to home for the round-up.

He clenched his teeth. Jesse didn't know how, but he was going to see that the thieves were brought to justice.

~

As dusk fell, the sun painted the grassy hillside and white siding of his gorgeous home with the hues of rosy gold. Jesse felt the familiar swell of pride at the sight of it, and the accompanying eagerness to see Annette. But as he remembered her silence on the ride home from town, it faded. She had seemed content with him, right up until she was reminded of the man she truly wanted. He wished she would have said something to put his mind at ease, but her silence had spoken volumes.

His shoulders slumped. He took his time unsaddling and currying his horse, then reluctantly turned his feet toward the house. Lucky was tied up near the door and ran to greet him, straining at the rope until Jesse was within reach and wagging his tail so hard his entire body moved back and forth. He leapt up in excitement, covering Jesse's chin with wet kisses. Comforted by the warm welcome, Jesse rubbed his head and scratched him behind the ears.

"Glad somebody loves me," he told the dog, patting his head one more time before heading to the bunkhouse to tell Claude of his discovery.

"He's brazen," Claude shook his head in disbelief. "He must think that since you're new to the territory, you won't know what he's up to. I've heard of rustlers using what's called a 'running brand' to freehand one brand into another. It's small enough to carry in their pocket, and they can heat it up over a campfire and brand the cattle at night."

"How are we going to catch him?" Jesse wondered aloud.

Claude shook his head. "I'm not sure. Let me think on it."

Jesse nodded wearily. He rubbed his hands over his face and bid his foreman and ranch hands good night. He paused to scratch Lucky behind the ears one more time before climbing the stairs to the kitchen entrance.

The tempting smells of savory beef and freshly baked cornbread wafted to Jesse nostrils before he ever opened the door. Annette turned at the sound of his entry and smiled in greeting. The table was set, and a vase of wildflowers was placed in the center.

"You're just in time," she smiled. "I'll prepare your plate while you wash up."

One of the modern conveniences Jesse had insisted upon was an indoor pump. He walked to it now and pumped water into the white porcelain basin, splashing his face and scrubbing the scent of horseflesh from his fingers.

Jesse took his place at the table, sensing Annette had put more effort into dinner tonight and suspecting he knew the reason why. She felt guilty. And that motivation did nothing to ease the ache in his heart.

He bent his head and said a prayer of thanks, then focused his attention on the plate before him. He didn't think he would ever tire of the flavor of a prime cut of beef.

"How was your day?" Annette asked, breaking the silence.

Jesse grunted in response, not wanting to divulge his discovery about the cattle thieves. He didn't want to give her any cause to worry about their financial situation.

But Annette persisted. "I think Lucky was disappointed you didn't take him with you today. He whined and whined after you rode out."

Jesse simply nodded.

"He's been doing well with his training, hasn't he? I think he enjoys it. Do you think he'll be ready to go with you on the fall round-up?"

"Maybe," was all Jesse gave her, reaching for another slice of cornbread.

"You're coming up on your second fall here in the west," she continued, and Jesse listened as she prattled on and on. But he could only resist her pleasant company for so long before he found himself drawn into conversation with her. And as they fell back into easy dialogue, he found some of the pain began to subside.

After the meal, he went out to milk the cow and check on the chicken coop. When he returned, he found her lighting the oil lamps in the living room. They usually passed the evenings together, and so Jesse took up his place in the armchair and Annette positioned herself on the couch under a lamp, situating the mending in her lap. Lucky sat at his feet, gnawing happily on a bone.

Jesse opened the pages of a book he had carried with him from back east. It was one his mother had given him, and though he had little interest in the story, he searched for a distraction from his own thoughts and concerns.

Feeling Annette's attention, he glanced up. Several times throughout the evening he had the odd feeling she was studying him. She seemed… nervous. He watched her out of the corner of his eye. She was holding the fabric in one hand and needle and thread in the other, but obviously her thoughts were elsewhere as she hadn't completed a stitch in minutes.

Finally, he stretched, yawning as he came to his feet. "I'm going to bed. Good night."

"Good night," she answered. Her voice sounded strained and anxious. Jesse considered asking if everything was alright, but she had already bent her head to her work and was now stitching as if her life depended on it.

Wondering if he would ever understand her, Jesse climbed the stairs to his bedroom.

Chapter Twenty-Six

*A*nnette waited several minutes, then put aside her mending, turned down the oil lamps, and followed behind him to her own room. With shaking hands, she changed into her long white nightgown, unbraided and brushed out her waist length blond hair, and picked up the candle.

She paused to check her reflection in the mirror on the vanity. With her blond hair cascading around her shoulders, wearing only her night clothes, she looked more like a little girl than a woman. The eyes that met hers in the mirror were round with trepidation. Annette wondered what Jesse's response would be to her sudden appearance and the vulnerable picture she presented.

The flame flickered in the darkness, shadows wavering around her as her hand trembled. She took an unsteady breath as she stepped out into the hallway and paused before Jesse's door.

Lord, let him want me.

Her knuckles wrapped softly against the solid wood. She bit her lip, waiting. No answer. Perhaps he was already asleep. After all, he'd had a long day in the saddle and he'd looked exhausted when he'd left her downstairs.

Letting out her breath in a sigh of mingled disappointment and relief, she returned to her room and sat on the edge of her bed. She paused for a moment to imagine what might have happened if Jesse had answered the door and welcomed her into his arms. But the cold floor beneath her feet was enough to ground her in reality. She placed the candle on the nightstand and swung her legs up onto the bed and beneath the covers.

But just as she leaned over to blow out the candle, a sound outside the door leading to the second level porch caught her attention. Her pulse quickened.

Jesse was out there. That's why he hadn't answered the door.

Before her courage failed, Annette took up the candle and went to the door. She opened it slowly, not wanting to startle him. He was leaning heavily on the railing, and he turned and straightened as she approached.

"Couldn't sleep?" she asked him, her voice sounding breathless to her own ears.

"No," he answered. "You couldn't either?"

"No," she said softly. Her heart thudded against her rib cage and she swallowed nervously. Then almost laughed, remembering how he used to do the very same thing and she had worried of his sanity.

"Are you alright?" he asked, studying her silently.

"Yes, I…" she faltered. "Jesse," she rested the candleholder on the railing and stepped toward him. "I want to ask you something."

His eyes narrowed with speculation.

She took another step toward him, and wasn't surprised when he took a step back. But she quickly made up the lost ground and gently rested her hand upon his chest. She could feel his heart thumping wildly through his shirt. She looked up into his eyes, wide and panicked.

"Jesse, please, will you make me your wife in the truest sense?" she whispered, her gaze slipping from his eyes and fastening on his lips. She leaned forward, willing him to kiss her, to pull her into a tender embrace—

He pushed her away roughly, taking a step back and putting distance between them.

"Nettie!" he exclaimed, running a hand through his hair and looking away from her out into the darkness of the empty prairie. His breath came heavily.

She tried to choke back her disappointment. After all, she had expected this response. But hot tears of rejection burned her eyes just the same.

"Why not?" she asked so softly that the words were almost lost to the sounds of the rustling wind.

She saw his hand come to his cheek in that all too familiar gesture. He traced the scar running the length of his right cheek, then his hands dropped to his side. His head hung and he let out a sigh so ragged that Annette's heart broke for him.

She waited in silence until his eyes moved back to hers. Then, in complete silence, she beseeched him to put aside his wounded pride and simply love her. But he only searched her face, as if unable to find the words.

"Why not?" she repeated finally.

He turned away to lean over the railing and released another broken sigh, presenting her with his back, as solid as any wall.

~

"Why would you want me to?" he finally demanded, though his tone was more wounded than harsh. "I thought it was Bryan Hunt you wanted."

"Then you were wrong," she replied quietly, but firmly.

"Why *would* you want me? Look at me," Jesse turned to face her, shame written in the line of his bowed head and the regret haunting his gray eyes.

Annette closed her eyes and turned away from him, releasing a sigh of deep frustration. When she lifted her chin and turned to meet his gaze, Jesse saw the sorrow that resided there.

"You still don't understand," she said sadly.

"I saw the way you looked at him," Jesse began.

"No," she corrected. "You saw the way *he* looked at me. You only saw my back."

"You were oddly silent the rest of the way home," he retorted, hearing the accusation in his voice and instantly regretting it.

"Yes," she admitted. "I was. I was thinking about my past, and about the way my decisions have shaped my life. But—"

"You wish you could have married him."

"I never said that."

"Of course you didn't have to," Jesse lashed out, a deep fury welling up inside him and taking voice.

"You still don't understand," she said softly, her blue eyes penetrating his with a steady calm that left Jesse baffled.

She stood there in the flickering candlelight, wearing only the thin cotton nightgown he had remembered her in many times since their last moonlit encounter. Her hair was loose and fell in blond shimmering waves. The shadows played over her face, highlighting the soft angles of her features and the hollow at the base of her throat. She was so exquisite it pained Jesse to look at her.

"What is there to understand?" Jesse's words held defeat. "Look at me," he whispered, tortured by the self-loathing that arose at the awareness of his own appearance.

He swallowed back tears, his eyes lowering to her bare feet on the wooden planks. But the tone of her voice brought his gaze sharply back to hers.

Gone was the gentleness that had characterized her speech before. Now her eyes snapped with anger. "What? You think I can't love you because of the way you look?"

"You're so beautiful..." his voice trailed off.

She leaned back against the railing, shaking her head. "Is that all there is to me? If I fell ill with the pox and my face was badly marked, would you believe I loved you then? Sometimes I wish I had been born ugly so men were forced to love me for who I *am*, and not just want me for what they *see*."

"Don't be absurd," Jesse argued. "You could never love me when you could have a man like Bryan."

Her head jerked up and she stomped her bare foot upon the wooden floorboards. "*Don't you see?* You took me when no one else would have wanted me. You knew the truth, and yet accepted me anyway. I don't care what you look like! I don't care how big a house you've built for me or how many head of cattle you own! I just want *you*!" she shouted, spinning on her heels and running to her room.

The thud of her door closing was followed by instant silence. Jesse stared after her, his mouth agape.

Disturbed by the noise, Lucky crawled down from the bed to join Jesse outside. Jesse sank down onto the porch floor and the dog flopped beside him, resting his chin on his master's knee. His tongue lolled out, and he looked up at Jesse with questioning brown eyes.

Jesse reached down to tousle the brown fur of Lucky's head. He shook his own head, trying to comprehend what had just taken place.

Had he missed the most important thing? Had he failed to see what he had in front of him all along? He had thought Annette was the prize of the territory for her appearance, when what truly made her special was the tenderness of her heart.

She did love him. Despite his amputated leg and his scarred face. She loved him for who he was. And she wanted to be loved the same way.

She *deserved* to be loved the same way.

~

After a while, Jesse had retreated inside and gone to bed. But sleep had been slow in coming. In the morning, he wasn't surprised when conversation over breakfast was stilted. He resented the awkward tension in their relationship, but had no idea how to relieve it.

As he strode out to the barn, Lucky by his side, he replayed the night's encounter in his mind and wished he could go back and respond to her differently. She had come to offer herself to him, and he had let his pride make a fool of him. He had pushed her away when he'd had the chance to pull her close.

His thoughts were interrupted as he entered the shadowed interior of the barn and a voice declared: "Lawd, Mr. Jesse, but you don't look fit for trainin' no dog today. You look more like a man ready to march into battle. And I feel sorry for those folks, I do."

Jesse let out a small laugh, trying to relax the scowl he now became aware contorted his features. He rubbed a hand over his face and forced a smile. "That better?"

"Some," Jim Ingram answered, "but you must've been havin' some dark thoughts to be wearin' such a fierce face. You sure you up to training that dog this mornin'?"

"Yes, I still want to train Lucky. It would be great if he could come along on the round-up and the drive to Cheyenne," he said, dropping to one knee beside Lucky. Excited by the attention, the bull terrier jumped up to lick his face, planting his large paws squarely on Jesse's shoulders and nearly knocking him to the ground.

Jim's laugh came out like a low rumble. "That dog ain't sure yet who's the boss, here. You gots to fix that problem 'fore you can take him on no drive."

"He knows I'm the boss," Jesse argued. "He can come, sit, and stay. He still has some puppy in him, that's all."

"All right then, Mr. Jesse." Jim grinned as if he still didn't believe a word of it, but wasn't going to force the issue. "I brought some jerky bits to give him as treats when he listens good. You been havin' him ride alongside that horse of yours, but you got him tied to the saddle. When he goes on a round-up or cattle drive, he ain't goin' to be tied up. He's got to know his job and get it done. So let's see how he does."

"All right," Jesse agreed, moving to saddle his mount.

Jim had already saddled his own, and now he pushed back his hat and leaned down to scratch Lucky behind the ears. Jesse couldn't make out the words, but he could hear the black man talking to the dog in a low, soothing voice.

Jesse had his doubts about the dog's readiness, but was hopeful Lucky could learn what he needed. He wasn't sure why it was so important that the dog come along, but it was.

He swung up into the saddle and rode over to Jim. "Mount up," he grinned. "We've got work to do."

Jim just shook his head and climbed up onto his roan stallion. "Let's see just *how much* work we gots to do."

"Come on," Jesse called to Lucky as he urged the appaloosa forward. Obediently, Lucky bounded forward, falling into step next to Jesse. He looked over at Jim with lifted eyebrows as if to say, "I told you so."

Three or four more steps, and something moving in the grass—a grasshopper or a prairie dog—caught Lucky's attention and he went bounding away after it.

"Umm-hmm," Jim laughed, his broad shoulders moving up and down with his laughter. "He well trained, that dog of yours."

"All right. What am I supposed to do?"

"Call him over to you, then give him one of these jerky bits," Jim passed him the bag of jerky. "Then, every few minutes he stays next to you, toss him another. He'll stick close to you if he knows you got treats for him."

Jesse did as Jim instructed, and Lucky stayed close, looking up at him expectantly as he pranced through the tall grass. His mouth hung open, and his sharp teeth were exposed in a happy dog grin. Jesse was just starting to think Lucky had mastered this skill, when off he went after another distraction. Jesse let out his breath in a frustrated sigh.

"That's all right. Just start over," Jim encouraged.

But every time they began again, Jesse couldn't keep Lucky's attention for more than five minutes. Then, to make matters worse, the dog refused to come when Jesse called him. He appeared to have something more enjoyable than beef jerky, and flopped down in the grass to chew it.

Jesse halted his mare and dismounted. *"Lucky! Get over here!"* he shouted angrily. He stomped over to where the dog lolled in the grass, a stick in his mouth. He took the animal by the collar and hauled him to his feet, pulling him back to where Jim and his mount waited.

"No good to be angry, Mr. Jesse. He's just a dog. You gots to be firm with him, but you gots to be gentle too. He don't understand what you's expectin' from him."

"Well, he should by now," Jesse replied through gritted teeth.

"Look, Mr. Jesse, he's just a dog, but I reckon he's a bit like a child. A good father gots to earn his children's respect, and he ain't gonna do that by yellin' at 'em. No suh. You gots to make more noise when he does *good* than when he does bad. Praise him when he's walking right. He gonna want to hear more praise from you, and he gonna try harder to please you. Just like a child, you gots *to earn his respect,* and he gonna do better than if you make him *fear* you."

Jesse let the wisdom of the Negro man's words sink in. He bet Jim Ingram had been a good father to his children. He glanced over at Jim, wondering if he was thinking of his children now too. Jesse couldn't imagine losing his wife and family the way Jim had. Planning to come back for them, to give them a better life, and never seeing them again.

Life was cruel to everyone, sooner or later, in one way or another. The measure of a man was how he met that cruelty, and Jesse wished he could say he had proven himself to be a man of strong character. The man beside him never grumbled or complained against life, against God, or even against white folks. Jim just did the best he could each day, and always with a smile.

Humbled by the strength of this man, who not only could lift three times as much as Jesse, but could endure three times as much hardship without complaint, Jesse simply nodded at his words and took a deep breath. He would try to emulate the patience he saw in Jim. He would try to earn Lucky's respect, and not simply demand it.

~

From the second level porch, Annette watched the distant figures of her husband and Jim as they worked to train Lucky. There was always something that needed to be done. Cleaning, cooking, laundry, ironing. But she didn't have the heart for it today. She'd known the odds were high Jesse would react to her invitation exactly as he had, but it didn't take away the sting of his rejection.

She leaned over the railing, watching him dismount and bring Lucky forcibly back to where his horse grazed. Lucky didn't appear to be doing very well with his training.

Annette watched, partly because she was curious how Lucky would do, but mostly because she wanted to see Jesse. It was silly perhaps, but she felt lonelier today than she had in a long time, and watching him took just a small sliver of that loneliness away.

Suddenly, an idea came to her. She spun on her heel and went down the stairs and out to the barn. She began to saddle Bella for a ride. Perhaps Sarah had returned from the reservation. Annette certainly hoped so, because she could greatly benefit from the woman's calm presence and wise counsel.

Leaving a note on the table for Jesse, in case he should return to the house before she did, she set off in the direction of the Gibson cabin. It was another bright, clear day and Annette tied a sunbonnet under her chin to protect her fair skin from the sun's rays. She thought of Sarah's brown face, and the way the color only enhanced her beauty. She wondered what she would look like if she quit wearing the bonnet and let the sun tan her face. Then smiled as she imagined her mother's reaction to such an idea.

Although the sun was high in the cerulean sky overhead, the air was brisk and Annette was thankful for the shawl draped over her shoulders. The summer's warmth was giving way to the coming of winter. The calendar read October, and she wondered if Jesse remembered they would soon be celebrating their first wedding anniversary.

She shook her head. No one would ever believe they had been married this long without sharing the intimacies of husband and wife. She could hardly believe it herself. And although she knew it was most likely because of Jesse's insecurities about himself, she still wondered if it wasn't partly because he didn't believe she was worthy. She told herself her past had nothing to do with his reticence, but what man would want a girl who just gave her innocence away to a married man like it was a worthless gift?

I'm so sorry, Lord. I sinned against You, against my own body, against Vivian, and even against Jesse, as my future husband. I know You've forgiven me, I just wish I could be free of this regret. Every time I remember, and every time I'm confronted with the consequences, I just wish I had done it differently when I'd had the chance. It was a shameful act, and so I do feel ashamed. But I know You've forgiven me. Please help me to take comfort in Your forgiveness and let go of the guilt.

A breeze stirred the tall prairie grass around her as the little black mare moved steadily across the open plain, and she felt the soft touch of it against her skin. God's presence seemed almost tangible around her, and she smiled her gratitude. She wasn't alone.

She longed to tell Sarah how the words she'd shared from the Bible had made such a difference in her life, but to do so would be to admit she had committed adultery. And while it was possible that Sarah already knew, that Vivian had told her, Annette wasn't sure she wanted to risk losing her friendship. It was difficult to imagine Sarah would have chosen to be her friend if she had known the truth about her from the beginning.

Shame once again began to whisper darkness in her ear—words of worthlessness and guilt. But Annette fought against it with this knowledge: *I'm forgiven. That is what matters.*

As the Gibson's cabin came into view, Annette noted it seemed smaller and more rustic than she remembered. She had gotten used to her own magnificent home, a virtual mansion set in the middle of the prairie. And while it may not make her love Jesse any more, she had to admit she certainly appreciated it.

The first thing Annette noticed as she approached the cabin was the absolute silence. Then as her eyes darted about, she saw there were weeds in the vegetable garden, a layer of mud and dirt on the front porch, and a film of dust covering the glass windows. There was her answer.

Nonetheless, she tethered Bella to a post on the front porch and knocked on the door. She wasn't surprised when she received no answer. Frank was probably out checking on the cattle.

With a heavy sigh, she turned to leave. She paused, looking about the place one last time. She wondered how Frank was managing without his wife and children. Sarah had been gone for close to three months. A long time to choose to be away from her husband.

Annette bowed her head and prayed for Sarah once more, then added another prayer for Frank and the children. She turned to mount Bella, wishing there was something she could do for this dear family who had given so much to her and Jesse.

As she urged Bella toward home, she spotted a rider in the distance. Deciding to take a gamble that it was Frank, she flicked the reins and turned Bella in his direction.

He tipped his hat in greeting and called out to her as soon as she was in earshot. But as he neared, Annette was appalled at the man's appearance. He was positively gaunt, and it didn't look as if he had bothered to shave or trim his hair since his wife had left him. His beard was entirely white, and she didn't remember his hair being so silver. He barely resembled the man Annette remembered. He looked old and worn out.

"Frank," Annette forced a smile, "it's good to see you. How are you faring?" she asked, although the answer was obvious.

"Not well," he admitted, reaching up to run a hand over his whiskered face. "I don't know what I did that was so wrong to send her away," he admitted, and the raw pain in his eyes cut Annette's heart.

"You didn't do anything wrong, Frank," she assured him.

"Well, I guess I didn't do anything right either," he concluded.

Annette remembered Sarah's words about Frank not understanding her grief, about going to her mother where it would be understood. She could only meet Frank's gaze with sympathy. There were no words that could remove his pain.

"Why don't you come home with me tonight and I'll fix you some supper," she offered.

"Thanks, Annette, but I'm not much company these days."

"She'll be back soon," Annette promised, although she could only hope her statement was true.

Frank nodded slowly. "I know. Soon."

Then he tipped his hat and nudged his mount toward the cabin. "Good evenin'," he called over his shoulder as he rode away.

Annette stared after him, noting the defeated slope of his shoulders. She truly hoped Sarah and the children did return soon. For Frank's sake, and for the sake of the entire Gibson family.

Chapter Twenty-Seven

*A*nother sleepless night. Jesse threw back the covers, secured his prosthesis into place, and pulled on his pants and boots. He needed some air.

Leaping from his place at the foot of the bed, Lucky wagged his tail as he joined Jesse on the porch. He flopped down on the white painted floorboards, resting his chin on his master's boot.

Jesse leaned his elbows on the railing, taking a ragged breath as he ran a hand through his disheveled hair. He wasn't sure which troubled him more: the awareness that he had pushed his wife away when she reached out to him, or the knowledge that there was a rustler getting rich on his beef.

His mind raced with memories of Annette's blond hair in the candlelight, only to be followed by the image of Harvey's wide, friendly smile. For a brief moment it had seemed that both love and success were within his grasp. Now it seemed they were both threatened.

Jesse closed his eyes, breathing in the sweet smell of the midnight prairie. *Lord, You've brought me this far. You've brought me and Annette this far. Show me how to walk the rest of the way, to hold on to what You've given me.*

Straightening, he gazed out at the rolling plains, steeped in dark shadows. Letting out a sigh, he stood and took a step toward his bedroom door. But a strange sound stopped him in his tracks. He listened and heard it again.

Lucky heard it too, looking up at him with his brown ears cocked in curiosity.

A cry of pain. The cry a cow made when its hide was seared with a hot iron.

Peering into the darkness, Jesse's eyes searched the horizon until they fixed on a small spark of light in the distance. A flickering, dancing orange light, like the flames of a campfire.

Hastily throwing on his shirt, Jesse buttoned it as he moved carefully down the stairs, a candle in his hands. Lucky followed eagerly at his heels. He paused at the exit to the kitchen to don his leather duster and clamp his Stetson on his head, tied the dog up, then ran toward the bunkhouse.

"Claude! Rattlesnake! Jim! Wake up!" he cried, turning the key to the oil lamp on the table and illuminating the room in a pale yellow glow.

"What is it?" Claude pushed himself up onto his elbow, squinting against the brightness.

"There's a campfire out there. I think he's branding my cattle."

Without another word, all three men sprang from their cots and reached for their boots. Jesse darted to the barn to saddle his horse.

Within minutes, the four men were making their way into the vast emptiness of the black night with their rifles in their scabbards. In his mind's eye, Jesse tried to visualize where he had seen that small prick of light in the distance and how he could lead them to it. If he hadn't stepped out onto the porch, he would never have been able to see the telltale flames of their fire. But from that vantage point, he could see for miles.

His heart thudded in his chest. If he was capable of leading them to the rustlers, they would have to approach in complete silence or give away the advantage of surprise. They would have to catch Simons and Harper with the hot irons in their hands, to prove their guilt, and then secure the thieves before they slipped away into the night shadows.

Jesse prayed his mount could see where she stepped in the darkness and kept her footing, because he had no choice but to trust her judgment as she plodded forward into the inky blackness. He began to question his sense of direction, fearing he had led his men astray and lost the opportunity to apprehend the rustlers. A cold sweat broke out on his forehead and upper lip. He might not have another chance.

Then, to his profound relief, a faint circle of light came into view as they crested a rise in the rolling landscape. Without a word, they stopped as one.

The men looked to him for leadership. He pointed to Claude and Rattlesnake, then indicated for them to ride around to the right. He pointed to himself and Jim, then gestured that they would close the gap to the left.

His heart caught in his throat at the creak of his saddle as he leaned forward to pull his rifle from its scabbard. He cocked the hammer, feeling the cold steel against his thigh as he rested the barrel across his lap.

It took every bit of restraint he possessed to keep the appaloosa to a slow, steady walk as he looped in wide arc around the rustlers, hanging back in the shadows. Then, when he saw his men were in position, he gave the signal and they all sprang forward to surround the two cowboys.

Harper's knee was pressed into the cow's shoulder,

sprawled on the ground with all four hooves bound to immobilize her. Simons leaned across her broad back, the running iron glowing red as he pressed it into the animal's hide. She bawled angrily in protest.

When they jumped back and released the wounded creature, they found themselves staring into the barrels of Jesse and Jim's rifles. Spinning around to flee, they realized they were hemmed in on the other side by Claude and Rattlesnake. Trapped, they lifted their hands in the air to signal their surrender.

"Tie them up," Claude barked.

Jim and Rattlesnake sprang to obey, while Jesse and Claude kept their sights trained on the thieves. But as the two men lowered their weapons and reached for their rope, Simons leapt into action, using the branding iron to knock Claude's rifle to the ground. Harper whirled toward Jesse, aiming to take him off guard and wrest the barrel of his rifle from his grasp.

But Jesse reacted instinctively to the charge and lifted the barrel forcefully into the thief's scraggly chin, sending Harper reeling backward. Jim and Rattlesnake pounced upon the two criminals, and they soon found themselves face down in the grass, bound by their wrists and ankles almost as they had imprisoned the cow moments before. Claude pressed his boot into Harvey Simons' back and spit on the ground, just inches from his face.

"What do you have to say for yourselves?" Jesse demanded, noticing that Harvey had lost his cocky grin.

He scowled at Jesse, but made no reply.

"They've nothing to say in their defense," Claude declared, eyeing them spitefully. "I say we get some rest and deal with them in the morning. Rattlesnake, you want first watch?"

"Sure, boss," the Englishman answered, settling down by the fire with his rifle across his knee.

Jesse, Claude and Jim unsaddled their horses, spreading their saddle blankets out around the campfire as makeshift cots and propping their heads against the leather saddles. Exhausted, Jesse lay down and closed his eyes, listening to the fire popping and crackling as the logs were consumed.

But, as weary as his body was, he found his mind would not quiet. The pursuit through the dark of night, then the sight of the two cowboys illegally branding his cattle and the fight which had ensued, replayed in his mind.

Thank you, Lord, he prayed, relieved that the rustlers had been apprehended and his hard earned investment had been saved.

Since he'd never mentioned his suspicions and concerns to Annette, she would wonder why he didn't come down for breakfast in the morning. It had never occurred to him to leave her a note of explanation. There hadn't been time.

Thinking of what the morning would bring sent a cold chill down his spine. He would be responsible for ensuring that the thieves were hung for their crimes. There was no denying their guilt. No need for either judge or jury, nor were such lengthy and legal alternatives available in this rugged wilderness. Justice would be served swiftly and surely.

Jesse rolled onto his side, watching the orange flames lick at the burning logs which had heated the running iron used for stealing his cattle. Right out from under his nose.

He sighed in frustration. He wished he didn't feel this

nagging sense of…

Of what? Obligation?

He glanced over at the cattle rustlers, leaning against one another, watching Rattlesnake for any sign of weakness. Jesse's rifle was within easy reach, should the cowhand be overtaken with drowsiness and nod his head. Jesse knew no sleep would come to him this night.

Everyone had a story, Jesse had learned. Behind every decision was a history and a past. A longing or a heartache. What was Simons' and Harper's story? What had prompted the men to take such a gamble, to believe it was wiser to steal another man's cattle than to take the time to build their own herd? To risk losing everything, even their lives?

He remembered his own overwhelming need to prove himself when he enlisted in the Union army as a sixteen year old boy. An awkward youth, unsure of himself and tripping over his own big feet, he had tried to follow in his brothers' footsteps. He'd desperately wanted to feel worthwhile, to be a gallant soldier and not a mere boy left behind with the womenfolk. And when he couldn't *be* that brave war hero he'd wanted to be, he'd settled for being *perceived* as one.

Yet God had forgiven him. If Providence did not withhold forgiveness from anyone—if Jesus made salvation possible for *all mankind* regardless of the sin they committed—then it was possible even for a man like Harvey Simons.

Jesse closed his eyes and turned away.

He was grateful for the second chance he'd been given. For the freedom he'd found. But to offer it to these thieves was out of the question. They deserved their fate.

Movement on the other side of the fire startled him into an upright position. It was only Rattlesnake looking for someone to take over his watch. Jesse nodded at him to indicate that he would take the next shift. Reaching for his rifle, he came to his feet and traded positions with Rattlesnake Rupert.

Settling down on the ground a few feet away from the rustlers, he studied their sagging postures. Their shoulders pressed into one another, bare heads touching. Simon's tall, thin frame was bent against the weight of his companion's thick form. Orange firelight danced over their dusty figures and gleamed on the dome of Harper's bald head. Although they were clearly worn out, they still had enough strength to glare at him with black resentment.

"Why'd you do it?" Jesse heard himself pose the question, surprised as they were by the tone of curiosity softening the inquiry.

Harvey Simons spat into the grass at his side, then released a string of vulgar profanities. His thick dark hair hung around his face, which might have been handsome when wearing a smile, but now was contorted into a violent scowl.

Jesse found an odd compassion overtaking him as he met the young man's hateful gaze. What drove a man to such a place?

"We all get lost sometimes," he said. "Make mistakes. How'd it happen to you?" he wondered.

"Mind your own business," George Harper growled, his bearded face cast in shifting shadows.

"I wanted to be like my brothers," Jesse continued.

Simons spit again. "Spare me the sob story. I don't need

319

your sympathy."

"Don't you want a second chance?"

"What? You gonna set us free?" Simons lifted his eyebrow in a defiant arch. Another foul expletive followed.

"They're going to hang you in the morning," he reminded the prisoners quietly.

"What's it to you?" Simons retorted.

"Nothing. But I thought it might mean something to you."

More curses.

"If you were given the chance to be forgiven, you wouldn't take it? Start over, do things right?" he pushed, baffled by their spiteful response to his offer.

"What's your problem?" Simons sneered. "I was gonna end up with close to half your herd. That would've put a pretty good dent in your profits."

Jesse shrugged. "I ran from my past for a long time, till I learned I was forgiven. I just thought anyone would want the same chance."

"Well, ain't you sweet?" Harper scoffed.

Jesse drew his booted feet closer to rest his elbows on his knees, the rifle still secure in his grasp. He fell silent, watching the men before him with profound sadness. He'd never imagined that Pride could be such a demanding taskmaster. That it could lead one to the brink of a cliff, then push him right over the edge when deliverance was offered.

Accepting the responsibility they had given him to see to their execution, Jesse felt no need for further conversation. They had been given a chance. They had chosen their fate.

Jim stirred, then came to sit beside Jesse. "I'll take the next watch, suh."

Jesse had a suspicion the Negro had overheard his dialogue with the thieves. He nodded and moved to stand, but Jim stopped him with a hand on his shoulder.

"Sometimes, there just ain't no other way," he acknowledged gruffly, his dark eyes solemn.

Jesse nodded once in agreement, then went to lay down on Jim's abandoned bedroll. He closed his eyes, but knew rest wouldn't come.

Jim was right. Forgiveness could be extended, but it had to be accepted.

By the time the rosy hues of dawn began to push back the purple twilight, Jesse's head ached with weariness and dread for the somber duty awaiting him. Claude had taken the last watch, and he sat with his rifle trained on the rustlers, slumped together in a defeated heap.

They knew their time was up. Any chance for escape was gone.

Silently, Jesse and his men saddled their horses and mounted up. Simons and Harper walked on foot behind them, Jim and Claude leading them by the ropes tied to their wrists. Rattlesnake led their horses.

About a mile away was a bend in the creek where a small copse of trees grew. That was where they headed.

They halted under the tallest, thickest cottonwood. A pall of gloom surrounded them as they prepared for their unwelcome task. Jim and Jesse took charge of the prisoners while Rattlesnake and Claude prepared two nooses. Then the men were assisted onto the bare backs of their horses and positioned under the dangling ropes.

The knots were loosened and lowered over their heads, only to be tightened under their chins. Simons' eyes briefly met Jesse's, and he saw the fear that blanched the young man's face of color. For a brief second, doubt and regret shadowed his gaze, then it turned cold and empty. The thief braced himself for the end.

~

The afternoon sun was high in the sky by the time Jesse was able to ride for home. The outlaws had been buried in unmarked graves, left to the merciless ways of nature and the relentless passage of time. Grass would grow over the loose earth, disguising the place where they lay. They would be forgotten, given up to obscurity forever, almost as if they'd never been.

There had been no one to mourn their passing, no one to shed tears or remember better times.

It reminded Jesse how thin the thread was that separated life from death, how fleeting the moments of breath on the earth. It made him think about the things that would matter to him when his time came to leave this world behind.

And when he imagined himself on his deathbed, he knew it wasn't his worldly achievements that would occupy his thoughts. How large his herd, how hefty his bank account, or how grand his house. It would be matters of the heart and soul that would entertain his thoughts.

Annette's pert nose and long eyelashes appeared in his

mind's eye.

He yawned, fighting to stay upright in the saddle as exhaustion overwhelmed him. The welcome sight of his home shimmered brightly in the distance, the sun reflecting on its white siding. He longed for the softness of his bed, the blessedness of sleep.

But first, he would sit down in the kitchen and grab a bite to eat while he told his wife the story of the night's adventure. Jesse wanted her to know that he was willing to protect their future, their interests, and their marriage against anything that might threaten to destroy it.

He didn't know how, but he would find a way to win her back.

Chapter Twenty-Eight

A week had passed since what Jesse had come to think of as *the night*. The night he had made a fool of himself, the night he had forfeited sharing the marriage bed, but perhaps most importantly, the night Annette had declared her love for him.

It was a shame she had to do it with her voice raised in anger. But Jesse was just grateful to have finally heard those words: *"All I want is you!"* He shook his head. He could almost understand it, but not entirely. He knew she felt indebted to him for marrying her and saving her from public shame and a life of spinsterhood. And they'd always enjoyed a comfortable friendship. She'd seemed quite impressed with the way he'd captured the cattle rustlers.

But that she would want to kiss him, to touch him, to be *intimate* with him... he just couldn't fully comprehend it.

He reached up to feel the way the skin tugged at the corner of his mouth, the way it ran a jagged trail up to his eye. He wasn't exactly a good looking man. But he kept thinking about what she'd said about having the pox. She's said if her faced was marred, he would believe her words. And she was right. He had been blinded both by her beauty and by his own pride.

Annette had become quiet and withdrawn, and Jesse knew she was waiting for him to reach out to her. And he wanted to— desperately. He just couldn't quite move past the fear that still immobilized him. He couldn't even explain what it was he feared, since he knew she wouldn't reject him. But every time he thought of going to her, he found he couldn't.

One time, he had made it as far as the hallway before returning to his own room, heart pounding.

But he could feel her drifting away from him, and he knew it was his responsibility to draw her close again. And there was only one way to do that. He needed to prove he did in fact love and want *her*, not just her face or her body, but all of her.

Dear God, he prayed, *give me the courage to overcome the disgust and shame I feel. Help me to see myself through her eyes, and to let go of pride. I need You to lead me in this, show me how to woo her and to make her feel cherished. Because I don't want to hurt or disappoint her anymore.*

He glanced over at her, silently eating her breakfast of eggs, bacon and biscuits.

Jesse reached for the another biscuit as he said, "Nettie, I'm going into town with the men to get some supplies for the round-up. I'd invite you along, but it won't be a pleasure trip."

She nodded, but he saw the doubt in her blue eyes. He hoped she didn't think he was afraid she would run into Bryan again. He realized now he had no reason to feel threatened by the man—whether or not it really made any sense to him. No, the real reason he didn't want her to come was because he intended to buy a gift for her for their first anniversary. And he wanted it to be a surprise.

Annette seemed lost in her own pensive thoughts, and Jesse hated leaving her that way. "Is there anything you want me to pick up for you while I'm in town?" he asked.

She looked at him briefly and shook her head before she

resumed eating. Jesse sighed. He was going to make things right.

"Thank you for breakfast," he said. Another nod. "I'll be back late tonight."

"Have a good trip," she managed.

"I'll see you tonight," Jesse said, wishing he could kiss her cheek before he left, but still feeling awkward about initiating any kind of physical contact.

He picked up his plate and fork and deposited them in the washbasin next to the pump, then retrieved his hat from the peg by the door. "Bye, Nettie," he said, still hoping for something more from her. But all she could offer was a sad smile.

Jesse paused to pat Lucky on the head before he went out to the barn, where the men were already waiting for him. The wagon was hitched and ready to go, and Rattlesnake and Jim were situated in the bed. Lucky was tied up, and he strained against the rope and whined at being left behind.

"You driving today or am I?" his ranch foreman asked.

"You go ahead, Claude," Jesse answered, climbing into the bed. "I'll just enjoy the ride."

"You do that," Claude Montgomery retorted, as he gave the reins a gentle shake and the wheels creaked forward.

Jesse settled back against the hard wooden frame and watched the prairie grass sway in their wake. The sky was dotted with clouds, but they were thin and wispy, and didn't portend a sudden change in weather. October in the Wyoming Territory could be volatile, and winter storms could blow in unexpectedly. He only hoped the clear, mild weather would hold out for the remainder of the week.

His thoughts drifted to Frank Gibson. Annette had said the man was looking like a ghost of himself, and Jesse had to admit he hadn't run into him as often as he used to. He wondered if Frank was still checking on his cattle, and if he was just being careful to avoid any run-ins. He felt sorry for the man. He'd been through a lot. He tried not to judge Sarah for her decision to leave, but it just didn't feel right to him.

Although he was beginning to understand that men and women just didn't see life the same way. So Frank's inability to understand Sarah's feelings of grief wasn't much of a surprise.

When they reached town, he told the men that he had some errands to run and suggested they meet back in an hour to purchase what was needed for the drive. The men nodded and took off in the direction of the saloon. Jesse shook his head and looked around. He wanted to stop by the post office to check if any letters from home had arrived, but he also wanted to buy a gift for Annette. He only wished he had some idea what she would appreciate.

He set off toward the dressmaker's shop, hoping something there would suffice. He didn't want to just get Annette *something*. He wanted it to be truly special.

As he walked past the jeweler's, he came to a sudden stop. When she had come to town with him, he remembered her attention had been drawn to the window display as they had walked by. He had noticed the way her eyes had lingered over each and every piece of jewelry, and she had almost leaned in to study them. She had clearly been pleased with the brooch he'd given her the night before their wedding.

He smiled as he imagined Annette's expression when she opened the gift box.

Entering the store, Jesse was immediately approached by a young man. "How can I help you today? Is there something in particular you would like to see?"

Jesse tried to ignore the way the salesman's eyes skimmed over his scar before darting away uncomfortably. The young man pasted a pleasant smile on his face and waited for Jesse's response.

He glanced around. His gaze settled on a case of glittering rings. Only the wealthy wore wedding rings, and it hadn't even entered Jesse's mind when they married. But unlike a brooch, a ring was something Nettie would see every time she looked down at her hands to wash dishes, scrub floors or mend his socks. It would be a constant reminder of his devotion to her.

He approached the glass case and peered inside. "That one," he said, pointing to a golden ring with a gemstone the same shade of blue as her eyes.

The salesman retrieved the ring and dropped it into Jesse's palm. "That's called aquamarine."

"How much for it?"

Jesse swallowed as the man answered. But he replied, "I'll take it."

"It's for my wife," he added, as the young man situated the ring into a velvet lined box. He didn't know why he had felt compelled to reveal that trivial detail. The man only nodded and smiled politely. Jesse supposed he wanted the young salesman to know that despite his scarred face, he'd found a woman who loved him. A woman who saw beyond the surface and thought he was worth her heart.

He found a smile was hovering over his lips as he replayed

those treasured words again in his memory: *"All I want is you."*

"Thank you," he smiled as he accepted the ring box, tucked into a bag displaying the jeweler's name. He had never imagined the simple knowledge that he was loved could be so transforming. Annette's love gave him new courage, new confidence, and even new hope.

He was going to be the husband she deserved. He would figure out how.

~

It was all Jesse could do to keep the ring a surprise over the next three days. He had hidden it in his coat pocket until he could situate it safely in his room, and then he had to think of a place she wouldn't find it when putting his clothing away or cleaning. He had finally concealed it in an old cigar box in the bottom of his wardrobe, where he kept all of the letters from home.

The morning of their first wedding anniversary, he could hardly keep his excitement contained. He hadn't felt this eager to give a gift since the Christmas he was eight years old and he had worked with his father's tools to make a jewelry box for his mother.

He went to the kitchen and found Annette already at work stoking the flames in the cast iron stove.

"Good morning," he said cheerfully.

She replied with less enthusiasm, barely looking up from her task. Jesse went to feed and milk the dairy cow, care for the chickens and gather eggs, and to join the men in feeding the horses. Then he hurried back to the house.

Breakfast was already waiting for him on the table, along

with a steaming cup of coffee. "Thank you, Nettie," he said, sliding into his chair and taking a swallow.

"I hope you didn't forget," he finally said, trying to calm the wild beating of his heart. Her blond eyebrows shot up, and the hope he saw flicker in her blue eyes made the cost of the ring in his coat pocket worthwhile. "Happy anniversary," he grinned.

"Oh Jesse," she smiled, as if the gift had already been given. She blinked away tears. "Happy anniversary."

"I was thinking," he said, buttering his biscuits liberally, "that we should go for a ride today. It's a bit cool, but the real winter weather hasn't hit yet."

He watched her eyes dart to the window, and was grateful for the warm rays of dawn filtering through the glass panes. It was going to be another clear day.

She looked back at him and nodded. "I would like that, Jesse."

He smiled, knowing his face gave away the secret that there was more to come and hoping she would notice it. He wanted her to enjoy this day, and anticipation was part of the fun.

"Why don't you pack a lunch for us? That way we don't have to hurry back."

"All right," she agreed. He saw the curiosity in her expression, but she didn't give voice to it.

Breakfast seemed to disappear faster than usual, and Jesse went to saddle the horses while Annette cleaned up the dishes. He returned to the kitchen to find her shrugging into her coat. Another item, he noticed, that could use replacing.

She reached for her scarf. "Are you ready?"

Her eagerness made him smile.

"Where are we going?" she finally asked.

Jesse offered his elbow and escorted her to the barn. "I found a special place that I want to show you. The other day, I was riding out to check on the cattle and I went further south than usual because that's where the cattle had wandered. And I found this spot where the creek shoots off from the Powder River and runs downhill over a course of jagged rocks, making a waterfall. I thought you would like to see it."

"Oh, I would!" she exclaimed, slipping her foot into the stirrup and mounting her little black mare.

"It's a long ride," he warned.

"Beats scrubbing the floor," she laughed. "Which is what I had planned for the day."

Jesse grinned. He loved the way her smile lit up her entire face and made her eyes sparkle with warmth. He noticed again their hue and was certain the stone called "aquamarine" matched it perfectly.

They spent the hours of the morning riding side by side over the miles and miles of open prairie. They passed herds of cattle, grazing on the hillsides and growing fat for market. Sometimes they rode in silence, but most of the time they shared easy conversation. Jesse knew he could never tire of the sound of her voice or the sight of her face.

When they reached a certain point, Jesse halted and Annette did likewise. She looked at him quizzically. He held up his hand for silence.

"Listen," he whispered.

In the distance, a low rumble could be heard, different from the rumbling and moaning of cattle.

"Is that it?" she asked, pushing back her sunbonnet in order to hear better.

"It will get louder as we get closer," Jesse told her. "It's the sound of the water rushing over the rocks."

When the full scope of the falls came into view, it wasn't the wild grandeur of nature that captivated Jesse, but the awe and wonder on his wife's face.

"Oh Jesse," she exclaimed, looking at him with wide-eyed delight. "It's beautiful!"

Jesse reined his mare in and dismounted, and Annette followed suit. They tethered the horses to the limb of an aspen growing along the bank of the rushing creek.

Procuring a blanket from his saddle bag, Jesse spread it out on a flat rock overlooking the pool into which the water splashed. Jesse sat down and indicated for her to take a seat beside him. She settled onto the blanket, tucking her feet under her skirt.

The water churned white as it flowed over the jagged layers of rock, foaming and spraying as it collided with the water below. It was indeed a spectacular sight, and the only regret Jesse had was the noise it created.

"Nettie," he said, having to raise his voice to be heard above the rushing water. "I want you to remember this day, as we celebrate our first year of marriage."

She smiled tremulously. "Thank you, Jesse."

"I have a gift for you," he said as he reached into his coat pocket. He opened the jeweler's box and held it in front of her.

She gasped, staring down at its contents in disbelief. "It's exquisite!" she whispered.

Annette looked up at him in sudden chagrin. "But I don't have a gift for you!"

Jesse lifted his left hand to gently graze her cheek with his knuckle. *"All I want is you,"* he echoed her declaration.

Tears pooled in her eyes, then spilled over to leave glistening rivulets on her cheeks. Jesse removed the ring from the box and slipped it onto the third finger of her left hand. "This is your wedding ring. To remind you how much you mean to me."

"Thank you," she held out her hand in front of her to examine the ring on her finger. "Thank you, Jesse," she repeated, turning her gaze to his.

He had been right. The color of the gemstone did match her eyes.

The love he saw in the way her gaze moved tenderly over his face gave him courage. He leaned forward, cupping her jaw in his hand. And to his great joy, she leaned forward to meet him halfway. Her lips were so soft against his, and he let his hand slip from her jaw to the back of her neck, his fingers tangling in her hair.

When he heard her breath catch, he realized his own pulse was thundering in his ears and a fire he had never felt before was burning inside him. He pulled away, searching her eyes and finding only longing there. He smiled, touching her lower lip with his thumb.

Suddenly his concerns about the night ahead receded, replaced instead by eagerness. He reached to put an arm around her shoulders and drew her against him. She leaned into him, and he heard a sigh of contentment escape her lips.

He closed his eyes, hardly able to believe his good fortune. *God, I know I've done nothing to deserve either your forgiveness or her love. But I'm so grateful for them both!*

Suddenly, all he wanted was to be close to her. It was intoxicating. He leaned over to kiss her cheek. "Would you like me to get the lunch? I left it in the saddlebags."

She nodded, and Jesse went to retrieve the cold sandwiches and water canteen, then quickly reclaimed his place by her side. He felt the warmth and softness of her shoulder as she leaned against him, and he smiled.

They spent another hour at the waterfall after lunch, climbing the rocks near the falls as well as clambering down the slope to the rippling pool below. Jesse didn't say so, but he planned to bring her back next summer and convince her to swim with him. It was a secluded and peaceful spot, perfect for such a sport.

Jesse held Annette's hand as she hopped from one slick rock to another, laughing with her when he lost his balance and nearly toppled into the cool water. They were having such a wonderful time, Jesse was reluctant to end it. But he had more plans for the evening, and he knew they would run out of daylight if they lingered overlong.

As they traveled back the way they had come, they rode in companionable silence. Annette smiled as he glanced her way, and Jesse was certain nothing would ever be the same. In that moment, he knew his life had changed forever. He finally understand what it meant to love and to be loved.

Dusk was beginning to fall on the prairie by the time they returned home. Even the sunset complied with Jesse's wishes and made a spectacular display of vivid color, splashing hues of violet and crimson across the great canvas of the sky. They paused and dismounted, standing hand in hand together and watching as the streaks of color shifted to darker shades and eventually gave way to nightfall.

They walked together to the barn, where Jesse took the horses and Annette went into the house to prepare dinner. Lucky was delighted by their return, and Annette paused to kneel down and scratch his ears and receive sloppy kisses on her hands. From the barn, Jesse smiled at the picture they presented.

He quickly curried, watered, and fed the horses, then went inside to wash for supper. Annette served reheated biscuits and salted pork, with squash and carrots retrieved from the root cellar.

"Did you enjoy the day?" he asked, having finished his first plate and reaching for seconds.

She nodded and smiled, offering him another biscuit. "Thank you for a wonderful and memorable day, Jesse. It was very special."

Reaching across the table, Jesse brought her hand to his lips. He swallowed, suddenly feeling nervous again. "It was a good day," he agreed.

While he helped her clean the dishes, his mind searched for clever and romantic ways to suggest they bypass the evening ritual of reading and mending and instead go straight to the bedroom. The bedroom he hoped they would share from now on.

Unable to think of any words, he simply caught her hand as she turned to exit the kitchen. She looked up at him with surprised and questioning eyes. Jesse caressed the line of her jaw, then slowly brought his mouth down to hers. Their second kiss was as sweet as the first. Jesse drank of her deeply, drawing her against him and feeling the thud of her heart against his chest.

"Come upstairs with me," he whispered against her mouth. "I want to be your husband."

She giggled. "You *are* my husband."

"You know what I mean," he almost growled, pulling the pins from her hair and watching the golden strands tumble down around her shoulders. He wove his fingers into the silken mass, which smelled faintly of lavender soap.

She wound her arms around his neck and pulled him closer to her, lifting her chin into the kiss. New desires sparked inside of Jesse, and he felt a combination of fear and exhilaration. "I've never... I mean, I don't know how..." he let the words trail off, embarrassed by his own incompetence.

"It doesn't matter, Jesse," she whispered into his ear, kissing his neck. "We'll discover this love together."

He tried not to think of her sharing a bed with another man, but the thought rose unwelcome to his mind. But as she began to unbutton his shirt and looked up at him with big, blue eyes full of adoration and desire, Jesse realized it didn't matter. That was the past. This was now.

She was his.

Chapter Twenty-Nine

Morning light slanted across the wood floor and cut a path through the shadows, spilling across Annette's closed eyelids. She blinked, covering her face with her hand. As the fog of dreams receded, she remembered the surprise of the night before and rolled over to find her husband still lying beside her.

His sandy blond hair fell across his forehead and his hand was tucked under his cheek like a little boy. She smiled tenderly as she watched the gentle rise and fall of his breathing. They were finally one, as God had intended.

Whatever Jesse had lacked in finesse, he had made up for in sincerity. Annette warmed at the memory of the way he had whispered his love for her over and over again, making every touch an act of reverence and not of mere passion. It had truly been a night to remember.

She wished it could have been her first experience with a man. For a few brief seconds she had been haunted by memories of Ricky Lawson. But Jesse's fervent devotion demanded her full attention and there was no room for memories. Only the present mattered, only this sweet and tender moment with a man who belonged to her and her alone.

In His wisdom and in His timing, God had been at work in both of their hearts to make them ready to fully love one another. Although she had felt confused and rejected by Jesse in the beginning of their marriage, she understood now that it had been a combination of his insecurity *and* his respect for her that had kept him away.

And Annette was glad they had waited until coming together was an act of love that honored their marriage and God, and was more than just a physical act of desire or obligation. She knew from her own experience that there was a decided difference between the two acts, even though they might appear the same.

The sunlight bathed the bed in golden light, and she leaned up onto one elbow to cast a shadow on Jesse's sleeping face. She wasn't ready yet for him to awaken. She wanted to savor this moment while he was unaware of the scrutiny.

She longed to reach out and gently trace the pink skin that formed his scar, cutting through the entirety of his right cheek. But she was afraid it would wake him, and so she merely studied him, the way his eyelashes fell across his cheeks, the contours of his nose and chin.

When she had first met him, all she had seen was his scar. Now all she saw was Jesse Stone, a handsome man who happened to have a scar on his cheek.

Everyone had scars, she realized. Some were visible for the world to see, while others were hidden deep within. Only Jesse and Vivian—and perhaps Sarah—knew of the scars she secretly carried. The rest of the world assumed because they couldn't see her scars, they didn't exist. They assumed that because she had been blessed with a comely face and a lovely form, her life was somehow charmed. Far from it, she thought. Her beauty had been the cause of her pain.

Her beauty and her own foolishness. She had failed to know her own value, had failed to save her heart and her body for a man who would love her forever.

But thanks to the inexplicable compassion of Providence, her past was forgiven. Though she didn't deserve it, she had been given a chance to know both her own value and Jesse's. She had finally been given the eyes to see beyond both their scars.

His eyelids began to flutter, and his gray eyes slowly opened, registering first confusion, then uncertainty. Annette leaned down to kiss his right cheek, pressing her lips against the scar that he had so long attempted to hide from her eyes. She smiled at him, offering reassurance of his place in her heart.

Jesse returned her smile sheepishly, then opened his arms, inviting her to nestle against him. The warmth and tenderness of his embrace was like a long-awaited balm to her heart, and she sighed as she pressed her cheek into his bare chest.

"I love you, Jesse Stone," she whispered.

He pressed a kiss into the crown of her head. "And I love you, Nettie."

~

That very day, Jesse moved his belongings from the spare room into the master bedroom. He hung his clothes next to Annette's in the wardrobe, and placed his comb in the drawer of her vanity next to her hairbrush.

He took every opportunity to kiss her cheek, hold her hand, or touch her shoulder. She was his wife, and he gloried in that awareness. Not because she was a gorgeous woman, but because she was the woman he loved.

Sharing a bed with her, however, came at a price. Annette

refused to allow Lucky to sleep with them. And although Jesse regretted the mandate, it wasn't much of a contest choosing between his wife and his dog. He put a blanket down in front of the fireplace and urged the animal to sleep there. It took the bull terrier several nights of whining outside the door to finally realize the rules had changed.

Jim had suggested Lucky wasn't quite ready to join the men on the round-up this year, and although Jesse was disappointed, he didn't want the dog to be a distraction or a detriment. The time flew by, and soon enough it was time to round up the herds for sorting and branding.

Jesse couldn't help but smile at his reflection in the mirror. Since coming to Wyoming, he had filled out with muscle and looked far more solid than he ever had. His skin had a healthy, ruddy color to it, and he looked every inch the cattleman he was. He placed the Stetson on his head, adjusting the collar of his leather duster. When he walked, the spurs on his boots jangled. He wished his mother, sisters and brothers could see the man he had become.

The cowboy staring back at him in the mirror bore little resemblance to the pale, thin fellow who had boarded the train in Springfield, Massachusetts. Not only in appearance, but in character. That young man had been out to prove himself through the acquisition of wealth and prestige, running away from his past and the guilt that dogged his heels. Now he understood that contentment came through having a relationship with a Heavenly Father and from the act of giving selflessly to another human being. He enjoyed the things that money bought for him, but he realized now those weren't the things that brought him joy.

He laughed. The pasty kid in a linen suit and bowler who had left Springfield was terrified of women and would never have imagined one day being married to the sweetest woman in the territory. Jesse shook his head, remembering how he hadn't had a clue what to do after they got married. Now they took every opportunity to hug and kiss and anything else time allowed.

He smiled again. And even though the skin puckered around his mouth, he continued to look in the mirror and grin. Because it didn't matter anymore.

Jesse went down to the kitchen where Nettie was preparing a bag of biscuits and salted pork for him to take with him. It was going to be a long day.

She kissed his cheek and whispered, "Be careful. I'll see you tonight."

Jesse kissed her mouth, tenderly touching a strand of hair that had worked loose from her braid. "I'll need a bath tonight, before I get into bed," he warned. "If you want, you could start warming some water after you eat your dinner."

"I'll do that," she grinned in reply. "Either that or you can sleep on the floor with Lucky."

"I don't think so," he put his arms around her and pulled her close. "I belong with you."

"Yes, you do," she agreed, wrapping her arms around his neck.

"I've got to go," he said, kissing her again. Then he grabbed his rifle, patted Lucky on the head, and ran out of the door.

This was his second year experiencing the fall round-up,

and he felt a combination of eagerness and dread. He loved the excitement of the day, the energy of all the men riding together, whooping and hollering, and the thundering of the hooves of so many Longhorn cattle. Thousands of the beasts, each weighing a ton or more, with horns that extended up to seven feet, all running together over the uneven ground was something to behold.

After the tedious chore of separating the vast number of cattle by brand, they would be driven to pens where the calves would be cut out from the cows and steers and placed in a corral for branding. The male calves would be castrated, a procedure which Jesse understood was necessary, but still couldn't endure.

His first year, he'd asked Claude to explain why on earth it was practiced. He'd been informed that it minimized aggression as well as improved the quality of the meat. Jesse just had to take his word for it. After all, Claude was the Texan.

Of course, some male calves were allowed to develop into bulls, for the sake of reproduction. This selection was made carefully based on the qualities of the calf and the potential he held for breeding.

Jesse wished the smell of blood and the sight of pain didn't affect him so strongly, but it wasn't something he could change about himself. Annette said it wasn't a sign of weakness, but rather an indication of a gentle nature. And she had been quick to insist that a man could be both strong and gentle. She certainly made him feel like a man, and although he wasn't as ashamed by his "gentle nature" as he used to be, he still hoped to one day overcome it. Just not this year.

After the calves were marked and castrated, the cows and steers were sorted to determine fitness for market. If they hadn't reached their potential weight, they would be given another year to graze and fatten up. All cattle deemed ready for sale would then be driven to the railhead in Cheyenne, a journey of several days.

Although the most grueling part of the process, it was also Jesse's favorite. It was an adventure, a challenge he was equal to meet. He could hold his own in the saddle, and since his amputation had healed over, he'd experienced less chafing and soreness. Although he did sometimes have tingling and twinges of the nerve endings.

He enjoyed the sheer power of the massive animals as they rumbled over the ground, making his teeth rattle in his head, kicking up dust and bellowing and grumbling as they went. All the cowboys worked together to keep them in a tight herd, going after any strays that wandered out of the circle. Dogs trained for the drive, as Lucky would be, were helpful at keeping the herd in line.

The evenings were filled with songs and stories. Jesse had never heard such songs as the cowboys sang, insisting that they calmed the cattle and prevented stampede. Jesse didn't know if it was true or not, but it soothed his soul. After a meal provided by the chuck wagon, who went ahead of the herd to prepare supper, the men gathered around the fire and shared stories. Some were of Indians and others were of mountain lions and rattlesnakes. Jesse suspected at least half of them were fabricated, but they made for good telling.

As he rode out with his men, his mind jumping ahead to the days to come, he had the funny feeling he was being watched. He turned in the saddle and looked back at his three story white house, where he saw his wife standing on the second level porch watching his departure. When she lifted her hand to wave, Jesse did likewise.

"You gots yourself a good woman," Jim noted.

"Thank you, Jim," Jesse replied, feeling greater sympathy for Jim's loss now that he knew personally how rewarding marriage could be.

As they joined the great troop of ranchers and cowhands preparing for the round-up, Jesse shifted eagerly in his seat. The air was charged with energy and excitement. He checked his rope and braided rawhide whip, draped around the saddle horn, and patted the rifle in its scabbard. He pulled the handkerchief tied around his neck up over his face to keep the dust out of his mouth and nose.

Urging his mount forward, he rode with the other men out onto the open range. Under the handkerchief, a smile touched his lips, and above it, a twinkle gleamed in his gray eyes. How could his brothers choose occupations that restricted them to a sunless room and hours in a chair? As far as Jesse was concerned, whatever risks he faced were worth the cost. And the sad fact was that his brothers didn't know what they were missing.

They rode through the morning, rounding up small herds all over the wild prairie and driving them back to the corral. After pausing for a quick meal, they were back in the saddles. Last year, Jesse had been mostly an observer, sticking close to Claude and learning what was expected of him. This year, he wanted to pull his own weight.

Sighting a group of strays in a valley, Jesse separated from the men driving a herd of about fifty. Claude touched his hat and nodded at Jesse, granting acknowledgement that he was up to the task. Jesse rode toward the animals, cracking his whip to get their attention. They grunted and bawled in protest, but slowly began moving away from the sound and up the hill toward the main herd.

One cow, however, lowered her tremendous horns and grumbled a warning. Jesse cracked the whip and she stepped back, then charged forward threateningly. Jesse raised the whip over his head again, then stilled as he realized her concern. Her calf was tangled in a scrubby sagebrush, his small legs twisted up in the branches. Jesse glanced up the hill, thinking to signal for help. But judging by the distant rumble of hooves, the men were out of earshot.

With a sigh, Jesse assessed the situation. How was he supposed to free the calf with the angry cow hovering over it? Would she understand he was trying to help, or charge him out of protective instinct? She lowered her head again, menacingly, as if to answer the question.

Finally an idea came to him. He wasn't sure if it would work, and if it didn't, he wasn't sure how he would fare. But he was determined to prove he was as capable as any of the other men riding today.

He swung the lariat in the air and sent it soaring to land with a swish around the cow's horns, then immediately tightened his grasp and wrapped the rope around the pommel of his saddle, tying it securely. The cow pulled and groaned, but Jesse urged his horse to lead her several feet from the calf.

His heart pounded against his ribs and he could feel a nervous sweat dampening his shirt as he dismounted. Cautiously, he approached the calf. The cow strained against the rope that held her, followed by the creak of leather as the saddle shifted and the horse stamped her feet.

Jesse knew he needed to move quickly. He took his eyes from the sharp horns of the protective cow and took slow, steady steps toward her calf. Speaking in low tones, which he hoped would reassure, he squatted down beside the calf to disentangle its thin legs. Uncertain of his intent, the calf bawled and squirmed. Jesse jumped back as the cow lunged, bringing her far closer to him than he preferred.

Sweat ran down his temples. He swallowed. He had to do this. He stood, wrapping one arm around the calf's neck, and the other under its belly. Then he lifted it up, knowing it would be scratched and bloodied, but at least it would be free. And hopefully its mother would let Jesse live.

When he felt it pull free, he quickly released it, pushing it gently in the direction of its mother. While the cow was distracted with looking over her calf, Jesse cut a wide circle around them both, edging toward his horse.

That was when he spotted the rider above him, halted at the edge of the hill. Although he wore a handkerchief over his face, the big white stallion he rode easily identified him. Bryan Hunt. Jesse touched his hat to signify that he saw him and had the situation thoroughly under control. He hoped Bryan would leave once he realized his help wasn't required, but he remained, watching.

Jesse quickly mounted his appaloosa, untied the cow, then circled behind her and cracked the whip. He had no idea what had happened to the other strays. But as he crested the hill, he saw they hadn't wandered far.

"Claude sent me back to see if you needed help," Bryan explained.

"I'm fine," Jesse answered, perhaps more defensively than

necessary.

"I can see that," Bryan answered, an edge to his voice Jesse couldn't miss. "I'll just help you drive these strays back to the herd."

Jesse nodded, and both men cracked their whips, sending the animals into a slow trot. They followed behind the strays, prodding them along as needed until the cloud of dust kicked up by the main herd came into view.

Neither man made any attempt at conversation. Jesse tried to calm the tension bunching his shoulders. He had to hide a chuckle as the thought occurred to him that they were just like two bulls fighting over the same cow.

And in reality, Bryan had far more right to be angry than Jesse. After all, as far as Bryan knew, Jesse had moved into his territory and disregarded his claim on Annette. Everyone knew Bryan had been courting her. For Jesse to move in and marry her had been a slap in the face. Not only had it been disrespectful, it had been hurtful.

Jesse shifted uncomfortably in the saddle as he considered this new perspective. He couldn't deny the truth of it. But it didn't make him feel any less like punching Bryan square in the jaw. The man just brought it out in him.

Chapter Thirty

*L*ifting a wet shirt from the basket, Annette twisted out the excess water, then smoothed it and hung it on the line, carefully placing the pin over it. The wind pulled and tugged at the clothing, and Annette fought to keep it from blowing away before it was properly secured.

Her skirts billowed around her, and her hair slipped free of its braid to whip around her cheeks. Glancing toward the distance horizon, Annette offered up another prayer for her husband and father's safety, knowing they were both on the drive to Cheyenne in this fierce wind.

She was glad Lucky hadn't been deemed ready to accompany Jesse on the cattle drive. Without Jesse, the house was lonelier than usual. Although the dog could sometimes be a nuisance, at least he was company. When she needed to be reminded that she wasn't the only one in the middle of the prairie, she would sit on the back porch and let the bull terrier rest his chin in her lap. She would scratch his ears until he flopped to the ground and rolled on his back, begging for a belly rub.

Reaching into the basket for another item of clothing, Annette paused and straightened as a sound reached her ears, mingling with the whistling of the wind. It sounded almost like the whinny of a horse approaching. Hopefully, she pushed the shirt aside and peered out into the billowing green buffalo grass.

She laughed in delight as she saw Sarah riding toward her, sitting astride her bay mare. Forgetting the wash, she ran toward her friend in excitement. "Sarah!" she exclaimed. "Sarah, you're back!"

Sarah dismounted and embraced Annette, laughing with her. "I am. I've been back for a few days and I thought I should pay you a visit."

Once again, Sarah wore a calico dress and her black and silver hair was wound up in a chignon at the base of her neck. Though her skin seemed to Annette to be darker than before, presumably from spending more hours in the sun.

"Oh, it's so good to see you!" Annette almost cried, surprised by the flood of emotions she felt at the woman's return.

Sarah put her arm around Annette as they walked toward the house. "How have you been?" she asked Annette.

"Just fine," Annette answered, wishing she could reply truthfully. There was so much she wished she could tell! But to share her joy at God's forgiveness would require admitting her sin; and telling of her new relationship with Jesse would mean revealing the truth of their marriage. And so she just smiled and added, "We're wonderful!"

"And Jesse's leg?" Sarah inquired.

"It's been doing well ever since you applied the bacon to it."

"I'm glad to hear it," Sarah replied. Annette noticed that the gray cloud of grief was absent from her friend's eyes. The heavy weight that had stooped her shoulders was gone, and her smile came easily.

"Where are the children?" Annette wondered.

"Elizabeth is old enough to tend them for a while. I can't stay long, but I wanted to speak to you."

"Please come inside and I'll put some water on for tea. I'd love to hear about your time away. Did you find your family?"

Sarah's cheerfulness dimmed for a brief moment. She nodded.

"I did. But first, let me ask this: is Frank on the cattle drive?"

Annette hesitated. "As far as I know."

"The cabin was empty when I arrived, and it's... it looks like..."

"I saw Frank recently. He didn't look well," Annette admitted.

"I'm not sure I did the right thing, leaving the way I did," Sarah admitted. She pulled up a chair to the kitchen table and sat down, watching as Annette placed the kettle on the stove and stoked the fire.

Annette joined her at the table, leaning forward silently in encouragement.

Sarah sighed. "I miss Frank. He's been a good husband to me. I just needed a woman to weep with me for the loss, to know what it's like to feel a child grow inside of you, to feel it kick, and then..." she paused, blinking back tears. "I am grateful for the three children I have. But I will always mourn Joshua's passing."

"I'm sure your family was glad to see you," Annette commented.

She watched as Sarah pursed her lips. "Yes, they were. Most of them, though not all. And I can understand why. To their way of thinking, I have befriended the enemy and forsaken my own people."

Sarah shook her head sadly. "I did not know what to expect on this reservation. But I was not prepared for what I found," she confessed. "My people have always been hunters of the great buffalo. They traveled to follow the herds and they lived off of the land and the beasts of the earth. Now they are forced to give up the way of life they have known for many generations and let the government provide meat and grain for them. Their pride is broken. They are prisoners on a land they once roamed free."

"What can they do?"

"Nothing. If they fight the white people, they will be annihilated. The white men have superior weapons and greater numbers. The time for my people has ended," Sarah acknowledged sadly. "I look into their eyes and see defeat. The meat brought to them is often rotten, and the grain is never the amount promised. Without the work of hunting, tanning hides, gathering food, the men grow restless and turn to spirits. Anger and drunkenness do not mix well." She paused when the tea kettle whistled and Annette rose to pour the water.

"Our way of life has ended," Sarah concluded. "The Lakota people must learn new ways to survive. The Indian Bureau says they are to be farmers," she laughed bitterly. "Even if the land were not hard and unfertile, the Lakota are *warriors*—not farmers! As if it did not wound their pride enough to herd them onto a plot of land and tell them they must remain on it, they want to make them *farmers*! It will never be so. It is not in our blood."

She accepted the steaming mug Annette offered with a nod of gratitude.

"The government will give them money, clothing, food… As if they are children to be cared for. My people are strong. They used what the land provided for them without causing it harm. They were one with the land."

She wiped a tear from her cheek. "My people are strong. Too strong. Like the oak that refuses to bend when the fierce wind comes. I worry for them."

"Oh Sarah, I'm so sorry," Annette offered weakly, her mind reeling to understand all that Sarah had disclosed.

"But," Sarah took a sip of tea and smiled, "it was good to see my mother and sisters again, and their little ones. It was good for my children to see their Indian family, to play with their cousins and learn there are many different ways to dress and cook and live. I am glad for the time I spent with family. And my mother did give me the comfort I needed, as I knew she would. It was not Frank's fault. I was like a lost child, and I needed to find myself again in my mother's tipi."

"Frank will be grateful for your return, and for your healing. He seemed lost without you and the children," Annette confessed.

Sarah nodded. "I only wish he could have come with me. But he needed to stay to tend the ranch, and it would have been difficult for him to share my Indian ways. And my family… not all of them think kindly of the white men after all that has been done to them. And I cannot fault them. But some men, like Frank, are good men and should not be judged for the sins of others who share the same skin coloring."

Annette sipped her tea, pondering Sarah's perceptive analysis. "You always have such wise words to speak."

The Indian woman pursed her lips briefly before replying: "Any wisdom I possess has been gained through heartache. In my tears and pain, I turn to God and listen for His voice."

Tilting her head thoughtfully, Annette considered the way the last few years of her life had been shaped by pain and suffering. And she wondered what other heartaches Sarah had endured to give her such insight into life and humanity. For a long time, Annette had listened to her own voice repeating words of scorn and self-disgust. Then, finally, had come the sweet words of forgiveness through Jesus Christ. Now she was training herself to listen to the still, small voice offering reassurance and hope.

"Sarah," she began slowly, "I owe you a great debt of gratitude. When you stayed with us that night, when Jesse's leg was injured, you brought much more than physical healing to our home. You brought us the words of truth from the Bible. And it's changed us. Thank you."

Coming to her feet, Sarah held out her arms and Annette stood to embrace her. "I am glad to hear it," Sarah said, tears shimmering in her almond eyes. "I have prayed for you, my friend, even while I was away."

Emotion choked Annette. She wished she could do more than merely nod and whisper, "Thank you." But it was all she could manage.

"Read the Bible," Sarah encouraged. "God will guide you."

After Sarah had left, and Annette remembered the unfinished laundry, she contemplated Sarah's advice. She and

Jesse read the Bible, but never together. When he returned from the cattle drive, she was going to ask him to read to her at night, the way Sarah had said Frank read to her. And not just on Sundays, as had been the habit in her own home growing up, but every night.

The image of her and Jesse sitting together in the living room, his head bent to the book in his lap, and his voice filling the silence as he read aloud almost brought Annette to tears. Only two, possibly three more days, until he was home.

She looked down at the aquamarine ring on her finger and smiled. Whenever she began to miss him so much that it hurt to breathe, she studied the way the sun glinted on the gemstone and he didn't feel quite so far away.

~

Pausing at the window to glance out at the rolling prairie had become habit. Any moment Jesse might be glimpsed riding over a distant hill with their ranch hands in tow. Annette studied the quiet landscape, then bent to stoke the fire in the stove. Another lonely supper.

She was thankful for Sarah's visit, but the silence since her departure seemed to thunder in her ears. She found herself talking to Lucky like he was a child. And, though she would never tell Jesse, the previous night she had been so lonely, she had slept on the couch so the dog could lick her hand and fill the quiet with the sound of his snoring.

Kneading dough for bread, Annette hummed a song as she worked just to hear the sound of a human voice. Suddenly her attention was snagged by a sound outside the door. Forgetting the flour that covered her hands and apron, she ran to the door and swung it open wide.

There on the steps stood her husband. She threw herself into his arms, mindless of the dust that caked his clothing, and wrapped her arms around his neck. "Jesse!" she cried. "Oh, you're home!"

Jesse laughed as he encircled her in his embrace. "Nettie," he whispered in her ear. "I missed you more than I ever imagined possible!"

She lifted her chin to look at him and laughed. Dust from the trail clung to his eyebrows and the stubble that had grown unevenly on his cheeks. His hair was a shade lighter from the film. And as she pulled away, she glanced down and saw that her dress was a shade lighter as well.

But it didn't matter. She pressed her lips to his in a welcoming kiss. Her husband was home.

He sat at the table to report that they had fared well at the market and he would be able to invest in increasing the herd. But the enthusiasm in his voice faded quickly and Annette looked up from her supper preparation to find his head nodding off.

"Shall I make you coffee?"

Jesse nodded. "I'm afraid I won't be much company tonight. Dinner and a bath, then a night's sleep in my own bed sounds like heaven right now. With you beside me, of course," he winked.

Annette blushed and grinned. She was grateful for this new side of him, this confident man who didn't hide his scar or worry about how his facial expressions might be affected by it. He knew she loved him, and that felt like a victory.

True to his word, immediately following his bath, Jesse fell into bed and slept well into the following morning. Annette had breakfast warming on the stove by the time he finally descended the steps. But she could hardly blame him. Days in the saddle had always taken a toll on her father.

Jesse spent the day with her, never leaving her side. They took their horses out for a ride in the afternoon sun, then stole an hour before supper to make up for the lonely nights he was on the trail. After supper, they retreated to the living room, where Annette removed the Bible from the table and offered it to Jesse.

"Would you read to me? It would mean a lot to me if we made that our evening ritual."

Jesse trapped her hand under his before she could release the Bible, then brought it to his lips. "I would like that," he said.

Annette smiled as she settled into the armchair under the oil lamp, retrieving her knitting from the footstool that doubled as a sewing basket. She leaned back and listened as Jesse's voice filled the evening with words written by a man who had been privileged to walk beside and listen to Jesus while He was on earth. She listened with every part of her being, enjoying the deep timbre of her husband's voice as much as the words themselves.

He read from the book of John. She recognized some of the verses they had read before. And every night he read another chapter. One evening, she found herself dropping the knitting and leaning forward. She couldn't recall every hearing this story before.

It was about a woman caught in the very act of adultery.

Annette held her breath. The people wanted to stone her.

She waited, wondering how Jesus would answer them. She leaned forward nervously.

Christ Jesus stooped down and wrote in the dust with His finger. Confused, Annette edged forward in her chair.

Her husband's eyes met hers briefly before he continued: *"He who is without sin among you, let him throw a stone at her first."*

Now her eyes were riveted on Jesse, waiting to hear how the story would end.

The Bible said that Jesus stooped down to write on the ground again. And without throwing a single stone, the crowd slowly dispersed, convicted by their conscience. When only the woman and Jesus remained, He asked her, *"Where are those accusers of yours? Has no one condemned you?"*

And the adulteress answered, *"No one, Lord."*

Annette felt the breath she had been holding expel in a rush of relief as Jesus replied, *"Neither do I condemn you; go and sin no more."*

She looked down at her hands, clenched tightly in her lap. She was just the same as the woman in the story. And Jesus hadn't condemned her. He had told her to sin no more. And in that moment, Annette realized she wasn't an adulteress any longer. Since Ricky's death, she had lived in abstinence, withholding herself from all men until the day that Jesse had been ready to fully become her husband.

Her attention was brought back to Jesse as he choked out the next verse: *"Then Jesus spoke to them again, saying, "I am the light of the world. He who follows Me shall not walk in darkness, but have the light of life."*

"What is it?" she asked, fearing that the reminder of her adulterous relationship with Ricky had wounded him.

"I'm sorry for my past, Jes—" she began, but he interrupted.

"No, it's not you," he wiped a tear from his cheek. "It's me. I have to return the medal."

"What do you mean?" she moved to sit beside him on the couch.

"He said to sin no more. Every day that I keep that medal, I'm lying. I'm lying to my family, to the Corporal's family, to the government of the United States. I have to give it back."

Annette linked her arm through his elbow and rested her head on his shoulder. "I'm proud of you," she whispered.

Chapter Thirty-One

*J*esse put his arm around Annette and drew her close. "Tomorrow I'll take it to the post office in Weston and return it to the Department of War." He closed his eyes, taking a deep breath. "I'll have to include a letter explaining exactly what happened, so the Corporal's family will understand."

She kissed his cheek, and he saw the pride shining in her blue eyes. For the first time in his entire life, Jesse understood the cost—and the reward—of courage.

The idea of returning the medal was humbling. He would have to confess to the United States Government that he had not only given false testimony in order to steal the medal, but was a coward in addition to being a liar. Yet the bravery it required to admit the truth and set the record straight was worth celebrating in itself.

As long as he kept the Medal of Honor in his possession, Jesse continued to be no more than a coward and a liar. Giving it up would change his identity. He would know he had chosen to be a man of integrity and valor in this time and place. There was no way to turn back the clock and undo the action; but he could take responsibility for it and live as a man of honesty and courage from this day forward.

And he would. The love and pride shining in his wife's eyes was enough to give him confidence and hope. Whatever shame might come with the admission, her expression at that very moment made it pale by comparison.

They walked up the stairs silently to prepare for bed. As he felt Annette's breathing change against his chest as she fell into sleep, Jesse rested his chin on her head and smiled. Just the decision to return the medal was like severing a rope that had hobbled him, the way a calf's legs were tied to bring him to the ground. Jesse had felt the heat of the brand on his heart, naming him as dishonest and weak. But as he closed his eyes and his mind drifted toward dreams, he saw that brand being washed away and replaced by one labeling him for Who he belonged to, and not what he had done.

He woke before dawn, the task before him filling his mind. Without disturbing Annette, he slipped from beneath the quilts and went to sit at the writing desk by the window. Lighting a candle, he placed a piece of paper on the desk and dipped the nib of the pen into a bottle of ink. He stared at the blank page for a moment, gathering his thoughts.

He addressed his letter to the Secretary of War, William Belknap. As he penned the words explaining his intention and purpose, as well as the reason for the medal having been issued to the wrong recipient in the first place, he felt a renewed sense of freedom. He knew God had already forgiven him, but now he felt like he had as a boy, when his father had placed his hand on Jesse's shoulder and smiled, "Well done, son."

Setting aside the first letter, Jesse retrieved another piece of paper and began a second. This one was addressed to the family of Corporal Lewis Adams, to be sent along with the medal. This one was more difficult to write because of the pain it would inflict. Although he didn't know this family, Jesse could well imagine the sting of betrayal they would feel learning another man had stolen the glory rightfully belonging to their son.

While Jesse could honestly say there was nothing he could have done to prevent the Corporal's death, he had altered the way Lewis Adams' death was remembered. But his letter would change that. Now it would not be remembered simply as another mindless sacrifice in the course of duty, but as an act of valor and bravery. It wouldn't bring Lewis back to his mother's table, but it would give her a snapshot of his courage to hold close to her heart.

"Although I do not deserve it," he wrote, *"I ask for your forgiveness. As a young boy, I wanted to be known as courageous, even if I had done nothing to earn the title. Now, as a man, I want to live courageously, even if it means being labeled as a coward. I am returning this medal to your family, not only so Corporal Adams can be remembered as the hero he was, but also so I can begin to live a life marked by true courage."*

As he concluded the letter and signed his name, he sensed he was being watched. He looked up to see his wife lying on their bed, her hands under her cheek, and her eyes intent upon him.

"Good morning," she said groggily.

Jesse left the desk to come kneel at the edge of the bed, drawing her into his arms. "Will you go with me today?" he asked.

"Of course, if that's what you want," she assured him, resting her cheek on his shoulder.

"I would like that," he said. "I just... I guess I just want you to see me do it and know I'm doing what I can to make it right."

She kissed his cheek. "I know you are, Jesse. I know who you are now. You don't have to prove anything to me."

Jesse closed his eyes, reveling in the feeling of her arms around his neck, loving and gentle. The feel of her cheek against his skin, and the silky blond hair that spilled over his arm. He wasn't sure he would ever understand her unfaltering love for him. But he wasn't going to take it for granted, either.

As soon as the morning chores and breakfast were finished, they saddled their horses to ride into town. The medal was encased in its velvet-lined box and wrapped with the letters in brown packaging paper. As he rode his mare across the uneven ground of the prairie, Jesse could feel its weight in his coat pocket thumping against his chest and reminding him of his mission.

They tied their horses to the hitching post and went inside, stepping into line to pay for postage. As Jesse handed the package to the old man behind the counter, he felt the weight of a burden he had been carrying for years lift from his shoulders. He squeezed Annette's hand and smiled.

"Would you like me to check for mail while you're here, sir?" the old man inquired.

Jesse nodded, then turned to Annette. "I guess we could get lunch at the diner before we head home."

"That would be nice," she replied.

"Here you are, sir," the postal worker handed a letter to Jesse and nodded politely at Annette before turning his gaze to the next customer.

Jesse turned the letter over in his hand. It was from his mother. He walked with Annette outside, then paused to open the envelope. He hadn't written in a while, and he felt a twinge of guilt as he unfolded the letter.

But it quickly dissolved as he read her words.

"What is it?" Annette asked worriedly, resting her hand on his arm.

"My mother is coming!" he exclaimed. He met her wide blue eyes. "She's taking the train to Cheyenne so that she can meet you and see my homestead." He shook his head, reading over the words again. "I can't believe it."

"Did you invite her?" Annette wondered aloud.

"No. I mean, I might have said that I *wish* she could meet you and see my homestead, but I never extended an actual invitation."

"How long will she stay?"

"Two weeks," Jesse answered, shaking his head again.

"When does she arrive?" Annette asked next, and Jesse detected a note of concern in her voice.

He scanned over the letter and announced, "In just a few days. Train schedules are hardly regular, so I can't say with certainty. Then she's taking a stagecoach from Cheyenne to Weston, so I'll have to ride out here to get her."

"I feel nervous meeting her," Annette admitted. "I suppose I should give the house a thorough cleaning. And what kinds of food should I prepare for her?"

"Don't worry yourself," Jesse reassured. "She's not here to judge you. My family thought I would never marry, so I guess she just wants to see you for herself."

"Why would they have thought that? You were such a charmer," Annette teased, and Jesse chuckled as he remembered how gruffly he had spoken to her when they first met.

But Jesse quickly sobered as he considered the Medal of Honor he had just left at the post office to be returned to the Department of War. "I was going to send a letter home, explaining the truth about the medal," he said quietly. "But since she's coming, I guess I'll have to tell her face to face."

His stomach twisted with anxiety as he imagined the look of shock and disappointment that would transform his mother's face when she learned the truth. He swallowed back the sudden tide of shame that rose with the image.

Reading his expression, Annette leaned close and said, "Jesse, I've never met your mother, but from everything I've heard about her, I don't think she's going to be angry or hold it against you."

"No," he agreed. "She'll just be disappointed in me, which is even worse." He hung his head. "She's always been there for me, Nettie. She raised me better than that, and I wish I hadn't let her down."

They had been walking arm in arm along the rough wooden planks of the sidewalk toward Maggie's Diner. But Annette pulled him to the side and looked up at him intently. "You were a boy then, Jesse, who wanted to be a man. Now you are a man, and you're doing what's right. If we're all defined by the mistakes of our youth, then what am I?"

Jesse pulled her into his arms, right there on the street. He pressed a kiss to her forehead and whispered, "You're right, Nettie. Thank you."

But the sick feeling in his stomach wouldn't subside.

~

Three days later, Jesse rode out alone to Weston to see if his mother had arrived. He presumed if she had arrived the day previous, she would have spent the night at a boarding house. Unfortunately, if her arrival had been delayed by mechanical complications or bad weather, he would have to ride out again to fetch her.

He reported immediately to the boarding house, and inquired if Mrs. Harriet Stone had registered there. He was informed that she had signed in two hours ago and was resting in her room. Jesse requested the room number and thanked the clerk.

As he climbed the stairs to her room, he puzzled again over her unexpected visit. It had never occurred to him to invite his mother out west because he couldn't imagine her braving the miles of travel by railcar, followed by the hours rocking over the uneven roads in a stagecoach. Or the expense. Not to mention the threat of Indian hostilities, although the Indians had been pretty quiet since Chief Red Cloud had agreed they would remain on the land reserved for them.

He knocked tentatively on the door, and wasn't surprised when the answering voice sounded bone-weary with exhaustion. He did as instructed and opened the door.

Harriet Stone rose from the chair with a small exclamation of joy as she came to him and wrapped her arms around her son. The travel had clearly taken its toll on her, although Jesse suspected his memory had been dishonest in the picture it held of his mother. She seemed much older than he remembered, her hair fully silver and her face, though still pretty, creased with wrinkles. She seemed thinner, too, the gray dress hanging loosely on her small body.

"Oh, it's good to see you, son!" she cried.

"I can't believe you came, Mother!" he laughed, pulling her close.

She looked up at him and grinned. "Neither can I!"

"How was the trip?" he asked, motioning for her to resume her seat as he pulled up a chair next to her.

"Fine," she smiled, as if they both knew it was a lie. "Well, perhaps a little frightening for this old woman, but all in all, it was fine."

"It's amazing how much of the world you can see from the window of a train," Jesse commented, remembering his own journey by train from Massachusetts to Wyoming.

"Yes, quite," she laughed, the thin skin around her eyes crinkling. "It is undeniably beautiful out west, Jesse, I'll give you that."

"Do you need to rest, or are you ready for a very comfortable ride on my buckboard wagon?" he grinned.

She shook her head wearily. "I'll think I need a short rest, if that's all right."

"Of course, Mother. I'll go get a cup of coffee and browse the mercantile. Is there anything you need?"

"No dear, just a chance to close my eyes for a few minutes. My old bones aren't used to this abuse."

Jesse was tempted to ask why on earth she had risked her

health simply to meet his wife, but withheld the question.

He returned to the boarding house two hours later and was pleased to find his mother looking rested and waiting for him in the parlor. He retrieved her luggage and led her out to the wagon waiting outside.

She lifted an eyebrow as she examined the contraption. "You weren't lying."

"No, Mother. I'm sorry to tell you it will be even worse than the stagecoach ride."

Harriet squared her frail shoulders and lifted her chin. "I'm sure I'll be fine," she assured him.

Jesse wished he was as certain.

On the long ride back to his homestead, he explained to his mother the details of cattle ranching and the attributes of the Longhorns. He spotted a small herd grazing in a depression and urged the wagon just a little closer to give her a glimpse of their proportions. Her eyes widened, and she looked at Jesse with new respect.

"And you can make these animals go where you want them to? And rope them?"

Jesse nodded, feeling the warmth of her pride.

As they crested a hill, the three story white house he had built seemed to rise up out of the prairie, standing tall and majestic among the miles of waving green grass. He simply pointed, watching as her jaw dropped.

"You've done quite well," she said. "It's even more impressive than the picture revealed."

Obviously watching for their return, he saw the front door

open and the figure of his wife emerged. She stood on the front porch waving, the blue dress she wore complimenting her thin figure, her blond hair neatly pulled back into a chignon.

"I'm very happy for you, son," his mother said, linking her elbow through his. "And very proud."

~

Jesse was relieved at the way his mother and Annette took to one another. He had feared his wife would resent another woman in the house, but instead she seemed genuinely grateful for the company. The two women had quickly fallen into working together in the kitchen, and in the evening, conversation had come easily.

Although all appeared to be going well, Jesse felt the tension of a coming storm. Just as electricity in the air would make his hair stand on end, portending an approaching storm even while the sky was still blue, Jesse knew the placid atmosphere would soon be disrupted. It was just a matter of time.

As they settled in the living room after supper on the second evening of her visit, Harriet declared, "I wasn't sure if I would survive the journey, but I'm so glad I could come and see your life here in the Wyoming Territory, Jesse. I was so heartbroken to miss your wedding, I knew I wouldn't be able to rest in peace if I never met your wife."

"Are you unwell, Mother?" Jesse worried.

"No," she laughed. "I'm just fine. But we have to face the fact that I'm not going to live forever. I thought I should make the trip before I was unable to."

"Well, I'm glad you did," Annette affirmed sincerely.

Harriet smiled. "I'm sure Jesse's told you about his home in Springfield, Massachusetts, and about the way our boys were the first to volunteer in the War Between the States."

Annette's eyes slid to Jesse's and locked. The clouds were about to break loose their fury.

"We're very convinced in our belief of the equality of mankind," his mother continued, obviously unaware of the exchanged glances between her son and his wife. "Our town gave up many sons and fathers to the cause, and although we grieve their loss, we're proud of their sacrifice."

She leaned down to retrieve a package Jesse had noticed resting by her feet. His stomach flip-flopped at the sight of it.

"This," she said as she unwrapped the paper, "is a plaque given to Jesse just after he left Springfield." Harriet declared proudly, "All four of my boys fought in the war, but only two of them were present to receive this honor." Her voice held regret. "So I brought yours here, Jesse."

Jesse swallowed. He looked into Annette's eyes and found encouragement there. "Mother," he began tentatively, "there's— there's something I have to tell you."

Harriet cocked her head intently, studying the strained expression on her son's face. "What is it?"

"I returned the Medal of Honor to the Department of War."

Her hand flew to her heart. Her mouth slipped open, and a full moment passed before she could issue the one word: "*Why?*"

"Because I didn't deserve it, Mother," Jesse whispered, the shame pouncing like a mountain lion upon his jugular. He swallowed anxiously, his throat spasming with the force of it.

"I—I don't understand," she said, her delicate white brows drawing together in confusion.

"I didn't volunteer to join the mission to acquisition a supply wagon. I saw the men running into the woods and I thought they were deserters when I joined them."

Her hand covered her mouth in shock, but Jesse continued. "I fought one rebel, and he cut my face with his bayonet. It was Corporal Adams who fought and killed three rebels to get that wagon. All I did is jump on while he rode away. And when he was shot, I..." he closed his eyes, forcing the words free, "I pushed him out and rode back alone to take the credit."

"Jesse..." she whispered, her eyes darting from his face to Annette's and back again. "I never imagined... You were just a boy." She shook her head, her brown eyes glistening with tears. "I never wanted you to enlist. But you wanted to be a hero, like your brothers. Jesse, you didn't have to go. Or be a hero. I'm sorry if I ever made you feel that you did."

Jesse shook his head. "It's not your fault, Mother. It was my own. All the men were joining, and only the women were staying behind. I felt like it was the only choice... I should have known I didn't have the constitution of a soldier. I thought in the heat of battle, courage would rush in. But it didn't. I was horrified by the sights, the smells, the sound of the..." he swallowed, feeling sick with the memory.

Harriet stood, her white hair gleaming in the lamp light as she held out her arms to her youngest son. "Oh Jesse," she cried as he came to her. "I never knew you carried this secret all these years. Now I understand so much."

"I'm sorry, Mother, so sorry," he sobbed into her shoulder.

"You returned the medal?" she asked quietly.

"I did. I want it to go to the family of Corporal Adams. I want them to know the truth."

"If I hadn't come…?" Harriet began, her eyes worried.

"I was going to write you a letter. I don't want to live with the lie anymore."

"You've grown into a fine man," his mother stated proudly. She looked over at Annette, watching the exchange with compassion, and extended her hand. When Annette stood and accepted it, Harriet repeated her earlier assessment: "You've done well, son."

Chapter Thirty-Two

*T*he remainder of Harriet's stay went better than Jesse could have expected. No further mention was made of his confession until the evening before her departure when she told him again how very proud she was of the man he had become.

Jesse shook his head, wondering why it had taken him so long to take the actions necessary to shake off the oppression of guilt nagging him for so many years. At least the truth was out now and he could look himself in the mirror without shame.

He couldn't help but wonder what his brothers and sisters would say when they learned of the truth, which he supposed they must. He decided he would write each of them individually, and when he suggested it to his mother, she agreed to remain silent on the subject and allow him to tell his own story.

Perhaps it was a bit of remaining cowardice that made Jesse relieved his family lived thousands of miles away and he would probably never have to look them in the eyes again. Unless he chose to visit Springfield one day, which was highly unlikely. Confessing his sins by letter was far easier than having to watch the expression of shock and disappointment that his words inspired.

Although Jesse was glad his mother had been willing to make the arduous trip to give her blessing on his new life as a cattle rancher as well as to meet his bride, even if it meant seeing that look in her eyes. She had further demonstrated her love by forgiving him for misleading everyone to believe he was a gallant soldier instead of an intended deserter.

Sadly, her words were true when she said she would not live forever. This could be the last time Jesse saw her in this life, and knowing she loved him unconditionally in spite of his secret would ease that loss when it came. It was a blessing to have been able to witness her forgiveness and to know she would live and die knowing who he really was, and loving him just the same.

The morning he was to take her to Weston to catch the stagecoach to Cheyenne, he felt the finality of the good-bye. He looked at her small frame, the white hair secured in a chignon at her neck, and the paper thin wrinkles on her face. Her time was coming to a close. Perhaps one day he would take Annette with him to see Springfield and visit his mother one more time.

He swallowed back tears, straightening his shoulders as he lifted her carpetbag and descended the stairs to the kitchen. She was just finishing helping Annette with the dishes, and she turned to smile at him as he entered the room.

"I'm almost ready, son. Let me just get my coat." Harriet hurried off to the living room to retrieve it.

Her cry of alarm sent Jesse and Annette running after her. They found her standing with her hands over her mouth in dismay. Her coat lay on the floor, half-eaten, the remains of it in shreds. Lucky looked up in concern at the noise, the fabric still hanging from his mouth.

"Oh, Lucky!" Annette cried.

"Bad dog!" Jesse fumed, grabbing the bull terrier by the collar and leading him outside. When he returned, he examined the coat on the floor. It was beyond repair.

The November air was biting, and he could hardly let his mother ride all the way back to Massachusetts without proper attire.

"Mother, I'm so sorry. When we get into Weston, I'll purchase a coat for you to replace it."

"No, no, Jesse, that won't be necess—"

"Of course we're replacing your coat!" Annette insisted. "And you can wear mine on the ride there. I'll just wrap up in a blanket."

"All right, but don't be upset at the dog. He's just an animal, after all. Why people let animals in the house, I'm not sure I understand, but..." she smiled, squeezing Jesse's arm. "You named him after your Grandpa's dog, didn't you?"

Jesse just nodded.

"Well, that monster was known to eat his fair share of things he shouldn't have, so I suppose he's just keeping with tradition," she laughed.

"Thank you for being so understanding," Annette answered, smiling at Jesse as if the origin of the dog's name pleased her.

Jesse scowled. He hated feeling like he was being sentimental and soft.

"Let's get ready to leave, then," he barked. "We've got a lot of ground to cover."

He saw the amused glance the women exchanged and his scowl deepened. "I'll be outside."

~

"We don't have a lot of time," Jesse informed the women as they stood outside the mercantile. "We can check at the dressmaker's shop down the street, but we can't be too choosy."

The mercantile only carried a few coats, and none of them were small enough to fit Harriet. The women nodded obediently and walked ahead toward the dressmaker's shop.

Annette linked her arm through Harriet's. She was sorry to see her mother-in-law leave. In a short time, she had come to love and respect her and she hated the idea that they may never meet again.

Jesse paused at the door to the shop, and Annette sensed his discomfort. "You can wait here," she offered. "We'll try to be quick."

He nodded in agreement, appearing relieved, and Annette followed Harriet into the shop. They certainly had more options to choose from than the mercantile, and far more fashionable.

The proprietor of the shop, a rotund gray-haired woman named Mrs. Heller, approached them amiably and inquired after their needs. Annette wondered if the lady had considered the way the purple gown she chose emphasized her girth. She tried not to stare as Harriet asked after a coat small enough to fit her frame.

Mrs. Heller nodded briskly and marched away. She returned very shortly with a gray woolen coat that looked promisingly small.

Harriet shrugged into it, and they all smiled as the sleeves reached her knuckles and the fitted waist gaped.

"If you like it, I have a seamstress on hand who can make quick work of the alterations," Mrs. Heller offered graciously.

Harriet glanced at Annette questioningly. "I have to catch the four o'clock stage."

"Oh, no worry," Mrs. Heller assured. "My girl is quick with her eyes and nimble with her fingers. She has a gift for it."

"All right then," Annette answered, "we would be pleased if you could have it fitted for her."

Mrs. Heller led them into a separate room and asked them to take a seat. She stepped to a door opening into the private section of the shop, calling "Elsie! *Elsie!*"

When a young Negro woman appeared, Annette glanced over at her mother-in-law, remembering her emphatic devotion to equality. From the way Mrs. Heller had referenced the woman as "her girl," Annette had assumed she meant her daughter. And she suspected Harriet had thought the same.

"Elsie, I want you to alter this coat promptly so Mrs. Stone can catch her stagecoach. But it needs to be done right," she added imperiously.

Turning her ponderous form to face Harriet, Mrs. Heller smiled graciously. "Please let me know if you need anything at all."

"Oh, one thing," Harriet stopped Mrs. Heller as she moved toward the exit. "I'd love an introduction, please," she smiled sweetly as she indicated the Negro woman.

Mrs. Heller's eyes narrowed. She stared in confusion.

Harriet remained nonplussed and offered her hand to the seamstress. "I'm Mrs. Harriet Stone," she offered.

The Negro woman's brown eyes shifted nervously to her employer. "I's Elsie. Elsie Ingram."

Harriet reached down to take the woman's dark hand. "It's a pleasure to meet you, Miss Ingram," she said politely, then turned to nod at Mrs. Heller dismissively, though all with such polish that Annette's respect for her mother-in-law only increased.

Mrs. Heller huffed out of the room, clearly offended.

"Now then, Miss Ingram," Harriet smiled kindly, "I do have to catch the stage at four o'clock, but you do what you can. I just need a coat to keep me warm."

"Yes ma'am," Elsie bobbed in a submissive curtsy, immediately grabbing a basket of pins and setting to work.

As she turned up the cuffs of Harriet's sleeves, Annette watched her curiously. She had seen very few Negros in her life, and never this close. She observed the rich brown color of her skin, pulled tight across high cheeks bones. Annette saw the intelligence in her eyes as she worked proficiently, moving to pin the excess fabric at Harriet's waist.

She remembered Jesse's words about the idea that had precipitated the war, that the darker a person's skin, the less human they were. Watching Elsie, Annette simply didn't understand. It was clear Elsie was every bit as much of a person as she was. Just with different coloring.

She wished Jesse could have fought to set the Negros free, to give them the same rights she had. But she knew he had done what he could. After all, he had just been a boy. She smiled, remembering the way he had scowled when Harriet revealed that their Lucky was named after his grandfather's dog. It revealed another glimpse of the tender man she so loved.

True to Mrs. Heller's promise, Elsie was a gifted seamstress and the coat was expertly finished in record time. "Thank you, Miss Ingram, for doing such a fine job," Harriet praised as she discreetly slipped a folded bill into the Negro woman's hand.

Elsie's eyes only lifted briefly before returning to the floor as she bobbed another curtsy.

Annette suddenly felt a surge of anger at the injustice of Elsie's place in the shop, and she wondered what the slaves had suffered in the South. She knew so little about it, having been raised on a cattle ranch in the west, so far from where the fighting had been. But this small glimpse into Elsie's life hinted at the bigger picture. And it both enraged her and heightened her understanding of Mrs. Stone's statement that she was proud of the men who had sacrificed for the cause of freedom.

She wished she could catch Elsie's gaze and give her a friendly smile, but the woman's eyes were riveted on the wooden floor under her feet.

After paying Mrs. Heller for the coat and alterations, the women exited the shop to find Jesse sitting on a bench, tapping his foot impatiently. At the sight of them, he sprang to his feet, exclaiming, "It's three-thirty already! I was considering coming in after you."

Annette smiled at the way he said it. "Actually dear," she laughed, "we were very impressed with the prompt service, and you may notice your mother's coat now fits her perfectly."

Jesse surveyed his mother and had to nod in approval. "Again, I apologize for Lucky's bad manners. I'm glad we were able to find something suitable to replace it."

"Never mind," Harriet replied. "If I had to shiver all the way back to Massachusetts, it would be worth it to see you again and to meet your lovely wife." She fought back tears. "I'm very pleased with your choice," she said affectionately as she linked her arm through Annette's.

"I'm so glad you came to see us," Annette said, her throat tight. "It meant a great deal to us."

When they reached the boarding house, the stage coach was already waiting. Jesse went inside to retrieve his mother's luggage and offered it to the driver, watching carefully as it was stowed on top and strapped down securely. Annette saw the way he scowled, fidgeting with the buttons of his coat, and knew he was fighting a battle with his emotions.

As his mother turned to say her farewell, he swallowed hard, holding back tears. Annette wondered why men felt the need to keep their feelings hidden. Why weren't they expected to feel the same emotions as women?

Harriet kissed his cheek, resting her hand on his scarred side tenderly. "I love you son," she said quietly.

Jesse nodded, clearly unable to speak.

Harriet then turned to Annette, who hugged her tightly and didn't worry about the tears streaking her face. "You are God's blessing to my son," she told Annette. "You're the answer to my prayers."

Annette suddenly found herself without words. If only Harriet knew why Annette had married her son, she might not feel the same way. But those reasons didn't seem to matter nearly as much as they once had. Whatever had brought them together wasn't as important as the love that *held* them together.

Jesse put his arm around her, and they stood together on the boardwalk waving until the coach rounded a corner and disappeared from sight. Then they turned to one another and shared a silent understanding. It was time to go home.

Chapter Thirty-Three

As they rode on the hard buckboard wagon through the dusty streets of town, Annette reflected on the time she had spent with her husband's mother. Meeting Harriet made her feel like she knew Jesse just a little better, knowing the woman who had raised him and imparted her gentleness and strength to him. It was a pity his father had died so young, something Jesse seldom talked about. And it was a shame she might never meet his brothers and sisters, their wives and husbands, or Jesse's nieces and nephews.

But she was grateful for the time with Harriet. Annette remembered the morning's fiasco, and felt embarrassment as she remembered the slobbery coat hanging from Lucky's mouth. She shook her head. Perhaps animals did belong outside for a reason.

But Harriet's graceful response to the situation had been inspiring, as had her interactions at the dress shop. Annette wouldn't have known how to manage Mrs. Heller so effectively. She remembered the way Harriet had slipped the money to Elsie, and knew she had given the young woman far more than just extra funds. She had affirmed the Negro woman's dignity with her kindness and generosity.

As her thoughts drifted to Elsie, Annette let out a sudden gasp. "Jesse!" she exclaimed.

"What is it?" he demanded, startled by her outburst.

"What is Jim's last name?"

"Ingram? Why on earth—"

"What are the chances his daughter is here, in Weston?"

"What are you talking about?" Jesse insisted impatiently.

"Jesse, the seamstress at the dress shop was a Negro woman named Elsie Ingram. What if she was Jim's daughter?" she said excitedly.

"That's extremely unlikely. Just because she is Negro and her last name is Ingram doesn't mean she's related to him. It could be a coincidence."

"It could be," Annette said slowly. "But I want to go back and talk to her."

"Are you serious?" he raised his eyebrows questioningly, glancing up at the sky.

She looked up at him, her eyes pleading, and for answer he leaned down to kiss her nose. Without a word, he halted the wagon and turned it around.

When they pulled up in front of the shop, Jesse said, "I guess you should talk to her alone. I'm not sure she'd feel comfortable with me."

"Do you know the name of Jim's wife?" Annette wondered.

"Martha," Jesse answered quietly, remembering the unfortunate details of Jim's story.

Annette squeezed his hands. "Thank you, Jesse. I'll be back soon."

As soon as she entered the shop, Mrs. Heller recognized her and looked down her nose. "May I help you, young lady?"

"Yes, ma'am. I was hoping I could speak with Elsie Ingram, please."

"Was the coat unsatisfactory?" the portly woman challenged in apparent aggravation.

"No, ma'am. I'd like to speak with her about a personal matter." Annette tried to hold her chin up with confidence and not be cowed by the woman's glare.

"I'm sorry, but Elsie's occupied at the moment," Mrs. Heller stated unapologetically. But a glimpse of Elsie peeking around the corner indicated otherwise.

"Oh, I'll only be a moment," Annette informed the older woman sweetly, brushing past her and striding purposefully toward the alteration room.

Elsie was waiting for her there, her dark eyes wide. "What's the matter, Miss?" she worried, her accent sounding strange to Annette's ears.

Annette hesitated, unsure how to broach the subject. What if Elsie had been separated from her father, but it wasn't Jim? What if she only opened a tender wound more deeply?

"I just wanted to ask you a question. It may sound odd, but would you mind telling me your father's name?" Annette began tentatively.

Elsie narrowed her black eyebrows at Annette. "Why you need to know my daddy's name?" she demanded defensively.

Annette took a deep breath. "I wondered if... I think I might know him."

"I haven't seen my daddy since I was a little girl. He runned off down in Alabama, when we wuz slaves," Elsie said, clearly unsure if she should trust Annette. "Why you think you know my daddy?"

"Is his name Jim? And your mother's name Martha?" Annette ventured, praying this was Jim's daughter.

Elsie's brown hand fluttered to her heart. She blinked back tears.

"I know your father, Elsie," Annette couldn't hold back her own tears. "He works on my ranch."

Elsie shook her head in disbelief, "How you know he's my daddy?"

"Jim Ingram works on my ranch. Elsie, he told my husband about how he had run away in Alabama, but planned to come back for his wife and children. When the war broke out, he couldn't get to them. After the war, he searched and searched, but he could never find you. And your last name is Ingram. I was in the wagon riding home when it occurred to me. And I thought, maybe…"

Tears flooded Elsie's brown cheeks and she sank down in a chair reserved for patrons waiting for alterations to be completed. She looked up at Annette, covering her mouth with her hands.

"My daddy's *here*?" she whispered raggedly. Her eyes reflected both longing and the fear of disappointment.

Her heart breaking, Annette nodded. "What about the rest of your family, Elsie? Your mother and brothers and sisters?"

Elsie wiped the tears from her face with trembling hands.

She took a shuddering breath. "Don't rightly know what happened to Mama. Reckon she's in heaven. Annie gone too. But Simon's here. He workin' at the livery in town, saving up money. He gonna file a claim for a homestead once he turn twenty-one."

"I'm sorry to hear about Martha and Annie," Annette said, hating to hear the news for Jim's sake. "But your father will be overjoyed to see you and Simon! Do you have off work on Sunday?"

Nodding, Elsie said, "I got off on Sundays. I ask Simon if he can take off." She rubbed at her hands with her face. "I just can't believe Daddy's here. I thought sure I'd never see him again neither."

"Well then, my husband and I will bring your father to town on Sunday. Where shall we meet?" She had almost suggested Maggie's Diner, but was unsure how the Negros would be received there.

Elsie rubbed at her chin thoughtfully. "We meet you right at the edge of town."

Annette smiled, grateful she could play a part in uniting Jim with his children. "Well then, I'd better go before Mrs. Heller marches back here and throws me out!" She came to her feet.

She was startled when Elsie grabbed her hand. "God bless you, miss, for what you done. You a good woman."

Annette squeezed Elsie's hand. "I think God led me to you, Elsie. And I'm just glad he did."

~

When Jim had been given the news that two of his children were not only alive, but residing in the town of Weston just miles away, he had fallen to his knees and wept. He removed the hat from his head, clutching it to his chest as he sobbed uncontrollably. Jesse had been startled by the open display of emotion and stepped back uncertainly, eyeing the top of the man's dark head uncomfortably.

Jim's massive shoulders shook with great gasping sobs, and the sound that tore from his throat was like a wounded animal. Finally he calmed himself enough to speak. He looked up at the expanse of blue sky above them, his white eyes round in his dark face. "Thank you, sweet Jesus," he rasped out.

Then, lifting his heavy frame from the ground, he stood towering over Jesse. He reached out to put his large hand on Jesse's shoulder. "You never know what you done for me, suh. I gave up hopin' I'd ever see my babies again. It's a miracle."

Jesse found that a lump had lodged in his throat and his eyes stung from unshed tears. He nodded in response, placing his own small white hand on Jim's muscled shoulder.

Sunday morning, Jesse noticed that everyone on the homestead seemed to share Jim's sense of anticipation. Even Claude and Rattlesnake walked Jim to the wagon where Annette sat waiting on the buckboard, offering their congratulations and well wishes.

Jesse knew Jim was torn between fresh grief over the loss of his wife, Martha, and their daughter Annie, and relief knowing the other two children were alive and well. Jesse tried to imagine what thoughts were running through Jim's head as the horse pulled the wagon over the grassy plain at what seemed like a snail's pace. It wasn't even his family, and yet Jesse felt a sense of urgency and resisted the inclination to push the gray appaloosa into a canter.

Finally, after watching the sun climb higher in the great basin of the sky above, the town of Weston came into view. At first it was only a brown smudge on the horizon, but with painful slowness, they drew near and the buildings began to take distinct shape. Finally, they were close enough to see two Negros waiting under a tree, just where the road began. A young man, as tall and broad through the shoulders as Jim, and beside him, a young woman.

Before they were any closer, Jim leapt from the bed of the wagon and ran past the startled horse toward his children. Jesse felt Annette link her arm through his as they watched Jim fly at Simon and Elsie, wrapping an arm around each of them and pulling them close. He heard Annette sniffling next to him, and looked down at her red face. She smiled up at him and laughed.

Halting the wagon under the shade of the lone tree, Jesse dismounted and offered Annette his hand. They both stood by watching the tearful reunion of a father with his son and daughter.

"Lord Almighty, but you all grown up!" Jim declared, looking over both his adult children. "You's just been babies in my mind all these years."

Simon stood a little taller, grinning broadly. The young man was the spitting image of his father, from the bulk of his frame to the way his toothy smile lit up his face. "You just the way I remembered," he told his father.

Elsie looked up at her father shyly.

"How old are you now?" Jim asked.

She looked up at him proudly. "Eighteen, suh."

"You every bit as pretty as your mama," Jim told her, pulling her into his arms again.

Annette nudged Jesse and he went to the bed of the wagon to retrieve the blanket and food basket they had brought for a picnic. She helped him to lay out the blanket and invited Jim and his children to join them there. While she removed the cold roast beef sandwiches, biscuits, and sweetened buffalo berry pie, Jim tried to explain the lost years to his children.

"You know I didn't leave you for good, not on purpose," he said quietly.

"Oh Daddy, we know!" Elsie cried. "Miss 'Nette here tell me how you planned on coming back for us."

Jim nodded gratefully to Annette. "I thought if I can get up north, I get some nice white folks to help me come back for you. It dangerous, running away like that, and I thought if I go alone, I learn the stops on the Underground Railroad and know how to keep you safe." He shook his head sadly. "But then the war come and ain't no way for me to get all the way back to Alabama. So I took up with the Union army to help fight for freedom. When that war ended, ain't nothing gonna keep me from gettin' back to my Martha and my babies. But it was too late. You was all gone," he whispered huskily.

He thumbed a tear from his eye. "What happened to you while I wuz gone?"

Simon and Elsie exchanged glances, and Jesse knew whatever he had to say was only going to bring more tears. "We go on like usual, but then them Federal soldiers come." He preceded to tell how word had reached the slaves on the cotton plantation that there were Union soldiers hiding out in the woods, and any slaves who joined them would be free.

Martha, along with three other slaves, took the children and went out under cover of darkness to find the Union camp. Jesse had heard the slaves were considered contraband of war could therefore be protected by the soldiers as well as providing them with labor and service.

Unfortunately, they were apprehended by a night patrol and returned to the plantation. Martha and the children, despite their young age, were whipped for their transgression. While they were still recovering from their punishment, the Federal army closed in on the cotton plantation and seized supplies necessary to sustain the invading regiment. They took what food was available, which apparently wasn't much as the Confederate army had already claimed their share. With supplies scarce, the slaves were left to their own to subsist.

Simon tried to provide for the women, but death by starvation seemed imminent. Finally Simon went to the invaders and offered their services to the soldiers in blue. They were taken to a contraband camp, near the army camp, and were given enough food to stay alive. It was not due to a lack of generosity on the part of the Union soldiers, but rather due to the overall shortage of supplies. In return, they washed clothes, cooked meals, and foraged for supplemental provisions.

Simon bowed his head.

"What happened to your mama?" Jim asked, as if sensing the next part of the story.

"Most of dem soldiers good men, but not all. You know Mama was pretty... She had that fair skin, from her papa."

Jim leaned over to rest his elbows on his knees, as if the weight of the truth had pushed him there. But he said, "Tell me, son."

"These two officers, they walk through camp and they tell her she gots to go with them. They talk to her like she gots a choice, flirtin' and laughin'. But she say she ain't goin,' then they ain't laughin' no more. They take her by the arms and drag her with them. We never..." Simon's eyes were full of regret as he studied the bent form of his father. "We never saw her no more after that."

Jim shook his head, tears spilling onto his lap. He groaned, "Oh, my poor, sweet Martha."

"Daddy, I looked for her—"

"You ain't to blame, son. I know you did what you could."

Simon wiped at his own tears. "I tried to take care of them all, Daddy, the way you would. But I's just a boy. Little Annie got sick. She so skinny, all her bones stick out. I tried, but, one day she don't wake up. She gone on to heaven."

Jesse had almost forgotten that Annette was sitting beside him. He had almost forgotten himself, so engrossed was he in the tragic story unfolding before him. But his wife's quiet sobbing brought his attention back to her, and he put an arm around Annette's shoulders and drew her close. She knew nothing of the harsh realities of the war.

"I got you and Elsie," Jim said finally, reaching out to engulf them both in another great bear hug. "I gonna thank God for that."

"How you get to Wyoming Territory?" he inquired after he had released them.

"We done stay with the army, following dem 'round, acting like dem slaves. But at least we's almost free. After Mistah Lincoln says we free, we's already in Pennsylvania, and the

Freedman's Bureau told us 'bout the land out here, how anyone could file for a homestead—no matter what color his skin. So we come by wagon train, gonna make a new life out here."

Jesse hadn't considered that the wagon trains still traveled across the rugged country when transport by railcar was so much faster and safer. But he presumed for those who couldn't afford the fare, it was the only way to chase after a better life.

"I reckon God brought you here," Jim said. "In this wide world, how else we gonna find each other?"

Elsie looked up at Annette. "If Miss 'Nette hadn't come in that dress shop, hadn't thought 'bout my name bein' Ingram, we never would have found you."

"Thank you, ma'am," Jim nodded at Annette and said solemnly, "You done give me back my babies."

Jesse chuckled. "I guess that dog of mine did us a favor, after all."

Annette laughed with him, "Imagine that. I guess he did."

Chapter Thirty-Four

Shivering as the winter chill crept into the house, Annette went to the back corner of the kitchen to retrieve some firewood. Cradled in her arms, she carried it into the living room and placed it on the floor in front of the fireplace. Using an iron poker, she stoked the coals until they were red hot, then added the fuel to the fire.

The floor needed to be swept. Although Lucky didn't shed as much in the winter, it seemed there was always brown and white fur collected in the corners and under the furniture. Retrieving the broom, Annette began in the kitchen with the intention of sweeping the entire downstairs before scrubbing the floor. Tomorrow she would tackle the upstairs.

As her hands worked, her thoughts were of Jim's reunion with Elsie and Simon. She had written a letter to Harriet, informing her of the unexpected sequence of events resulting from Lucky's bad behavior. Although her mother-in-law had only been gone for a week, Annette found she missed the female companionship.

She smiled as her thoughts turned to her husband. He had certainly been enjoying having the house to themselves again. She had never imagined a day would come when he would be so light-hearted and so completely unperturbed by the scar that marked his cheek or the prosthesis he strapped onto his leg every morning.

When they first began to share a bedroom, Annette had tried to shield his pride by looking away when he was working with the apparatus or when the rounded stump of his leg was exposed. But it was impossible to daily share the space with him and always keep her eyes averted. And it seemed silly, quite frankly, in light of the greater intimacy they shared. In time, the concern faded into the background, until neither of them thought to worry about it anymore.

Annette was grateful she'd had the chance to meet Jesse's mother, and she was pleased she could honestly say she both liked and respected the woman. She only wished Jesse's relationship with her parents could improve. She hadn't been to see them in months, and she hadn't bothered to invite them to her house after the way her father insulted her husband.

They were her family, and she would always love them. She only prayed one day her father would look beyond the exterior to see the man Jesse was inside. Her mother seemed to be willing to try, but was never given the chance when Jesse was always on guard in their company. She sent up a prayer to heaven for resolution.

A sound on the porch caught her attention, and she leaned the broom against the wall to peer through the window. It was only Lucky bounding around, his tail wagging against the door in his exuberance. With a sigh, Annette opened the door and brought him into the house. His rope dragged behind him, chewed through again.

The dog raced across the room, his nails biting into the floorboards as he slid around a corner and crashed into the wall. Hardly pausing to blink, the bull terrier leapt to his feet and ran into the kitchen with Annette in pursuit behind him. Grabbing hold of the rope, she planted her feet and brought him to a halt. Although her hands were raw from the rope sliding through, she did manage to stop him from causing further damage.

"Oh, you're such a beast," she huffed, leading him back outside and tying the rope again. "Now, leave that alone!" she admonished, but she paused to scratch him behind the ears.

Once inside, the silence engulfed her. She had hoped to find Sarah standing on the front porch, not her wayward dog. The sky outside was clear and the sun shone brightly on the prairie. It was November, and the weather could change suddenly and without warning, but there didn't appear to be a cloud in the sky for miles around.

Perhaps she would slip over to the Gibson homestead and see how they were getting on. Scribbling a quick note for Jesse, just in case he should return before she did, Annette grabbed her coat and scarf from the peg and went to the barn to saddle Bella.

Although the air was biting, the sun shone brightly overhead. Annette far preferred the wind in her face to the shadows of the house and a broom. She hoped Frank and Sarah had repaired the rift in their marriage and the children had settled back into their familiar routine. She couldn't fathom what it would be like to be taken from a cattle ranch and placed on an Indian reservation, introduced to dark skinned natives and told they were your family. Then, just as you became accustomed to sleeping in a tipi and hearing a strange language, having to return to the old way of life. She wondered how Elizabeth, the oldest, had fared with the adventure.

She smiled as she approached the cabin and noted the changes in it since her last visit. It was immediately apparent that a woman's touch had returned to the place. The windows sparkled in the sunshine and the front porch had been swept clean. The garden had been weeded and clothes flapped in the breeze on the wash line.

It was Elizabeth who opened the door for her, smiling broadly and rushing at Annette as if they were old friends. "Mrs. Stone!" she cried. "I missed you while we were away."

Annette was touched by the girl's warm welcome and hugged her tightly. "I'm so glad you're back safely, Elizabeth. And I think you've grown!" The girl was certainly an inch taller, if not two.

"Oh, Annette!" Sarah came bustling out of the back room to also pull her into a welcoming embrace. "I had hoped we'd hear from you soon."

"I'm sorry I haven't come sooner. We had an unexpected visit from Jesse's mother," Annette explained.

Sarah's dark eyebrows raised. "And how did that go?"

Laughing, Annette removed her coat and scarf and placed them in Sarah's extended hand. "Quite well, actually. She was a very dear woman, and I was glad to have met her."

Frank Jr. and Miriam lingered near Annette's skirt, looking up at her expectantly. She knelt down and pulled them into a hug, kissing their cheeks alternately. Satisfied, they scampered off to resume their play.

"Would you like a cup of tea?" Sarah offered.

"That would be wonderful, thank you. I enjoyed the ride over, but I could use warming up," Annette admitted.

As she pulled back her chair and took a seat at the table, she noticed an envelope with a letter beside it. She didn't mean to pry, but she couldn't help notice that the envelope was addressed to Vivian. Sarah must have been replying to a letter she received, which answered Annette's question about whether or not they still remained in touch.

The mere sight of that name, Mrs. Robert Hudson, scrawled on the envelope, brought a rush of emotions. The foremost being shame, followed quickly by embarrassment. But there was also remorse at having forfeited the opportunity to make a friend. She suspected that under different circumstances, she and Vivian could have gotten along rather well.

Sarah was preoccupied fetching water from the outdoor pump, filling the teapot, and situating it on a hook in the fireplace to boil. She turned to see Annette's expression as she glanced guiltily away from the folded pages.

"I was just writing a letter to Vivian Hudson," Sarah stated the obvious. "I haven't had time to sit down since I returned from visiting my family. I can see why you said Frank was lost without me," she smiled, but Annette sensed there was sorrow hiding behind it.

"The place was a bit untidy," Annette said generously.

Sarah nodded. "Poor man. I shouldn't have been away so long." She sighed with regret. "I love Frank dearly, and I'm so glad he's forgiven me for my selfishness. I didn't mean to be unkind to him... I just didn't know how to manage my grief. But he's proven to me once again what a good man he is and how blessed I am to have him as my husband."

Joining Annette at the table, Sarah retrieved the letter from Vivian as well as her reply and tucked them into the pocket of her apron. "I was pleased to hear from Vivian," she commented conversationally, returning to her earlier comment.

"And I'm happy to report that she and Rob are doing very well. You may have heard he wanted to go back east because he missed the water. He's started a fishing business, and it seems to be flourishing." She grinned then, "And Vivian is expecting a little one. Due around Christmas. Lily is very excited to be a big sister."

Annette nodded politely. "I'm happy to hear Mr. and Mrs. Hudson are doing so well."

Sarah studied her face intently, but said nothing. She instead rose from the table and went to stoke the fire, although it seemed more for the sake of activity than actual need. Annette looked down at her hands. She wondered what thoughts were running through Sarah's mind. Did she already know?

As Sarah used her apron to remove the teapot from the fire and prepare their mugs, Annette picked at her fingernails anxiously. Sarah and Vivian were such close friends. It didn't seem fair to allow Sarah to show Annette kindness without knowing how she had hurt Vivian.

"I don't think Mrs. Hudson liked me very much," she admitted cautiously as Sarah placed the mug of steaming tea before her.

Settling into her chair across the table, Sarah lifted her black eyebrows. "Why do you think that?"

Annette glanced over at Elizabeth, quietly reading in a corner.

"Elizabeth," Sarah seemed to have taken the unspoken cue, "can you take Frank and Miriam outside for some fresh air. Dress warmly."

As the children donned their coats and scarves, Annette

took a deep breath. Sarah wouldn't be sending them outside if she hadn't thought there was a conversation forthcoming that required privacy.

When the door closed behind them, she looked directly into Sarah's dark almond eyes and said, "You know what happened, don't you?"

Sarah pursed her lips, glanced down at the tea in her mug, then slowly brought her gaze back to Annette. "If you mean Ricky Lawson, I do," she admitted quietly.

Annette felt her cheeks flame. She had suspected all along that Sarah knew. And she had chosen to befriend her nevertheless. But the certainty of her knowledge brought a fresh wave of shame. She swallowed back tears.

"You—you never said anything," she faltered.

"What was there to say?" Sarah said kindly, reaching across the table to place her tanned hand over Annette's. "Vivian had forgiven you, so why shouldn't I?"

Wiping away a renegade tear, Annette remembered the odd conversation she'd had with Vivian that day by the creek. She'd thought Vivian was using talk of the weather to encourage her to make a fresh start, to communicate her forgiveness.

"But why should she forgive me?" she wondered. "I could never forgive a woman who slept with my husband!"

The Lakota woman nodded in understanding. "But with God, all things are possible."

Feeling once again like an adulteress and a whore, Annette felt hot tears flood her cheeks. "I liked Vivian. I never meant to hurt her. I tried to stay away from him, but he was just always *there*. And Ricky never would take 'no' for an answer. And then—and then I tried to tell him it was an awful mistake. That very day she found us, the day he died, I had gone to tell him how I felt horrible and didn't want to ever see him again. I wanted to do what was right, but he," she paused, remembering the day so vividly, "he knew how to make me do what he wanted."

Sarah didn't seem a bit surprised by the disclosure. "I'm sure he made it difficult," she admitted, and Annette bowed her head, hearing the unspoken truth: she was still complicit. She was still responsible for allowing it.

"I know I should have never let it happen," she said through the sobs that shook her shoulders. Sarah released her hand to scoot her chair beside Annette and placed her arm around the young woman.

Offering Annette a handkerchief, Sarah waited silently for her to regain control of her emotions.

Annette mopped her face with it, willing the tears to stop. After a moment, she continued, "I've regretted it a million times over. I've carried my secret shame with me every single day since then. If there was any way I could go back and relive that first day when he flirted with me, I would slap him in the face and never speak to him again. But I can't fix it! It's done!"

Sarah stroked her hair as if she were a child. "When I last saw you, you said I had brought more than physical healing to your home. You said the words of truth from the Bible had changed you. What did you mean?"

Annette took a deep, shuddering breath. She closed her eyes, trying to reclaim the peace she had known when first understanding the gift of God's forgiveness. "It did make a difference, Sarah. It's just that every time I'm reminded of what I did, what I am..." she blinked back fresh tears. "I still feel ashamed."

"Shame is from the Enemy of Our Souls. But there's something called 'godly sorrow,' and it leads to repentance. There's a difference. Don't get trapped with shame. Let that go," Sarah admonished.

Hearing the truth in her words, Annette nodded. "When you spoke of God's forgiveness—that *anyone* could be forgiven—it gave me hope. I wanted to be forgiven. We began reading the Bible, and we found in John where it says Jesus came into the world for that very reason. And it was like..." she tried to find the words to express it, "like watching the sun rise after a long, dark night. Vivian had said something to me about a 'fresh start' the day we were picking berries. I finally felt like it was possible."

"There was a man in the Bible who was an ancestor of our Lord, Jesus Christ. He was a king, and he used his power to have adultery with a beautiful woman," Sarah replied.

Annette's eyes widened. She wasn't sure she'd ever heard that story.

"He even committed murder so no one would find out." Annette listened attentively as Sarah continued. "He is known as 'a man after God's own heart,' if you can believe that. Because he repented. Psalm 51 was written after he confessed his sins to the Lord, and he writes, '*A broken and contrite heart—these O God, You will not despise.*' God forgave King David, and even allowed him to be in the family line of Jesus." She shook her head. "You don't have to read very far into the Bible to realize that it's full of sinners, and rarely a saint. We all need God's forgiveness. Every one of us."

"I just wish I could purge my memory of the whole incident," Annette confided. "Every time I'm reminded, I feel dirty again."

"Our memories can be a gift and a curse," Sarah agreed. "If I didn't remember losing baby Joshua, I could live without the pain and grief the memory brings. But I'm not sure I would treasure my three other children the way I do. And if you didn't remember your past, you wouldn't feel so grateful for God's gift to you. Or, I suspect, the love of your husband, Jesse."

Annette nodded. "Jesse knows. He knew before we ever married. I do love him, you know," she smiled, her heart warming at the very thought of him. She looked down at the blue gemstone ring on her finger. "He knew the truth, and married me anyway."

"I knew I liked that Jesse Stone," Sarah laughed as she pulled Annette into a hug.

~

Annette placed the cornbread on the warming tray at the rear of the stove, pushing a loose strand of blond hair from her eyes. She almost tripped over Lucky, who had decided to nap at her feet while she cooked. "Oh!" she exclaimed, catching her balance.

The dog looked up at her with wide brown eyes, his chin resting on his paws. She shook her head. How such a poorly behaved animal could master such a look of innocence was beyond her. But a smile touched her lips.

She knelt down to pet him. Immediately, the bull terrier rolled onto his back for a belly rub, his pink tongue lolling out of his mouth onto the wood floor. Annette complied, chuckling at the way his loose jowls fell back to reveal a sharp, toothy grin.

Dinner was already prepared, she was just waiting for Jesse to come in. She had seen him ride into the barn a moment ago. After they ate, she would tell him about her visit to Sarah's and the discovery that Vivian had forgiven her before moving back east. Somehow the knowledge lifted another brick from the load.

Annette stood, rubbing her hands on her apron to wipe off the dog fur. She endeavored to remember Sarah's words about the memory being as much a gift as a curse. She would try to let it move her to gratitude, and never shame. For she was forgiven and loved by her God.

And her husband. And that was another unexpected blessing she hoped to never take for granted.

Bryan Hunt was a fine man, and one day he would make another woman very happy. But knowing Jesse had chosen her as his wife when no other man would have, that he loved her knowing her darkest secret, was like a tie binding her heart to his. She could never love another man like she loved him.

The doorknob turned and Jesse entered the kitchen, his sandy blond hair rumpled by the wind and his nose pink from the biting cold. Annette waited while he removed his coat and hung it on the peg, then came and wrapped her arms around his neck.

"You're a sight for sore eyes," she said, smiling up at him. "I missed you today."

He grinned as if he had been given the deed to a thousand acres. "You're a welcome sight for my eyes, I can promise that," he said, brushing the errant strands of blond hair back from her face and pressing a kiss to her forehead.

Annette reached up with her left hand and cradled his cheek in her palm. "You never need to worry about being enough for me, Jesse."

"Is everything all right?" he narrowed his brows suspiciously.

"You will always be the man I choose to love, Jesse. Never doubt that," she persisted.

"You would still choose me to be your husband if you could choose *any* man in the world?" he pressed, a half smile tipping his mouth.

Despite the teasing tone, Annette sensed there was doubt in the question. Her thumb tenderly traced the tight, pink scar lining his face. "I would be a fool to choose anyone else. You've been such a gift to me, Jesse. Don't you see that? You're the first man who's ever loved me for who I am."

Jesse gathered her into his arms and she breathed in the smell of horseflesh and autumn air that clung to his chambray shirt. He reached up to cover her soft hand with his, rough and callused against her skin.

His gray eyes caressed her lovingly. "I suspect it was more difficult for you to love me for who I am."

Annette tilted her face upward and gently turned his face away, leaving a feather-light kiss on the puckered scar that had tormented him for so long.

"I disagree," she countered. "I loved you first."

Of Wind and Sky Series

Book 1: Through Every Valley

Vivian Lawson came to Wyoming because it was her husband's wish. But the discovery of his true nature leaves her bitterly determined to never trust a man again. And his sudden and timely death leaves her widowed on the western frontier, burdened by betrayal and guilt.

Rob Hudson returned to Annapolis, Maryland after years of fighting to preserve the Union and set the slaves free. But when the pursuit of his dreams leads only to loss and disappointment, Rob sets out on a westward adventure that will test his courage and reshape his character.

Book 3: As Eagles Soar

Catherine Gilbert can't stop looking over her shoulder. She only did what was right, but the decision has cost more than she bargained for. Now, all she wants is to make a new life for herself and her younger sister, Lydia, in the Wyoming Territory. But someone is determined to prevent her at any cost.

Bryan Hunt lost everything when he was drafted into the Union Army. Although his loyalties lay with the south, duty compelled him to fight for the unity of the nation. But in the end, the war took everything he loved. He thought he could forget the past and find peace in the west, but his heart still longs for something more.

 *Rebekah Colburn* calls Maryland's Eastern Shore her home, but has always been drawn to the romance of the Western Plains. Her earliest memories include stories about wagon trains, cattle drives, and the pioneer lifestyle. Her idea for the series, *"Of Wind and Sky"* was conceived on a visit to Wyoming and a cold, sleepless night camping at Yellowstone National Park.

Her desire is to bring history to life with rich stories, compelling characters, and inspirational themes which will both entertain and encourage her readers.

In 2001 she obtained a B.A. in Biblical Studies from Washington Bible College. Rebekah loves being outdoors and enjoys mountain biking, cycling, and cruising the local waterways with her husband.

She lives on the Eastern Shore of Maryland with her husband, teen-aged daughter, two sweet dogs, four spoiled cats, and a whole lot of chaos.

You can contact Rebekah Colburn via:

Email: rebekahlynncolburn@gmail.com
Website: http://rebekahcolburn.weebly.com/
Facebook: https://www.facebook.com/ColburnRebekah
Twitter: https://twitter.com/RebekahColburn

Made in the USA
Coppell, TX
03 September 2022

82586881R00246